"There is a finely robust quality about Norah Lofts' new story of eighteenth century adventure . . . It moves fast, its people are not the stagey swash-buckling types so often to be found in such romances, and it holds your attention . . . Hester is a most likable creature and this picturesque record of her changing fortunes reads remarkably well."

SUNDAY TIMES

"The life of the inn, and of the rough, dangerous times becomes our life; and we follow with unrelaxing interest the adventures of this lovely valiant girl . . . It is the sure character drawing and close knowledge of eighteenth century conditions that give the novel its distinction."

COUNTRY LIFE

Also by Norah Lofts

JASSY
THE BRITTLE GLASS
A CALF FOR VENUS
QUEEN IN WAITING
SCENT OF CLOVES
THE LUTEPLAYER
BLESS THIS HOUSE
THE DEVIL IN CLEVELY
OUT OF THIS NETTLE
TO SEE A FINE LADY
THE ROAD TO REVELATION
MADSELIN
I MET A GYPSY
HERE WAS A MAN
BLOSSOM LIKE THE ROSE
WHITE HELL OF PITY
THE LOST QUEEN
HOW FAR TO BETHLEHEM?
REQUIEM FOR IDOLS

The House Trilogy

THE TOWN HOUSE
THE HOUSE AT OLD VINE
THE HOUSE AT SUNSET

Norah Lofts writing as Peter Curtis

DEAD MARCH IN THREE KEYS
YOU'RE BEST ALONE
THE LITTLE WAX DOLL

and published by Corgi Books

Norah Lofts

Hester Roon

CORGI BOOKS
A DIVISION OF TRANSWORLD PUBLISHERS LTD
A NATIONAL GENERAL COMPANY

HESTER ROON

A CORGI BOOK 552 08252 X

Originally published in Great Britain by
Peter Davies Ltd.

PRINTING HISTORY
Peter Davies edition published 1940
Peter Davies edition reprinted 1940
,,   ,,   ,,   ,,   1957
,,   ,,   ,,   ,,   1967
,,   ,,   ,,   ,,   1968
Corgi edition published 1969
Corgi edition reprinted 1972

This book is set in 10 pt. Garamond.

Corgi Books are published by Transworld Publishers Ltd.,
Cavendish House, 57–59 Uxbridge Road,
Ealing, London, W.5.
Made and printed in Great Britain by
Hunt Barnard Printing Ltd., Aylesbury, Bucks.

"When he was four years old he was sent
to a Dame's school, where he and his
maid were taught for the absurd sum of
6s. 6d. a quarter."—BAYNE-POWELL,
English Life in the Eighteenth Century.

"To Lizzie, one year's wages and for tea
also ... £2 12s. 6d."
Parson Woodforde's Journal.

For those who might question the existence
of Miss Peck's school and the lowness of
Ellie's wage.

N.L.

Part One

CHAPTER I

WHEN Ellie Roon was brought to bed in the furthermost attic of The Fleece, she hoped devoutly that the baby would be born either dead or a boy. Things were easier at any time for a male creature, and when, as in this case, the newcomer was to receive, not only the gift of life but the heritage of bastardy, it was doubly desirable that it should be male.

Not that Ellie, grunting and groaning up there in the rat-ridden attic, gave her thoughts this precise form. In her muddled, inarticulate and tormented mind she merely knew that women had a hard time in this world: and that when a woman was illegitimate people remembered the fact and watched and waited for her to go the way her mother went. With a boy they often forgot. She knew: she was illegitimate herself. And wasn't she proving, at this very moment, that the expectations of the watchers were often fulfilled?

But the baby, roughly helped into the world by an old hag who made part of her living by such amateur obstetrics, was a girl, and far from dead. In fact her earliest cries were so loud and lusty that the other attic dwellers, starving for sleep, banged upon the dividing walls and shouted to Ellie to strangle the brat if she couldn't keep it quiet. Ellie stirred and sighed and obediently pulled the thin blanket higher around the red wrinkled face and hairless scalp of the infant, and tried to hush it with gentle words that sounded strangely upon her unaccustomed tongue. The word "strangle" made an impact upon her mind and she thought sadly that perhaps that was what she should do, since the baby was a girl and alive in spite of all her hopes: but she was neither desperate nor energetic enough to

7

take such a course, and as the tiny thing snuggled against her an unknown and hitherto untapped source of tender feeling within her sprang into being and she pressed it closer with her work-roughened hands and formed all kinds of plans for its future and well-being. The child should be called Hester and she, Ellie, would see to it that the life this day begun should not be wasted as her own had been.

But after four days of such fondling and planning Ellie was bound to return to the world and learn anew that her personal feelings and hopes and intentions were less than the dust which it was her duty to remove from the flagged floors of The Fleece's many rooms. She descended from the attic into a world where she and her baby counted for nothing and realised before the first long morning was ended that she might think herself very lucky if she were allowed to rear her baby within the walls, which, though dedicated to hospitality, were not accustomed to giving it.

The Fleece stood at the point where the London–Norwich road made its most definite swoop eastwards towards the Norfolk coast, as though desirous of catching up and including the traffic from the sea. Almost opposite its front door a narrow track, so worn that the heads of the horsemen hardly showed above its banks, led away to Southwold, Kessingland and Lowestoft. Left and right it was flanked by the main road which ran, North to Norwich, South to Ipswich and thence to London.

Standing as it did where the three roads joined, The Fleece did a brisk and prosperous trade. Every morning while the roads were passable the pack-horses toiled, sweating and blowing, into the yard bringing dripping creels of fish from the coast. Unpacked, reparcelled and loaded again, the harvest of the sea was dispersed to feed the hungry towns through which the coaches passed. The custom brought by this means alone would have kept The Fleece busy. But that was far from all. There were the bundles of leather from Norwich, the bales of woollen stuff from Lavenham, the chickens, turkeys and beef-on-the-hoof from the rich farmlands of Norfolk. All these made their way through the great yard of the inn. And these inanimate or involuntary passengers were supplemented by the proper travellers, the coach passengers, the packmen and the pedlars who regarded The Fleece as a stage in their journey.

The inn belonged to and was kept by a vast man whom many thousands of people in the course of the years doubtless remembered as the ideal host. He was round and fat and jolly and when he laughed his bright shrewd little eyes lost themselves in the folds of his mirth. He welcomed in the coach passengers and the regular pedestrians with such good humour and warmth that the journey, cold, or wearisome or even dangerous as it might have been, seemed to have been well made if it brought one at night to a place where such a genial spirit presided. But the fishermen and the other dealers who disposed of their goods in his great yard, and the people who worked for him for their bread, saw quite another side of him and knew that he was cruel, mean, avaricious and a bully. No one who had seen him hasten on his short stout legs to welcome in a cherished customer, with "Aha, now Mr. Harrison, sir.—Very pleased to see you again.— And glad to say that your same room's empty and the very spit of the home-cured that you so enjoyed last time, on the cut again.—And how are things with you, sir?—And what's the news from London?"—would have imagined that that same voice could have struck terror into any heart as it did into Ellie Roon's, and many a dozen more.

He had his pound of flesh, too, out of every man whose trade touched the inn's property and custom, however glancingly. Repeatedly some stockman or fisherman, smarting beneath a sense of grievance, would pluck up courage enough to point out to Job that the oxen, the turkeys, or the fish, never entered his property, but were loaded up across the road. Something unforeseen and unfortunate always befell the wares of such a dealer in logic. His next consignment would not be wanted : his sale would be forestalled : his oxen would stampede suddenly, for no known reason, his turkeys would be run over. Job was not even above inspecting a load of fish awaiting transport on the free side of the road, clapping his hand to his nose and ordering its owner to take his stinking manure out of the wind. Experience taught that it was far better to pay the innkeeper's exorbitant charges and keep on the sunny side of his temper.

Within his limits Job was, though grasping, honest above the average. No Gentleman of the Road had ever received information or encouragement from him. It was not unsafe, as it was in so many places, to display any evidence of wealth before the innkeeper. Word never went out of The Fleece that Mr. So-and-so, in a green chaise drawn by grey horses, would be passing Foxhall Heath during a certain afternoon and that he would be worth stopping. All Job's ways of making money were strictly legal, and though these included the over-working and the under-paying of his staff, and the levying of heavy tolls upon those who used his yard, they were less offensive and far less dangerous than the tricks indulged by men of less honesty and greater generosity.

He ran The Fleece himself, overlooking everything but the cooking, which he left entirely to the stout, irascible but not ill-natured Mrs. Bridges. If he had ever had a wife The Fleece had no knowledge of her; and the mistresses who came and went were installed for his pleasure, not for their knowledge of domestic arts. The last of these, a florid young woman who had expected far more than she had received, had run away with a packman, and after that Job had embarked upon a period of celibacy that had done nothing to help his temper. Occasionally Mrs. Bridges' assistant, a strange dumb country-woman with a certain placid comeliness, would be absent from her bedroom on the attic floor. Next day she would be idle and inclined, by passive resistance, to shirk some of her duties, but Mrs. Bridges soon dealt with that.

"Martha," she would say sternly, "how you spend your nights is your own affair, but what you do in the daytime is mine. Mr. Wainwright hired you to help *me*." And Martha was easily quelled.

On the first morning of her return to the lower regions Ellie filled a pail and set to work to scrub the floor of the kitchen and the flagged passage which led to the dining-room and the rest of the house. It was quite evident that no one had touched it, except with the feet, since the morning, five days before, when panting and groaning, she had cleansed it as her last task. Grease and mud and cinders were stamped about it, mingled with straw and horse manure from the yard. She felt very ill and weak and her head swam when she stooped. Despite the October chill of the early morning, drops of sweat fell from her forehead and mingled with the dirty water upon the floor. But she scrubbed on. When suddenly the space next to be scrubbed was occupied by two wide feet in enormous buckled shoes and looking up she saw the white stockinged calves, the homespun breeches, the round sagging paunch and still higher, the treble chin and the great red face of her master, her one comfort was that, at least, being so hot she couldn't look pale and her one fear that she might not be able to speak for breathlessness.

"Aha," he began, as she scrambled to her feet and wrapped

her dripping swollen red hands in her sacking apron. "So you're about again, Ellie. And nearly time too."

"Yes, sir," she agreed meekly.

"You feel it's about time too, do you?"

"It's only five days, sir," she pointed out, wringing her hands round and round in the sacking.

"Well, isn't that long enough to have the floor left in this state? You've got rid of your trouble I see."

"Yes, sir."

"Where is it?"

"Upstairs, sir. In the attic."

"God bless my soul, in the attic indeed! Well, get it out, do you hear me? Get it out. It's bad enough having you tabbies spawning all about the place without putting the result in our attics. If you've got to misbehave yourselves you should at least make some preparations for disposing of the bastards. What's Mother Fenn for, eh? What's Mother Fenn for?"

"But sir, you know . . ."

"What's that? Speak up, you're talking to me, not the bucket. What do I know?"

"Mother Fenn," said Ellie faintly. "Those babies always die . . ."

"And ain't that a good thing? Ain't that as it should be? What else do the mawthers take them there for?"

"But I want mine." Very faintly and apologetically the words formed on the pale dry lips of the scrubbing woman. A wave of sickness swept over her and she put a furtive hand behind her to touch the wall. The cold stone on her hot palm was like a tonic. A shudder ran through her.

"It shouldn't be a nuisance," she said. "Nobody'd need to know that it was there."

"A likely story indeed. And even if you could keep the noise and the stink of it away from people's noses and ears, you'd be neglecting your work and running up to it four and twenty times a day."

Another shudder ran through her. The stink of it . . . that soft, intimate, endearing odour, like nothing else on earth. The noise . . . the little wailing that told of life within it, the little nuzzling contented noises with which it settled at her breast. She was weak with longing for it. Oh, to be able to turn round to mount the many crooked stairs to the attic, to snatch up the little warm bundle in the old blanket and escape, be free to devote

11

herself to its service.

Job Wainwright, staring at his serving wench with hard blue eyes that missed nothing, saw that she was wrestling with unaccustomed emotion, guessed that she was on the verge of rebellion. The knowledge pleased him, titillated his over-weening vanity and sense of power.

"Well," he insisted, "wouldn't you?"

"I wouldn't go near it, sir," said Ellie, raising her tormented eyes. "I'd get up early and feed it. And during the day I'd only feed it again when I should be eating myself. Oh please sir, give me leave to keep it. I'd never forget your kindness, sir. I'd be grateful for ever."

"Bah," he spat out the repudiation. "What good is your gratitude to me . . ."

The dimness of the passage was suddenly lightened by the opening of a door at its upper end.

"Ha, Wainwright," cried a cheerful masculine voice, "there you are. The coach is just leaving and I was looking for you to say goodbye. Lord man, what a fount of energy you are. You even overlook the scrubbing, do you?"

The blustering tyrant of the moment before was gone. In his place stood the stout genial figure, radiating cheer and good humour.

"I'm just having a word with the wench here, Mr. Coldham. I'll come and see you off." With one hand he signed to Ellie to remove the pail to one side and let him through. But Ellie, with the failure of her pleading heavy and bitter upon her heart, merely lifted the hem of her sacking apron and attempted to staunch the hot tears that suddenly poured down her pallid cheeks.

Young Mr. Coldham's easily engaged attention switched to her.

"Why, what's wrong, lass?" he asked kindly.

"My baby," sobbed Ellie, crying even harder because of the kindness in his voice. "My baby."

"Ill? Or dead?" he asked uncomfortably, half regretting his first unnecessary question and forced to ask another against his will.

Job Wainwright broke in : "Ellie here has been a naughty girl, I'm afraid, Mr. Coldham. There's a baby but no father, if you understand me. We were just discussing what to do with the poor little thing."

"Well, well. That's nothing to cry about, you know. Not now, when it's all over. I'm sure the baby will have a good home here, eh, Wainwright? Room for everybody and everybody welcome. That's the motto at The Fleece. Cheer up girl. See here," he fumbled in one of the many pockets of his great swinging topcoat and drew out a coin between finger and thumb. "You buy something to make the baby look pretty and when I come next time I shall expect to see you and the baby, both smiling. Come on now, Wainwright, they'll be gone without me."

With the gold guinea piece sticking out of her moist palm Ellie watched her employer step over the pail and waddle away. In a few moments the clatter of hoofs and wheels over the cobbles of the great yard and the tootle of the horn as the vehicle turned out under the arch informed her that the coach had gone. Stooping, she lifted her skirt and tied the coin in her petticoat. Then she flopped down again on knees that felt like jelly and went on scrubbing.

Moving slowly, inch by painful inch, she had almost finished the passage before the upper door opened again.

"How much did that young fool give you?" Job's voice, harsh and hopeful.

"A guinea piece."

"Hand it over."

The skin on her fingers was sodden, wrinkled and almost numb from long immersion. She fumbled as she untied the knot. Her employer tried to speed her by saying, "Quick now. Don't be all day," and when at last the coin had changed hands he slid it into his capacious breeches pocket without a word of acknowledgement. But as she lowered the sodden apron he said, "Remember, if it makes a noise, or you go wasting time on it, out it goes."

Ellie, thankfully and humbly assuming that the guinea had paid the baby's way for a time at least, sank down on her knees and scrubbed on.

CHAPTER II

A QUIETER baby than the young Hester never breathed. Perhaps, laid away in the distant attic with no human being near her, she learned the futility of any vocal discontent. Fed by Ellie in the early darkness of the winter mornings and again in the breakfast spell and once more during the late afternoon when Ellie should have been feeding herself, she lay for the rest of the time on the hard straw pallet, uncomplaining, neglected and dirty. Ellie, who had entered The Fleece kitchen as a worker when she was nine years old and had worked seventeen hours a day ever since, had never a moment of her waking day to call her own. From five o'clock in the morning until ten at night she scrubbed floors, laundered linen and scoured dishes. Because she was meek and slightly simple she was liable at any moment to be called upon to perform any other task which some less meek and simple person did not feel inclined to do. When she climbed the final twisting stairs and reached the draughty attic where the rush-dip flickered in the icy air she was too tired to do more than suckle the baby for the last time and perform the merest bare essentials of its toilet. For the first two years of her life Hester had no clothes at all, and in winter this fact ensured that she stayed in the comparative warmth and shelter of the bed. In the summer, when there was danger that she would leave this shelter, Ellie guarded against such a possibility by tying her to it.

No one came near the attic : she had no toys. When it was time for Ellie to wean her, she moved, without any gradual stages of transition, on to a diet composed of anything that her mother could unobtrusively purloin from the kitchen. If it suited her it became incorporated into her wiry little frame : if not she returned it almost as effortlessly (sometimes more so) as she had assimilated it, and by that time Ellie was on her way down to work again and so was spared the worry of knowing that Hester was sick. Fortunately, in that great kitchen, there was plenty of food and to spare; the pease-pudding, the fat bacon, the coarse fish upon which the child throve and the hard crusts of bread upon which she cut her teeth, were not missed.

With every passing day Ellie loved the child more passion-

14

ately. She might climb the stairs and crawl along the passage in a coma of weariness; her voice, as she replied to this or that person's final order might be rough and harsh; but when the attic door was shut at last and the faint light of the dip fell upon the eager, expectant face and the tousled bright hair of her child, a change came over her. Her "See what mother's brought for her good girl to-night" was soft as a wood-dove's cooing. Her rough hands, raw in the winter from chilblains and constant immersion in water, were deft and gentle as they laid the broken viands within the child's reach and straightened the tumbled bed.

And all around and below the attic where Hester lay and dozed and crawled and tumbled and waited, the teeming life of the inn went on. In the brewhouse across the yard the ale was made, brown and potent. In the chimney of the smoke-house the great hams grew ripe. In the enormous ovens gargantuan meals were cooked day after day for the satisfying of the many mouths, the hearty appetites of the house's changing population. The straining exhausted horses were turned with a final flourish into the archway and were led away, fed and watered. Others, freshened by a stay in the dim vast stables, were led out and hitched to the heavy vehicle. Pedlars and packmen, honest men and rogues sank thankfully upon the settles in the parlour and quenched their thirst. The fishmongers and the drovers passed through the great yard, expostulated at Job Wainwright's charges and paid in full. And Job himself added guinea to guinea in the hiding-place below the loose oak plank of the floor beneath his huge bed.

To Ellie's unbounded relief her master seemed to forget the child. All through the first long winter she had drawn a tremulous breath and felt her unsteady heart bang in her breast every time he passed her as she went about her humble labour and he made his meticulous rounds of inspection. She was prepared each time to hear him say, "Got rid of that brat yet?" But he never did, and after a while she was hopeful that he had forgotten the child's existence. Ellie was careful never to remind him of it. The few utterly essential pieces of washing that had to be done for the child in the early days were washed and dried in the attic, a lengthy and troublesome procedure, but worth while, for even a fluttering diaper upon the long line in the drying-ground might not have escaped his carping eye.

Ellie, already almost incredibly overburdened, never dreamed of grudging the extra labour, the pails of water carried up and down, the delays before she could fling her weary body upon the hard bed and gain the paradise of unconsciousness. If she could have been shown Job's treasure, shining and golden in its canvas bags in the cavity of the floor, she would not have exchanged it for her own treasure, the hungry, dirty little atom of humanity secured by a strip of linen to the leg of the bed in the attic.

Ellie was happy. But one day, as she stood by the clothes-tub, the "dolly" between her hands, vigorously thumping the clothes that lay in the steaming, soapy water, Job, on his way across to the smoke-house, paused and addressed her.

"Hey, you Ellie. What's become of that brat of yours?" The moment she had dreaded!

"She's upstairs, sir. She don't give a bit of trouble, sir. And I feed her off my own plate."

"Don't gabble woman. Did I ask what she ate? Mr. Coldham is here again, waiting for the Newmarket coach. He seems to remember something about you and her, and I think he'd rather like to see her. Gentry take queer fancies . . . unless"—he paused and for once he looked at one of his menials with the humorous face which his customers so much admired—"it isn't his bye-blow by any chance?"

"Oh, sir! No, sir."

"Well anyway, bring her down—it is 'her', ain't it? And see to it she's clean and well-behaved."

"But, sir. She can't come down. She hasn't any clothes."

"Well, for God's sake! Get her some. Borrow some. Make her look tidy and bonny. Tidy up yourself as well. Go about it now. Don't gape at me. Leave that tub. Hey there, Rosie, come and take over this tub. Yes, it's you I mean, you shiftless idle besom."

Rosie, a buxom girl, with frizzy shining hair and trim clothing, who served in the bar and the dining-hall and scorned more menial duties, came forward reluctantly, but obediently and with a venomous glance at Ellie, took the "dolly" from her hands.

"And you, Ellie," said Job Wainwright, suddenly remembering something and pausing, "don't start whining as soon as you think you've got an ear turned your way. Perk yourself and look as though you appreciate your good home."

Ellie, drying her hands upon her apron, went into the kitchen where Mrs. Bridges, the cook, was basting an enormous joint of

16

beef that hung before one of the fires on a spit. Mrs. Bridges, as supreme mistress of the kitchen, must be addressed with circumspection, so the scrubbing woman waited until the beef was dealt with and Mrs. Bridges, iron dipper in hand, turned back to the table. Then she said in her timid, hoarse voice:

"If you had to get some children's clothes in a hurry, ma'am, where would you go?"

"That sort of thing isn't likely to happen to me," retorted Mrs. Bridges sharply. She turned and eyed Ellie up and down. "You in trouble again?" Ellie, with her hands rolled in her coarse apron level with her stomach, might have been in any condition, and the cook blamed herself for not noticing the obvious before this.

"It's for Hester, the one I've got, that I want the clothes," Ellie explained. "There's a gentleman in the parlour takes an interest in her and Mr. Wainwright said I'd got to make her look nice."

"Dear's sakes," exclaimed Mrs. Bridges, "so that's how it is. You'd better get some clothes for yourself, too, and straighten up that hair of yours. Then maybe he'd make an honest woman of you."

Ellie was too bothered and worried to explain any further. She sighed and was turning away to the passage that led to the back stairs when Mrs. Bridges said, "Why'n't you ask Mother Fenn? She sodded one last week, tidy size it was too. And less the ragman's been that way she'd have its things."

The idea was distasteful to Ellie, who loathed Mother Fenn and her trade, but she could think of nothing better and the Fenn house was not far from The Fleece, so she turned away from the stairs and went into the yard again. Once outside she hurried, breaking every now and then into a flat-footed trot, and by the time she reached the spinney where Mother Fenn lived in a tumbledown hovel she was breathless and had a stitch in her side.

Ellie's ideas upon cleanliness were not very definite, but even by her unexacting standards Mother Fenn was disgustingly dirty. She earned her living by acting as midwife and layer-out. A strange combination of function, as though the two extremes of human experience, birth and death, were so remote from ordinary human living that they must be relegated to the care of one whom those living in the space between the two extremes avoided and disliked. No one went to see Mother Fenn for the pleasure of seeking her company. Even Ellie, asking aid of her, turned her eyes away from the long, skinny talons with their sharp, dirt-encrusted nails, from the wart that decorated the old woman's nose, the filth-filled wrinkles on her neck, the black, broken teeth within the sagging purplish lips. She was surprised at her own feelings of repulsion. She had accepted Mother Fenn's ministrations during her labour, with resignation and a modicum of gratitude. She was not self-analytical enough to realise that it was from the old woman's trade that she shrank : that her love for her own baby was the measure of her loathing for the creature who "cared for" unwanted babies in such a way that no infant survived for longer than three months.

In her hoarse meek voice she explained her errand, her eyes sliding furtively around the filthy, cluttered room, half expecting, half fearing to see a little corpse tucked away in one of its corners.

Mother Fenn, in her reedy old-woman's voice, expressed her ability and willingness to oblige with the loan of some baby clothes. Ellie unwillingly watched her as she opened a chest and took out some neatly folded garments, which, with a leer and a sniff the hag shook and held up for display. Pleasure and cupidity replaced the furtive disgust in Ellie's eyes. The little garments were just what she wanted for Hester, about the right size, beautifully made, clean, and of good material.

"Four shilling to loan, five to buy," said the old woman. Ellie, who upon the tenth of October which every year marked the conclusion of her year of labour, received twenty shillings and a length each of flannel and print, shrank back and seemed to grow smaller as the sum was mentioned.

"It's too much," she said.

"It's no more than the ragman will give me," declared Mother Fenn, shaking out and holding up again the little dress which was the most decorative piece of all. "Sheer Indian muslin this is, and the flannel of the petticoats is the finest that has come my way for years. Came on the last baby, they did, and you'd be surprised if you knew where *that* came from. No village girl's bye-blow I may tell you."

Ellie felt a pang for that unknown child, unwanted and disowned, who had come upon such untimely and unnecessary death. But hard upon the heels of this feeling of compassion and compunction, came the thought of how fine Hester would look in the clothes, and the memory that time was short.

"I won't have any money until the tenth of next month," she said. And then recklessly she added, "I'll pay you then, five shillings, and keep the things."

"It'll be six, if I have to wait for the money," said Mother Fenn, taking advantage of the desire so plainly shown upon her customer's face.

"Oh, all right," said Ellie, bundling the things together hastily and making her escape.

In a frenzy of haste she ran back to The Fleece, dipped a bucketful of hot water from one of the coppers which it was her duty to keep full and boiling all day long, and mounted the stairs as fast as her burdens permitted. With the maximum of speed that was compatible with tender handling she stripped off the ragged shift of her own which had been Hester's only wear, washed the child from head to foot, towelling the yellow curls into a foaming mass of beauty and arrayed the small body in the exquisite clothes. Then in the same water she washed her own face, neck, ears and forearms and put on a clean print dress and cap.

"Now we're ready," she said gaily. But before opening the door she spent one long gloating moment in looking at her darling. Never before had she regarded Hester with dispassionate or critical eyes, but now for a moment she looked at the baby as the strange Mr. Coldham in the parlour would look; noticing the soft pale baby skin, slightly flushed from the hot water and the towelling; the wide eyes of indeterminate colour, the silky lashes and faintly pencilled brows above which the tumbled yellow curls clustered. It was with a sharp feeling of surprise that she saw that the baby was beautiful, lovely as a flower that had unaccountably strayed into the squalid attic. She raised the child in her thin strong arms and showered several passionate kisses upon the little face and the yellow hair. Then she opened the door and with careful tread descended the stairs.

Mr. Coldham, who had idly asked after "the scrubbing wench and her baby", and voiced the desire to see them that had set all this activity in motion, had been joined by an acquaintance in the parlour. They had discovered that they were both bound for the races at Newmarket, and were deep in race-course gossip and the discussion of form. A bottle of Madeira wine, two glasses and a plate of biscuits stood on the table between them.

Ellie opened the door timidly and peeped in. For a moment neither man noticed her and she hesitated, poised for flight.

19

The stranger, aware of a current of cold air from the doorway, turned, saw Ellie and said, "Hullo, what's this?" Young Mr. Coldham craned his neck around the back of the settle and said :

"Aha, it's the inn's inhabitant, born when I was here last. Come in my dear and let's have a look at you."

The baby's beauty, of which its own mother had only just been made aware, was obvious even to two young men with race-horses in their minds.

"Well, that's a beauty and no mistake," said Coldham, "isn't she, Fenton?"

Fenton, whose wife had thrice blessed him in the four years of their married life and who had learned that even baby-clothes cost money, stared at the Indian muslin, so beautifully embroidered, contrasted in his mind the baby's appearance with that of Ellie, weighed up the unusual interest that a young spark like Coldham was showing in the offspring of a serving wench and came to his own erroneous conclusion.

"She's a beauty," he admitted, "a credit to her sire."

"And to her mother," said Coldham, ignoring the thrust.

Hester, upright upon her mother's arm, stared calmly at these strange creatures. If she reached her second birthday, late in the next month, she would have spent two whole years in the attic. Occasionally one of the other women about the place had looked in at her for a moment. To a friendly chambermaid Ellie would say, "Just pop in and look at Hester when you're upstairs, will you?" but she had never seen a man before. Shyness, however, had been completely omitted from her make-up, and she stared at them with her wide, queerly coloured eyes, unafraid, uncurious, calm.

When Mr. Coldham, at a loss to know quite what to say to her or to Ellie next, picked up one of the biscuits and held it towards her, she took it in her dimpled little hand, set her brand new teeth in it and ate it with gusto and utter abandon of concentration with which she honoured most of her food.

"Can she walk?" inquired Mr. Coldham.

Ignoring Mr. Fenton's, "My dear fellow she must be two years old, they scramble about at a year," Ellie set Hester on her feet. Hester, who had never been so free, even in the attic, started off on a tour of inspection that brought her eventually in contact with Mr. Coldham's high, brilliantly polished boots with the tassels at the top. She tugged at the bright object, tasted it, rejected it in disgust and looked up laughing into his face. He laughed too and swung her up, shoulder high.

Mr. Fenton poured himself another glass of wine, withdrew to a fireplace and stood looking on with the cynicism of a seasoned father and of a man who imagines that he knows another man's secret.

Mr. Coldham tossed Hester in the air, she crowed and smiled and pulled his hair. Ellie stood watching, thinking what a good-looking pair they were, and remembering, quite suddenly and for the first time in many months, the laughing, yellow-haired foot-soldier whose brief stay in the stable-loft across the yard had resulted in Hester's begetting. Her short moment of passion and desire had been overlaid by the bearing of its consequences and by her life of gruelling labour, but now, for a little while she could picture him quite clearly, so young, so yellow-haired, so trim in his tight uniform of red and blue with the pipe-clayed belt and leggings. She did not yearn for him, even now. His visit had been like the visit of the angel to Mary amongst the lilies, something remote, detached from ordinary life. It had had its delight, she had borne the result, the whole thing was over and could never be repeated. But now, just for a moment, she remembered.

Suddenly, as everything did with him, the baby palled upon Coldham. Once more he fumbled in his pocket, furtively drew out a coin and tucked it down between the soft flesh of the child's neck and the frilled muslin that encircled it so prettily. Then he plumped her back into Ellie's arms, ready crooked to receive the burden.

"She's a grand child," he said kindly. "And you see that there was nothing to cry about, after all."

"No, sir," said Ellie, remembering Job's exhortation, and willing to allow Mr. Coldham to go on believing that she and Hester were welcome and kindly treated in a place where the baby's very existence must be concealed and ignored, even by herself, for long hours on end.

"Well, I shall hope to see you next time I pass here, both flourishing and the baby twice the size. Good-day to you."

Ellie made her little bob. "Good-day to you sir, and thank you. Good-day sir," she added to Fenton.

The door closed behind her. Fenton, after a few attempted witticisms which Coldham flatly ignored, returned to his seat and the interrupted conversation was taken up again.

21

CHAPTER III

WITHIN half an hour Coldham would be on his way to New-market. Ellie and the baby would be forgotten, and would remain so until some time in the future, when, drawing near to The Fleece, he would suddenly remember : "Ah, yes, this is the place where that little pinched thing had the baby that she shouldn't. I must ask after her." But the little episode, so simple, so quickly ended, was to alter Ellie's whole life, and through hers, Hester's.

Ellie, in greater haste than ever now, since her work was awaiting her and the brief hour of leisure ended, climbed the stairs again and, anxious to preserve the clothes, stripped Hester rapidly. As the last garment came off a guinea rolled out and across the floor. Hester gurgled and stretched out her hands for it, but Ellie, fearful lest she should swallow it, picked it up, said "No" in the firm voice that Hester knew and respected, and tucked it away amongst her own clothes. Then she replaced the torn old shift, sat the child on the bed and fastened the piece of linen which restrained her perambulations.

She shut the door firmly and went down to the kitchen, where a bucket of potatoes and one of onions had to be prepared be-fore she could return to the washing which Rosie had left as soon as Job Wainwright was out of sight. All day, washing and hanging out, taking in and folding the linen, tidying the kitchen, cleaning the great stove, scouring the dishes, she worked like an automaton. For almost the first time in her life she was occupied by abstract thought. That guinea, rolling for a foot or so before the irregularity of the attic floor brought it to a standstill upon its edge, had started something far bigger than itself, just as the first strain of coach horses against their collars started the heavy vehicle upon its destined way.

Ellie began to think about the future, about the baby and about money. Her first vague intentions that Hester should not spend her life scouring and scrubbing as her mother had done, had quickly died under the influence of the scrubbing and scouring, and up to this day Ellie had only thought about the child in terms of love and concealment and nourishment. Now

22

she looked ahead. In order to give Hester a proper start in life she must have money. That guinea must be the foundation of a nest-egg, it must be put away and added to. But how?

Next month she would receive twenty shillings. Six were already mortgaged to Mother Fenn. Six more, at least, would go, as usual, to the sempstress who converted the lengths of material into wearable form. That left eight shillings for the miscellaneous expenses of the next twelve months. She would have to break into Mr. Coldham's guinea for the shoes which she needed. For although she wore clogs in the kitchen and the yard, Job would not allow such footgear in the other parts of the house. They were too noisy and they marked the floors. Shoes she must have.

Except for the expenditure upon Hester's clothes, and that more than compensated for by Mr. Coldham's unexpected largesse, there was nothing new in Ellie's budget. Autumn after Autumn had brought, with pay-day, the same old problems. What was new was the manner of her thinking and the way in which her mental processes had brought her, every time, to the same conclusion. She must get some money. The guinea must not be touched : it must be laid away : it must be added to. But how? How? How?

Ellie, now in her thirty-first year, had toiled at The Fleece for twenty-two of them. Until she was twenty she had received no wage at all, merely her board and the two lengths of cloth. Illegitimate and orphaned, she had considered herself—when she gave the matter any thought, which was seldom—to be very lucky to have been taken into the inn at all; and she had never questioned the generosity of her employer, who after having worked her hard for eleven years for nothing, had, without being asked, given her twenty shillings a year from the time that old Anna, the previous scrubbing woman, had died over her pail in an icy December. Now, for the first time, Ellie asked herself whether she had been contented, too easily satisfied and whether it was too late to aspire to some less humble occupation about the place. There was Rosie, for example, younger than she certainly, prettier, more sprightly, but at the same time far lazier and less conscientious, who served in the bar and the great dining-hall and received fifty shillings a year, three aprons and caps ready-made as well as the lengths of material for dresses, and in addition was often given small sums by travellers whom she had served. Mrs. Bridges, too, had come into The

Fleece in a very humble capacity, had married a coachman who had been drowned in the wet February when the Stour had washed away its bridge, and had returned as cook, head of the kitchen and mindful only of Job Wainwright himself. And all the time Ellie had patiently scrubbed and scoured, not lifting her eyes above the tub and the pail which seemed her destiny. But now, just as that unknown fount of mother-love had sprung within her flattened bosom, so did ambition, belated but vigorous, take possession of her mind. She must have a better job, in order that Hester might be properly clothed and started in life.

To ask for promotion and a rise in wages was not easy to one of Ellie's natural diffidence and humble station. The mere asking implies the possession of means to seek the desired rise elsewhere should it be refused : and the very meagreness of the wages paid to underlings at that time denied the possibility of movement and of choice. Even the wealthy Rosie would have found it difficult to leave The Fleece, pay her way to another inn of the same size and look for a similar job there. Ellie would have found it impossible. Moreover she was handicapped by the child. Here at least Hester seemed to have been accepted and forgotten. The more Ellie thought about it the less hopeful she became : but her need was imperative and when at last the day of payment came and the rolls of grey flannel and bright prints were laid out upon the white scrubbed table in the kitchen, and one by one the female employees came forward in order of precedence to take their choice and then went along to the end of the table where Job sat, paying out the paltry sums with very ill grace from one of his canvas bags, Ellie, at the end of the line, knew, from the madly beating pulse in her throat, that she was going to speak.

Every other year she had watched the prettiest print being taken and the more sombre being left until as usual she picked up the dullest bundle, with envy in her mind. This year she hardly noticed. The harsh, hairy flannel clung to her palm as she took it in one hand and put it under her arm, the dampness of her fingers marked the grey and black folds of the print, but as she watched Job count out the twenty shillings and pull the draw-string of the canvas bag with a relieved air, she drew in her breath sharply and said in a voice that sounded hard and arrogant to her ears, though it was only the meekest whisper, "Mr. Wainwright, sir, could you give me a better job?"

Baalam, whose ass turned in the narrow path and asked,

24

"Why strikest thou me?" was hardly more amazed. Job's face turned redder and he spluttered, "Eh. What's that?" as though he doubted his hearing.

"It's like this, sir," said Ellie, hearing in the rhetorical question an invitation to explain, "I've been scrubbing for a long time now. Ever since I was a little mawther. And I don't seem to be getting on, sir. I don't make no headway."

"You make the only kind of headway that matters, my girl, headway with the scrubbing. What would you like to do—take a turn with the punch-bowl?"

That was Job's own speciality and to his mind the satire closed the conversation. Pushing back his chair he rose. The satire was lost upon Ellie, who hurried round and with unparalleled audacity put herself in his way. "Oh no, sir, not that, sir, but if you could find me a place in the still-room, sir, or in the hall. I'd work very hard, sir, indeed I would."

"You put your hard work into the floor," said Job with unusual patience, "and don't go getting ideas into your head."

Ellie, completely defeated, dropped back and as she left the kitchen, laid flannel, print and wages on the corner of the dresser where she could keep an eye on them, and filled the inevitable pail. She had asked, she had been refused, she must bear the disappointment. She dashed the back of her scarred hand across her eyes and plunged into the scrubbing without loss of time or noticeable slackening of effort.

Mrs. Bridges, who had received her wages first and was attending to the bubbling pot of stew while Ellie pleaded with Job, looked down on the thin bowed back with a scornful but not unkindly gaze. Of all the women about the house she liked Ellie best. True, she despised her as well, but then she despised them all. She knew, however, that Ellie was a good worker who did not resent being imposed upon, and Ellie, moreover, accepted little favours, such as a baked apple, a little cake or a scrap of candy sugar for the child, with an extravagance of gratitude that flattered the cook's vanity. To-day she attended to the stew, mixed flour and water for the dumplins known as "floaters" and dropped them into the bubbling brown mass before she showed any signs of interest in Ellie's petition, but as the scrubbing finished by the kitchen door and Ellie turned her attention to the crocks and knives used in the morning's cooking, Mrs. Bridges said, "Would Aggie's job suit you?"

Aggie, Rosie's sister and even prettier and vainer than she,

25

was seldom seen in the kitchen. Her work lay amongst the bedrooms—clean, warm, delicate, womanly work compared with Ellie's.

Ellie, who had missed the satire in Job's question about the punch-bowl, thought she heard irony in Mrs. Bridges' voice and said defensively, "I wasn't meaning that, you know I wasn't. I only thought perhaps I could have a job like Rosie or Maria. I want a little more money. It's not that I mind scrubbing."

"You can have Aggie's job if you'd like it," Mrs. Bridges persisted. "Mind you, that ain't all honey. Lots of people don't think that the bedroom maid's work is ended when the bed is made. But you know all about that and I don't suppose you're particular. Well, speak up, would you like it?"

"But Aggie ain't leaving, is she?"

"Not that I know on. Still, you leave that to me."

Ellie, in common with the rest of the people at The Fleece, knew that Mrs. Bridges was fond of her drink, and dismissed the conversation with the thought that the cook had been drinking early in honour of its being pay-day. She gave a timid, half-hearted smile and turned to the washing up. She did not see Mrs. Bridges separate one liberal portion of the stew into a little crock, added extra onion and pepper and something out of a jar that she took from the cupboard. And when Aggie came down to her dinner Ellie was hanging dish-clouts in the yard and missed the almost affectionate way in which Mrs. Bridges said, "Here's yours, Aggie. I put it aside to keep it hot."

Aggie, all unsuspecting, ate the savoury dish. By midnight she was seized with violent pain and purging. Mrs. Bridges, informed of this in the morning, recommended an egg beaten up in warm milk and went so far in the goodness of her heart as to prepare it. The potion, warm and soothing, had at first the desired effect and Aggie rose from her bed and dealt languidly with the slops and beds in two rooms. Then the unknown ingredient got to work again and Aggie's state was even worse than before. Declaring that she was dying and meant to breathe her last at home, she set out on foot for the village. A friendly carter gave her a lift in his wagon, and her mother, when she reached the cottage, put mustard plaster on her stomach, forced half a pint of hot elderberry wine down her throat and asked her suspiciously what she had been up to. By morning Aggie was pale and limp but greatly restored and would have made a perfect recovery could she have resisted the temptation to eat the jellied calves' feet which Mrs. Bridges sent by Rosie when she came to enquire how her sister was faring. Still quite unsuspicious Aggie was appalled and surprised by the rapid and thorough return of her symptoms.

Meanwhile Job Wainwright, with the Ipswich coach about to arrive in the evening, and all the beds but two unmade, sent an urgent message to Mrs. Bridges to send up which of the kitchen maids could best be spared, and Mrs. Bridges with a beaming smile and a significant nod to Ellie, bade her strip off her sacking apron and depart to the upper regions. "Work a bit extra for the first day or two," she advised, "then you'll be well dug in before yon besom is better."

In order to delay that eventuality she set about preparing a jug of beef-tea, so strong and good that it had set in a jelly before it reached the cottage, where it was delivered with the message that Aggie must drink it all as it was very strengthening and would make up for what she had lost. This cryptic message confirmed Aggie's mother in her worst suspicions and she gave it as her opinion that Aggie would be better to leave The Fleece and go into private service at the Rectory. Aggie, in no state to resist suggestion and remembering that the Rectory gardener was a handsome and eligible young man, an ex-soldier, who even if he had a wooden leg had a pension of a shilling a week to compensate for it, weakly agreed.

As soon as this news was retailed by Rosie, Mrs. Bridges lost interest in Aggie's state of health, with the result that Aggie recovered with rapidity, went to the Rectory and married the gardener before the daffodils bloomed in the borders that he tended.

Ellie, happily ignorant of the fact that Job Wainwright intended her to mind the bedrooms for the same wages that she had received for scrubbing, was delighted beyond measure by her sudden promotion. Job was also delighted. Aggie, with a home in the village making as it were a headquarters from which to operate, had been far more independent than he liked his employees to be. On that account she had managed, in two years, to screw up her wages to sixty shillings a year and had, although nobody but himself knew it, asked for another rise on the last pay-day. Now she had gone and Ellie was taking her place and keeping everywhere upstairs far more clean and shining. Ellie's scrubbing was being done by a youth of eleven, lately flung upon the charity of the world by the deaths of his

27

father and mother from typhoid due to drinking ditch water. Ellie sometimes passed him as he struggled with the pail that she had so lately abandoned, and when a pang of pity smote her as he strained and grunted she soothed herself with the reflection that he was both bigger and older than she had been when she first went to work.

Mrs. Bridges was also pleased with the new arrangment, because, when she explained the situation to Ellie and showed her that it was entirely through her good offices that promotion had come, Ellie had agreed without protest that a portion—a third —of the little extra she received, was due to the kindly cook. Ellie, imagining herself to be in receipt of sixty shillings a year and surprised to find how generously people bestowed pence, fourpenny pieces, even shillings upon her, felt rich enough to meet even greater demands than this. She had managed to pay Mother Fenn and buy herself some shoes—ordered but not yet delivered—without breaking into the precious guinea, and as she added the small change given her by generous travellers to the little hoard that she had started, she conceived a wild, fantastic, audacious ambition— Hester should go to school.

She thought of it, not because she had any ideas concerning the value of education, or the desirability of being able to read and write—such things were beyond the scope of her imagination. The resolve grew from her desire for Hester's happiness and her fixed determination that the child should not, at an early age, drift into the world of work. During the last year it had become obvious that Hester could not remain for ever in the attic. Already she had learned the knack of escaping from the bonds that held her to the bed, and had ventured out more than once, running along the passages like a little ape, swarming down the stairs on hands and knees. Soon, Ellie knew, the time would come when some different arrangement must be made, and so she thought of school. She pictured Hester sweeping, scrubbing, dusting, and contrasted that picture with one of her bent above a book, holding a pen. What book, and what she would do with the pen escaped Ellie's imagination because her experience was so small, but she knew that the latter vision utterly eclipsed the former.

CHAPTER IV

THE year passed. The annual pay-day came and Ellie was handed twenty shillings. Her disappointment was so bitter that it was some hours before she could make a protest. And when she did Job Wainwright brushed it and her aside with impatient contempt.

"If you ain't satisfied," he said roughly, "you can go back to the kitchen, or get a job elsewhere. Find somebody else who'll give you and your brat house-room and the run of your teeth. And that'll take a long time I'll warrant."

Ellie was effectively silenced. The knowledge that he had not forgotten Hester crushed her utterly. All her bright hopes faded. She knew that never, never would she be certain of more than twenty shillings a year; and of the uncertain pickings of her office a third was mortgaged to Mrs. Bridges. She would never be able to send Hester to Miss Peck's school. Never, that was, by any honest means.

For the first time in her humble, honest life Ellie began to consider other means. And to no one in an inn was the path of dishonesty more open than to a chambermaid. Most people were astonishingly careless of their belongings. Men would turn out the contents of their breeches-pockets on to the dresser and then go down to the privy across the yard, leaving the bedroom door open. Sometimes horsemen, arriving wet and muddy, would hand her clothes to be dried before the morning and it was not at all unusual for the pockets of coats and breeches to contain money, watches or seals. For the first year of her new duties Ellie had never touched a penny that was not her own, but now hope was dead in her, Hester would be five very soon and the clothes that had been purchased from Mrs. Fenn were completely outgrown.

With the concentrated and qualmless singleness of purpose of which only the simple mind is capable, Ellie began a course of petty thieving. Her work which took her in and out of the bedrooms offered her many opportunities and she availed herself of them. Within limits she was crafty enough and she seldom took much. A fourpenny piece, a shilling or even a few pence if the pile of money were small, a florin or even a crown piece if the pile were large. She grew bolder as she realised that the people who were careless with money generally carried their carelessness so far that they never knew to within a shilling or two how much their pockets held. The ones who were careful—and there were several such—generally gave her no opportunity at all. They kept their money in purses or bags, carried them with them always and slept with them under their pillows. Even when one such obviously careful traveller suffered a momentary aberration and gave Ellie a chance to help herself she seldom took advantage of it. It was too dangerous. She became almost uncannily adept at judging which traveller was safe spoil and which not.

To the blatant and obvious form of stealing—direct taking—she added another. It was easy enough, often, to knock over a few coins laid out on table or press, to let a pair of breeches slide to the floor accidentally and in such a way that the contents of the pockets rolled about the uneven floor. After such an accident she was humbly and anxiously eager to help to recover the scattered coins, and if one of her finds slipped into her own shoe or pocket it merely meant that the search was prolonged until the traveller tired of it and said, "Well, if it turns up when you're sweeping you can keep it." On such occasions Ellie's thanks were genuine and heartfelt, for she considered that such permission absolved her from the guilt of theft.

When Hester was six she began to attend Miss Peck's school. Miss Peck had come to the village some thirty years before with her father who had been a lecturer at Cambridge until he lost his sight. Miss Peck was not only literate beyond the common, she was a scholar of no mean order, and since her father had always spent everything he had earned and was now dependent upon her, she had opened a little school. In the early years she had not been able to give it her full attention, because the old man had demanded her help in the writing of a book called *The Lamp of Learning*. It was a history of learning and culture in England from Roman times to the present. It was a wild combination of sheer erudition and guesswork, and although when it was finished it brought him very little in the way of guerdon it was bound in course of time to become one of the classic sources from which subsequent surveys were derived. Its author died in penury, and his daughter, though competent by this time to have followed it with several volumes of her own, decided that there was little to be gained by setting down what you knew on paper, it was far more profitable to pass on the light of learning by teaching the young the mysteries of the alphabet, the handling of the quill and the rule of three. To this she devoted the whole of her time. Thrice a week she rose at seven and trudged through dust, mire, wind, rain, frost and snow, to the Hall at Fulsham where, in an unheated schoolroom she taught the seven children of Squire Moreton. Before she left, at eleven o'clock she set them tasks, equal to their ability, which kept them occupied and out of mischief until her next visit. On two evenings a week she had her men's class; young farmers and dealers, an ambitious boy who wanted to go in for the Church, an elder man who wanted to be able to read the Bible for himself. They paid twopence a session. In between times Miss Peck taught any child whose parents were willing and able to pay a shilling a week for the six days. On Sunday she attended service in the church—somewhat unwillingly but she was anxious to keep in the good graces of the Rector—and during the rest of the day she did what washing was needed, baked herself a fresh batch of bread and gave her cottage a perfunctory cleansing.

She was a tall, gaunt woman, past middle-age by the time Hester joined the ranks of her disciples, with a lined, parchment-coloured face and thin grey hair covered by a cap. Her eyes were already failing and there was a milky line around their dull brown pupils. Her upper lip was decorated by one or two coarse black hairs. She spoke English free from local accent or idiom and sometimes her pupils did not understand her, although long experience had made her conversant with whatever they might say. She taught with passion and if necessary punished with vigour, and it probably never occurred to her that she was doing a mighty work in keeping the lamp of learning alight in a very dark corner. When, as sometimes happened, one of her pupils proceeded to the Grammar School at Norwich and did well, she was pleased, but neither surprised nor elated, nor anxious to claim any credit. "Harry," she would say calmly, "was always a good boy. He deserved to do well," and then she would immediately divert her attention to another good boy who needed encouragement, or to a bad one who needed correction.

Her pupils were mostly boys, but there was a girl or two amongst them. This unusual fact was due to the Rector having three orphaned daughters with whom, by habit and temperament, he was quite unable to deal. He sent them to Miss Peck in

31

order to have peace in his home, and his parishioners were encouraged by this example to expend a few shillings upon the education of their daughters.

Miss Peck much preferred boys to girls, but she was too shrewd to say so or even to show her preference. The shilling a week was too precious. She even went out of her way to teach the girls a few embroidery stitches and some plain sewing. Every girl who attended the school was, moreover, given a little note-book bearing a label and the words, written in Miss Peck's prim slanting hand, *Rule Book*. Within, copied by the girl herself, were rules for behaviour, plain cooking and simple medicines. The little books travelled far, to remote farmhouses and distant cities, and many were the appetites tempted, the social problems solved and the pains assuaged by the application of "Old Peck's Rules."

In order to attend Miss Peck's classes Hester was fitted out with new clothes, made by the village dressmaker from a roll of material purchased by Ellie from the pedlar. The dress, the hood and the cloak were of duffle grey; the shoes, also the product of local talent, were clump-soled and buckled. From the shadow of the hood Hester's narrow white face, yellow curls and bright black-fringed eyes gleamed out, and Miss Peck, seeing her for the first time, was conscious of a strange movement of the heart. She excused the feeling to herself by thinking that she could read unusual intelligence in the child's face. Subsequent events proved her right, but by that time she would have admitted, though only to herself, that she would have been attracted to Hester had she been stupid.

On three days a week school began at eight o'clock and continued until three: on the other three days, when Miss Peck attended upon the Moreton family, it began at twelve and went on until six. Nobody could complain that Miss Peck did not give value for her shilling.

Hester, rigorously instructed by Ellie, slid down the back-stairs of the inn, and up them again with as little display as possible. She carried a small satchel in which, beside her slate, pencil, pen and Rule Book (already begun with instructions as to how to address one's superiors) lay a packet of food put up by Mrs. Bridges. During a good part of the year Hester managed to supplement this provender by going through the garden and orchard of The Fleece, unknown to Ellie, and helping herself to anything that offered. As a last resort she did not scorn the raw green produce of the onion bed and when, on such occasions, she took her place upon the bench, reeking to Heaven, Miss Peck did not treat her with contempt as she would have done any other onion-odorous scholar, but gave her home-made peppermint drops with a flavour equally pungent and a scent almost as far-reaching.

Hester's educational progress went forward at a phenomenal rate. Could she have seen into the future and realised how short a time was to be allowed her for availing herself of Miss Peck's tuition she could hardly have learned more rapidly. Her mind responded to the dry facts of learning as a plant, transferred from a cellar, responds to the sun and changes colour in the course of an hour. For six years she had been virtually a prisoner in that distant attic, a tethered body and an unoccupied mind, now it seemed as though all that fettered energy was released. She never forgot anything that Miss Peck said, she picked up every crumb of knowledge, even when it was not meant for her, as a winter-famined bird pecks around the nose-bag of a horse.

Miss Peck, used and resigned to her uphill work, was enchanted and enamoured with Hester's responsiveness. Almost every day she seized an opportunity to say, "Hester, if you will wait a little after the others have gone, I will explain that more fully." And when the last clumping step had gone gladly away, Miss Peck would unlock her tea-caddy, spoon out a precious measure of tea, put the pot on the hob "to draw" and then the two heads, one so young and so pretty, the other so old and ugly, would bend together over the page and the two cups of tea would steam and grow cold as the teacher explained the mysteries of the world and the pupil listened as though spell-bound. Just occasionally Miss Peck would give way to un-academic weakness and lay her thin, purplish-veined hand upon Hester's shining hair, murmuring, "You are a good child, Hester." And at such times, through the dry and dusty reaches of her virgin and learned being a tiny trickle of tenderness and regret would begin to flow. If only Hester were her own, how she would teach and cherish her, to what esoteric paths could she not lead her. And when Hester at last had clumped away in the wake of the others Miss Peck, for the first time in her self-contained and unemotional life, was conscious of loneliness and frustration.

Hester did not love Miss Peck at all. She used her as she used the inn garden, plucking what she wanted as she passed, calm, greedy and completely ungrateful. She did not even appreciate the hours of personal attention, the peppermints, the costly cup of tea. She was not, despite the doting old lady's verdict, a good child. Unless she were busy, as soon as she had mastered her own task she upset the other children by shuffling in her seat, dropping her tools, drawing on the margin of her book and holding it up for exhibition. Such behaviour in another child would have brought unmistakable proof of Miss Peck's righteous indignation. In Hester it brought mild reproof or sometimes besotted praise.

"There, Edgar Goodchild, Hester has finished her sums, you've hardly begun. Fancy letting a little girl get ahead of you like that. Make haste now."

Solid, stolid Edgar Goodchild would grunt and look at Hester with intense dislike. Hester would look back, and after a crafty, rapid glance at Miss Peck, would wrinkle her nose at him or stick out her tongue. But going home Edgar (or another smarting dunce) would be avenged upon the infant prodigy by tweaking her nose, throwing mud on her clothes, pulling her hair, or, sweetest revenge of all, pursuing her with a frog caught in a ditch. Hester's horror of anything that crawled was intense and unaffected. She would fly along the path as fast as her thin legs would carry her, pausing every now and then to shout, "Oh don't. Don't. Put it down, and you can copy all my sums to-morrow." Sometimes the bribe worked, sometimes it didn't; and there was once a dreadful day when, after the bribe had been accepted and met and all Edgar's sums were right, he approached Hester and said smoothly, "Will you take this for helping me?" He held out a blue sugar-bag, doubled over at the top. Hester, pleased and flattered, accepted it and opened the fold. At the bottom of the bag a large warty toad lay breathing visibly and watching her with a wary, beautiful eye. Hester with a scream dropped the bag, threw up her hands and fell forward in a white faint. Edgar, with the loud guffaw which Miss Peck was always denouncing as the mark of a lout, ran away and left Hester to come round by herself.

Hester came round. The empty blue bag on the ground reminded her of the horror. She got up quickly, shaking out her clothes and shuddering at the thought that the reptile might have taken refuge amongst them. She could feel the stealthy movement of it upon her legs and her stomach for hours afterwards, and each time a strong rigor shook her. But she was not thinking of that to the exclusion of everything else. As she went quickly home her seven-year-old face was set in an ageless mask of hatred and fury. Edgar Goodchild should regret that act.

With the matter-of-fact acknowledgment of weakness that is the beginning of all strength she accepted the fact that she herself, seven years old to his twelve, and a girl to boot, was not qualified to punish him adequately. Since body could not, mind must, and all through the next day she was quiet and subdued, to Miss Peck's delight, as she brooded over her problem.

Edgar Goodchild's father had a farm at the far end of the village. Edgar had been sent to Miss Peck's in order that he might learn to read and write in the simplest fashion and be able to count quickly and correctly, for Goodchild senior had often felt the lack of these abilities. On the other hand he resented the loss of Edgar's labour resultant from the demands of education; and if Miss Peck had been less enamoured of Hester's yellow head she would have realised that to compare the work of the two children was unjust, since Hester attended school regularly every day of the week while Edgar came only on the days when school was over at three o'clock in the afternoons. After that hour, and upon the other days, he helped about the farm, where he did much better work than in the schoolroom. Amongst his jobs was the tending of geese on the stubble-fields.

Hester knew that Edgar kept geese and she knew where. She also knew, with the sharp knowledge of the country child concerning essential matters, that the geese were valuable. Edgar's treatment of her, the need for vengeance visited upon him by some stronger hand than her own, the geese and their value, merged together in her mind and by the end of that day's school she had a plan all ready for execution next day.

School did not start until twelve, and Edgar was to spend the day minding the geese. Early in the morning, driving his flock before him, he set out for the distant field, bearing with him a slice of bread and cheese, which he devoured as soon as he was out of his mother's sight, and two pocketsful of bright red apples. It was a bright October day and he settled down to exert himself as little as was compatible with keeping the geese together. At about eleven o'clock, after what seemed like half a lifetime already spent, he was surprised to see Hester picking her way delicately, but with haste, between the lines of the stubble.

He now bore her no malice, and boredom made her a welcome sight. He selected the largest of the apples and polished it to even greater brightness upon his sleeve. As she came near he gave it to her and she smiled a Delilah smile and set her white teeth in it.

"I now saw such a funny thing," she said, with admirable casualness.

"What was it?" asked Edgar, rising to the bait.

"Ben Stowe in the stocks on the green, and Lolly had taken off one of his shoes and was tickling his foot with a turkey feather. Everybody did laugh. You should have heard Ben saying what he'd do to Lolly when he got out. Awful things. And Ben is coming out this afternoon."

"My, I wish I could be there to see," said Edgar wistfully. "But I've got to mind these blamed geese all day to-day. I never do see anything. All school and work my life is."

Hester tilted her yellow head on one side and looked at him with an expression of deep commiseration. Not too soon and not too eagerly, she asked, "Could I mind geese?"

Edgar made a noise that was like a preparation to spit.

"Anybody could mind 'em," he said scornfully. "Anybody *could*; but I've *got* to."

"I could mind them while you just ran down to the green. You might just get there when Ben got out. Oh, I wouldn't like to be Lolly when he does!"

The gloating in her voice and the sparkle in her eye made Edgar the more eager to be there, in the forefront of the scene of interest.

"You got to go to school," he said in a hopeful voice.

"I don't care. I'll say I had toothache. I have got a funny tooth, look."

She swallowed the last fragment of apple and opened her mouth to show a loose milk-tooth hanging precariously by a shred of flesh. Edgar weakened even more.

"If the geese get away me father'll flay me. Gor, he can't half lay it on too, when he's riled."

"Would he really? Would he flay you?" Hester's eyes would have betrayed her to a more astute protagonist.

"But I'll mind them, Edgar. He'll never know."

Edgar did not stop—as wise people do—to question the gods what he had done to deserve such favour from one whom he had little to bind to him. He merely accepted the Grecian gift. He took out three more apples, laid them in Hester's small hands

36

and departed as fast as his legs would carry him. Hester watched until he was out of sight. Then, with method and patience and dispatch, she scattered the geese.

The heavy spoiled birds, almost aware of their value in the approaching Christmas season, were disproportionately alarmed when she set about them. They had never been hurried, much less stampeded in their lives. They fluttered and squawked and waddled. They spread their wings and attempted to remember how the lean, unspoilt, wild geese fly. They were like a rich, spoilt, effete people when the barbarian hordes swoop down. And Hester was the barbarian. She flung clods of earth and stones. She snatched a hazel twitch from the hedgerow and beat every bird she could reach, she screamed and stamped and shouted. In an hour the birds were scattered far and wide. Returning, time after time to the attack, Hester drove them in all directions. Not a single goose remained in the original feeding-place. She widened her circle of terror, she ran, jumped ditches, pushed through gaps in the hedge.

Then suddenly she stopped. By this time, she thought, regretfully, Edgar would have reached the green, learned that the whole comic scene had existed only in her vivid imagination, and would be on his way back. Well, let him come. October days are short and he would have to run for many miles before even half his flock was gathered.

Hester made her way to Miss Peck's cottage which was in the opposite direction from the green.

Her smile was angelic as she said, "I've had toothache, Miss Peck, please. But it's better now and I did want to come." Miss Peck laid a cold dry finger on the smooth oval cheek.

"Poor little girl," she said with more tenderness than she was aware of. "Which one is it?" Hester obligingly opened her mouth and Miss Peck, with a sleight of hand worthy of a conjurer, tweaked it out and held it up aloft. "There," she said triumphantly. "That won't trouble you again. And I think a peppermint would do the place good, don't you?"

The other children, who had lost their milk-teeth without help from anybody and without peppermints, looked on in wonderment. Their feelings that there was something queer about this Hester Roon, who was never seen except at school, and was so much favoured there, increased.

Next day Edgar Goodchild, a little puffy about the eyes still, though his expression was defiantly stolid, returned to the class.

37

He did not sit down, but elected to stand by the table and do his lessons leaning forward on his elbows. In the short break allowed for the eating of the food the children had brought with them, the boys gathered about him and he exhibited, not without pride, the stripes which marked his posterior. He also related, in short surly sentences exactly what had happened on the previous afternoon.

Hester held herself apart. At first this aloofness was her own choice, but as the tale spread child after child looked at her coldly and avoided speaking to her. They had no terms of abuse with which to meet the occasion. They could not call "Tell-tale tit, your tongue should slit," because she had told no tales. "Cheat" or "sneak" was equally unsuitable. "Treachery" was outside their vocabularies. To these soil-born youngsters, destined to deal always with realities, Edgar's confession that although he had searched until darkness drove him home in despair with less than half the flock, the story of the geese deliberately scattered was appalling. No normal child, they felt dumbly, could have acted that way. And despite themselves they were a little frightened. The spite that could so over-avenge so small an injury, the ingenuity that could invent so convincing a story as that of Ben and Lolly, the energy and determination which could have made so thorough a job of the geese's dispersal, all these were outside their understanding and they feared it as all ordinary people, children and adults alike, fear the unknown. The immediate result of this was fortunate for Hester; not even Edgar contemplated revenge. Dimly and dumbly he felt that whatever he did to her would be rewarded again, a hundredfold. The stripes upon his buttocks healed and were more or less forgotten, but his mind remembered, and even when, in his late twenties, he fell in love, he found himself unable to trust his chosen because she was a woman. Mrs. Edgar Goodchild suffered many things through Hester Roon although she had never seen her.

Isolation hurt Hester not at all. She was used to it, born and reared and grounded in loneliness. She lived in the centre of the busiest community for miles around, but she was bound, by Ellie's orders, to pass through it, unobserving and as far as possible unobserved. Nevertheless, she knew more of the comings and goings in the great yard than Job himself. Beneath the attic window she had dragged a stool, and standing upon it with her elbows on the stone sill, she leaned down, like an imprisoned lady from a tower, and as long as daylight lasted watched the changing cavalcade as it passed below the window. She saw the swift light chaises bound over the cobbles, the heavy goods wagons with their wooden wheels, iron shod. She saw the horsemen and the dealers, the drovers, the fishermen, the coach passengers. And when the light failed and the scene faded she turned away, unregretful, calm, self-contained as ever and lay upon the hard narrow bed. She turned off her outer eye and began to use the inner. She saw the people in the books that Miss Peck talked about; the up-thrust ranges of mountains, the wide expanses of sea, the sunny lands from whence came the tea and coffee, the raisins and the oranges and figs. She saw the ram appear to Abraham, Lazarus emerge, stinking from the tomb, Jonah swallowed by the whale. She was quite happy and well able to dispense with the company or approval of noisy little children who caught frogs in damp places.

CHAPTER V

MEANWHILE Ellie was headed along a path that could have but one ending. With her means her desires had grown. She was no longer content for Hester to possess one tidy outfit of clothing. She must have garments in reserve so that when it was wet she could change her clothes. She liked to slip down and inspect the pedlar's tray and buy the child ribbons and goodies. The book-packman, too, found her an unusually willing customer. And over and above all there was Miss Peck's weekly shilling to find. But, strongest incentive of all, was the love of the game for itself. Ellie had become a jackdaw, she stole for the pleasure of it, for the thrill and the excitement, for the triumph of making a successful haul. Until she had embarked upon her criminal career she had never tasted power, never known excitement, except for the brief interlude of her illegal passion for the passing soldier. She had been like a working animal, overladen, unrewarded and completely unassertive. And since every human nature, however humbly it may conduct itself, has some instinct of assertion, Ellie's, driven underground for so long, was doubly dangerous now that it had found an outlet. She took pleasure in slipping away the unmissed coin, and in seeing the unsuspecting traveller depart. "You little know," she would think. If she had been suddenly reduced to the kitchen ranks again, even at a vastly superior wage, she would have been less happy.

But the simple path of petty larceny took an unexpected twist.

There arrived at The Fleece one evening in the January of Hester's tenth year, a little wiry man in a shabby overcoat. He alighted from the Ipswich coach with five other travellers and was installed, with his valise, in a small bedroom at the end of a passage. Ellie did not pay him much attention, his coat was too shabby and his valise too small. But the night was very cold and he called for his fire to be lighted. The door of his room opened outwards and fitted badly, and as Ellie shifted the basket of logs with which she was laden from one arm to the other in order to allow the door to swing open past her in the narrow passage, she could see, through the gap between door and lintel, the little man, full in the light of two candles, pouring a stream of coins from a leather bag into his palm and back again. His face bore a look of intense pleasure. So did the watching Ellie's, though she did not know it. Fascinated, she stood by the door, her eyes following his every movement. The careless gloating way in which he handled the money informed her experienced mind that the coins were uncounted. He looked swiftly round the room as though searching for a hiding-place. The sticks of kindling were already crackling on the hearth, searching for the logs that were still in Ellie's basket. He went towards the fire, bag in hand and passed from Ellie's sight. When he stepped back into her range of vision again the bag was gone. Her jackdaw instinct told her that he had not slipped it into his pocket— it was in the chimney somewhere. She was quite sure of that. She opened the door and stepped down the three oak stairs into the room. With a quiet deftness of service that was all her own she laid the logs in position, and through the resultant bellow of smoke asked if there was anything else she could do. The little man said that there was. She could bring him up a bottle of Rhenish and a glass and then she might inquire how long it would be before the pigeon pie which he had ordered would be ready for serving.

Something in the manner he said "Rhenish" and "pigeon pie" informed Ellie that his more usual fare was ale

40

and bread and cheese. He was very pleased with himself and was treating himself well. Ellie, herself a thief and a hoarder, came straight to the correct conclusion; his pleasure was in some way connected with the bag of money, and it had been ill-gotten. She smiled as she climbed the stairs again. It would be hard if she could not gain possession of a tithe of his haul to-night.

Savoury odours began to steal through the distinctive and persistent atmosphere of the inn, imposing upon the underlying scent of wood smoke, tobacco, ale, onion and well-worn clothing the drifting and ephemeral perfume of cooking food. The pigeon pie was served and the little man summoned to eat it. Ellie armed herself with a new basket of logs. Hardly ever did she enter upon her depredations without excuse. The fire was burning brightly, so that with the light of the two candles as well the room was well lighted. She set down the basket upon the warm hearthstone where the guest's damp boots were already steaming, and ducking her head a little she stood within the hood of the great open chimney. Above her an unevenness of the brickwork made a soot-coated shelf. She raised her arm and ran her fingers along it. Twice the clotted soot deceived her, feeling soft and heavy to the touch, but the third obstacle that her groping fingers met with was the bag. She opened her hand and grasped it carefully, and as she did so two strong arms closed about her waist; she felt herself dragged backwards, her head caught the overhanging chimney breast, and then she was standing on the hearthstone, bag in one black hand and the little man, still holding her, was staring at her with a look of humorous accusal.

"So that's the game, is it?" he asked, taking the bag from her nerveless hand. "A common thief, eh? And can you find gold like a water-diviner finds a spring? What do you use, your nose?" He flicked his fingers across that feature and held them up to show Ellie how she had blacked them. But his banter gave her time to recover herself.

"I didn't know it was yours, or that it was gold, sir," she said, bending her head meekly. "The fire was smoking so I thought perhaps a bird had nested in the chimney, I looked up to see, and I saw that. I didn't know you'd put it there."

"So the birds hereabouts nest in January, do they? Come, come, my good girl, you must do better than that. Besides I'm not such a zaney as to put the thing where it showed. You were searching for it, weren't you? Own up now, or I'll get my host

41

and the constable to deal with you."

"When I came in with the wood, the first time," said Ellie, trying another tack, and vaguely relieved because he was showing some reluctance to call Job, "I saw you put something up the chimney, and I wondered what it was. I wasn't going to take it away, sir, honest I wasn't. It was just my curiosity. I'm sorry."

"You're not a bad liar," the little man admitted. "But that wouldn't save you, you know. The law's very strict on dishonesty in inns, and so by God, it should be. I've no doubt if they searched for your little hiding-place, even if they were only looking for birds' nests, they'd get a surprise. Wouldn't they, eh?"

Ellie thought of the straw mattress which held her treasure, and it seemed to her that the small grey eyes of the stranger could see it too. He was playing with her, that was what he was doing. Perhaps the coins had been planted there just to tempt her. Perhaps, even, he had heard from other travellers, less unsuspecting than they appeared, that things had been missed at The Fleece. Her natural pallor increased, so that the soot marks on her face showed up ghastly on the waxen skin. She began to tremble in every limb. Her chin quivered.

For an appreciable time the little man watched her, his eyes amused and sardonic. Then he ducked back, reached up and restored the bag to its hiding-place.

"Pour out some water," he ordered. Ellie obeyed. He washed his hands carefully, dried them slowly and then tossed the towel over to her. "You'd do as well to wash too. I'm going down to my supper now. Take away that wood and bring it in again in an hour. You and I have something to talk about." He mounted the two steps to the door and then turned back. "I'm forgetting the snuff I came back for. Bless you, snuff-box, you saved me that time." He took it up from the table and slipped it in his pocket. "Be quick with that washing woman, if you want to use my room for your ablutions. I've my reputation to consider." He went off along the passage smiling to himself.

Ellie spent the next hour in trepidation. The more she thought about it the more desperate did her case seem. She came to the conclusion that the little man was prolonging his triumph, playing with her as a cat plays with a mouse, intending all the while to devour it in the end. The thought that her room might be searched made her heart tremble, but her mind was so distraught with terror that she did not even attempt to hide the incriminating evidence elsewhere. And where else was there? She stole back upstairs once and found Hester bowed above her books, straining her eyes to read by the light of the rush-dip, her hair falling forward and hiding her cheeks.

"What's the matter?" she asked, looking up reluctantly.

Ellie gazed around the attic. No, there was nowhere else that would be safe.

"Nothing," she said vaguely.

"There's been another robbery on the Foxhall Heath," said Hester, who had been leaning out of the window in the darkness, listening while she could not see until the cold drove her to shut herself in.

"Oh," said Ellie, not interested, and shaken by the mere word. If this, her lastest victim reported her to the constable and set the law upon her, would it be the stocks? Flogging? Norwich gaol? "It's very cold up here, Hester," she said, shuddering. "Would you like me to ask Mrs. Bridges to let you sit by the fire for a little? Mr. Wainwright won't go in the kitchen any more to-night."

Hester pulled the blanket which she had taken off the bed, higher around her, she thrust her thin blue hands into its folds. "I'm all right. It's quieter here." She bent over her book again and her hair fell forward, hiding her face.

Ellie stood for a moment looking at her, and love and admiration banished anxiety from her mind for just that moment. For the thousandth time she fell into wonderment at the idea that she should have produced anything so clever and so beautiful. To see Hester reading made something warm and strengthening swell in Ellie's heart. It was like, and yet unlike the feeling that took possession of her when some unsuspecting traveller went on his way short of a florin : it was another manifestation of her power. But to-night, as she remembered how and why it had come about that the printed word held no mystery for her child, her mind leaped away and landed uneasily upon the thought that this power had been bought at a heavy price, and that in a moment or two the bill would be presented. One word from the little man and the least that could happen would be for Job Wainwright to turn her out and she and Hester might starve before she found another place. Ellie sighed audibly, but Hester did not raise her head. Robinson Crusoe had just discovered the print of a naked foot in the sand and Hester was oblivious to the fact that a figure in a drama just as tense and exciting was standing within reach of her hand in her own attic. Ellie sighed again and stole away.

Down in the oven the hot bricks that heated the beds were absorbing the warmth left over from the cooking. Two by two she lifted them out, wrapped the grimy flannel around them and carried them upstairs. She left the little traveller's until last. Through the crack of the door she could see the light of his candles and knew that he was within.

He was standing upon the hearth, his coat-tails lifted, his legs and back bathed in the red glow of the firelight. Ellie turned back the bedclothes, deposited the brick and covered it. Then, with her heart trembling like a bird, she stood, empty hands to her sides, and waited. The little man dropped his coat-tails and spoke as though he were for the first time aware of her presence.

"Ha," he said, "you've forgotten to bring back the wood." More delay, thought Ellie, scuttling away for her basket. Her breath came and went so quickly and her fingers shook so ungovernably that she mended the fire badly and the little man pushed her aside and set the logs in order himself before he spoke.

"Now," he said, "suppose you sit down and let me have a look at you."

For what seemed to Ellie an age of suspense he studied her. He saw the pale face with its vague blunt features, the nondescript brown hair already scanty at the parting, the frightened eyes that tried to meet his with defiance. He saw the deceptive frailty of her small hard body, the hands, widened and reddened with perpetual work. And while he stared steadily at her, Ellie, in swift, frightened glances took in the contours of his small brown face. It was seamed with exposure to the weather, the mouth was hard, the eye calculating, the nose coarse, yet it was all redeemed from ugliness at the moment by the twinkle which softened the calculation in the eye and touched the lips with a smile.

"Why do you steal?" he asked at last. "Necessity or pleasure?"

Too eagerly Ellie made her confusion. "From necessity sir, dire necessity indeed."

The twinkle broadened. "Well, since you confess that you *do* steal there need be no more beating about the bush. What's your name? Ellie Roon. Well, you know Ellie, you were caught in the act, and if I'm not to lay a complaint about your behaviour,

44

I shall want you to do me a favour in return."

Involuntarily Ellie's eyes turned towards the bed. She knew, as did everyone in the inn, that Aggie's charms had often led travellers to make advances, advances which she had been quite willing to meet; but Ellie's lack of beauty had protected her from such suggestions; ten gruelling years had passed since the soldier had found her desirable. While she hesitated the man saw the drift of her thoughts and laughed.

"Nay, lass," he said, with unflattering promptitude, "it's not that sort of help I want. I want someone who is spry and sly, used to using her ears and her eyes and capable of moving about quietly in the dark. And someone who isn't over-scrupulous about how she earns a guinea."

Ellie, who had used her eyes and ears to advantage and did not fear the indoor dark that she knew, or the prickings of conscience, was kept silent by a doubt as to whether she were spry or not. The word suggested someone like Aggie or Rosie, moving lightly on their feet, upright, swift and bouncing.

"What did you want me to do?" she asked at last, timidly, feeling that some response was expected of her.

"Supply me with information," said the little man promptly. "To a man like me it would be a god-send to have somebody in a place like this, who would slip me a word now and again."

"Yes," said Ellie, "and what sort of word?"

"Now, now, if you're going to be stupid you'll be of little use to me. I'll give you an example of what sort of word. Do you know Dick Tench?" Ellie nodded. "Well then, come on now, tell me what does he do, what does he trade in, where does he go?"

"He trades in horses. Good ones, because he always has one stable to himself and a groom guards it all night. Sometimes he takes them to Norwich, sometimes Cambridge, sometimes Ipswich. He looks after his money as he does his horses, and he never gives me anything except a lot of running to and fro."

"Excellent," exclaimed the little man, bringing his hand down on to his thigh with a sharp smack of delight. "I felt that I wasn't wrong about you. There's just one thing you didn't mention about him. I wonder can you think of it."

He waited, and Ellie, recalling what she hardly knew she knew, continued : "He has a boast that he has never lost a horse yet, not even to Little Tom!" And with that name a light seemed to burst into her mind and as she mentioned it her hand

45

flew to her lips as though to catch it before it was heard.

For this was Little Tom, himself. Sitting here in The Fleece, cool and calm as you please and giving no sign of knowing that the sheriffs of four counties had set a price on his head. Little Tom Drury, whom rumour credited with being the no-good kinsman of the Moretons up at Fulsham. Though, if rumour were right in that, the blood bond had not prevented the Squire from contributing to the prize money. The list had hung upon the door of The Fleece and in similar prominent places throughout Norfolk, Suffolk, Cambridgeshire and Essex, bearing witness that a large number of gentlemen were so concerned for the safety of the roads that they were willing to dip into their private purses in order to enable the sheriffs to promise two hundred pounds to anyone giving information that would lead to the arrest of the felon known, indifferently, as Little Tom, Tom Drury, or Tom Common.

But Little Tom had powerful friends, as well as enemies, and his nefarious exploits were profitable enough for him to be able to buy silence. Two hundred pounds was a good round sum, but once it was received the source from which it came was dry, whereas Little Tom might go on dripping guineas for ever. Moreover there was the fate of Bob Mullet to stand as a warning against informing. Bob Mullet, a farmer out Swaffham way, had found seven horses instead of six in his stable early one morning, and not having sufficient faith to believe that anyone loved him enough to make him a present of so goodly a steed, had set to work to find the rider. He found him, Davy Price, the Welsh highwayman, curled up in a hay loft, sleeping late after a night's activity. Bob Mullet had a magistrate and two soldiers at the foot of the stairs before he waked the sleeper, and on the day of Davy's hanging Bob received fifty pounds in gold. And little good it did him, for he never even lived to get it home. In the morning he was found with his head clean drilled with a bullet; and in the place of the fifty pounds was a paper saying that as the writer credited him with less conscience than Judas, he had not given him the chance to hang himself. And the farm that had been Bob's was known as the Potter's Field to this day.

All these thoughts flowed through Ellie's mind with the swiftness of running water and yet it seemed that the little man broke a long silence when he said : "Quite right, my dear. But I propose, with your help, to remedy that state of affairs. And you'll find that helping me will be far more profitable than

46

stealing an odd coin here and there. Less dangerous too."

"What do you want me to do?" she asked again, rather less timidly.

"Be my eyes and ears in this place," said Little Tom succinctly. "I have them in several places, but not here. Job Wainwright has the reputation of being incorruptible from the outside." He laughed harshly. "Prefers to do his own robbing in his own way. But you, now, you could be a sight of use to me, if you liked." He hesitated for a moment as though wondering how far to trust her, remembered that she was a self-confessed thief, and plunged on. "Four miles or rather under, along that lane across there, there's a place called The Honest Lawyer. I daresay you've heard of it?" Ellie nodded. "It's a mean little place, good for nothing but a glass of ale, though you can get a horse there if you want one. But Slomey Candler doesn't make his living selling ale or letting out horses, see? He's in with *us*, me especially. Now I'll tell you what you have to do. We'll say Dick Tench arrives with a string of horses. It shouldn't be impossible for you to find out, one road or another where he's bound for. He'd open his mouth in a place like this that everyone knows is honest. Then later on you slip out and pass the word to Slomey. He mounts a man that'll take a night ride if he's paid for it and lets me know. That's how it's done, my dear, all the world over, and Job's about the only innkeeper I know who doesn't give somebody a word sometimes. And you needn't squeak on Tench alone. Keep your eyes and your ears open and tell what you think'll be useful. Young bloods who boast what they've won at Newmarket, women travelling with their jewels, folks who've done a pretty bit of business of any kind. You let me know, and I'll see you get your share."

"But," said Ellie, who had hardly listened to these instructions, so eager was she to state the insurmountable objection, "I never have time to run four miles with a message. I ain't been out of this place for more'n an hour, ever. I'd be missed."

"Good God," he said, quite earnestly. "What a life! I knew old Job was a driver but I never . . . But look here, *after* they're all fed and bedded down for the night, you're loose then, ain't you?"

"But then there's Hester."

"Who's the devil she?"

"'My little girl. She's ten. She'd notice."

"Why, that's the very thing. Send her. Why, if you can scare

47

a child into holding its tongue it's the best messenger in the world. Slip through anywhere."

"I wouldn't send Hester out alone at night for anything you could offer me," said Ellie flatly. Then, as she watched the anger dawn upon his face she remembered that she had other duties toward Hester besides guarding her from the perils of the night. She wanted to make money for the child's sake, and here she was baulking at the one good chance ever offered her, or ever likely to be.

"But I'll go myself, somehow," she added.

Immediately he brightened.

"That's a sensible lass," he said. "And by the way, if at any time Slomey shouldn't be home you can give the message to Kate. She'd take it; she'd ride with it too at a pinch."

"All right," said Ellie. "I'll do as best I can."

CHAPTER VI

So FROM petty pilfering Ellie graduated into the fellowship of the road.

She began, that very night, to dread the coming of that other night when she must make some excuse to Hester and then face the journey in the darkness. Horrible things, as every woman knew, lurked in the night, and the lane that led seawards was as lonely as any in England, and even on a moonlight night dark as a tunnel between its high banks.

The day of ordeal arrived before Christmas. On a day of sleety rain and biting wind Dick Tench arrived with a string of six glossy horses which his groom led away to the usual stable. Dick himself came blowing and slapping his hands together into the warmth of the inn parlour, and quenched Ellie's one hope of reprieve with his first words.

"Well Job, old cock," he exclaimed, beating the innkeeper upon the back, "here I am again and as much in need of a good draught of mulled ale as ever. Have you ever known Norwich Fair to fall in a decent spell of weather?"

So he was bound for Norwich. And with her own ears Ellie

48

had heard him say it. Up till then she had cherished a feeling that was half hope and half fear, that she might not be able to discover the horse-dealer's destination. Then, through no fault of her own she would have nothing to communicate, and nothing to reproach herself with. Now, knowing, she had to choose between making the dreaded journey and admitting that her fear of the excursion was more powerful than her love of her child.

She finished her work, put the hot bricks in the beds and saw that those fires that had been ordered were burning and supplied with fuel. Then she went down into the kitchen and stayed by the fire until Martha, at Mrs. Bridges' order, raked over the embers and led by the cook the last lingerers trooped upstairs. It was bitterly cold upon the attic floor and Martha, as she opened her door and felt the resulting outrush of draught shuddered and said, "I 'ouldn't like to be out to-night."

Ellie, shuddering even more violently, passed on to her own little room. Hester was curled up in the middle of the bed, sound asleep. For a moment Ellie contemplated the easier way of slipping out without waking her or explaining. But there was a possibility that Hester might wake in the night and discover that she was absent; she might make a fuss that would draw someone's attention to the fact. Ellie decided to wake her, and bending over shook her, gently at first and then more violently. Hester woke and blinked at the candlelight.

"Listen, darling. I got to go out. I shan't be long. You'll be all right, won't you? I don't want anyone to know I'm gone."

"Oh, all right," said Hester sleepily and quite without interest, and was asleep again before Ellie had struggled into an extra skirt and a shawl. Going out so seldom and never on a long journey or in inclement weather she lacked suitable clothes, but that was hardly worth considering. She had her clogs, the extra skirt and the shawl and she intended to walk quickly enough to keep warm. She kissed Hester's sleeping face, waited a little until all sound had ceased and then crept, timid and silent as a mouse, down the stairs.

The journey was all that she had dreaded. The thick mud in the lane sucked at her clogs, the wind plucked at her skirt and shawl and flung handfuls of icy sleet at her face. She stumbled into deep holes full of water, tripped over stones and was clawed at by briers. However, she pushed on, breathless, but hurriedly. Perhaps the physical difficulties of the journey kept her from feeling too fearful, she was too absorbed with the need to make progress, to keep her feet in her clogs and the shawl upon her head and shoulders, to have time for fancies.

She came to the little stream, spanned by a plank for the convenience of the infrequent foot-passengers and knew that she was nearing the place. Soon the little low house was on her left hand, crouching like an animal beside the road, a shed or two and a stable near-by pressed up to the main building like cubs to their mother's body. There was no light in the place and no sign of life, and after Ellie had felt for and found the door and battered upon it for some moments she thought, with a sickening sense of futility, that the journey had been in vain.

She stepped back and stood looking up, willing and willing that some sign should answer her. But she had grown tired of waiting and was turning away, deeply dejected, when the creak of an opening window halted her in her tracks and a female voice, low and cautious, inquired, "Oo's there?" Doubting that her reply would mean anything Ellie nevertheless said, "Ellie Roon." The young woman had evidently been warned. There was no caution, and considerable warmth in the voice as she replied, "Is ut indeed? Wait a minnit, I'll be down."

Drawing the sodden folds of her cloak more tightly around her, Ellie waited. Several minutes passed and then the door-hinges screamed and the oblong of yellow light framed the figure of a woman, her body shapeless in a long cloak and her head bristling with knobs of hair curled up on strips of rag.

"You poor girl, you. Come right in," she said kindly, and seized Ellie by the elbow to hasten her, shutting the door behind her with a well-directed thrust of her foot.

She went swiftly over to the fireplace and taking a handful of chopped faggot from a basket, threw it on to the few pinkish embers, reached for the bellows and plied them vigorously. As the flames leaped and crackled she fed them with more faggot and then finally dropped on a small dry log. Soon even Ellie could feel the warmth. The strange girl stood up then, pulled forward a broken chair and said, "There, you sit down, spread out your skirt and give me that shawl."

She shook the drenched garment with the same vigour with which she had worked the bellows and then stretched it over a piece of string which hung, looped from nail to nail all over the ceiling. Several other articles of clothing were already suspended in various parts of the room.

"Now you'd better have sommat to take to. Brandy suit you? It's what I' ave meself. T'ain't nothing extra, but it's better than the rot-gut we sell." She bustled about as she talked and whisked round from the cupboard in the wall with a bottle and two cracked and chipped brown measures in her hand, before Ellie could either accept or refuse.

She had lighted one candle from another, set one on the dirty bare table and the other on the shelf above the fire and to Ellie's dark-accustomed eyes the dirty little room was brilliant. She took the measure of brandy which the girl had poured out and over its brim regarded her. She was a tall, broadly-built creature, twice Ellie's size, though not fat and her features were bold and well marked. The twisted tortured hair was black and plentiful,, her eyes a deep brown, her lips and cheeks naturally red. She had, all about her, an air of vigour and determination, and as soon as she had dealt with the simple arrangements for Ellie's comfort she came straight to the point.

"You've come about a message for Tom Drury, I reckon. 'E said you might. You'd better let me 'ave it. There might be summat that ought to be seen to at once."

"It's about Dick Tench," said Ellie. "He's got six horses at The Fleece and he's bound for Norwich."

"The crafty old devil," exclaimed the girl, "fancy going that road to Norwich from his place. It's as near again for him to go Swaffham way. Still, that's the way 'e's done business all these years and it's worked till now. My word, Tom is pleased with getting you into the game and no mistake. It'll make a world of difference to 'im, and to us all. And I'll tell you this about Tom, he don't forget who 'elped 'im. That's more than could be said for a lot of them. Well, I'd better get young Willy on to this right away. Don't you disturb yourself. Sit and get warm, you need it."

She rose up swiftly and opened a door at the back of the room shouted, "Willy! Willy!" at intervals until a voice answered. Then she said, "Job for you. Now. Tom." Returning to Ellie, peering into her mug and replenishing it, she added, "I don't 'alf like sending him out and that's the truth. But there's no one else. My father's out already. And God knows how we'd live if it wasn't for Tom and 'is like. I tried for years to keep Willy out of it, but you know what boys are. Still he only do the errands and such like. I 'on't let 'im really take to it. That's one thing I 'old against Tom, he will *talk* to Willy so much. And to

51

'ear him talk you'd think that slitting a man's throat was no more than slitting a pig's. Not that Tom's violent as a rule."

The warmth and the brandy had combined with Ellie's weariness to cast her into a pleasant somnolence. Her eyes half closed and she nodded forward. She hardly heard a word of the girl's discourse, but the sudden cessation of it brought her to herself wiht a start. She mustn't go to sleep yet : she must drag herself out of this sheltering warmth, set her feet upon the long muddy road again, face the wind and darkness. Reluctantly she stood up.

"Yes," said the garrulous girl, "I s'pose you must." She consulted the clock that hung upon the wall, the one whole and reasonable clean thing in the room, "My, yes, it's after one." Graver matters made her forget Ellie. She went to the door at the back again, "Willy! What are you at? Are you ever going to be ready?"

A petulant voice, thick with sleep replied, "All right, Kate, dammit, I can't ride in my shirt a night like this."

Kate turned back to Ellie and said indulgently, "He 'ates being got up. I've known 'im sit up some nights when we expected a message, rather than get up again. There now, I'm afraid this ain't dry yet, but on the other 'and it ain't any the worse. Would you like my cloak?"

"It'd drag on the ground on me," said Ellie, "and somebody would be bound to notice it and wonder where I got it. I ain't supposed to be out."

"Well, you can always say you've popped over to see your friend Kate Candler, can't you? I dessay we'll see each other often enough. Good-night, and thanks. Dirty old night, ain't it?"

Ellie's answering 'Good-night' was torn away by a swoop of the wind. Kate stood for a moment with the door held against the blast, looking out into the night, and then she turned back and set about speeding Willy upon his way.

Ellie slopped and buffeted her way back to The Fleece. She was soaked to the skin and almost senseless with cold and exhaustion by the time she reached it. She had not even energy left to wring out or hang up her dripping clothing. She dropped it on the floor and crept into bed, drawing Hester close to her for warmth. In the morning she ached in all her joints and had the sniffling beginnings of a heavy cold; but beyond a repeated injunction to Hester not to mention the matter, she made no reference to her nocturnal journey.

Dick Tench rose early, breakfasted hugely, shrugged himself into his heavy coat, retrieved his whip from the peg where he had hung it and bustled out into the yard. The six horses, all in fine fettle, awaited him. In full view of all whom it might concern—and you never knew which of your fellow-guests that might be—he and the groom set off along the Ipswich road. Less than a mile along it they turned off through the property of a friendly farmer, made a slow detour across a field, along a lane and through a ride in the wood and struck the Norwich road again about a mile and a half above The Fleece. It wasted time but Dick did not grudge it.

Such naïve subtleties had saved him from the danger of premeditated attack, and experience had taught him that most attacks were premeditated. Few people attacked on the spur of the moment. Confident that if he were being watched for, it would be along the Ipswich road, Dick spoke cheerily to his groom and sang and whistled as he made his way to Norwich.

For two days Ellie waited to hear whether her alliance with Little Tom had been crowned by success or not. Although she wished Dick Tench no harm she did not like to think that the discomfort of her journey, and the violent cold she had taken, had been borne for nothing. On the third evening, with the incoming of the coach from Norwich, came the news that Dick had been set upon as he paused to allow his horses to drink at the Winwood water-splash. He and the groom had resisted, but the groom had been shot in the leg, Dick through the eye, and all the horses had been taken. Dick was lying, in very poor case, at The Maid's Head in Norwich, whither he had been taken by a chaise which had happened to reach Winwood within an hour of the assualt.

Rosie recounted all this to Ellie and the others when they met in the kitchen for supper. Ellie was suddenly unable to continue her meal. Her throat felt thick and dry and her stomach jumped uneasily. The bit about Dick being shot in the eye was largely responsible for her feelings. It sounded such a brutal thing to do. Three days ago he had set out, a stout, well-set-up, happy man, and largely through her perfidy he now lay, shot through the eye, "in very poor case." The groom's wounded leg caused her less concern, for the leg, less sensitive a member, is not so easily injured in the imagination. She felt obliged to put her

53

own hands over her eyes and press them gently. Then, plate in hand, she stood up and looked towards Mrs. Bridges. The cook understood the evening ritual. She eyed the plate and said, "Not much to add to that, to-night." Then she piled upon Ellie's unfinished portion the extra bits that she had reserved for Hester, and Ellie bore the brimming plate away.

Hester had finished *Gulliver's Travels* and was sulkily awaiting Ellie's arrival. She wolfed down the food and then said, "Can I go down now?"

"I think so. It's fairly quiet in the kitchen to-night. And Hester, if Mrs. Bridges asks you to do any small job while you're down there try to do it with good grace, won't you? We owe her a great deal and she might make things very difficult."

"You pay her for everything we have," said the child hardily. She had once seen her mother give Mrs. Bridges her "share."

"That's nothing to do with it," said Ellie rather wearily. Really, she thought, Hester could be very difficult. Things were less easy now than when she was a mite of a thing, tied to the bed.

Hester, tucked away in a warm corner of the kitchen, accepted, with obvious pleasure, a piece of rock sugar from Mrs. Bridges, and with equally obvious displeasure, a little later on, a bowl of raisins to stone. It was the kind of slow, fiddling job that she detested, and the monotony and the stickiness were not compensated by eating every fifth raisin. But to-night, as people drifted in and out of the kitchen, she was delighted to hear, with much repetition and some variations, the story of the assault on Dick Tench at the water-splash. Not for the first time in her life she regretted her sex. A stirring story was always concerned with men, never with women, she reflected fiercely. Women did all the dull, dreary, boring things, like stitching and cooking and scouring. And stoning raisins, she thought, disgustedly, licking her sticky fingers for the twentieth time. No one could read her mind, so no one thought to tell her that blood is sticky too.

Discontent with her sex had been born in Hester with her ability to read, and had grown side by side with it. A girl could never be a soldier, a sailor, a pirate or a highwayman. And although, according to Miss Peck (a feminist long before her time) England had risen to heights of greatness never surpassed in the reign of a queen, queens were not encouraged. The eldest daughters of kings (Miss Peck insisted upon all their names being memorised) were married off, and as often as not banished for ever from their native country. Whereas the sons . . . Not even rank or wealth could salve the sting of being a woman; Hester realised that already. It was easy to see that ladies had a duller time than poor women; that accounted for the interminable fine stitchery that they did. Even the wife of the King with the proud and enviable title of "The Conqueror" had nothing better to spend her time on than the Bayeux tapestry. And who, in her senses, could compare the pleasures of winning the battle of Senlac with embroidering the story of it?

Even at that early age Hester realised that she was singularly fortunate in being sent to school at all, but she did not realise for several years that she was even more fortunate—in view of her particular disposition—in having Miss Peck for a teacher. More than a century and a half was to pass before the world looked upon her like again But as an antidote to the bitterness which was beginning to devour her most brilliant pupil Miss Peck was not a success. Her own bitterness had been dulled by time, but the memory of it lurked. If she had been a man, not a woman, she might have followed her father, became a light in the Cambridge firmament, instead of wasting her undoubted talents in the wilds of Suffolk teaching louts their alphabet, guiding clumsy hands in the making of pothooks. It was useful work, she admitted that, and one day it would be universally recognised as such, but the fact remained that she did it, not from choice, but because the world forced her to fit herself into so narrow a sphere, merely because, by some strange, inexplicable fate, by some unreasonable pre-natal influence, some of her organs had been fashioned in one way instead of another. This being so, Miss Peck's tuition was not likely to be such as would resign Hester to her fate. Miss Peck knew all the disadvantages, and none of the pleasures of being a woman. Plain, capable women seldom do. She did not point out to her glowering pupil that William's conquests were thrown into Matilda's lap like jewels, that Elizabeth's triumph lay, not in her queenship but in the inspiring nature of her femininity, that Charles the Martyr lost his head because of the counsels of his little French queen. Of these things Miss Peck was hardly aware. For her the state of womanhood had been a tragedy : if it became that for Hester too, well, that was the fault of a stupid, one-sided world, not of Miss Peck, to whom the stories of Jael, who smote Sisera with a nail through the temples, and of Deborah, without whose support Barak would not venture into battle, were far more sweet and inspiring than the story of Mary amongst the lilies at the Annuniciation, or of the other Mary listening at the feet of Christ.

So Hester, shooting up like a sapling, becoming eleven, becoming twelve, stuffing her head with old stories in which men walked like gods and women flitted like pale shadows, brooded and rebelled, and risked offending Mrs. Bridges by her aversion to simple household tasks and caused Ellie many a sigh as she realised with every passing month that it had become impossible to keep this life confined to the attic, and equally impossible to control its actions once it had left that retreat. Before long Hester discovered that the yard and the stables offered greater opportunities of entertainment and less risk of being burdened with a job than the kitchen, and after that Ellie's worries increased. She thought sometimes of the risk she had taken, and was taking still, in order that Hester should have the advantages that the Rector's girls had, and reflected sadly that she might as well have let her become immersed in the life of the inn from which she had tried, for a time at least, to save her.

Soon after the assault on Dick Tench a parcel was handed in at The Fleece by a young man whom no one seemed to notice. It was addressed to Ellie, and inside many wrappings were tucked five guineas, which Ellie, hardly believing her eyes, took and, when Hester was absent, added to her hoard. New ambitions sprang into being, new dreams came to life as she added the coins, one by one, to the collection of copper and silver for which she had, literally, risked her life. If this could only continue for a little while she would have enough to leave The Fleece. She might even take a little ale-house somewhere and run it with Hester's help. And she would let it be known that Hester would have a neat little dowry when she married, that she was no penniless girl, made for a man's passing sport. And then an eligible suitor would come along and Hester would be married by the time she reached a dangerous age.

In this oblique fashion Ellie admitted the existence of a problem which every day was going to increase. Hester was twelve years old, her arms and legs shot disconcertingly out of her sleeves and skirts, though her girth seemed to remain the same, but even the leanness and the legginess, the poor patched garments, lengthened with bands of contrasting material, could not hide the fact that Ellie had mothered, if not a beauty, a child of unusual attractiveness. The round, babyish contours had gone from her face, leaving that long narrow oval which not even age itself can destroy. It was cunningly, lovingly moulded in frail clear lines. Beneath the sharp jaw, before the neck began, there was a hollow in which a pulse was visible, a pulse which quickened with anger or excitement. The brows were thin and dark and had an upward leap and spring, the like of which Ellie had never seen on any other face. Beneath them, fringed with dark lashes were the eyes, a greenish amber in colour but traced with darker lines, quite symmetrical and oddly reminiscent of daisy petals. Little escaped those eyes; they were equally swift to record, or to convey an impression. A pleasing face so far, a young, attractive face. But did Ellie, so blindly wise in a few matters, so near the soil, so dumb, read danger in the mouth? Already those wide full lips had the curves of maturity; firm red and satin smooth, beauty dwelt on them, and passion, and determination. Was it because of them that Ellie's mind hovered around thoughts of marriage and a dangerous age and made them twin?

Grinding toil, robbing the woman of so much, gave her at least a spurious peace of mind, and for long days on end she did not worry about Hester for the simple reason that she had so many other, more pressing things to think of. Only now and then did she pause to plan and dream, and those occasions were chiefly when Little Tom cropped up, either as a master to be served, or a benefactor to be blessed.

For the imaginative pain of Dick Tench's lost eye did not drive Elllie from her bargain. Time after time, as opportunity occurred, she made the journey to The Honest Lawyer and handed, either to Kate, or to Slomey, her scrap of information. She much preferred dealing with Kate, whose robust cheerfulness could lend an air of ordinariness even to the underground exchange of espionage. Ellie found that Slomey, with his battered nose, cauliflower ears and generally villainous appearance, drove home her own sense of wrongdoing. Without being in the least self-analytical she realised that when she handed her information to Kate she expected to get home safely and hear that the assault had been a success; whereas when Slomey received the message, she knew more terrors on the way home and expected the assualt to be disastrous for Little Tom, her own share in it to be exposed and herself either flogged or hanged.

Hanging and flogging were often in Ellie's mind at this time.

CHAPTER VII

TWICE during the next two years Tom Drury visited the inn in person, appearing as an ordinary, respectable traveller and regarded as such by all who came into contact with him. The second time was immediately after an affair which had roused an outcry and caused a good deal of uproar even amongst a community that was hardened to the danger of the roads. A man and wife, people of wealth and substance, had attended their son's wedding and were returning in their own chaise, driven by their own man. They were stopped. The driver, whom they might have expected to trust, had stolen away into the dusk. The lady was ordered to hand over her jewels. Her husband protested and drew his pistol. Without further parley the highwayman had shot him through the heart, and as he gasped out his life on the floor of the chaise the robber had collected everything of value, cut the horses out of the shafts and left the lady to spend the night alone in the chaise with her husband's corpse. That, everyone felt, was carrying the thing a little too far, and when the lady, almost demented from her ordeal, recovered and described her assailant in such a way that other victims recognised Little Tom, voices were loud in their demand that something should be done. The reward for him was increased by fifty pounds.

Soon after, in his modest anonymous garments, bearing his little valise, the wanted man alighted from the Ipswich coach and walked into The Fleece, where he demanded a room and a meal immediately. Job Wainwright gave him the welcome that he reserved for persons who had visited the inn before and spent well, and addressed him as Mr. Burroughs. Only Ellie, spreading the clean linen on the bed, recognised him as the cold-blooded ruffian for whom four counties were on the look-out. Once again she had the feeling of nausea which had assailed her when she heard of Dick Tench's eye. It seemed impossible; he looked such a merry, harmless little man. His husky voice was so kindly as he said, "Well, my dear, here I am again, you see."

Ellie thought of the extraordinary growth of the hoard in the recesses of her straw mattress, and realised that it was not for her

58

to judge him. She remembered the old country adage, "The receiver is as bad as the thief". Nevertheless she could not banish from her mind the picture of that unknown woman, watching through the night with her skirts dabbling in her husband's blood, her only company his corpse. When she regarded Tom now Ellie saw less the humour in his eyes and more the recklessness, and decided that there was a ruthlessness about him even when he smiled. When he congratulated her upon her perspicacity and the way in which she delivered her information, Ellie's heart was shaken, not elated.

And yet, after he had gone, and everything had quietened again, she went on playing her part. The surreptitious visits to The Honest Lawyer continued.

Ellie's work was not rendered easier by Hester's growing interest in the reason for her mother's absences. Hester at twelve years of age had reached a point where everything under the sun held interest. She was extremely wilful too, and increasingly subtle in getting her own way. After almost every one of Ellie's absences Hester (without saying so) drove some kind of bargain as the reward of her silence.

"I shall go out again, to-night, Hester. Stay in bed, won't you and forget all about it."

"Then can I go down for my food? And if Mrs. Bridges doesn't mind, can I sit by the fire for a while? Otherwise the time will seem so long."

Or—"I won't say anything. But Mother, can I have some new shoes? These nip my toes."

Ellie, only half suspecting that she was being bargained with, always gave in. The only cheering thing about Hester's growing reluctance to be confined to the attic lay in Mrs. Bridges' increasing affection for the child. Despite the fact that Hester was idle and greedy, the cook seemed to welcome her presence.

Few indeed were the days when she did not save her some titbit from her cooking. The kitchen fare was varied by little tarts with a large H marked on them in pastry, spiced cakes of which Hester was fond, the succulent "oysters" which Mrs. Bridges had whisked out of fowls served on the guests' tables. And the only return that Hester gave for such favours was the all-embracing interest with which she listened to Mrs. Bridges' reminiscences. And there was nothing personal in that. She extended it to any and everyone who made a bid for her ear. The one story of all others—the one which dealt with Ellie's doings in the hours of her absences in the night—was the one story which Hester most earnestly desired to hear, and the one which was denied her. Ellie had engaged in crime in order that Hester should have a "better" life, and she was determined that the child's innocence should not be smirched with the knowledge of her mother's dishonesty.

Ellie herself regarded her lapse as a purely temporary affair. Let the association go on successfully, let Little Tom evade the law and share his spoils for another year or two, and she and Hester would be gone from The Fleece and would be set up on their own. This dream, crystallising with every remittance from the highwayman, inspired Ellie to a far wider and firmer interest in life than any she had taken before. She knew that the tavern she hoped to take would be much smaller and humbler than The Fleece, though she pictured it as cleaner and more prosperous than The Honest Lawyer; nevertheless she thought she would profit by knowing how the larger establishment was run. She began to neglect her own province whenever she felt it safe to do so, and haunted the brew-house and the smoke-house, trying to learn how ale was brewed and hams cured. She begged Mrs. Bridges for the "rules" by which she cooked, and made Hester add them to Miss Peck's, with which they were often oddly at variance. She even questioned the ostlers in the yard about the diet of horses and what they cost to stable for a day. Money and a trifle of secret power had worked their infallible alchemy and transformed the cringing, hopeless drudge, whose chief thought had been how to get through her daily toil, into a woman with a life, a future and dreams of her own.

So the two years passed with their varying seasons. Travellers came, halted and went on. Ellie listened and watched and continued her secret warfare. Hester grew out of her clothes, completed her subjugation of Mrs. Bridges, and was at last considered worthy, to Miss Peck's inexpressible delight, of sharing with her her contemplation of the glory that was Greece and the grandeur that was Rome, with an occasional excursion into Babylon and Egypt.

Ellie made her journeys, through winter, spring, summer and autumn nights, and came home, often enough, with substantial proof of Little Tom's reputed honesty in sharing. The sums varied from half a guinea to five. And every time, whether there was money for her or not, she received a warm welcome from Kate. Slomey was drinking more and more steadily and seemed to be less in evidence.

And then one evening—it was in the autumn after Hester's twelfth birthday—Kate opened the door of the tavern without smiling and did not offer Ellie her usual refereshment. It was a warm night, full of fluttering leaves and the scent of apples and garden fires.

Ellie stood (Kate had not asked her to sit down) and said :

"There's a young man who won a hundred pounds at the races yesterday. I heard him shouting to Job to come and split a bottle with him. He's starting out for Felsham tomorrow at ten o'clock. Will you let Tom know?"

Kate did not reply and Ellie felt that she had not been sufficiently explicit.

"He's a fair young man in a mulberry coloured suit and he rides a cream mare. He's armed too."

Kate still said nothing; her face bore a look of almost over-emphasised unconcern, but her mouth and her brow were surly.

"What's the matter?" asked Ellie at last, timid as ever in the face of anything that looked like disapproval.

"I'm sick of this game, that's what's the matter. I wish I'd never set eyes on Tom Drury and that's the truth. 'E's got clean 'old of Willy. And I've asked 'im again and again to leave the boy alone. Oh, I know 'e used to carry messages, but that couldn't be 'elped. It's 'is going on the road that I object to. Tom Drury'll be sorry he crossed me, too. I been a good friend to him, and you know what they say about good friends—they're good enemies, too."

Her usually merry mouth was set in a hard thin line. Ellie looked at her and reflected that she must feel about Willy as she herself did about Hester.

"You don't understand," said Kate, misinterpreting Ellie's glance. "A thing may be all right for you, when you're grown up and know what you're doing. But it's different when it's somebody you brought up. I 'ate the very thought of it. 'E's out now. 'Ow do I know if he'll come back?"

"I do understand," said Ellie earnestly. "I've got a daughter, she's twelve now. I ain't never told her anything about all this. Tom Drury once said she could take the messages. I reckoned that was a horrid notion."

"I reckon so, too," said Kate, "but Tom Drury wouldn't give thought to that. There's only one person in 'is little world and that's 'isself."

She went off into a drift of thought wherein Ellie had no place, and Ellie, conscious of the passing night and the return journey yet to be made, shuffled from foot to foot, indecisively. At last she said, "Well, will you give Tom the message?"

"I'm not sure that I can. There's nobody here but myself."

Ellie remembered Tom's words, "And ride with it too at a pinch," and realised that Kate was no longer a willing servant of the highwayman. "Looks as though I've had a journey for nothing, then," she said with a lightness she did not feel.

"There's a lot of wasted work and worry in this world," said Kate in reply.

Ellie made for the door. Kate roused herself and accompanied her. At the very threshold she remembered and, turning back, lifted a packet from the cupboard.

"'Ere, wait a minnit, Tom left you this last time he come."

The coins in the packet clinked as she laid them in Ellie's eager palm. "Funny, ain't it? He's very honest in some ways and got no conscience at all in others. Damn 'im to 'Ell."

"Thank you," said Ellie. "Good-bye."

"Maybe it's a longer good-bye than you reckon on," said Kate. "If Willy don't want me no longer I shan't be here to watch 'im go down'ill. I been a mother to that boy, and now Tom's making a mock of me to 'im. Good-bye."

She did not linger to watch Ellie out of sight this time, but slammed the door upon her last word, leaving Ellie alone in the empty blowing night.

Ellie made her way back to The Fleece, full of thought and doubt. There was good reason to imagine that Kate, as a medium between herself and Tom, had ceased to exist. The angry brooding woman who had slammed the door was not going to pass on any message; she was going to bed, to lie and ponder her wrongs. And Ellie could not really blame her. Suppose someone should lead Hester astray. Wouldn't she feel the same?

At ten o'clock next morning the young man in the mulberry suit mounted his cream mare and Ellie felt positive that he and his winnings would be unmolested, by Tom at any rate. And the races would cease now for the winter. Before they started again who knew what would happen? Ellie had a feeling that she too would have deserted Tom by then. When she had a chance she would take the paper-wrapped bundles of coin from the mattress and count over her hoard. If it seemed even almost sufficient the Spring would find her and Hester far enough away.

On the Thursday of that week, before Ellie had had time to reckon over her money, the postboy, on his weekly journey to Norwich, stopped to change his horse and to refresh himself. He poked his head into the kitchen and inquired for Ellie Roon. Martha, despatched by Mrs. Bridges, found Ellie in the dimly-lighted, airless little apartment where she mended linen.

"Postboy's asking after you," she said. Ellie looked up from the sheet that she was darning and surprise was plain upon her face. It changed immediately to consternation. Who, she thought, who on all this earth, save Tom Drury, would have need to communicate with her? She bundled the sheet hastily together, jabbed in her needle and with a brief word of thanks to Martha, hastened down to the kitchen.

The postboy, a wedge of Mrs. Bridges' famous currant cake in one hand and a mug of steaming coffee in the other, stood by the fire.

"You asked for me," said Ellie.

Somewhat handicapped by a lump of cake in his cheek he tried to look at her with a significant expression. Then he laid one finger to his nose and winked prodigiously.

"I brought you the parcel what you ordered," he said, and winked again. "You know, when I was here last you asked me to fetch you . . ."

"I'd quite forgotten," said Ellie. "I wasn't expecting it so soon."

With an air of relief he dipped into the leather satchel which he usually carried on his saddle and handed her a small flat parcel. "There's nothing to pay," he said.

"Thank you," said Ellie; and then, aware that both Mrs. Bridges and Martha were regarding her with interest she made her escape from the kitchen. Safe back in the sewing-room, with the sheet huddled on her knee as a shield between the parcel and anyone who might disturb her, Ellie opened the paper. Within was more paper, sealed, and within that yet a third layer, tied with twine. In the heart of the third wrapping was a sheet of stiff white paper, folded over at either end and sealed, and marked in several places with the print of a dirty thumb. Impatiently Ellie broke away the seals and spread out the paper. There was nothing within but its inner side bore some lines of writing.

A dew of perspiration broke out upon Ellie's forehead and upper lip, as she looked at the black irregular letters. They meant nothing to her in themselves, and yet she was certain that they were written by Tom Drury—or perhaps Kate Candler. She clung hopefully to the alternative. If Kate had gone away she might possibly have taken this means of letting Ellie know and perhaps of saving her a fruitless journey to The Honest Lawyer. And in that case the letter had already fulfilled its purpose and the actual words were of no importance. But if, on the other hand, the message was from Tom she could not guess its meaning and there was nothing to do but to ask Hester to read it. Dear God, it might even be a warning! Bewildered embarrassment gave way to terror, and her heart began to thump so hard that the repercussion of its beat made the folds of sheeting tremble and the paper crackle as she held it again before her straining eyes. If only she could read. If only she had had the wit and energy to learn with Hester when she was first struggling with the mysteries of A B C. But she hadn't thought about it then, never imagined a contingency when her inability to read might even be a danger. She must wait until Hester came home.

She took a few more stitches, controlling her hand with an effort, but she was too nervous and impatient to finish the job. She folded the sheet and laid it aside. The letter she tucked into her bodice and went down to the kitchen. There at least she would see Hester's arrival.

Mrs. Bridges, with the light cool touch of the born pastry-cook, however hot or heavy she may appear herself, was preparing the covering for the pies. Marth was slicing apples into the deep brown dishes and made no demur as Ellie took up a knife and began to help her. The boy who had taken on Ellie's work with the scrubbing-brush came in and out bearing baskets of logs and faggot wood. Every time the door opened Ellie looked up. Each time as it admitted only the panting laden lad, she dropped her eyes again and counselled herself to patience.

At last, however, there came the step there was no mistaking, the light bounding step of unburdened youth, and Hester tripped into the room. Her bright indifferent smile played over the three women alike, but when the cook said, "Hungry lovey?" in a voice that counted upon an affirmative reply, she edged around to Mrs. Bridges' side of the table and watched with bright eyes and absorbed attention as the stout woman took from the cupboard a dish of deep brown gingerbread cut into slices. She said "Thank you" and bit into a piece at once. Mrs. Bridges laid another slice beside the pies and returned the dish to the cupboard.

Ellie watched with a feeling of jealousy stirring in her heart. She was able to give Hester so little, though she bought her some trifling thing from almost every pedlar who made his way into the yard. Mrs. Bridges' oblations were daily and all concerned with food, which played a great part in Hester's life just now when she was growing so rapidly. Once again Ellie stayed herself upon the prop of her dreams. When they were free of The Fleece and she had a kitchen of her own, she too would have little treats and surprises to greet Hester's home-coming. But to-day the prop of dreams broke beneath pressure and Ellie remembered the letter. Those straggling black letters might contain a message that would make the future uncertain, or even dangerous. She could wait no longer.

Hester took up the second slice and bit a semicircle out of it. "Bring it upstairs," said Ellie, "I want to fit your new petticoat."

"Bring it down and let her fit it in front of the fire," said Mrs. Bridges, unwilling to curtail the pleasure she took in watching Hester's appreciation of her culinary skill.

"Somebody might come in. She's too big to be seen in her petticoat," said Ellie a trifle sharply. "Come Hester."

Outside the door she laid a hand on her daughter's shoulder and almost hustled her upstairs. And yet, when the attic had been gained and the door safely shut, she drew out the paper with a gathering reluctance. She was about to let the child into a carefully guarded secret : to do exactly what she had so studiously avoided. She felt her hands begin to tremble again. The new petticoat hung over the broken-backed chair, all ready for fitting, and Hester was already unbuttoning her bodice. Should she fit the garment and not mention the paper? For a moment she hesitated. But necessity overcame her. For safety's sake, perhaps for Hester's sake, she must know what the paper had to say. And whom else could she ask? Whom else trust?

"Wait a minute," she said. "The petticoat can wait. I want you to read this to me."

With an effort of resolution like that required for the plunging into a cold pool whose depth is unknown, she proffered the paper, crumpled now from confinement in her bodice. Hester took it, walked to the window and bent forward to catch the fading light. Ellie watched her. Hester was silent for so long that the woman's impatience became agony, and she said :

"What's the matter? Can't you see? Shall I light the candle?"

"I can *see* it," Hester answered touchily, "but it's such bad writing, and I can't understand what it's about."

"Just read it out, darling. Just as it is. I shall understand."

"All right. It says, 'K. C. has turned runty'—that's right, r u n t y—'runty and split on the game. They are after me. Keep your light burning and sleep with one eye'—it just says a small i like i for ink, but I suppose it means eye—'open for a night or two. I look to you.' That's all. What on earth does it mean? Where did you get it?"

She turned from the window and looked at Ellie, who, at this confirmation of her worst fears, had sunk down, white and shaken on the foot of the bed. She straightened herself and said, with a commendable show of calmness, "Oh, is that all? It doesn't mean anything."

"Who is K. C.?"

"Nobody that matters."

"Then who are *they* who are *after* whoever it is?"

"Oh, nobody! Don't ask so many questions, Hester."

"It's something to do with where you go at night," said the child confidently associating the old mystery with the new one.

"Ssh," hissed Ellie, "you don't know what you're saying. Come along now, finish undressing and try on this petticoat."

Momentarily baffled Hester took off her bodice and let the skirt of her dress fall to the floor. She stood more than usually still and quiet while Ellie marked the place where more tucks were needed.

"You don't seem to thicken out at all, for all you're for ever eating," said Ellie. "This ain't a bit bigger round than your last one."

"I don't want to be fat," said Hester, skipping agilely out of the new petticoat. "Look at Mrs. Bridges. Why, Martha has to help her into her shoes. I'd starve to death before I'd look like that, like a store pig."

"You're a naughty girl to say that," said Ellie with a reproval that was quite mechanical, "she's very kind to you."

"Did I say she wasn't? I said she was too fat. And she is."

This proof that Hester was not blindly enamoured of her benefactress was balm to Ellie's heart.

"You needn't worry. You'll always be thin, like me," she

said, drawing Hester's attention to her own possession of the quality that the child evidently admired.

"You work too hard. And then you often stay up half the night," Hester pointed out with a naughty glint in her eye. "That'd keep anybody thin."

"Don't mention that outside this room, Hester, please. Now more than ever." Her harassed eyes shot a glance at the paper.

"There you are," said Hester triumphantly, "I knew it had to do with that. Is it smuggling?"

"Oh for the dear's sake! Ain't I worried enough without you nagging at me? Sit down and learn your lessons and keep your nose out of what ain't your concern."

She had seldom spoken so roughly to Hester in all her life, and it was quite meekly that the child said :

"Make a light, then."

Ellie lighted the candle and set it out of the draught. Then she took up the letter and folded it across and held it to the little flickering flame. She had folded the writing outwards and beneath Hester's watching eyes the brown scorching heat ran up and engulfed, one by one the words, "Keep your light burning." It was like Miss Peck's finger moving, word by word along an unfamiliar page.

Left alone, Hester ignored her book. From the rough shelf where she kept her personal belongings she took down a dirty red handkerchief that had, until lately, adorned the brown neck of Sam, the youngest of the ostlers. It was full now of woodnuts, ripe and freely separating from their withering husks. She opened the door a trifle and inserted the nuts one by one in the hinge, cracking the shells by giving the door sharp little pushes. When she had a good supply cracked and shelled she threw the shells out of the window, laid the kernels on the counterpane and threw herself down beside them. Munching steadily she gave herself up to thought. She found that a supine position, stomach downwards and face propped on her hands was conducive to this activity.

Ellie went out at night, secretly, thought Hester, tackling the problem in logical fashion and marshalling the known facts first. Ellie had been impatient to have the letter read, she had not been able to wait for the second piece of gingerbread to be eaten. Yet she had hesitated before producing it, once they were alone. That meant that she could guess what was in it and knew that it was connected with the secret. Now for the note itself.

67

Somebody had "split on the game". Given away the secret that Ellie shared. Was that it? And the other somebody had somebody else after him. And he wanted Ellie to leave a light. Why? So that he might know her room from the others? Maybe. Again why? Well, if he had somebody after him it seemed likely that he needed help. And from Ellie of all people. Strange. Hester thought again of the form of the letter. It had been written by somebody who could just write and that was all. Miss Peck would have rapped any knuckles responsible for such strokes, and described, in no flattering terms, the brain that could have allowed "i" to stand for "eye."

A man who could not write very well, a man in danger, a man in some way concerned with Ellie's nocturnal errands. Who moved in the night? Smugglers and highwaymen and footpads. And Ellie had not denied the smuggling. She had merely gone bad-tempered. Slowly, but with relentless mental progress Hester was arriving at the realisation that Ellie had not been making her nightly journeys to meet a lover. That had been the explanation which she had offered herself and accepted, basing it upon the slightly squalid and intensely earthy knowledge of sex relationships which was the heritage of four years' of hanging around the kitchen and the stable. Men and women met for some purpose, half veiled in mystery, but the subject of shrewd guesses after the witnessing of certain proceedings in the pig yard. Martha went to Mr. Wainwright; the barman, John, was known to visit Rosie; and Hester herself, one evening during the last spring, had gone in search of her friend Sam and found him in the hayloft with one of the village girls. After that she had accepted Ellie's absences with nothing more than a slight disgust. Ellie little knew to what brand of suspicion she owed her sudden freedom from her daughter's inquisitiveness. Hester knew that such things were furtive and secret, and had accepted them in silence.

Now that was all altered and she suddenly saw Ellie as the participant, not of some uninteresting mawkish intrigue, but of something stirring and exciting, men's stuff, real, vital.

She was conscious of a tingling of her skin as she considered that she was so near, next door, so to speak, to a real story. Somebody was being chased, wanted help from Ellie, had driven an unaccustomed pen in words of appeal. And Ellie hadn't been able to read a word. She, Hester, had had to do that. So she was in this now. Not outside, as one was outside a story in a book, however carried away one might be, however much one might pretend, but walking about, living and breathing, in the very heart of a drama. She finished all the nuts in one crowded mouthful, crushing them as she wanted to crush the marrow out of the bones of life.

CHAPTER VIII

It was with the deepest sense of disappointment and frustration that Hester learned that her mother did not intend to burn the signal light.

"But, Mother, he asked you to."

"Well, I shan't," said Ellie, flatly, shaking out her skirt before laying it carefully over the seat of the broken chair. "And unless you want to make me savage you won't talk about it any more."

She, like Hester, had been giving the matter her whole attention all the evening, and she had come to the comforting conclusion that she had only to do nothing and all would be well. The first shock of hearing that Tom was in trouble was offset by the knowledge that he would not have asked her to keep a light burning unless he had intended to come to The Fleece himself. And he would not contemplate that if she herself had been in any way involved by Kate's betrayal. If the inn was safe, Ellie was safe, and she had only to keep her window darkened, and if he came he would go away again and she would be left in peace. Sound reasoning so far. But her subsequent plan was faulty. If she had taken Hester into her confidence and told her that there was danger—for both of them—in taking any action, things might have been very different. As it was she left the child knowing at once too much and too little, aquiver with curiosity and surly over being excluded.

She pulled back the bedclothes, set the candle on the floor beside her and extinguished the flame with a well-directed puff. Then she lay down, and as the warmth of the bed crept about her grateful bones she thought first a little about Kate, who had, she knew, betrayed Tom because he had, despite her wishes, allowed Willy to share in his criminal exploits; and then about herself and her own immediate plans. She knew that with a puff of breath she, no less than Kate, had betrayed Tom. Sooner or later, as soon in fact as he felt himself safe again, she would have to answer for that. If he came and found no window lighted and she, by that sign, unwilling to render him whatever aid he had planned to demand of her, he would go away, but unless he were taken that would not be the end. Well, she didn't intend to stay there and await her punishment. The mattress did not hold as much as she had hoped to secrete in it, but there was enough; she would manage. On Saturday she and Hester would leave the inn, separately and unobtrusively and catch the London coach, or if that were full, a goods wagon, somewhere along the Ipswich road. She would carry nothing with her except her money. As a runaway servant, leaving at the very beginning of her year, she would probably be liable to fearful penalties, but they would have to catch her first, and although she would pay fares to London she would not be so simple as to go there. At some inn on the way she and Hester would sneak away and take another coach, going in a different direction; and if necessary she would repeat the trick until she was far away and out of Job's reach. She pictured a pleasant village somewhere, remote, tucked away, where she and Hester, alone at last and at peace, should take up a new way of living.

The plan, bold and energetic, showed exactly how far Ellie had come since the morning that the guinea had dropped from Hester's borrowed baby clothes. Life and experience, in the shapes of Hester and Tom, working upon the unshaped and the uninformed, had made Ellie a woman. Ten years ago, without question or complaint, she was resigned to scrubbing floors, in one place, all day long, for all the days of her life. Now, like a slave who suddenly perceives that he is shackled with straw chains, she was ready to burst them and make a bid for freedom. This was Thursday. Only one more night in this attic. One more night . . . one more night. The words made rhythm in her sleepy mind, and their music lulled her to sleep.

Less than a foot away lay Hester's head, bone of her own bone, flesh of her flesh; the head whose first thrust into the world had rent her body and transformed her soul. Between no two heads in the world should there be less distance; yet, although the basis of their thoughts was the same, between no two heads was a greater gulf fixed. For Hester lay despising her mother and planning desperate things. She was sure now that Ellie was retreating from adventure because she feared to carry it through. Out there, in the night somewhere, there lurked a desperate man who looked to Ellie for aid. And Ellie had blown out the candle and gone to sleep . . . refusing, denying, retreating. The elementary romanticism of the young, fostered in Hester's case by the stories with which, through eyes and ears, her head was stuffed, was alert, wakeful and troubled. Here was a chance for something to happen, for the drab everyday life to touch something from the exciting outer world. Here, moreover, was mystery : and Ellie blew out the candle and went to sleep.

Impatiently Hester twisted over in bed and lay upon her back, watching the moonlight brighten upon the ceiling and the whitewashed wall, tracing the dark lines of the leading of the panes. Out there, out there, something was happening—something that was the outcome of Ellie's midnight excursion. And Ellie, who had tried adventure and tired of it, had shut it out. What was it? Who was it? What did he want? Who was after him, and why? She must know.

Trembling at her own daring and yet no more able to restrain herself than a puppy can help gnawing things Hester crept, inch by inch, out of bed. The tinder-box, ready to Ellie's hand in the morning darkness, stood by the candle. Hester picked them up and felt her way to the furthermost corner of the room. There, with her back to the bed, she struck the flint and steel together with timed, nervous strokes. The bit of cotton-waste ignited and she held the candle upside down in it until the wick was alight. Then—just for a moment, she thought, just for a moment to see what will happen—she held the candle to the window. And as though, out of daredevilry and ignorant curiosity, she had held a stick of dynamite in the fire, she blew up the foundations of her little world.

It was very small, merely a pebble that fell short of the window and bounced away with a rattling sound down the sloping roof of a built-on bedroom on the floor below. But it showed that someone was moving and watching. Hester would not have been Hester if she could have refrained from looking out. And far below, in the courtyard she saw the foreshortened figure of a man dart back into the shadow of the building as though anxious to avoid attention that he himself had attracted. Hester drew back. After another full moment a second pebble, more accurately and violently aimed, hit one of the little diamond-shaped panes dead in the centre and a shower of glass tinkled on to the bare boards of the attic floor and on to the roof of the room below. Instantly, with great presence of mind, Hester nipped the candle wick between her finger and thumb, and stood still. No more pebbles were thrown. Once more she leaned forward and looked out and saw the man, this time looking up. She saw the gleam of his eyes and teeth in the moonlight. She was too far away to see the anxiety on his face, yet she was conscious of it. It was as though he had sent out tentacles, reaching for her, drawing her down, absorbing her in his agitation of mind. She drew back again and with her fingers pressed to her mouth, stood indecisive.

She had an impulse to creep back into bed, draw the clothes over her head and shut out all thought of the man down there in the moonlight who was willing her to do something, what she did not know. The white light of the moon and the blackness of the shadows were full of sinister menace. The outside world might be exciting, it was frightening too. Perhaps Ellie had found it so. Perhaps Ellie was right to sleep, and behind her dark, anonymous window deny adventure's call. But a little while ago she had been despising Ellie for this same denial. Hester stiffened her soul. Here was her chance to solve the mystery. If her courage served she could go down, just peep, at least, perhaps get an answer to her questions, and then come back and share Ellie's peace and oblivion.

Drawn, or driven, by something far stronger than herself she began to cross the floor. The door hinges, well exercised from cracking nuts, swung without a sound. The passage was completely dark, and she set each foot before the other with the utmost care, for the attic stairs were unrailed, and it would be all too easy to fall down them sideways. The landing below had one small window and the moonlight threw its shadow on the floor and lightened the whole of one end. It was hard to turn one's back on the light and face the darkness of the next flight. Her feet, unconsciously performing their natural but well-nigh forgotten function, adjusted themselves to the varying surfaces she trod, going lightly over the treacherous boards, confidently on the rugs, shrinkingly over the cold stones. Every hair on her body, recalling its animal origin, was raised and taut. She walked with hands stretched out, like a sleep-walker or a person blind. At any moment, she thought, someone waking or lying sleepless in the night, might hear her and cry out. But no voice

72

came, no sound of creaking bed or opening door. The shadows that suddenly barred her way melted at her approach or turned into pieces of furniture that warned her that she had lost her way. And so at last she reached the kitchen, comfortable with the stored warmth of a thousand fires.

Here once more she hesitated, and reason and caution made one last bid for her hearing. But the memory of that white, up-turned face, that furtive darting back into the shadows, the very things that should have warned her, drew her on. She put her hand to the bolts of the door and eased them along their track. With its customary, but hitherto-unnoticed, shriek of iron on iron the heavy door swung open, and with it came the body of a man. He had been pressed close against it, and its sudden opening upset his balance so that he fell into the kitchen striking Hester as he fell. They tottered together for a moment before they regained their feet. As soon as he was steady he said in a weak, gruff voice, "My God. I thought you were never coming. Shut the door, quick."

Hester closed the door and stood still, feeling that the situation had got beyond her. The man was indoors now; and the short sharp way he spoke did not encourage her to think that she would easily be rid of him. She could think of nothing to say and waited for him to speak again.

"Well," he said at last, in an impatient hasty whisper. "Have you got me a place to hide? Show me. And then look sharp with something to eat."

"But," said Hester, faltering, "but I haven't found . . ."

The childish voice, so unlike Ellie's hoarse meek tones, arrested his attention. He stretched out his hands, found her body in the darkness and took her shoulders in a hard, urgent grip.

"You're not Ellie Roon," he said. "Who are you? Why did *you* come down?"

"I'm Hester," she said in a very small voice. "And I'm afraid you can't stay here. Mother doesn't want you. She wouldn't even keep the candle."

"What she wants be damned," he said fiercely. "Here, can you make a light without rousing the house?"

Feeling her way Hester crossed over to the stove, broke a twig from a piece of faggot and stirred it amongst the ashes of the fire. One ember winked a red eye. She held the twig to it until a small flame blossomed upon the tip of it. Shielding the flame

73

in the curve of her hand she held it to the wick of a candle that caught her eye as she searched the cluttered mantelshelf.

The flame crossed from twig to wick, leaving the stick dead in her hand. She dropped it into the hearth. For a moment or two the candle flickered, then suddenly it burned clear and bright, and Hester and Tom Drury looked at one another for the first time.

Hester's first feeling was one of violent disappointment. Adventure, to her unformed mind, was concerned with the handsome, the tall, the swaggeringly courageous. Tom Drury was small; he was shabbily dressed; at some time, not far distant he had taken refuge in the vicinity of pigs; he was, worst of all, furtive. His eyes now slid round the lightened kitchen as though he expected to find it full of enemies. The last justification for Hester's interference dropped away. If he had been exciting, tall, handsome and romantic, she would have been right to come down. As it was her sense of ill-doing rose, her spirits fell, her sense of adventure retreated and even her curiosity was quelled. This dirty, oldish, small man and her mother had no story worth exploring. Her one idea was to be rid of him quickly.

He in turn inspected her, but without emotion. He saw in this tall thin, inadequately clothed child with the wide eyes and tumbled yellow hair, merely the intermediary between himself and Ellie, the bridge between him and safety.

"Where's your mother?"

"Upstairs. Asleep. I'm not supposed to be here. I don't know what made me come down. I think you'd better go away."

He showed his teeth in a smile that held no mirth and reminded her uncomfortably of a picture of Satan in a woodcut in one of Miss Peck's books. Hester shivered suddenly. It was all rather like a moral story. Satan tempted you by appealing to your curiosity, or some other weakness, and then he had you in his power, and though you struggled and resisted you were bound to obey him.

"You fetch your mother to me, or take me to her. I'll talk about going away to *her*."

"But she doesn't know you're here. She blew out the candle and went to sleep. . . . She'll be angry. . . ."

"So shall I be if you stand blathering there. Come on. Lead the way."

There must be some means of getting him on the other side

of that door! If once she could, how hurriedly would she shoot the bolts again, and run upstairs, not caring very much who heard her. The bare cold attic, with Ellie sleeping heavily in the hard bed seemed like a very haven of safety. She must think. She must be crafty and get out of this awkward position like one of the heroes in the stories that she read so avidly. Ulysses now, who taught the Cyclops to call him "Nobody" : what would he do? Inspiration came.

"But you said that you were hungry. There's nothing to eat upstairs. I know where there's a mutton and apple pie."

"Are we safe here? Anybody sleep near here?"

"Nobody." Alas, nobody! Or should she be glad of that?

"Fetch it out then."

Silently on her bare feet Hester padded to the pantry, brought out the pie, a pitcher of milk, the pewter salt cellar. She put them on the hearth end of the table and turned to the dresser to take down a plate, a tumbler, and to lift a knife and fork from the drawer.

"Don't bother," said Little Tom, and turning she saw that he was falling upon the food like an animal, tearing the crust with his fingers and scooping up the mixture of tender mutton and soft apple in his hands. He lifted the jug and drank from it greedily between the mouthfuls. Beneath her horrified but fascinated gaze both pie and milk disappeared in a twinkling. He wiped the back of one dirty hand across his lips, rubbed the resulting smear of mutton fat and milk on the seat of his breeches and returned to the attack long before Hester had thought of a way to parry it.

"Now," he said, ominously.

"Now you must go. I've done all I can. I've fed you," said Hester with more confidence than she felt. "I daren't take you upstairs. If Mother had wanted to see you she would have stayed awake, and . . ." Her voice faltered before the fury in his face.

"Are you going to take me to your mother?"

"No," said Hester, retreating a step or two.

He came close to her and with irresistible swiftness and force slid one arm round the back of her neck so that his hand held her mouth tightly shut, while with the other he twisted her arm outwards and backwards. She bore it until the muscle in her shoulder cracked and it felt as though her arm were being torn from its socket. Then, just as the agony reached its crisis she nodded her head. He freed her, lifted down the stump of candle and said :

"Lead on then, and don't try any tricks."

Her arm fell to her side, heavy and helpless. She felt sick; but her mind was still active. Across the yard, over the stable, Sam slept at one end of the loft. If she could reach him he could deal with this intruder. She said in a voice, which, though it dealt with ordinary words, was laden with hatred : "I must shoot the bolts again. And you can't come upstairs in your boots."

He stooped and began to loosen the boots whose shining lacquered surface was scratched and crusted with mire. Hester crossed the floor, snatched the door open and had taken two flying steps across the yard before he reached her, dragging her backwards as though she was a half-filled sack of sawdust.

"You little bitch," he said through his teeth, "you bloody little bitch." His hand was over her mouth again and he shook her savagely to and fro until her head wagged limply. He shifted his grip, dragging her head down between his elbow and his body and holding her so, reached with his free arm and bolted the door himself. Then he fumbled inside his greatcoat and produced a large black pistol. It was unloaded, but Hester was not to know that .

"See this?" he asked. "One sound or wriggle and I'll blow you to Kingdom Come and take pleasure in it. It'll rouse the house, but it'll be the end of you as well as me. Now, up you go."

There was no help for it. Completely cowed, Hester led the way upstairs, even holding the candle low at any unevenness of the floor or staircase in case he should stumble. And all the time she could feel the hard round mouth of the pistol pressing against her spine. Only when they stood inside the attic and the candle, shuddering in her unsteady hand, showed Ellie peacefully sleeping, did he move from behind her. He gave a great sigh of relief as Hester, stepping back, closed the door. It told her that the ordeal of the ascent had not been hers alone.

He went to the bedside, laid one hand on Ellie's mouth lest the sudden waking and the appearance beside her bed should make her scream, and with the other hand shook her shoulder. Ellie's eyes opened, swerved wildly in the candlelight from the face of the man to that of her daughter, and then with her two hands pushed away the one that muzzled her mouth. "What

. . ." she whispered, and the sibilant sound was more urgent than a shout. "How . . . Oh, Hester. What have you done?"

"Your work,' said Little Tom shortly. "I warned you. But you tried to rat, like the rest. You've got to hide me, do you hear? You've got to hide me, here, in the one place where I shan't be looked for."

Ellie struggled up into a sitting position and then closed her eyes against the sudden dizziness which smote her.

"But I can't. I ain't got nowhere to put you. Why, there ain't even a lock on that door."

"Listen to me. I'm a desperate man. If I don't get shelter here I'm dead and damned. But I shan't go alone. In the eyes of the law you're as guilty as I am. For the sake of your own skin you've got to help me. I must stay here till it's safe for me to move. Under the bed if there's nowhere else."

"But someone'll see you."

"You must see that they don't then. So stow your gab and give me a pillow and a blanket."

All this time Hester had been standing nursing her wrenched arm with her other hand and listening hard. The threat against Ellie's safety, and her obvious, pitiful terror, shook her to the core of her being. While Ellie still hesitated she moved forward, took a pillow in her sound hand, threw it under the bed, followed it with a blanket and then stood away to allow him room to wriggle under. He was small and agile and a few convulsive thrusts took him out of sight beneath the sagging mattress.

Then Hester threw herself upon her mother and began to sob the tearless, rending sobs of nerves overstrained.

Ellie, who had never laid an ungentle hand upon her in all her fourteen years of life, reached out and smacked her cheek, hard.

"You're a bad wicked girl," she said, "and you've ruined us. You've spoilt everything."

Immediately she was appalled at what she had done. Shock and panic and penitence struggled for mastery in her mind. She too began to cry. She took Hester in her arms and rocked her to and fro as though she were a baby. "Oh, Hester," she moaned helplessly, "what shall we do now? Whatever shall we do?" For several minutes they mingled their tears. The younger mind recovered its balance first. "We'll manage, Mother. We'll manage somehow. I'll think of something." Ellie shook her tortured head, pressed her hands to her face and sobbed on. Hester, who

77

had shifted the need for plan and thought into the future, soon found herself growing sleepy. She yawned to relieve the pressure of sleep in her throat. The candle flickered, burned high for a second and went out. Hester lay down in the darkness.

"Go to sleep again, Mother. We can't do anything till morning," she mumbled, yawned again, and slept.

Ellie lay awake in the whirling darkness. Every now and then the thought of Tom Drury, alive, fugitive, life-sized, hiding below her very bed, set her heart thumping, and she felt that she must scream. It would have been a relief to have screamed and screamed, roused the house, poured out the whole story and let them do with her what they would. Her restless fingers plucked at the bedclothes, she sweated and shivered. What, oh, what, should she do in the morning? The relentless morning drawing every moment more near. Watched and busy as she was every hour how could she feed him, hide him, clothe him, and get him away? Oh, why had she ever begun this thing? Why had she not been happy and contented in the old days when life was at least safe and uncomplicated? What should she do to-morrow?

The maddening procession of thoughts went round in her head like a whirligig. Sometimes the thought of Hester joined them, adding bitterness to fear and bewilderment. Hester, whom she loved, Hester for whose sake all the wrong had been done. Hester for whom she had braved the terror of the night journeys, the risks of brutal punishment. Hester for whom she was planning a new and better life that was to have started on Saturday. Oh, why had Hester interfered? Anger stirred again uneasily at the bottom of her troubled mind. But it did not stay long. Whatever she did, and whatever came of it, Ellie loved Hester, the dear soft little baby who had lain at her breast and stolen her heart. Hester had meant no harm. Once again Ellie raised herself, bent over and laid upon the cheek that she had smitten the kiss of peace. Her hot, dry lips lingered upon the cool, smooth cheek; her rough fingers touched the soft tousled hair. Ellie knew a brief respite as she gave evidence of her love and repentance. Then she thought of the man under the bed, of the morning that was approaching even as she thought, and she started off on the whole maddening round again.

When she left her bed in the morning her eyelids were swollen and discoloured, her face puffy from lack of sleep. She dressed slowly, pausing to eye the bed that hid her secret and to

78

sigh.

When she was ready she waked Hester.

"You'd best not come down to breakfast. And what I bring up you must share with him."

Hester remembered the night's activities. She sat up in bed. "I am sorry. I only went down just to see. And I did try to get rid of him. But he shook me and nearly broke my arm, and then he had a pistol."

"You shouldn't have gone down. But it ain't no good talking about that now. You *did*. Now we must think of something and keep our heads. I'll tell Mrs. Bridges that you got a lesson still to learn. And if you pushed the bed to the wall there'd only be one side for him to show under."

"I'll do it," said Hester. "I'll do anything if you'll forgive me."

"I forgave you last night," said Ellie, mustering her pitiful smile. "You didn't know. I shoulda told you."

She went off to her morning's work, and Hester pushed back the clothes and began to dress herself. Her twisted arm was still very painful, even her fingers seemed stiff and swollen, and by craning her neck she could see that her shoulder was black. Her face hardened into a mask of hatred. She wished, oh how heartily, that there was some way in which she could hurt the man without injuring her mother. But the few words that had been exchanged in those burning whispers last night had shown her that there was some mysterious link between the two of them. She did not understand its reason or its implications, but the man had pointed out that in the eyes of the law Ellie was his equal, and Ellie had not contradicted him.

Hester finished dressing and moved to the window. Grey light was stealing about the yard. Sam came out and washed in a bucket, splashing the water about his face and neck. Then he stretched several times, twisted and tied his neckerchief and hitched up his breeches. In the empty yard he looked big and powerful. If only she could have reached him last night! No use wishing. Now he was letting the bucket down into the well, she could hear the squeaking of the chain as it uncoiled. He might yet be of help to her. For to get away the man beneath the bed would need a horse, and that Sam might help her to procure.

There came no sound from the hiding-place where Tom was sleeping off his exhaustion; but suddenly Hester remembered

Ellie's instruction about the bed. She would move it before her mother brought up the breakfast. Hunching her shoulders she turned from the window and stretched one long thin arm beneath the bed. Her hand closed ungently on the part of Tom's body that was nearest the edge, and she shook him, saying s-s-s-s-h, as she did so, lest he should call out at the sudden awakening. He muttered a few indistinguishable sounds. Then with the consciousness of his stiff and aching body laid amongst the fluff and feathers of the twilight space under the bed, returned the consciousness of his position and his danger, and he shot a startled head out of the sagging droop of the bedclothes and looked at Hester with an expression of terror which faded as he recognised her.

"I want to move the bed back against the wall. Mother said that would be safer. But you hurt my arm last night, so you'll have to help me." Her voice was cold and unfriendly; the glance which she turned upon him as he crept, stiff and slow in his damp-wrinkled, fluff-covered clothes, out from beneath the bed, was eloquent of scorn and hatred. Nevertheless, as he pushed against the foot of the bed she applied her sound arm and the pressure of her thigh to the head of it and heaved with a will.

The sound of a step on the passage sent him scuttling back into hiding, and Hester, pulling down the edge of the patchwork counterpane, sat on the side of the bed and bent over as though fastening her shoes. But it was only Ellie who entered, shut the door carefully, and stood with her back against it as she held out to Hester a brown bowl filled to the brim with porridge.

"Eat first," she said, "and save half for him. Mrs. Bridges wouldn't send up your coffee, she said you were to drink it by the fire and get thoroughly warm before you went out. Is he awake?"

Hester nodded, and Tom, reassured by the sound of Ellie's voice, stuck out his head like a tortoise. If he and Ellie had been engaged in lechery, instead of larceny, and he hiding from an outraged husband instead of from the law, the scene would have been comic. As it was the tension in the attic could be felt. Even Hester looked wan and worried in the morning light, and Ellie's face was ghastly. Hester looked, with no great pleasure, at the porridge. Her usually voracious appetite had failed her. But the top of the enormous portion had been liberally sprinkled with brown sugar, and she decided, more from spite than from hunger, that she would eat all the sweetened part. Carefully, in order not to mix the sugar with the bulk of the porridge, she spooned off several sugary mouthfuls and then, ramming the spoon into the remainder, she handed it down to Tom. He attacked it as eagerly as he had devoured the pie on the previous night. Soon the bowl was empty.

"Carry it down, Hester, and have your coffee. And try to behave as if nothing had happened. And, Hester, don't mention a word about this, don't even think about it. What there is to do, I'll do."

Hester threw her cloak over her arm, tucked her books under it and with her sound hand pulled the heavy, numb one into position, thrusting the thumb of it into the button of her bodice in order to lend it some support. Then she took up the bowl, said, "I'll come straight home. Good-bye," and made her way downstairs.

"So you've come to your senses," sneered Tom as soon as the door had closed behind Hester. "And what there is to do you'll do. May I ask *what* you're going to do?"

"What can I do?" asked Ellie, spreading her hands in a gesture of helplessness. "If this was my place it'd be different. I could hide you somewhere safe. But it ain't. Anybody might come in here. What then?"

"I'll lay still enough. But you'll have to look lively. You've got to get me some clothes, different to those I wear. Something bright, and a tall hat, make me look like a gentleman. And I want a horse, a good one."

"And where do you think," asked Ellie with some asperity, "that I'll get things like that?"

"You got money, ain't you? God knows I've sent you some good splits in the last two years. You ain't spent it all in a place like this, surely."

With a great and determined effort Ellie prevented her eyes from moving to the bed. There it lay, her precious hoard, within two inches of his head.

"I earned that money," she said stubbornly. "That ain't nothing to do with you now. 'Sides, even I wanted to I couldn't get hold of it in time. It's with a friend who's minding it for me. And you got to go this afternoon, soon's it's dusk."

"Go, go, go. That's all you can say. How can I go, less you help me? And mind, if I'm found here it'll be as bad for you as for me. My God, I picked some friends! That tatty bitch at The

Honest Lawyer, and now you. I wish to hell I had her here. I'd knock some sense into her, and she had some guts, which is more than anybody could say for you. Can't you see that unless you help me to get away we'll both hang?"

A great anguished sigh tore itself out of Ellie's body. She could see that, only too well. But she saw too that if she absented herself from her work, began trying to get the clothes and the horse that he demanded, she would bring instant notice and suspicion upon herself. On every side she was hemmed in.

"I'll see what I can do," she said, without the slightest idea of what that might be. "Get in under there now and I'll make the bed. Mr. Wainwright ain't above looking in here to see that it's tidy."

Her hands were unsteady, but hasty as she straightened out the bedclothes and pulled the patchwork quilt so that its edge swept the floor. Already she felt that she might have been missed in the lower regions, and she made haste to get away. As she left she remembered that the imprisoned man had another need, one which she could, at least, meet.

"There's a pail you can use," she said shyly, and then vanished.

CHAPTER IX

No DAY had ever been so long in its dragging hours of harassed thought, nor so short in the way it sped away without bringing the problem to solution. Her hands, her feet, her very tongue went on their usual track. She did her work, answered when spoken to, remembered all her errands. But all the while, her mind, like a tethered animal, went round and round in a circle. Once or twice she stopped and pressed her hands to her head, trying to relieve, by outward pressure, the pounding and pushing that was going on inside her head. She had not been able to eat anything, but had, like a person in high fever, swallowed great draughts of water which seemed to refuse to be incorporated in or even warmed by her body, but to stay in her stomach, a vast, cold, quivering pool that shook in unison with her steady heart. A footstep approaching, a voice raised to call her, made her start. She was certain each time that Tom had been discovered, that the whole secret was out and that the cart's-tail and the noose awaited her. Every grisly story, the common exchange of conversation about the kitchen, about felons being flogged until their spines were bare, about hangings which had not been successful at the first or even second attempt, rose up in her memory and repeated themselves. And some such fate would be hers unless she could work a miracle and get Tom Drury safely away.

Just before midday she found herself alone in the kitchen and snatched the oportunity to saw a slice from the loaf and a round from the joint of beef. She slipped them into her apron pocket and stole up the stairs. This time Tom, upon whom the enforced inaction and confinement were beginning to tell, pestered her with questions which were the very expression of her own terror. Had anyone mentioned him? Had any soldiers been seen? Had that old devil Moreton been hanging about the place? To all these Ellie was able to return momentarily comforting negatives; but the mere mention of such possibilities increased her terror almost past bearing.

She went down again and collected from the scattered bedrooms the candlesticks which were arrayed every evening upon a table at the foot of the stairs, so that guests could light themselves to bed. Several needed new candles, all should be scraped free of tallow and polished. But at the moment she was too restless to settle herself to the lengthy work. She wandered into the kitchen again, giving herself the excuse that if she could once get thoroughly warm she would feel better and more steady.

"You've got the ague, that's what you've got," said Mrs. Bridges, noting the pallor, the tremors and the hot dry lips. "Why, you're all of a shake, and 'tain't a cold day at all. But I know what'll just meet your case."

From the peg where it hung in line with others of varying size, she unhooked a large pewter jug. She stood it in a warm place on the hearth, at the same time thrusting the poker deeply into the fire. From her private cupboard she lifted a bottle of red wine and emptied it into the jug, adding a pinch of pepper, a stick of cinnamon and a clove which she smashed with one well-directed blow from her iron spoon. Soon the poker was red-hot and she withdrew it, banging it upon the hearth to knock off a clinging fragment of wood. Then she plunged it into the jug and as the mixture hissed and seethed and bubbled she said, "Hand me two drinking measures."

She divided the liquid fairly and handed one measure to Ellie.

"There, that'll drive the cold out. Drink it while it's hot. And this'll save me from taking it."

She drank her own scalding portion in a few experienced gulps, looking tolerantly upon Ellie, who coughed and spluttered.

"You do make a fist of it," she said.

But the hot heartening brew was having its effect.

There were often some clothes, left by the more careless travellers, upon a row of pegs near the stairs. Ellie resolved that she would take a topcoat and a hat from there. And there were always horses in the stable. True, Sam slept just above, but Sam was friendly with Hester. If she could, without being observed by Tom, just slide a coin or two out of the mattress, she could tell Hester to give them to Sam, with a message that somebody had said that he was to buy himself a drink. He'd do that like a shot. Then he'd sleep sound and not hear as she let Tom out into the yard and added horse-stealing to her other crimes.

As the wine fumes mounted to her head she began to see that the plan was feasible. In fact that was what Tom had meant her to do. By to-morrow morning he would be out of The Fleece and by the middle of the morning she herself would be gone. So even if he didn't get far it would be no concern of hers. Once he was gone she and Hester would turn out the mattress and remove the money.

Ellie gave a great sigh of relief. Mrs. Bridges heard it.

"Feeling better?" she inquired. "There's nothing like it if you feel a bit low. Many's the time I've saved myself from bed with a good hot posset."

"I can do my candlesticks now," said Ellie gratefully. "Thank you, I'm sure." She smiled at Mrs. Bridges as she set down her beaker and turned to leave the kitchen. It was a pale and watery smile, and one which the cook was to remember.

As she went towards the table where the candlesticks awaited her she glanced up at the pegs. It seemed that fortune was in her favour, for there hung a bright blue coat with many collars and full flared skirts, and a tall hat of shiny beaver. On a separate peg were lodged a pair of fine gloves with gauntlets and a riding-crop, unmistakably a gentleman's, with a handle of mother-of-pearl. If only they had come to stay! They were enough to disguise even Tom Drury as a gentleman. As she stood gazing up at them she thought she heard Job's voice, raised in anger, and at this reminder of her duty she scuttled towards the candle-table, which stood in a little recess beneath the stairs, and set about her work. Job was certainly in the vicinity. She listened. Yes, the voice was coming from the private parlour, the door of which was separated from her only by the angle of the wall.

It was mid-afternoon and the inn was quiet : the coaches would not be due for another hour. At various points of the compass at their varying hour's journey from the inn, the drivers of chaises and coaches and the horsemen were urging their steeds, making the most of the last hours of daylight, steering for The Fleece. Mrs. Bridges was stoking her fires and getting out her cooking things. Rosie was in the dining-hall laying the tables with napery and silver. In the bar John was sanding his floor and setting his drinking-vessels in order. The boy who had replaced Ellie was scrubbing the cellar steps. Martha was ironing, so languidly that, as the cook said, "You have to look hard to see which way the iron is going." Far away upstairs Tom Drury kept his narrow hiding-place under Ellie's bed, and further away still, Hester, in Miss Peck's stuffy cottage, had forgotten all about The Fleece and its problem, in listening to her teacher's description of the pagan age. For some reason best known to herself Miss Peck, that wise and elderly virgin, grew lyrical in her discourse upon Pan and urgently bade Hester note that even that lecherous and goat-footed god had had no power over a pure virgin.

"Always remember that, my child," she said, gazing fondly at Hester's rapt, attentive face, "there is a great truth there, allegorically expressed."

The inn was very quiet and as Ellie's ears adjusted themselves to the one sound within hearing she found that she could make out the sense of the conversation within Job's room. She could even hear how righteous anger was at odds with respect in his voice. She had listened on Tom's behalf before and now her attention was almost mechanical.

"But I tell you, your honour, I 'a never set eyes on the man in my life. I don't know him by sight even. Why should he come to me?"

85

"That, Wainwright," returned the fruity, arrogant voice which Ellie could not recognise, "is not a question that I can answer. I only know that Sir Nicholas himself sent me a message this morning, saying that they had discovered that the man had been in close touch with someone in this place over a period of time, and that his horse, completely foundered, was seen and recognised not five miles from here, late yesterday afternoon. The conclusion is obvious."

They were talking about Tom and about her! "Someone in this place'" Ellie Roon. Perhaps they even knew that. The solid table swayed and danced before her eyes. She dropped her polishing cloth and the candlestick upon which she was working and clutched at the table's edge, hanging on with both hands, not breathing, not stirring, just listening.

"We'll soon know," said Job. "I'll have every man Jack of 'em, and the women too, brought before your honour and you can question them as you wish. Aye, and we'll have the truth out of 'em if I have to wring it out with these hands. My inn mixed up with a common cut-throat like that one! Really sir, you could fell me with a feather I'm that moithered with the very thought of it. Five and thirty years have I held The Fleece and never a breath of that kind of scandal near it. God's blood, asking your pardon, your honour, if it's true and I find the culprit there'll be little left for the hangman."

"Softly, Wainwright, softly. Walls have ears in such places. And I'm not sure that it wouldn't be better to search the premises first. The man is the quarry, the person who has helped him can be dealt with later. I suppose we can count on your full collaboration in the search? And there's one thing, if we once raise him he won't get far even if he makes a dash for it. I've men posted at all points."

The threat in the magistrate's voice was deliberate, and it was directed at Job. Squire Moreton had been as shocked as it was in his nature to be, by the information that Tom Drury was taking refuge in his own village, under his very nose. And he did not believe such a state of affairs possible without the inn-keeper's connivance. He was trying to tell the innocent Job in diplomatic language that it would be of little use his warning his highwayman friend. But Job, strong in his innocence, was as furiously keen on the pursuit as the squire, and rose at once, knocking his chair backwards as he did so, so impatient was he to prove that Tom Drury was not in the place. The threat fell with all its implications upon the listener, who, but for her grip on the table, would have fallen prone. The two stout men passed through the door and Job himself stood within reach of her hand while the squire went to the door and called two of his men to come and help in the search. Job followed him with his eyes and so missed the sight of Ellie, stricken and paralysed amongst the unpolished candlesticks.

"The cellars first, I think. We shall need lights."

"There are lanterns on the shelf inside the door," said Job, and drew out his tinder-box.

They passed from Ellie's sight and hearing, and with their passing came the knowledge that she must act, act at once.

Relinquishing her grasp on the table she made her way to the main stairs and forced her trembling legs to climb them. Hurry, hurry, said her racing heart. Stairs, passage, stairs again, another passage, already growing dim with the twilight, and the last twisting flight of attic stairs. Her own door. She opened it, fought for her breath, spoke, without any sound, and followed the soundless words with a despairing, choking cry. She must speak, she must. She drew in her breath again; moaned out:

"They're here and the place is surrounded."

The bed shot away from the wall as Tom Drury clawed his way from under it. He made a rush for the door, but Ellie barred the way. "You'll run into them." He turned and made for the window. Only a third of it opened and that third was too small for the passage of his body. But Tom, in desperation, had become a living battering-ram. Two frenzied thrusts and the whole rickety framework gave way. He went with it. Ellie rushed forward and saw his body bounding down the sloping roof of the built-on bedroom of the first floor, much as his first pebble had done the night before. At the very edge of it, when it seemed inevitable that he should pitch over, he checked his fall, halted for a second, and then came crawling back. The bare steep roof offered no shelter. He turned his head from left to right, came to a lightning decision, crossed to the right-hand side of the roof and jumped. He cleared the space between the bedroom and the kitchen, sprawled, and began to slide downwards again, dug in his hands and toes and crawled to the peak of the kitchen roof. For a moment he sheltered behind the kitchen chimneys, and then, upright once more, went scrambling and slipping towards the stable roof, which joined that of the kitchen at an angle and at a slightly lower level. Ellie, her lips parted and her sweating fingers clenched together, watched him; lulled from a sense of her own danger by the sight of his. If he reached the stable roof safely, kept to that side and dropped into the meadow beyond there was just a chance, a frail, negligible one, but a chance, that he might get away.

But as he braced himself for the jump, downwards and sideways, somebody down in the yard let out a yell. Little Tom hesitated and tried to turn back to the shelter of the chimney. He was too late, somebody down there, out of sight, fired. The hunted man threw up his arms, spun round, and dropped.

At the same moment there came the sound of heavy, eager feet, speeding up the stairs. It was only one of the squire's men, sent up to shoot from a window should Little Tom have proved difficult to dislodge. But to Ellie it was the sound of doom. They were after her; they would whip and hang her. Something cracked in her brain. Like a stag at the moment when the hounds encircle it, she looked wildly around her. No way of escape, no hope. Screaming in the sudden loosening of control, screaming so loudly that the sound carried to every end of the straggling building, she clambered through the space where the window had been, and threw herself downwards and outwards.

(For almost two centuries Ellie's story lingered on, though she herself, her name, the details of her crime were forgotten. Vague stories were passed from mouth to mouth. The attic floor was supposed to be haunted. Maids refused to sleep there, and were inclined to cling together and after darkness to move in couples even in other parts of the inn. Footsteps were heard, and heavy sighs, doors opened by no human agency; and one woman swore that she had wakened to find all her bedclothes on the floor and somebody trying to move her mattress. The strong-minded laughed, the weak shuddered. But in the twentieth century belief in ghosts rose suddenly from the level of ignorant superstition and became a cult with a learned name. Men whose names were famous in two continents listened gravely to the tags and pieces of story of The Fleece's haunted floor, and in the autumn of 1933 the place was honoured by an official visit. The result of the investigation found its way into journals specialising in the reporting of supernatural occurrences and was finally enshrined in the second volume of *Verified Instances of Psychic Phenomena*. From its rather coldly scientific pages the curious may learn that Ellie was as shy and evasive in the spirit as she had been in the flesh and refused, even to the sympathetic and credulous ear, the full explanation of her earth-bound state. But that she lingered, that she was still troubled and still in search of something, the learned men established to their complete satisfaction.)

The two broken bodies were picked up from within a few yards of one another and thrown into an outhouse. One was known to have been a murderer, the other a suicide. For them no bell would toll, no sonorous voice promise that though worms should destroy the body the spirit should return to the God who gave it.

The sunset light of the autumn afternoon found its way through a few chinks in the unsound roof and showed them lying there side by side, the man who had terrorised a district, the woman who had been terrified. Small difference between them now. Why he had robbed and killed his fellow men, at what malleable age he had become set in an evil mould, would never be known now. The roads were safer for his passing. Ellie, less vicious, had been led astray by her love for the yellow-haired child who was at this moment making her way home across the fields. She had done evil as the sword murders and the hammer strikes. And now, master and tool, driver and driven, they lay together quietly, while the night fell and around their resting-place life gathered itself together again and went on.

Martha fainted and had to be revived by burnt feathers held under her nose by Mrs. Bridges, who was at heart far more shocked and shaken. Rosie remarked of Ellie that still waters always run deep. Job was merely concerned with the establishment of his own innocence in the eyes of the squire, who was also a magistrate.

The squire dived into his pocket and presented the man who had fired at Tom with a guinea, there and then. Everybody settled down to drink at Job's expense, the men in the bar, the squire in Job's own parlour, where the mystery of Ellie's complicity was thrashed out over and over again.

"She seemed such a steady wench," said Job rather regretfully, as he remembered the years of ungrudging and uncomplaining service which he had had from Ellie. "Apart from one other little business I've never known her have a thought out-

89

side her work."

"And what was the other business?" asked Squire Moreton, growing mellower with his drinking.

"A baby. Twelve or more years ago."

"Then he's the father, I'd wager. That'd explain why she threw herself out after she'd seen him fall, wouldn't it?"

"It would that, your honour. Nothing escapes you—as our late friend Tom Drury has learnt to his cost." Anxious to banish any lingering suspicion the squire's mind might hold against himself, Job was exerting himself to charm. As if absent-mindedly he pushed the brandy a little nearer to his guest : as if absent-mindedly the squire replenished his glass. The brandy was as undoubtedly excellent as his host's motives were transparent. And it was just possible that Ellie had been dispatched to warn the wanted man and had fallen out of the window in an endeavour to watch his progress. Mr. Moreton shelved that idea for future consideration. There was still something odd, to his mind, in Tom's being found in the one place where he had never been suspected of having any connection: and this old devil Wainwright was a crafty as he was fat. But he could be watched, and should be, sharply, in future. The squire raised his glass, sipped appreciatively, settled his coat-collar and picked a bit of straw from his sleeve. He would have something to report to Sir Nicholas, by God. If the night kept clear he would ride over and tell him the whole story. He'd show him how to catch highwaymen, the insinuating old dog! Speaking as though he had believed that cock-and-bull story about Tom Drury being a Moreton on the wrong side of the blanket and owing his long immunity to his kinsman's protection. He drained his glass and rose.

"Well," he said comfortably, "we've done a good day's work. I'd advise you to keep a sharper look-out on your wenches in future, Wainwright. We've certainly saved the hangman a job." A brief and pointed epitaph.

CHAPTER X

HESTER hurried home as she had promised. The problem, forgotten during Miss Peck's discourse, loomed again as soon as she had shut the cottage door behind her. She walked swiftly, the brown and yellow leaves scattering along her path, with a sound like the swishing of stiff silk petticoats. To some beeches and hawthorns the amber and crimson leaves still clung and when they stood before the lowering sun they burned. Like Moses' burning bush, thought Hester. Every spring the bare twigs blossomed like Aaron's rod : every autumn they burned. Perhaps those stories, too, contained, like the story of Pan, a great truth in allegorical language. But this was no time to pursue fancies. When she reached home she must persuade her mother to let her confide in Sam. Sam would help if he were asked properly and Hester considered that she had, in the country phrase, "got the measure of his foot." Seldom did he refuse her anything. Of course, she had never before asked him to betray his trust and lend her a horse. Still, she was fairly confident. And as she looked up just before entering the yard and making her way to the back door ,she saw one bright early star wink out in the slowly darkening sky. She took it for a sign. It promised that all would go well, that the evil that she had done in a moment of silly curiosity should be expunged and leave no mark.

The largest meal of the day had been served in the dining-hall and the staff were gathering in the kitchen for their own repast. At The Fleece the midday meal was unimportant, travellers were on the road then and anxious to press forward. So Mrs. Bridges seldom cooked until both guests and staff could share the result at once. She sat now at the head of the big table. dishing up stewed mutton and onions. Martha, quite recovered, was serving the steaming potatoes. Rosie, whose time was limited because she would soon have to clear the guests' tables, was ladling food into her mouth with more speed than politeness. The barman had just taken his place. Hester's stool was placed at the foot of the table, near the end of the bench upon which the menials sat. Only Mrs. Bridges used a chair.

She had opened the door upon a babble of talk. Speculation and recrimination and memories of things that they had all considered strange at the time but thought best not to mention, flew about the table. They were all talking at once and all at the top of their voices. But when Hester opened the door and stood amongst them, her eyes searching for Ellie, to whom she meant to propound her suggestion without delay, there was as sudden a silence as if they had all been struck dumb.

Hester, thinking to find Ellie upstairs, began to cross the kitchen to the door that opened upon the foot of the back stairs. Mrs. Bridges recovered in time to stop her.

"Come and have your food while it's hot. You can hang your things on the door."

Hester obeyed and sat down on the stool at the foot of the table. The stew smelled extremely good, and after all there was no hurry, they had the night to work in. Sam would be busy for quite a long time yet rubbing down the horses that had come in hot and sweaty, looking over their feet and harness and obeying the orders of careful owners about bran mashes and linseed oil.

The queer silence persisted. True, Mrs. Bridges asked whether she was enjoying her supper, an unnecessary question, since her enjoyment was obvious, but the general uproar of conversation did not break out afresh. There was nothing unusual about that, however, for Mrs. Bridges had once shown very plainly that she considered some subjects unsuitable to be discussed before Hester. In that she was right but rather over-late. Hester ate steadily and waited for Ellie to appear. Perhaps something upstairs had happened to detain her. Perhaps she should have gone upstairs and seized upon the chance for a quiet talk.

Then she noticed that there was no knife, no spoon and no chunk of bread in the place next to her. Nor did any crumbs remain to suggest that Ellie had taken her meal and gone. Memories of her mother's pallor and shakiness returned to her and she broke the queer silence to ask, humbly :

"Has my mother been down, Mrs. Bridges?"

For answer Mrs. Bridges rose from her place at the honourable end of the table and came and with difficulty inserted her bulk between the bench where Ellie usually sat and the table.

"You'd better know, child," she said, in that same kind voice. "There's been an accident, and your mother was hurt. To tell you the truth, she's dead."

"Dead." Stunned, Hester repeated the word. "But what happened, what kind of accident was it?"

Before Mrs. Bridges could answer, Rosie, who had been wiping up the last drop of gravy from her plate with a gobbet of bread, popped the soaked morsel into her mouth and spoke through the impediment. Her voice was an odd blend of venom and hysteria.

"Go on," she shouted, "tell the brat the truth, she'll have to know it. Your mother was shielding Little Tom Drury and when he was caught this afternoon she chucked herself out of the window. Good riddance to bad rubbish, too, I say, bringing a bad name on the lot of us."

Mrs. Bridges reached out and took Hester's plate. She hurled it straight at Rosie's face and found her mark with satisfying assurance. The edge of it took Rosie upon the nose and split it to the septum, fragments of meat and potato buried themselves in her frizzy hair and a shower of rich brown gravy descended upon her neck and bosom. "You bitch," she said, "you heartless bitch, get out of my sight before I limb you!"

Screaming loudly and regularly like an automaton, Rosie obeyed and Mrs. Bridges turned to Hester, trying to draw the rigid little body into the comfort of her over-upholstered embrace.

"There, there," she murmured, "never you mind her. She's as full of spite as an egg is of meat. Your poor mother wasn't to blame, that I do know, and if she got into trouble it was because she didn't know what she was up to. And she fell out, craning to see what had happened to that vagabond. You believe that, my dear."

Through tight white lips Hester said, "It doesn't make any difference." Once more, in the nightmare light of remembered folly, she was seeing herself lighting the candle, descending the stairs, letting in the stranger, and Death with him. Once more she heard Ellie's futile frightened protests, felt upon her cheek the stinging proof of her mother's terror. As surely as though she had plunged a knife into her heart she had killed her mother.

Mrs. Bridges held her and patted her, trying to woo her to the storm of tears that she expected and hoped would ease the first pangs of sorrow. But no tears came. Hester sat, rigid and white, with self-reproach eating into her soul. They sat together, physically linked and yet utterly alienated from one another until Job flung open the house door.

"Leave pampering that spawn," he bellowed. "It's work she needs, not petting. We'll see if we can't work her mother's devil out of her, aye, and her father's too."

Part Two

CHAPTER I

IF WORK could have done it Hester would have been free of the
devil within a month of Ellie's death. The half-witted orphan
boy who had taken on Ellie's work with bucket and scrubbing-
brush eight years before was sent to work in the garden. Hester
was presented with the bucket, a new scrubbing-brush and cloth
and told to get down on her knees and "put some elbow-grease
into it."

There is seldom justification for bullying : and perhaps less
of it is done consciously than is sometimes imagined. Many
people are cruel to their fellows because of some nagging
frustration, some nervous strain in their own lives. But Job
Wainwright considered, with some reason, that Ellie had injured his reputation, and for months after her death he was
unable to look at Hester without wanting to hurt her. For five-
and-thirty years, as he had proudly told Mr. Moreton, his inn
had been famous for its honesty and safety. He was not a
generous man, he never gave anything away : but the lives and
property of his customers were not amongst the things he sold.
That Ellie should have collaborated with Tom Drury, and that
the highwayman should have spent his last night of freedom
at The Fleece were things that Job could neither forgive nor
forget.

He was more fortunate than many people who have to nurse
a grudge helplessly. His spite had an outlet. And when a faceti-
ous or merely tactless traveller mentioned Tom Drury in his
hearing, and his anger sent the blood roaring to his head, he was
always able to go and find Hester and vent his hatred upon her.
Even after the psychological need to relieve his anger had

passed with the passing of time, it was too late for Hester. Job's treatment of her had become habitual : his attitude towards her fixed.

Even her physical appearance, which seldom failed to have effect upon beholders, moving them to admiration, infatuation or jealousy according to their nature, enraged him. And one day, coming upon her bent over her scrubbing, he stooped down, looked hard at the parting in her yellow hair and then straightened himself, announcing loudly and untruthfully the one word, "Lousy." With the sharpened insight of hatred he did not pass on this information to Mrs. Bridges, or even to Martha, but to Rosie, bidding her take a pair of scissors and crop the girl's head before giving it a good dressing with vinegar.

Hester fought violently, scratched and kicked and screamed, and perhaps it was not entirely Rosie's fault that the scissors missed their objective more than once, and that the points dug a short deep groove above one eye on Hester's forehead, marking her for life with a little white scar. One by one the short thick curls fell to the floor. After the first few grinding slices Hester resisted no more, but gave her attention to the checking of the trickle of blood that ran down her temple. A partially cropped head would be as unsightly as a wholly cropped one, so she gave up the struggle and Rosie considered her victory fairly easy. Edgar Goodchild might have warned her, but he was not there, and the scissors ground on.

So within a very short time of Ellie's passing Hester, with her hair at uneven lengths all over her head, her face strained and weary, her thin body wrapped in a sacking apron and her hands already sodden and broken, was in exactly the position that Ellie had given her very life to save her from. She was even less fortunate than Ellie had been at her age, for Ellie had had no enemies.

But if Hester had enemies in Job and Rosie, one made by malice and one by retrospective jealousy, she had friends. For between her and complete subjection stood Mrs. Bridges, between her and complete depression there was Sam. Job might hustle and harass, even strike her (to discipline his servants was then a master's privilege), but he could not be for ever in the domestic part of the building, and as soon as his presence was removed the old kindnesses were forthcoming from the cook. And although Hester supposedly chopped faggot and carried, wood, filled the copper and took the household swill to the pigs, there were few days indeed when Sam did not take chopper, bucket and logs from her hand and put his greater strength to her service.

Lessons, of course, had ceased abruptly on that autumn afternoon, but often when Mrs. Bridges said, "You look peaked, child, run out and get some air," Hester would make her way to the cottage, where Miss Peck would put aside her book or her work, unlock her tea-caddy and the riches of her conversation and share both with the only pupil whom she had ever loved. Precariously supporting herself upon the brink of penury, she had little else to give, but the hours spent with her varied Hester's deadly round of labour and kept her mind awake.

One evening the talks centred around the sonnets of William Shakespeare, which Miss Peck had been reading when Hester arrived. It became, as always, a monologue by Miss Peck upon the subject, and she mentioned the "Dark Lady" and from that drifted on and gave Hester the interesting information that dark ladies were rare in fashionable circles in Elizabethan London, since as a compliment to the red-headed Queen, most ladies of style dyed their hair to auburn with a preparation of henna. In this, she added, one thing leading to another, they did but imitate certain clay-plastered savages reported in Captain Anderson's account of his Pacific voyages; and also certain Hindu ladies who must, according to custom, have reddish tips to their fingers.

Hester's brain took in and docketed these miscellaneous and casual scraps of information and she went home thoughtfully, after extracting the valuable fact that henna was doubtless procurable in England from any good apothecary.

Her own hair was growing again and curling as it grew, but whenever Rose felt ill-disposed towards her she made pointed comments about hair being a woman's crowning beauty, the horror that she, personally, felt for lice, and other similar slow-witted expressions of spite. Never once did Hester betray the depths of the wounds which Rosie's barbs made in her vanity; her face remained stolid; she went on attending to her food, if she were at table, to her work if Rosie chose to annoy her at other times; but Mrs. Bridges knew that she was hurt, and on one occasion said sharply, "I shouldn't say so much about hair, if I was you, Rosie. Yours is wholly thin on top, but I s'pose you can't see up there."

Rosie went straight upstairs and almost dislocated her neck

with her frantic endeavours to study the crown of her own head.

That was some weeks before Miss Peck's timely mention of henna. Soon after it the subject cropped up again. Rosie had, in the interval, counted all the hairs that had come out in her comb, and mourned each one. Her nose had never been the same after Mrs. Bridges' attack upon it with the plate, and if she were now losing her hair the future was black indeed. When next she mentioned Hester's hair, pointing out that it would soon be time for its next cutting, she spoke from envy. The wretched child's hair would soon be as long, as plentiful and as beautiful as ever.

"You'll soon be lousy again," she said unkindly, "your hair grows like weeds."

Hester, for the first time, deigned to notice the subject of the conversation. She ran her fingers through her lengthening curls and said, "You may cut it down to my scalp. While there's henna in the world I can grow it again."

Rosie gulped at the bait. "*What* did you say?" Obligingly Hester repeated the word. "Henna."

Nothing more was said at the time, but for four or five days Rosie refrained from taunting Hester, and was even painstakingly civil to her when they came into contact with one another. Finally she came into the open.

"That stuff you mentioned the other day. Where do you get it?"

"What stuff?" asked Hester innocently.

"What you put on your hair. Mine's coming out something shocking. I thought I'd try some."

"Oh, you mean henna. I was thinking of getting some for myself, because I supposed you'd be coming at me with the scissors again very soon. If you like I'd get you some at the same time."

"P'raps you mightn't need any for yourself. Old Job didn't say anything about *keeping* it short that I can remember."

"Nor that I can," said Hester in a voice that would have made a more intelligent protagonist pause. "All right, I'll get you some."

"And tell me what to do with it?" Hester nodded, noting that there was something that she had yet to discover for herself.

Sam, who occasionally went to Norwich on business connected with the horses, readily consented to take a note to the apothecary, and to bring back a parcel. Hester penned her request for "a good quantity of henna" and for instructions how to use it in order to redden hair.

The loyal Sam promised to pay the charge and to take Hester's word for it that she would repay him some day. But the sweet day of revenge was delayed, for the ladies of Norwich apparently knew not the art of hair dyeing in the ancient manner, and the obliging apothecary sent back a message that he would obtain a supply and instructions from his brother-in-law in London.

The delay sharpened Rosie's anxiety. She went on counting hairs, which hitherto she had never noticed, and pestering Hester to know when the stuff was coming. There was no further mention of re-cropping Hester's yellow head. And at last Sam returned, bearing the parcel with a carefulness that argued its value, an argument borne out by his remark to Hester that it was "damn dear" and that she had better start saving right away. He did not, however, as a serious creditor would have done, tell her that he had parted with a precious five shillings to pleasure her.

Wrapped around the pound of greenish-brown paper was a paper giving directions for mixing the henna into a thick paste with very hot water, applying it hot to the hair and leaving it on until "the desired shade is attained."

Rosie, faced with the puzzling paper, appealed to Hester, first to read them to her, and secondly to help her to put them into action. But Hester was not so simple as Rosie. She refused to take a hand in any proceedings which might have strange results. "I do mine myself, so can you," she said, and obviously lost interest in the whole affair. Eventually Rosie appealed to Aggie, who came to the inn one afternoon, flaunting her wedding ring before Mrs. Bridges and Martha, and the two girls, giggling and excited, disappeared into the upper regions, bearing a kettle of boiling water and one of Mrs. Bridges' pudding basins.

It was a cold winter afternoon. Hester's last job before darkness fell was to take in the linen from the line in the drying-yard. She had recently been afflicted with chilblains. As she took down the stiffened linen and punched the rigid shapes into the basket, the sharp air bit into her fingers and little bloody cracks appeared in them. She licked them without, for once, either rancour or self-pity. Sam, appearing from nowhere and heaving up the big basket while she took the pegs, looked with commiseration upon the little cracked hands.

"Hedgehog grease, that's what you want," he said. "Bit late in the year to get hold of one now, though. They lay up all winter."

"Never mind my hands. Just wait till you see Rosie's hair," said Hester happily.

"Why, what'a she done? Cut off her own?" (It was largely Sam's matter-of-fact and humorous acceptance of her cropped head that enabled Hester to bear it.)

"I *think*, and I hope that hers will be worse than *cut*," said Hester confidingly, "but don't you show that you know anything about it, will you, Sam?"

"You could trust me by now, I should think," said Sam fondly.

At the kitchen door Hester took the basket, put the pegs on top of it, and entered the kitchen, giving, for the benefit of any who might be watching, a good imitation of a half-grown girl who has carried a heavy burden for several hundred yards. But nobody was paying her any attention for the moment. Mrs. Bridges, her hands covered with flour and bits of pastry, was rolling about the kitchen laughing as only a fat woman can. Gusts of mirth shook her to the last outpost of her bulk. Tears of mirth squeezed through her wrinkled eyelids and were brushed away by the floury hands. Martha, with meat-chopper poised, was staring open-mouthed and open-eyed, and now and again letting out a squawk of horror. Aggie, in genuine tears, cowered by the pantry door. And in the centre, the stained towel upon which she had been drying her hair still around her shoulders, her face plum-coloured and distorted with rage and misery, was Rosie. Her frizzy hair still dripped on to the towel, and there was every shade in it, from bright amber to its original black. Aggie, lacking both experience and sense, had taken no care to spread the paste evenly. Where it had lain thickly it had worked violent changes.

Hester set down the basket of linen and tucked her cold hands into the warmth of her armpits. Rosie became aware of her presence. She let out a shrill scream and darted towards her, every nail poised to scratch. She slavered like a dog with hydrophobia. Mrs. Bridges, without ceasing to laugh, put out a restraining hand and Hester dodged round to the other side of the table.

"You can't blame the child," gasped the cook, "p'raps she didn't know what it'd do to black hair. Oh, you do look a sight and no mistake. No, you don't my girl! You calm yourself and get that hair dried and your cap on. You'll be glad of your cap to-night. He-he-he!"

Rosie, baulked of physical revenge, exhausted in two minutes her complete repertoire of abuse. She threw at Hester every foul term, culled from stable and stye, that experience had taught her. She dragged up Ellie and Little Tom. She vowed vengeance that had much to do with the more intimate portions of Hester's body. As soon as she was silent for lack of breath or further things to say or threaten, Hester turned to Aggie.

"How long," she asked mildly, "did you leave it on?"

"Forty minutes. I came down three times to look at the clock. But she would have it on a long time because she wanted it to work good."

"You done it a-purpose. You both done it a-purpose," screamed Rosie. "Now I shall be a sight for the rest of my days. I could kill you. As for you, you snotty little . . ."

"Now, look here," bellowed Mrs. Bridges, recovering entirely from her amusement. "That's enough. You've said all that once, and I listened because I was having a good laugh. You get your speckled head dried and let's hear no more about it."

With a last glare of baffled hatred in Hester's direction Rosie departed. As soon as she had gone Mrs. Bridges burst into another gust of laughter, and only then did Hester permit a smile to curve her lips.

"You're a lixer, a proper little devil," said the stout woman fondly. "Not that it don't serve her right. But you look out, my dear, she'll want her own back on you, you know."

"I know. I expect she'll get it, too," said Hester with the air of accepting the inevitable.

But beyond administering a pinprick upon every possible occasion, there was little that Rosie could do. Her mind was not inventive, and in her heart she was, like the children at school, long ago, frightened of Hester. Moreover, beside a stout partisan in the cook, Hester had a valuable buffer in Martha, who secretly suspected Rosie of setting her cap at Job. Lately his interest had waned, and Martha was unhappily aware that Rosie was much younger, more sprightly, richer in florid charm. She was delighted to see the girl going about with her hair dragged back unbecomingly and her cap pulled down over her ears. And since Hester's work lay mainly in Mrs. Bridges' province and she slept in Martha's room, Rosie's half-hearted attempts at vengeance never did her a great deal of harm.

She was frequently unhappy enough. The work was hard and dreary. Job's hatred seemed implacable. Many times during the next four years did she fling herself down on the floor of the room where she slept and long to die; or, preferably, to find some means of getting enough money to make practicable her escape from The Fleece. But she found none, and she earned nothing. On the other side of the wall, in the room that had been Ellie's the damp was rotting the mattress in which the unhappy woman had hidden her hoard. Nobody went there now. The window had not been mended and birds fouled the floor and even nested upon the shelf where Hester had kept her books.

CHAPTER II

VERY soon Hester was sixteen, and in the spring that followed her birthday Mrs. Bridges was smitten with apoplexy. Job Wainwright had tired of Martha, and the cook had found her assistant more than usually lethargic. One afternoon, just before the busiest hour of the day, Mrs. Bridges discovered that Martha had neglected to put the loaves in the oven. There they lay, shapeless masses of dough, at a time when they should have been ready to lift from the oven and set to cool.

"Now they'll either have to go in, just when I want the oven for the pies, or else stand there and ruin. And there'll be hot bread for the tables and they'll kill themselves with belching. Of all the idle, useless tools for a busy woman to be wrapped up with, you're the very worst. I'll speak to Mr. Wainwright, that I will. I've put up with you long enough, you shiftless, senseless besom. Now he's done with you I'll have you ousted, mark my words. Bread in the oven at four o'clock!"

Martha, stung to unusual resentment by the cook's reference to her fall from favour, which was indeed largely responsible for her absentmindedness, said miserably :

"You only want me gone so that you can have Hester to help you. I've seen it coming a long time."

The truth of the statement was the last drop in Mrs. Bridges's seething ocean of fury. She picked up one of the wilting loaves and flung it at Martha, shouting, "So now you'd answer back would you? I'll show you, you . . ." And as the dough draped itself around Martha's head, the cook's face changed suddenly, the rating voice fell silent and quietly, almost gradually, she dropped from an upright position on to knees, and from there crumpled on to the floor, where she lay still.

Martha, still struggling with the adhesiveness of the dough, tore open the house door and ran screaming to Job. He silenced her roughly and returning with her to the kitchen, applied to Mrs. Bridges every restorative that the inn offered. But the stout body still lay supine, breathing noisily and showing no sign of returning consciousness, even when Job waved a glass of his best brandy under its nose.

At last he gave up the struggle and called Sam and John to come and carry Mrs. Bridges into his own parlour. Her bulk made the negotiation of the stairs quite impossible. While they struggled to carry out his orders Job stood a little apart, pulling out his lower lip and letting it go again as if it were the elastic of a catapult. He was much exercised in his mind. It seemed to him, in view of the cook's physique and the fact that the seizure had been brought on by anger, that the services of a surgeon were called for. But there was none nearer than Dixon of Winwood, and he would demand a heavy fee for riding so far. If the cook died the money would be wasted. On the other hand she was a good willing woman, though she had latterly annoyed him several times by her partiality for Hester Roon.

By the time Sam and John had laid the heavy body upon the large settle which Job had had made expressly for the comfort of his own vast bulk, he had made up his mind. "Sam, you take the black mare and ride to Winwood and bring Dixon back with you. Tell him to bring his tools."

Sam obeyed with alacrity .He was grateful to Mrs. Bridges for her kindness to Hester, and in the shortest possible time he returned with the little surgeon bouncing behind him. Mrs. Bridges was bled. She did not, as such cases often did, recover consciousness; nor did the heavy breathing, drawn in with a hiss and released with a grunt, change. After two hours he bled her again; but except that her colour changed and her nose seemed to become suddenly pinched, there was no result. At midnight she died.

Meanwhile Martha had taken on the responsibility for the evening meal. The pies stood where Mrs. Bridges had left them. The bread went into the oven and came out, a flat and unsuccessful batch, to join the cold ham with which the guests had to content themselves. She was helped by a meek and subdued Hester. For some years now the stout, hot-tempered cook had been her friend, and Hester's concern for her well-being was not so selfish as it would have been at the beginning of that time. The years had brought their inevitable changes to Hester, in mind as well as body, and she was, though still hard, far more vulnerable than she had been when Ellie died.

The guests, from whom, at all costs, the presence of sickness and death must be hidden, went to their beds, but around the kitchen fire Martha, bearing no spite to the cook, Hester, and Maria, who had taken on Ellie's work, sat and waited. They had forgotten Mrs. Bridges' irascibility and remembered only her kindness. Hester with her hands tightly clenched in her lap, willing, with every nerve in her body and every fibre in her brain, that her friend should recover. It seemed to her, as it has to so many who have been in her position, that if the will was strong enough and the concentration sufficiently fierce, events must go the way that she desired. Her fingers were bruised, her jaws ached from being clenched so tightly. But Mrs. Bridges, who had always noticed this when Hester was troubled or unhappy or overwearied, was beyond her reach now. Very quietly Mrs. Bridges died, and the little surgeon came through the kitchen to break the news. Job had told him that he might share the barman's bed, and Martha, crying noisily and loud in self-reproach, led him away to it. Rosie, sniffing, followed in their wake.

Hester, dry-eyed and beaten, took her shawl from the peg behind the door and let herself into the yard. She had only Sam now.

A flight of shallow wooden stairs led up to the loft where Sam slept. She climbed them and pushed open the door at the top. Within there was the scent of hay, the dry musty fragrance of corn, and the all-pervading odour of horses. Sam slept in a corner on a heap of straw, which he changed as regularly as he changed the horses' bedding. In cold weather he burrowed into it and pulled a horse-rug over himself. It was cold to-night, and he was deeply ensconced in his bed, weary from his hard riding to Winwood and happily, deeply asleep. Hester had to call twice before he stirred, rustling in his strawy lair. Then he was, after the manner of the country-bred, suddenly and completely awake.

"What's the matter? I ain't got to take that little bastard back, have I? Not to-night."

"No. He's sleeping with John. But she's dead, Sam." He scuffled out of his straw and reached out and found Hester's hands.

"You're frozen," he said. "Where you been?"

"In the kitchen. But the fire died down. Can I stay with you a little while?"

For answer he pulled her across to the pile of straw, warm from his body, spread the rug across their knees and slid one of his arms around her shoulders. Like Mrs. Bridges, years ago, he hoped that she would cry and so soften with tears the hard core of her sorrow. But the relief of tears was one of the things denied to Hester. She leaned against him, shuddering now and then, mute and miserable and yet feeling the comfort of his warm physical presence.

It was utterly silent in the loft except for the soft, muted rustle of the straw on which they sat. Hester stared straight ahead of her into the darkness, musing upon life and death and the difference between them. One minute you were there, a living entity with appetites that must be catered for, moods that must be respected, and then you were suddenly just a body that must be shovelled away as quickly as decency permitted. Mingled with these thoughts was selfish speculation as to what life in the kitchen of The Fleece would be like with Mrs. Bridges' friendly influence removed.

But while her mind was thus engaged her body was becoming conscious of a change in Sam's grasp and touch. Slowly and with the gradual movement of an incoming tide something unknown, untold, unguessed at, crept over her. Although the loft was as dark as ever, she seemed to see Sam's lean, brown young face, his leathery neck, the way his hair broke into a little wave above each prominent ear, the kindly humorous look in his hazel eyes. The weight of his arm over her shoulder had pulled down her head and under her cheek she could feel the steady rapid thudding of his heart. But the warm dissolving tide that was bearing her away had little to do with any of these things.

She had seen them many times. It was something else, it was being alone with him, like this in the darkness, being held so warmly, so close. It was the memory of Sam's kindness; and the knowledge of his maleness, that hard, unknown, unexplored quality.

Sam was less ignorant. He had been aware of the approaching crisis from the moment when his arm had slid around Hester and she had leaned against him. He had liked her for a long time, ever since she was a curious, yellow-haired, bright-eyed little girl whom he lifted into an empty manger so that she could watch the horses without being in any danger of getting beneath their hooves. He had pitied her over the matter of Ellie and done what he could to soften her lot. But he had not known, and never guessed, that this moment would arrive; when the touch of her flesh would burn him, the nearness of her breathing rend him apart. Without his intention, almost without his knowledge his big brown hand slipped from her shoulder where it had lain comfortingly, down, under her arm until it touched her breast with the hot fingers of desire.

With its touch a strong shudder shook Hester. It passed, and left in its wake pain where she had never known a capacity for pain existed. Her mouth, her breast, her throat, and her fingers all yearned towards Sam as an empty stomach yearns towards food. With the blind instinct of a shoot that presses through the cold, damp earth into the light and the sunny world where its existence has purpose and significance, she lifted her face to his. His came down and his lips closed hard upon hers. She put her arms around his neck, pressing him to her. For her this moment was the consummation and the goal of sixteen years' growth and change. For this moment were her lips full and warm, her breasts soft, her thighs hard and long. Without a doubt or question she was prepared to yield herself.

But Sam was twenty-four and neither inexperienced nor without conscience. He had never heard of Pan, but he knew that virginity, especially in the very young, should be respected. With a great effort, the measure of his affection for her, he tore his mouth away, and pressed back his head against her encircling arms. In a hard, breathless voice he asked:

"Do you know what you're doing, my little dear? You better get away down afore we get into wrongdoing together."

Hester was beyond speech; but her flesh spoke for her. Her hands, wise with the wisdom of all the women since Eve who

106

had gone to her making, closed upon the back of his head and dragged him down. And like someone who has learned to play upon a rough strong fiddle that has survived many learners and is then presented with a violin, frail and exquisite, he dealt with her with a gentleness and consideration that he had never shown his village loves.

It was morning when Hester crept, dazed with ecstasy, into the room she had shared with Martha since Ellie's death. Martha was still awake, or had awakened very quickly, and said, as Hester flung herself down, "So it's you." Hester understood the phrase to imply that Martha recognised her bedfellow. But the three words had another, more sinister meaning.

Martha's lethargic manner and slightly cow-like exterior concealed an ardent nature. She had lived now, for many years, upon the anticipation, the realisation, and the memory of her nights spent with her master. Now they had ceased. She had done what she could, put fresh ribbons in her cap, risen early on summer mornings and gone into the orchard to wash her face in dew, even curled her thick, straight hair into ringlets round the poker. But all in vain. Job was tired of her. And as Hester crept to bed in the early hours of the morning Martha imagined that she knew the reason. Slowly, through the remaining hours of the night all the placidity, the energy, the frustrated passion of the woman's nature, melted together into anger that was different from Mrs. Bridges' flashes of temper as any two emotions bearing the same collective name, could well be. She had stayed at The Fleece, not through necessity but from choice. Her brother, a widower, owned a prosperous leather-merchant's business in Norwich and had repeatedly invited her to go and keep house for him. But, for the sake of those secret nights in Job's bed, she had stayed on in a menial position, worked like a servant, and borne without resentment, until yesterday, the cook's reproaches about her idleness. All that was ended now. Even her passion for her master shrivelled in the slow white-heat of her anger. To-morrow—no to-day, for it was already morning—she would pack her things and leave; and before leaving she would give Job a piece of her mind.

As soon as it was light she rose, hauled from under the bed the chest in which she kept her things and began stuffing into it everything that was hers. She washed and did her hair carefully and then, dressed in her best, sat down with folded hands until the moment to strike should arrive.

Hester went down into the kitchen before Martha stirred and kindled the fire, while the boy whose work it was, polished boots and whistled through his teeth, interrupting the noise now and then to throw out some remark about the suddenness of Mrs. Bridges' passing. To these, and his speculations as to the effects of the cook's removal, Hester vouchsafed no answer.

A glance at the clock on the wall told her that the time for breakfast was approaching. She filled the kettles and pulled forward the pan of porridge that had been simmering since the previous afternoon at the back of the hob. Still her superior did not appear, and at last Hester climbed the stairs and was confronted with the vision of Martha, dressed as if for an outing, idly looking out of the window.

"I thought you'd overslept," she said. "I've started the kettle and the porridge."

"Oh," said Martha without turning her head.

"Well," began Hester : and then the box, closed and corded, and Martha's clothes conveyed their message. "You aren't coming down. Is that it? Then who'll make the breakfast?"

Even Martha's fury could not hold her silent before such an opening.

"Why don't you?" she asked in a calm, bitter voice. "You're fond of taking other people's places."

"I don't know what you're talking about," said Hester. "But somebody's got to get it. I want mine, for one."

She had not eaten since the previous midday, and the night's events had made heavy demands on her. She felt hollow. Now and again there shot through her consciousness a voluptuous memory that made her dread her next meeting with Sam in the broad light of day. There was also, equally recurrent but less sharp, the thought of Mrs. Bridges, for whom no other day would dawn, lying behind the locked door of Job's parlour. A good meal would help her to resist the sorrow of that thought, too.

Maria and Rosie, appealed to in turn, refused to have anything to do with the cooking. They were busy already, and until Mr. Wainwright ordered . . .

Hester returned to the kitchen, heaved down the side of bacon, slashed it into rashers with the carving knife, lifted the heavy iron frying-pan into a central position, and set about the job herself. When Job came into the kitchen twenty minutes later he found Hester, wrapped in one of Mrs. Bridges' white aprons, her face flushed with the heat of the stove, slapping eggs and bacon on to a dish held for her by the odd-job boy.

"What d'you think you're doing?" he asked, searching in vain for any sight of Martha.

"Making the breakfast," said Hester sharply. "Nobody else would."

"Where's Martha?"

"Upstairs."

"The hell she is," he shouted, and strode away.

He confronted Martha, who had been hoping for just such an opportunity, in peace and privacy to speak her mind; and learned, in five minutes, far more about the nature of his discarded mistress than all the nights in the big bed had taught him. Icy, calm and deadly, Martha's voice went on, heedless of interruptions. She told him just how fat, how mean, how vain, how old, how increasingly impotent he was. She showered upon him some of the choicer nicknames with which the overcharged fishermen and stockdealers relieved their spleen in his direction. She referred to Little Tom Drury, and said outright what the squire and others had only hinted. Only one pleasant thing—and that not intentional—did she say.

". . . and then to take a child like that, young enough to be your grandchild—if you'd ever had the guts to get a child yourself. You should be ashamed. And on the very night that Mrs. Bridges died. You didn't dare do while she was alive, did you? She'd have sorted you proper, you dirty old goat. Little girls with the marks of the cradle still on their bottoms, that's all you're up to now, you old lard bladder. . . ."

She was still talking when Job, seeing that there was only one way of stopping, or escaping, the tirade, took it, and walked away.

Martha left on the Norwich coach which passed the inn at about midday, and Hester remained in supreme command of the kitchen until, on the day after Mrs. Bridges' funeral, two new workers were installed. One a dry, wizened little woman who took over the cooking, and the other an orphan girl, provided by the parish, who inherited Hester's pails and mops. Without anything being said, it was understood that Hester was to take Martha's place as assistant to the cook.

When these exterior and disturbing matters had been settled Hester was free to indulge her secret life.

The moment of the meeting with Sam, so dreaded, had not,

of course been avoided. He had appeared on the next morning and taken his breakfast from Hester's hand. And she had been busy and bothered with her unaccustomed responsibilities and had dished up two more slices of fat bacon and another egg without any emotion whatever. It was not until Sam was half-way through his meal that she remembered. She looked across the table and met his eye. He smiled a trifle sheepishly, and she smiled too, noting anew, and loving, everything about his face and figure which last night she had only been able to see with the eye of the mind. Dear Sam, she thought, not at all embarrassed as she expected him to be, but rather eager, pressing forward to the delights that their next meeting would bring. (So some men cherish lion cubs, delighting in their softness and innocence; ignoring the day when the playfulness will turn to fury, and the cuddlesome pet become a thing of claws and fangs and terror.)

As soon as Hester knew that Phoebe, the orphan, was to share her room, she set about putting Phoebe in her rightful place.

"Sometimes I sleep here, sometimes I don't. When I do, I have this side of the bed and I keep the candle as long as I need to read. So you must turn the other way if the light bothers you. When I don't, my whereabouts are none of your business, and if you mention my absence to anybody, even to me, you'll be sorry."

The orphan, extremely anxious to do well in this, her first place, and overawed by Hester's size, assurance and appearance, said humbly, "Yes, ma'am," and with that meek acceptance of the situation, set Hester free.

CHAPTER III

THEN came the halcyon days, the days of the kingfisher, the spring, the fitting season for young love. Hester was never one to remember much, to live in the past or brood; but all her life a hawthorn hedge, bright green with young leaves, a cherry tree dazzling white, the call of the cuckoo across the cowslip pastures, was to recall, for a brief, bright, nostalgic moment the

110

very scent and sinew of her first love. Hester's life was easier now, Phoebe was the drudge; and with the coming of warmer weather and the sprouting of the meadows Sam's evening work was reduced, the horses could be turned out. And Mamie—everybody called the cook by her rather unsuitable name—had never exercised the motherly control upon Hester's comings and goings that Mrs. Bridges had done. In the spring nights the pair forsook the loft and took to the woods, where the silence was so deep that the flight of a bird could startle them, and the thick drifts of last year's leaves made a bed fit for lovers. Around them the pale oxlips and later the wild hyacinths spread wide pools of loveliness. Above them the hawthorns, the crab-apples and the wild roses hung their garlands. And Hester and Sam, hardly aware of the beauty around them, beneath flowering skies and starry trees, walked as though this were Eden, and they indeed the first to discover the pleasures of love.

But the spring, coaxing to growth the wayside plants, the meadows and the woodlands, brought to ripeness the seed planted unwittingly in Job's mind by Martha. She had accused him of seducing Hester, and by that natural mistake had implanted within him the desire to do so. Until that moment he had seen in Hester only the reminder of her mother's ill-doing, and his only interest in her body had been to chastise it. Martha's accusation had brought to his attention the fact that Hester was a pretty nubile female, completely in his power. And not young blood alone is subject to disturbances with the rising sap and the opening bud.

He made no immediate advance. He hesitated for a while, savouring the flattery of returning desire. He had been tired of Martha, unwilling to make a change, and half-convinced that his age was to blame. Martha, by accusing him of dalliance with Hester, had restored him. Like a branch that will, in a warm November, bloom again, untimely, the old man's lust sprang into belated activity.

Close watching—unsuspected by Hester and therefore not guarded against—revealed that the first swathe had fallen to the young groom's sickle. Job did not consider this a matter for regret. There were drawbacks to virginity. But Sam's removal was desirable. And that presented no difficulty at all.

It was easy enough, one bright sweet summer morning, for Job to look into the bins where the feeding-stuffs were stored and to declare that they were far below the level that they

111

should be.

"You bin selling any of my stuff behind my back?"

"'Course not," said Sam, easy and confident in his knowledge of his innocence. Job passed on to another bin, looked in, grunted, came back and said flatly :

"No wages for you, you thieving little rat, come pay-day. And I'll get locks put on these so you have to ask for every skepful. That's what I'll do. You fellows are all alike. You'd sell your grandmother for a shilling."

Sam's face reddened to the very tips of his ears. Almost without his knowing his hands clenched and he moved towards Job menacingly.

"Nobody's going to call me a thief," he said in an angry, high-pitched voice. "Every mossel of fodder in them bins has gone into the bellies of the horses that 'a paid to be here. Nor you ain't going to dock my wages neither. You take both them words back, Mr. Wainwright."

"What I said I mean. And don't you double your fists at me, you dishonest little devil. You get outa here while your skin's whole. And if I find you on my premises after this I'll get the constable to you. Thirty shillings-worth of good fodder you've robbed me of, and you're lucky to get off so lightly."

"Why, there worn't thirty shillingsworth . . ." Sam began, and then it dawned upon him that reason would not serve him. If by a miracle he could suddenly have filled the bins to over-flowing, Job would still persist in his monstrous accusation. He shot out one fist and smote Job on the jaw. The fat man gave a strangled bellow of rage, reached out and seized the first thing to hand—the chopper with which Sam sliced the hay—and, holding it aloft, drove Sam out of the stable, across the cobbles of the yard and out through the archway. Once, while they were in the yard, Sam turned at bay, driven to the folly by the know-ledge of his own undignified appearance in the eyes of anyone who might be watching. He tried to get in under Job's guard and fetch him a wallop in the stomach, but without compunc-tion Job brought the back of the chopper down hard on the brown forearm. An ominous crack testified to the force of the blow and Sam, clapping his other hand around the suddenly limp and useless arm, beat a hasty retreat.

Bemused by the suddenness of his eviction—for surely Job had been pleasant enough yesterday afternoon—and at a loss for a reason to account for the change, and in increasing pain from his arm, he made his way, disconsolately to the smithy, where the smith, who in his rough and barbarous way was also a horse doctor, inspected the arm and announced that one bone in it was broken.

"An almighty smite it must 'a bin, and all," he said, ripping off a length of sheeting with a sound that set Sam's teeth on edge. "You're lucky both bones didn't go, then you'd 'a needed a splint."

"I'm sick of hearing that I'm lucky," said Sam sourly. "That old devil said I was lucky to get off lightly for something I never done. Now you say I'm lucky to have only one bone broke. I'm lucky all right, I am! And what's it all about. Can you tell me that? The old swine see the corn bins yesterday and never said nothing. Now here I am with no job, the best part of a year's wages took from me and a broke arm."

"Hold still," said the smith in the voice he used to the horses; and Sam held still while the arm was tightly bandaged and the linen smeared with glue that set the folds as hard as wood. Then, with his professional duties performed to his satisfaction, the smith turned his attention to the psychological aspect of the case.

"He've took against you," he said at last. "Like old Saul Dyer's wife did. Sweet as pie she was all the time they was courting, took everything he gave her and behaved that meek. Then the minute they was married she wouldn't let him near her. Took the rolling-pin up to bed, so she did. And all she could say was that she'd took against him. Reckon that's what happened to Job and you. Must 'a bin a rare take against too, for him to fetch you that swipe. Not violent as a rule, is he?"

"Not that way," said Sam thoughtfully. "But he's a bloody liar and all. Said I'd robbed him of thirty shillingsworth of stuff and the bins don't hold that much atween 'em."

"Plain took against you," said the smith again as he followed this reasoning. The repetition of the unhelpful phrase was annoying and Sam was about to leave the forge, when he remembered that he had nowhere to go and had not had his breakfast. The smith was renowned as a hearty feeder, and it might be worth a little irritation to be asked to share his meal.

"What are you going to do now?" inquired the smith.

"I dunno. Get a job somewhere out of reach of Job's tongue, I s'pose. I don't want to go around with thief tied to me like a rattle on a dog's tail."

"Well," said the smith, satisfying himself that his fire was going to burn. "You'd better have a bite alonga me. I got a beaning job directly arter breakfast."

"I don't hold with that job," said Sam firmly. "If a horse is lame it should be let be lame and turned out till it's better. Why, it's like breaking my other arm and pretending that you've cured this one."

"That stops the limping," said the smith. "A nice dry bean or a little pebble under one shoe'll keep a nag treading even."

"I don't hold with it, all the same," said Sam. "Some of you fellows act as if a horse didn't have no feelings. That's bad enough to have one lame leg without somebody laming another."

"Do you want some breakfast or do you want to stay here and argufy? Because if so you can stay alone," said the smith, slightly resenting this slur upon his trade.

"I might as well eat," said Sam. "Lord knows when, or where I'll get my next meal."

He followed the smith through the low door that joined the forge to the little house, and was given a plate piled with slices of fat salt pork, a dish of fierce brown pickle, half a loaf, a lump of butter and a tankard of ale. The smith's wife kindly cut the pork and bread into pieces for him.

"That's all wrong he should be let do that to you," she said when she had heard the reason for Sam's disability. "If the boot had been on the other leg and you'd 'a hurt him that way there wouldn't half 'a bin a rumpus."

"That's the way in this world," said Sam sourly. "I ought to be able to go to the constable and say that he's robbed me of my wages. That's be true, too."

It was not until he had satisfied the needs of his stomach, and for the pleasure of the smith's wife re-told the whole tale from the beginning, that the thought struck Sam that separation from The Fleece meant separation from Hester. Then he alarmed his hosts by springing up and shouting, "God dammit."

"What's bit you now?" asked the smith, still chewing with the steadiness of a cow in a field.

"I just thought of something. Thank you very much for tying this up. And for the breakfast, too. I got to go now."

He sped out of the shady little house into the sunny morning. Half-way to The Fleece he passed a man leading a limping horse which was going to be cured, not of its lameness but of the relieving limp by the brutal process of beaning.

Sam, who liked horses and was in pain himself, gave a shudder of sympathy. A damned rotten world, that was what it was, a damned rotten, unfair world. And yet as late as last night he had been perfectly happy in it. Happy in his work, sound in his body, and blessed in his love. Now it was all spoiled, and his most earnest scrutiny of the situation did not provide him with a clue to the reason.

Back at the smithy cottage the smith was, for the fifth time, replying to his wife's voiced wonder as to what made Mr. Wainwright behave like that to the lad, with the phrase, "Just took against him, like old Saul Dyer's wife."

"But that don't explain anything," said the woman. And Sam, hearing the same words in memory, returned the same demur. Clearly Job had taken against him, but why?

He came to a standstill in the road before the inn and sat down on a low wall on the other side. That, as least, as he had heard many disgruntled dealers point out to Job, was not inn property. And he waited there until Phoebe came out to wash windows. Then he beckoned her across.

"When you get a chance just tell Hester I'll be waiting in Lownde Wood, will you Phoebe? Ask her to come as soon as she can." The orphan, honoured by the trust, nodded vigorously and returned to her work.

Sam, for the first time in years, had a whole day on his hands, and at least twelve dragging hours to get through before he could hope to meet Hester. She was seldom free before nine, and he could tell by the look of the inn that it was about nine in the morning now. It seemed impossible that just across the road and through the archway, all the tools of his trade awaited him. The broom with which he swept out the stables, the buckets, the harness, the curry-combs and the chaff-chopper, the last put to such strange use an hour ago! Suppose he went back, took up his things and went on with work. Would Job notice? Or would things be as they had been before that strange incident? For a moment he needed his injured arm to assure him that he hadn't dreamed it all.

He shuffled along the wall until he had a view of the yard through the archway, and saw Job and Jerry, his fellow-groom, rushing hither and thither in a great flurry, helped, or hindered by the orphan boy, Tom, who had been in turn odd-boy and gardener and was now completely bewildered by his sudden

115

promotion. It had fallen to his lot to harness a frisky young horse to a light chaise, and the directions bellowed across to him by Job and Jerry confused rather than they helped him. At least Sam had the pleasure, seldom experienced by the dismissed, of watching the scene of his late labours and seeing how he was being missed.

Then young Mr. Enoch, Lord Loddon's agent, rode out of the yard. He was a pleasant young man whom Sam knew by sight. His Lordship owned some property in Norwich and Mr. Enoch visited it at varying intervals, always breaking his journey at The Fleece. His main duties lay in the Newmarket district and he and Sam generally talked about horses each time they met. Their love for the creatures was a strong link.

He rode out to Sam's side of the road, restraining his mount because there was considerable activity in front of the inn, and as he drew level Sam slid to his feet and said :

"Mr. Enoch, sir, just a minute, your girth's twisted."

"Oh, hullo Sam," said the rider in a surprised voice, pleasurably surprised. "What are you doing out here?" Then his eye lighted upon the stiff, bandaged arm. "You've hurt yourself."

"You'll have to get down, sir. I'm afraid. Anyway I doubt if I can do it with one hand."

"No, no. Of course not. I didn't notice what you said. Girth twisted, eh? Damned careless. You know, even with a bad arm you might be across there seeing that that little beggar didn't turn people out like this, mightn't you?"

"I'm sacked, sir. Sacked this morning, and my arm broke just by way of parting."

"Sacked with a broken arm. That's bad," said Mr. Enoch, straightening the strap and preparing to shoot it home. "Here, just hold her head, will you, she's dancing mad this morning."

He buckled the girth. "Now then, what's all this? Why should a broken arm lead to your dismissal, my lad? It'll mend, won't it? And as I said, there's several things you could see to meanwhile."

"I know. But I'm sacked. Mr. Wainwright said I'd stolen some corn, sir. I hadn't, before God, sir, I'd never sold or given away or even wasted a grain of it. But he called me a thief and then I . . ." Sam poured out the whole of the tale. Before it was ended Mr. Enoch said :

"You'll have to walk alongside me, Sam. I can't hold her still any longer. All right, go on."

Sam finished. As an employer of labour Mr. Enoch was bound to say, "You shouldn't have struck your master, you know."

"I know, sir. It was being called a thief that did it." And if, the man reflected, you weren't as honest as the day you wouldn't have admitted that you had done so. I'd have had no means of knowing.

"So now you're out of a job, eh?"

"Yes, sir."

The road was quieter here and it didn't matter if the mare did sidle round until her heels were in the middle of it. Mr. Enoch stopped, and Sam imagined that he was going to fumble out a coin and dismiss him with that and his good wishes. But the agent was silent for a moment. He had always liked Sam, admired his way with horses and his knowledge of them. And he believed his story.

"Would you care to come to Newmarket, Sam? I could find you a job in the stables. But you'd have to come at once because I'm going to look over a pack of lads to-morrow. If you like to come it'd be as well that you should have time to learn the job while your arm's out of use. They aren't coach- or pack-horses there, you know."

"I'd love it, sir. I'd just love it." His breath was short with excitement and his eyes shone. "Would to-morrow do, sir?"

"To-morrow would be excellent. All right, Sam. I'll see you. At Newmarket take the road towards Ely and after about two miles you'll see the gates—you can't miss them, the pillars have eagles atop. You'll get in if you ask for me, and I'll have some-body on the look-out for you."

"I'll never be able to thank you, sir. But I am grateful, indeed I am."

"Thank your sharp eye that noticed the girth, lad. You'd better go back and watch for the horse with the bridle on its tail. By the look of things when I left it'll be along before so long Good-bye."

The mare, released at last, went off at a sharp trot. Sam turned back. He had a job, and he'd go to sea if it wasn't a better one than he had lost. Now he must wait in patience to see Hester and to persuade her to come with him. It would have to be done quietly, for in a way it was robbing Job; a girl in Hester's position belonged, more or less, to her master, but it could be managed. Sam's mind went off down the track worn almost

117

smooth by Ellie's dreams. To steal away with Hester and start a new life somewhere else.

Far happier now, though his arm pained him still, the young man wandered off to Lownde Wood, where he lay down and slept in a sunny clearing with his head on a pile of green bracken. When he awoke he was surprised to see, by the slant of the sun, that the evening had come. The level rays fell through the trunks of the trees, not through the leaves. Hester would soon be finished in the hot kitchen and free to join him. A clump of honeysuckle, with a few bees still busy about it, caught his attention. He gathered some sprays that were within reach and sauntered along to the edge of the wood, keeping a sharp look-out for any other clusters. He would gather a bunch of it and when they met and went to their usual place she should have it beneath her head. He was half ashamed of the fancy and glad that there was no one to see him, wandering along like a zaney with a bunch of flowers in his hand; there was little of the "rural shepherd" about Sam. Nevertheless he did not throw away the sprays he had gathered, nor fail to find others, and by the time he had reached the gateway from which he could watch the path by which Hester would come, his hand was as full of scented blooms as his heart was of eager longing.

CHAPTER IV

BUT Sam, in his innocence of Hester being in any way connected with his fall from favour, had neglected to caution the orphan to secrecy, and when the timid child, after twice attempting to speak to Hester and twice being brushed away with "Don't hinder me, I'm busy now," came on the girl emptying a dish of broken pieces into the pig-bucket, she thought that here was her opportunity and did not even notice that Job was standing near, watching with a sharp eye to see that nothing that could be used in the kitchen was thrown away to the pigs.

Her "Sam says you're to meet him in Lownde Wood," was as audible to Job as to Hester, and Hester, equally ignorant of any undercurrent, and devoured by curiosity to know the whole story of the morning's scene, said graciously, "Thank you, Phoebe." The fact that Sam was in disgrace with Job meant nothing to her, and it was in order to let Job know this that she added, "I'll go as soon as I've finished." Phoebe, pleased at being thus taken into the confidence of the one whom she considered the epitome of every virtue and charm, said :

"I'll do anything you don't want to," and blushed at her own temerity.

All through the summer day the kitchen had been very hot, for no matter how the sun shone people seemed to want hot meals, and there was the bread to be baked and the linen ironed. By the time that Hester, aided by a willing and panting Phoebe, had put away the last platter and laid the sticks ready for the stove in the morning, she felt limp and sticky and unpleasant. But her heart bore up her body, and she sang a tuneless song to herself as she dipped a pan of greenish soft water out of the butt by the corner of the house and ran upstairs. She wished as she ran that she had a new dress, or that she had had time during the day to let down the hem of her old one. In the four years since Ellie's death she had had only one new dress, and that was of warm, thick crimson cloth bought for her by Mrs. Bridges. Her summer dresses, repeatedly lengthened, were faded with washing, tight around the chest and far too short. One was of pink print and faint traces of the colour remained under the arms and in the folds, though all the rest was a neutral grey colour; the other, which Ellie had bought especially for Hester and paid the excessive price of five shillings to have sewn, was white with little lilac-coloured sprigs all over it. It had been lengthened with bands of lilac cloth, harmonious in colour, but too thick for the purpose, and Hester regretted, as she remembered the cobbled appearance of it, that she had put so much careful labour into the sewing of it. Reviewing her two possible changes of clothing, she reached the attic stairs and climbed them, wishing passionately that she had a dress of white muslin with many frills and ten yards of stuff in the skirt, and a sash of shining yellow ribbon and a string of yellow beads. It would be nice to appear before Sam in a dress that he had never seen before, and she would like him to see, by her care in her appearance, that she didn't mind what he had done, or that he had lost his job.

Well, it was no use wishing. She must wash her face and hands, hold her face under the water, indeed, to cool it properly,

119

put on the lilac-sprigged frock, which was, at least, less faded, and get to Sam as soon as possible. She hopped up the last two stairs and slopped a little of the water. As she held the pan out away from her dress Mamie's door opened and the little wizened woman, with a towel in her hand and her thin arms and neck poking out from her underbodice, said, "Hester, I been waiting for you. The master wants you to move your things into the room over the arch. He said to tell you."

"When did he?"

"Just now, as I came up. I met him."

"Oh, all right. I'll do it in the morning. I can't stop now, I want to get out."

"He said at once."

"Well, you can forget that you saw me. Tell me again in the morning, there's a dear. I haven't the time now."

Mamie remembered, just in time, that she was the cook, and Hester only her assistant. But it is very difficult to exercise authority over somebody who is head and shoulders above you in stature, unless you yourself are of the arrogant, fussy type of miniature. Mamie was a flutterer.

"You'll get me into trouble and yourself as well. The master said you were to move at once. And after all I have told you, so it's no good pretending I haven't, and if you don't do it don't expect me to take any blame, and I can't see what you've got boiling over that you're in such hurry."

"Besides," said Hester ruminatively, "none of us sleep *there*. It's a guest room. And I'm all right where I am."

She had remembered that the room over the archway was next to Job's own. And he would know, if he cared to notice, every night that she went out, and the nights when she didn't return. If Sam obtained, as she hoped he would, a place somewhere in the neighbourhood, she might have to be out for even longer periods of time.

"Hester, will you do as I told you?" It was Mamie's last bid for obedience.

"To-morrow," said Hester good-naturedly but firmly, and opened the door of the little room that she shared with Phoebe.

"Very well." Mamie retreated with dignity and shut her door. It took her hardly a moment to don her dress again, and she was still buttoning its front when she hurried downstairs to tell Job that Hester had flatly disobeyed her.

Job, naturally, had issued the order with a view to his own

convenience. Martha had always come down to him; but that affair had started so long ago that he could not remember the words or the circumstances in which he had first suggested that she should do so. Probably she had gone so far to meet him that the thing happened without anything being said at all. But instinct and commonsense informed him that he could not go up to Hester and make the same suggestion. It was too blatant. He wanted her near him so that he could visit her. That was subtler; and less dependent upon her doubtful co-operation.

Ignorant of all this, Hester had shut the door of her room, regretting for the hundredth time that it did not lock and resentfully certain that Phoebe would rush upstairs as soon as possible and creep dumbly about the room, picking up a pin or a ribbon that she dropped, pushing her shoes about the floor in order to make it easy for her to step into them, making a dozen little offerings of slavish service and adoration, flattering to the vanity but maddening to the concentrated mind.

She laid out a clean petticoat, stiffly starched, an underbodice that she had worn only once before, and the sprigged dress. Her other clothes she threw down in a heap, happily conscious that she would find them all neatly folded or hung on pegs in the morning. Then she stepped into the bowl of cool water and began, with her piece of flannel, to dribble the coolness over her shoulders, back and breast in little streams. It made her gasp a little, but it was lovely. Sam was always trying to persuade her to stand with him in the little gurgling stream that ran through the wood, but she could never do it because frogs lived in the water and she knew that if one touched her naked flesh she would die of horror. She sat instead, on a piece of the bank that Sam had trodden over, and inspected carefully and watched him while he splashed and poured handfuls of the shining silver water over himself. She thought of him now, and remembered that during supper Phoebe had said that his arm was bound. The thought of any injury to that precious flesh moved something deep and hidden within her. How she would comfort him!

She was too engrossed to notice the stealthy opening of the door until, at a certain point, it creaked. Then she looked towards it, prepared to tell Phoebe to hurry in and not leave her on view from the passage. But instead of Phoebe's timid head, the aperture held Job's great red face and his little greasy eyes were devouring her. She gave a shrill cry, snatched the stiff petticoat

121

off the bed and held it before her and shouted, "Go away."

"I want to speak to you," he said, without moving.

"Not now," she cried. "I'll come."

She stepped out of the water, sprinkling a shower of drops, and still holding the petticoat before her, rushed towards the door. It was closed before she reached it, but she stood with her back pressed against it defensively for a moment before, seizing the towel, she made all possible haste to dry and clothe her body. Job stood outside and waited. The window at the end of the passage was high and faced westwards and a long ray of sunset light struck through. Within the golden shaft the dust-motes danced, exaggerated and beautified. Job looked at it, unseeing; his eye still held the vision of softened, sunless light of the room, of the bowl of dark water, and rising out of it the slim, long drawn lines of the girl's body, washed in tones of warm ivory and deeply shadowed, every muscle taut and poised as she raised her arms to pour the water downwards, and the whole, stemlike, supporting the bright yellow head, like a sunflower. It was the nearest he had ever been to pure beauty, and there was little wonder that he should stand there, staring at, but not seeing, the fading shaft of light, gloatingly savouring the memory and dreaming of promised delight, until the door opened behind him, and Hester, smoothing down the folds of the sprigged print over her hips, came to the passage. He turned round, and because the necessity to touch her was imperative within him, took her elbow in a hard, painful clasp.

"What do you mean by refusing to obey me?" he asked harshly. "Get your things together at once and go where you're told."

"I didn't refuse," said Hester. "I said I hadn't time just now. I'm going out."

"You're going to do what I say. Get back in there and gather your truck. I shall wait and see that you do it."

Momentarily defeated, Hester shook off his hand, shot back into the room, and with rough, impatient movements collected her few belongings. The clothes she threw over her left arm, her few books she piled precariously upon them, keeping them in position with her chin, while in her right hand she held her piece of flannel for washing, a scrap of soap, her comb, and a small wooden box, given her by Mrs. Bridges for holding her bits of ribbon and trinkets. Thus laden she emerged upon the passage again. Without speaking Job took the books from her and led the way down the attic stairs, along the passage on the next floor, and up the seven steps, at the top of which lay his own room and the room that had been built out over the archway.

It was, as Hester had pointed out to Mamie, a guest room, comfortably furnished, vastly superior to the attic. At any other time the thought of having so much space to herself, being free of Phoebe, and enjoying the comfort of the small four-poster bed, would have given Hester great pleasure, as well as speculation as to why she was thus favoured. But to-night Sam was waiting, and the light was already fading. So she hardly glanced round her new apartment, flung her things in disorder on the bed and turned to Job with a look that said plainly, "There!"

"There," said Job, answering her unspoken word. "Now you can put your things away neatly. There's a press and a chester drawers. There's no call to be untidy here."

He himself began arranging the books on either side of the little swinging mirror that stood on the top of the chest.

"I'll do it later," said Hester, desperately ."I want to go out before dark."

Job's precarious patience gave out.

"I know. You think you're going out to meet that worthless little thief of a groom that I got rid of this morning. Well you're not, so you can get that idea out of your head, my little beauty. You're going to settle down here and do what I want you to, in future. Do you understand that? Sam may have been all right for a romp under a hedge, but he's no use to a girl like you. You want a man now, a man who can give you things, fill that press over there with pretty dresses. You want a silk gown, and some fine stockings, and a pair of little shoes with silver buckles. And you shall have them all, aye, and lots more, if you just settle down and be pleasant."

The words, innocuous enough upon the surface, were spoken with such significance and accompanied by such an unmistakable leer that Hester's ignorance of his motives fled away and she was able to see, with a thrill of mingled fear, fury and disgust, exactly why Sam had been dismissed and she herself brought down from the attic. To do what she had done with Sam with this gross old man! Why, if it had not been so horrible it would have been laughable .

Instinct informed her that it was not the moment for argument. There shot through her mind the memory of the way in which Job's eyes had played over her as she stood in the water. He meant it. Nothing could save her except swift and determined action. Job stood by the chest where he had been arranging the books. The way to the door was clear. Suddenly she shot across the space and had the door-latch in her hand, tearing at it. But she had forgotten that this latch pulled upwards instead of pressing down, and in the second wasted before she remembered it her master had thrown himself at her and with as little effort as he would have needed to expend in order to lift a kitten, had lifted and flung her backwards, so that the edge of the bed caught her behind the knees and she fell back on to it with her feet in the air. She rolled sideways and was upright upon the far side of the bed in a second, but Job, moving with surprising agility, considering his bulk, was upon her at once, cuffing her ears until her head buzzed and shaking her as though she were a doll.

"You've got to be tamed, my girl, and it might as well begin now. If kindness don't answer in your case we'll try the other thing. Oh, you would, would you," and there was even an echo of delight in his voice as Hester, dropping her head, bit him sharply in the hand, "we'll see. You've got to learn who is your master."

He was not even angry. Her resistance, even the pain of his bitten hand, was delightful. After Martha's calm, overwhelming, one-dimensioned passion, to deal with Hester was like drinking old brandy after flat ale. With a perverted pleasure that had its roots in sexual passion, he mauled and smacked and hurt her, thinking all the while of the moment when she would lie, tamed and accepting. As long as there was strength in her, Hester struggled, squirming, kicking, scratching, like a trapped cat. Trapped she was, and at last she knew it and in the kneeling position to which he had forced her, dropped her head and her hands and stayed still. Job would have stayed and pursued his pleasure to the ultimate goal then and there, but it was early and he had things to see to. There were guests with whom he must talk and joke and drink. He must see that the cellar was locked and the doors bolted, the windows, open because of the day's warmth, closed again and latched. And he had no intention of hurrying over his ultimate triumph. He said, quite gently, "There, you'll learn," and stooping, assisted her on to the bed. Then he went to the door, opened it and closed it behind him. Hester heard the grate of the key in the lock.

124

Immediately she sat up, pulling together the remains of her dress, far too old and frail to withstand such handling, and recovered her shoes which had been kicked off in the struggle. She felt dizzy and sick. One side of her face, where Job's hand had fallen heavily, was swelling, and there was a bruise below her breast that ached dully. But she had no time to consider her physical distress. Through that door he had gone, and since he had the key, through that door he would return unless she acted quickly.

The press defied her; but if she took out the drawers she might be able to move the shell of the chest. One by one, with the neat movement that she had inherited or copied from Ellie, she drew out the drawers and stacked them one above the other on the floor. Then, with her thin arms thrust into the spaces they had left she tried to push or pull the chest itself across the doorway. It was built of solid oak, heavily carved, and put up a stout resistance. It dug its great feet into the thickness of the carpet upon which it stood, and refused to move. After a moment Hester stood back, catching her breath and pressing her hand over her bruised side and looked at the piece of furniture with hatred and fury. Then, with her lips drawn back from her teeth in a snarl, she flung herself upon it again, heaving with her shoulder, putting the whole force of her body and soul against it, sobbing out, "You shall move, you shall!" And the chest moved about four inches and came to a standstill with a great fold of carpet upon its further side.

In the little wooden box which held her treasure was a pair of scissors, slight pointed things, and the knife with which, in happier days, she had sharpened her pens. With these poor tools she set to work, cutting the carpet into strips and pulling it away. The sweat poured off her, mingling with the tears of rage and impotence that sprang unchecked from her eyes. At last the carpet was free and she stood up without a pause and launched another attack upon the chest. Inch by inch she pushed and pulled and heaved until it stood across the doorway. With one last effort she lifted and replaced the drawers and then fell back across the bed, temporarily safe at least and completely exhausted.

The light had been fading fast as she worked, and when she lifted her head again she realised with sudden panic, that she must take stock of her position while there was still enough light to see by. Dragging herself wearily she went across to the

125

window. It was a small casement window divided into three parts by two stone mullions. Half the middle section opened. A small and exceedingly active person might, by twisting his body diagonally, hope to wriggle through it. But outside there was a sheer drop of wall before the arch was reached, and then there was empty space down to the cobbles of the road in front of the inn. A nasty drop in any light, and in the dusk, terrifying. There was no hold for hand or foot, and Hester stood back in despair for a moment before she remembered that there was the wherewithal for ropemaking in the bedclothes.

There was no candle in the room and no means of making a light. She had, in her impatient removal, forgotten to bring her tinder. She must get to work while she could see. Driving herself, she retrieved the scissors from the floor where they lay amongst the shreds and tatters of the carpet's edge, stripped back the bedcovers, and with the ruined, blunted tool began hacking the sheet into wide strips. It must be strong, so the strips must be wide, and when the sheet was used she tore down the hangings of the bed and used them also. Her fingers were stiff and her nails broken, there were white blisters rising on the thumb and finger which, thrust into the small handles of the scissors, had had to exert fierce pressure in order to drive the inadequate blades through carpet, sheet and cloth. But at last the strips lay separated on the floor and, setting her teeth into her lower lip, she began to knot them together.

It was quite dark by this time, and when the last sheet was knotted Hester sat down in the middle of the coil and cried, fiercely and miserably, because before she dared to make her attempt at escape she must wait until Job was asleep, and by that time Sam would have concluded that she wasn't coming and would go—where she did not know, since he could not return to his loft—and she would not see him. Damn and blast Job Wainwright, she thought, amid her gulping sobs. May ulcers devour his flesh and worms his bowels. Spoiling and trampling the only thing she cherished, the only sweet and lovely thing that had ever come her way. (She forgot, in that hour of savage misery, Ellie's love, Mrs. Bridges' affection, Miss Peck's passionate tuition.)

Meanwhile Sam had lingered until the honeysuckle withered in his hand and the great white owls came swooping by in soundless flight. Too agitated to stay in one place he visited in turn the stream, the little clearing where they had lain upon the

126

bracken, and the opening where the field path met the wood. He cursed himself for hoping that Hester might have come into the wood by another entry and be sitting by the stream. He knew that she always came the one way, yet when he found the stream running lonely he was aware of disappointment. When it was much too dark to see any distance along the path, he left the wood and began to walk towards the inn. It might even be that she had stumbled and sprained an ankle, put her foot in a rabbit hole, hurt herself getting over a stile. But there was no sign of Hester along the path, or in the lane, or in the orchard when he reached it. He was now on Job's property, but he gave no thought to that. The dark mass of the stable buildings loomed up before him. He skirted along them and reached the door in the corner which connected the orchard with the great yard. It was bolted upon the inner side. Still with a half hope that Hester might have been delayed, forced somehow to make an appearance of going to bed, and that she would steal out later, he sat down with his back to the door and waited. She would come through there if she came at all.

As Sam sat down amongst the rough grass and the nettles of the orchard, Job put his hand on the key in Hester's door, turned it and pressed down the latch. He pushed. The door stayed in position. He heaved against it with his shoulder. It still resisted. What on earth had the little hussy done? He called her name.

Hester, on the safe side of the door, became crafty. Unless she answered he might think that she was gone already, and sheer curiosity might lead him to have the door removed. She opened her mouth in a wide yawn and called through it sleepily, "What do you want?"

"I'll show you what I want, my girl. Open this door."

"I can't. I'm sleepy. And you've hurt me. I'll open it in the morning." Her voice, except for a plaintive note when she said "hurt", was placating. Job reflected. To get the door lifted off its hinges and whatever stood on the other side removed by force would mean calling for help, and letting somebody into his not very creditable secret. To-morrow would also be a day and a night. He was quite sure of her now. To-morrow, when her little injuries had been forgotten, and only the futility of resistance remembered, and with half a bottle of wine inside her she would be amenable enough. And he himself was tired. It had not been an easy day. Without resentment he turned away from the barred door, entered his own, put on his nightshirt and his cap with the tassel atop it, turned back most of his covers, very neatly, and got into bed under the sheet. The picture of Hester bathing came to him, and the memory of the way in which her little slender bones had seemed to crumple under his hands. In ten minutes he was fast asleep.

Sam got up from amongst the nettles and stretched himself. Hester wasn't coming and he must know why. For some reason that was even more important than that he should tell her about his new job and ask her to get up early and join him on the road. Had Phoebe forgotten to give the message? Or—surely Hester wasn't fool enough to believe, or believing, to care that Job had accused him of theft! Sam's usually merry eyes were troubled, his candid brow puckered as he puzzled over what could have kept Hester from her tryst.

Well, there was one way to find out. He knew a way into the stable, from the back, a shuttered opening whose shutter was mouldy and rotten. He removed it, bit by bit, scrambled through and dropped into a manger. As he crossed the stable, the black mare, Job's property and in permanent residence there, recognised the step of Sam whom she knew and loved, and whinnied. Stepping up to her Sam fondled her nose and hushed her. If he had not had graver matters on his mind he would have felt sorry that he was stroking her for the last time. She dropped her nose to his pocket, which had, in the past, often contained a tit-bit for her.

"There's nothing there, old dear," said Sam ruefully, "everything's gone wrong to-day."

He came out into the night again in the yard and stood looking up into the jutting shapes and gables of the inn, sticking up like cardboard silhouettes against the night sky. With so many doors and windows it should not be impossible to force an entry. If his arm had been sound he would have tried the reverse of Little Tom Drury's scheme and made an attempt at reaching the window of Ellie's room. As it was, that was impossible, and he began walking round, trying every door and window, hoping to find one forgotten and insecurely fastened. And here Hester's tryst with him served.

Since Hester had taken to going out at night she had always used the kitchen door. In the winter, when she had gone out late and only across the yard to the loft, she had left the bolts back and thought that there was little danger of any one shooting them in her absence. But in the light evenings, when she and Sam went out earlier and farther afield, she had considered the risk of someone, going later to bed, bolting the door against her. It would have caused her little inconvenience, for she could have shared Sam's straw, but it would have meant the betrayal of her secret to others, less sunk in thraldom than Phoebe. So for three days immediately after her promotion to be cook's help she had spent every moment when she found herself alone in the kitchen, working upon the sockets of the bolts, with the result that though the iron defences shot home much as before only their tips reached the sockets, and as these had been put back very loosely a sturdy push was enough to make the door swing. Sam, trying this door in turn, found that it gave before him, and with a feeling of surprise as well as relief, he found himself in the warm dark kitchen.

He had seldom been in the upper part of the house, but his few errands there, when he had been called to help to move something, enabled him to find his way, with only a few false moves, to the attic floor. Hester's room was next to the empty one which was at the end. He opened the door of it softly, but the orphan, who slept lightly and whose nerves were not of the steadiest, woke with a start and cried out. Luckily for Sam, she had, since her arrival at The Fleece, more than once awakened the floor by crying out in a nightmare, and if any of the others heard her now they thought, "That dratted Phoebe again," and turned and slept once more.

Phoebe, cowering down amongst the clothes and regretting that she had betrayed her existence by that involuntary cry, shivered and shook, a pitiable prey to terror. She had hated going to bed alone, had wept when she found that Hester, so much bigger and braver, was not there to stave off the terrors of the dark. And now what she had always dreaded had come to pass. The door had opened. Someone was in the room.

Unable to move or even cry out again, she lay there and would have died had not Sam said softly, "Are you there Hester? It's me. Sam." Then Phoebe, released from terror's chains, crawled out of bed like a puppy and threw herself at him, moping and mowing, incoherent with relief. Sam, knowing now that Hester was not in her usual place, and torn with impatience, anxiety and the awakening pangs of jealous suspicion, calmed her as well as he could and then put his question.

"Did you give Hester my message?"

"Yes, Sam."

Then by God! he had missed her. How?

"Did she go out? How long ago?"

"The master took her away. She don't sleep here no more. She've gone to the room over the arch.'

"What did you say?"

"Oh, there was a to-do." Phoebe had recovered herself, and was now ready to share with Sam the gossipy delights of the evening. "The master say she weren't to sleep here no more. He come up hisself and helped her to take all her things away. And she ain't been seen since. And Mamie say she reckon Hester got better work now and on't be in the kitchen no more. And Rosie's ever so savage, she say that's what Hester been aiming at all along, and why should she have one of the guest rooms? Martha never did. Who was Martha?"

Shock held Sam silent for a moment.

Mamie, who had told Rosie and the rest of them what she knew they wanted to hear, had carefully omitted any mention of Hester's refusal to move or of the fact that Job had helped with the books more in the manner of an armed escort than of an assistant. It had not taken Mamie so long to learn that Hester was disliked by the other maids or that they would far rather think that she was wanton than that she was unwilling. Phoebe, of course, had received no information beyond what her ears, sharpened by her interest in Hester, could pick up.

"Are you sure that you've told me all the truth?" asked Sam at last in a flat, beaten voice.

"Oh, no," said Phoebe naïvely. "There was a lot more. John say that thass easy to see why you was sent off. And Rosie say that Hester is a lot more fly than Martha and 'll get lots of dresses and ear-rings and things. Right savage Rosie is. Then Mamie say Rosie's jealous and they started a row and told me to get outa the way."

"All right, Phoebe. You get back into bed again. And don't tell anybody you seen me. I ain't supposed to come in here you know."

"What'll happen if the master see you?" queried Phoebe, curling back into her place, but anxious to prolong the interview.

"He'd break my other arm, no doubt. Or shoot me. He sleeps with a gun by his bed. Good night, Phoebe."

Sam stole quietly along the passage and down the stairs. On

130

the lower passage he paused. Injured love and vanity did their best to urge him on to its end, to mount the seven steps and burst into the room where he had little doubt Job and Hester were lying together and to kill the pair of them. He could have done it with pleasure. Of all the filthy dirty tricks he'd ever heard of this was the very worst. Every atom of the tenderness that he felt towards Hester because she was frail and young, turned to gall. She'd fooled him properly. And he'd believed in her as he had in himself.

Then he remembered Job's gun and his own broken arm. Likely he'd only get himself killed or into some trouble. He'd broken into premises that he'd been warned off; nobody would wonder a bit or think it at all wrong if Job did shoot him. And he'd rather live and go to Newmarket. Hester wasn't worth risking anything for.

He turned stairwards and very soon was in the yard again, crossing towards the orchard gate. Out here he could tread without caution and he trod hard, trampling under angry feet the wreck of his dreams, the sweetness of his memories. Now and again he recognised a fragment of one of them; that first night when she had been so ignorant and yet so ardent. He trod that down too, though he groaned as he did so, and once the words, "Oh, my little love, how could you?" broke from his lips and startled him. He walked quickly across the orchard, anxious to leave behind the scene of his love and his youth, of his betrayal and disillusionment.

He gained the road again at the place where Hester used to jump over the ditch on her way to school. His face was towards Newmarket. He'd walk through the night and chance getting a lift from something or somebody in the morning. And if, in the future, he ever got hold of a girl again, be she never so young and small and seeming-innocent, by God he'd let her have it.

CHAPTER V

AT THE moment when Sam unbolted the orchard gate and let himself through it, Hester decided that it was safe to move, and that the move must be made now or never. She took off the tattered dress and pulled on the pink one, bundled her warm dress and one or two other things into her cloak and dropped them cautiously out of the window. Then she tied one end of her improvised rope round the leg of the four-poster, tested it by sharp pulling and let the other end out of the window. Even in the darkness she could see its white track along the wall, marking the terrifying depth of the dark ravine into which she must launch herself. Then, with her heart thudding sickeningly and her hands slippery with sweat, she put her legs over the windowsill and hung there for a second, face downwards, balanced on her stomach while she got the sheet between her hands. Now she must cling with one hand while she felt for a hold, below the windowsill, with the other. There was no hold where the sheeting pressed against the stone. The rope swung a bit as it took her weight, her one arm felt as though it must break, and then she had a second hand-hold and was ready to descend. She seemed to go down very quickly, without time to change her grasp as she had imagined, for her weight was too great for the strength of her arms, and the sheet, growing hotter, seemed to tear itself through her palms. It was a great relief to come to a knot, for then she could pause just long enough to convince herself that she was in control of the situation, not merely falling through space. The brickwork ended and the dark gap of the archway was before her; now she was level with the iron spikes on top of the gate, now the gate itself was before her eyes, and now, at last, oh glory! her straining toes touched the solid ground. The weight was off her aching arms, and she was free.

She felt round and found her bundle, picked it up and started running toward Lownde Wood, inspired by the hope that Sam might have fallen asleep there. The way by the road was far longer than across the orchard and the field, but she had escaped into the road and must keep to it. Her strained nerves and her

132

weariness, even her horror of things that crawled the road and the footpaths by night, were obliterated by her pressing need to find Sam. They would come together, hand to hand, face to face, and find comfort and strength in the meeting. They were both outcast now, and both free. They could go away together and live somewhere where Job would never find them. This shattering upheaval would mark the beginning of a new life. If only Sam had waited. If he had gone she did not know what she would do. She dared not hang about the village for fear of Job. But she thrust that thought away, it weakened her legs and she needed all her strength. Stumbling and slipping in the darkness, she hurried on. One shoe came off as she ran and flew away, so that it took her several moments to find it. The few things in the bundle grew heavy as lead, and where the bruise was in her side a perpetual stitch seemed to be nagging. But it would be all right, everything would be all right, if only she could find Sam asleep by the entrance to the wood, or by the side of the stream, or in the clearing.

And all the while Sam was hastening, with hatred in his heart, in the opposite direction. Every moment and every step was widening the distance between them, carrying them farther and farther apart through the night.

When she had failed to find Sam in any of their meeting-places, Hester indulged in a hysterical outburst. She pushed her way amongst the trees, screaming "Sam! Sam!" at the top of her voice. The wood, so pleasant a meeting-place, so delightful a background for loving play, became terrible. The trees seemed to be holding their breath for fear, they even took her cries, echoed them hushfully and deadened the sound into the all-embracing silence. The very spirit of the wood was abroad, alien, primitive, unfriendly. She had been able to withstand it while there was hope of stumbling upon Sam's sleeping body, but now, the only member of the human race, the only intruding personality there, she stood affrighted. With little incoherent cries she began to push herself out of the wood, running into tree-trunks, catching her clothes on the brambles and undergrowth, frantic with disappointment and distraught with terror. But for the stream she would have lost herself and might have wandered in the woods for days, for it stretched far, almost without a break to Winwood. But she followed the stream, leaping away to this side and that as she thought she saw movements in the grass by its sides, and so came at last to the clearing where Sam had planned to lay her head on a pillow of honeysuckle, and so on to the edge of the wood where the hazels hung over the field path. It was much lighter there and a great deal of her reasonless terror fell away, leaving her to bear the onslaught of practical problems.

Where was Sam? Sleeping somewhere, no doubt. She tried to remember whether he had any friends in the village, but she could think of none. Sam, like herself, had led a life bounded by the inn's premises. She had never heard him mention his home or his parents. Unless he returned to the wood he was as lost to her as if he had been drowned at sea. She had just one hope. He might come back to-morrow, to spend an idle day in the shade of the trees, or to bathe in the stream. It was clearly her duty to wait there; to brave the terrors of the darkness, to take the risk—not very great—of being seen during the day. And with that settled, a great weariness came on her so that even her thoughts were incoherent. She stayed awake just long enough to take the cloak off the bundle, repack her things in the crimson dress and lie down, her head on her bundle and the cloak spread over her. Then she slept.

When she woke the sun was high and she realised that some-one might have seen her there on the edge of the wood and reported it to Job, who would be on the look-out for her. Look-ing warily about her she drew back into the shelter of the trees and walked into the heart of the wood, where she hid her bundle in an easily-marked spot. She found the stream and drank from her cupped hands, but there was nothing to eat, and by afternoon the emptiness of her stomach had become a pain. At intervals, throughout the day she visited the clearing, the stream, and, with great caution, the wood's entrance. There was no Sam.

Hope rose again as the sun sank. This was their hour. Now, if ever, he would come, but sunset and twilight passed and the darkness descended and her loneliness was not disturbed. She made a wild dash back into the wood in order to retrieve her bundle before the darkness thickened amongst the trees, and the menace that the night loosened was upon her. Then she settled down again at the wood's mouth, so that there was the open field in front of her, and spent the hours of the night alternately sleeping lightly, waking hopefully and bearing dis-appointment. As soon as the blackness turned grey she rose, tightened the sleeves of the dress that held the other things to-

134

gether and without looking backwards, walked briskly away in the direction of the road. She had given Sam every chance. What had happened, where he was, she might never know. But two things she knew. She must get well away from the village before morning brought people from their houses, and she must soon find something to eat.

She chose the London road instinctively. Between the first gleam of the coming dawn and full daylight she had covered eight miles and was on the verge of collapse from hunger and exhaustion. The road was growing more frequented now; a string of packhorses loaded with fish turned out of a lane and with lowered, dogged heads began to plod up the hill, the sight of which had brought Hester to a standstill, measuring her weariness. A light chaise, drawn by two horses, overtook and passed the others. Hard after it rode a horseman. She began to consider leaving the road for a while. She was not far enough from The Fleece to feel safe yet. The bank that bounded the road was crowned with blackberry bushes, covered with their delicate mauve blossom. She edged her way through them and continued her journey along the fallow field.

The untilled soil lay beneath its summer burden of short-lived vegetation. Red poppies, white daisies, pink ragged-robins and blue bugloss raised their heads above the mat of green, making the field look, to Hester's fancy, like a wide spread of delicately coloured print. The sun was warm now; it was going to be another hot day. She took off her cloak and wrapped it around the bundle, wished for the hundredth time that she had left the inn by the usual way, through the kitchen, and brought away a supply of bread and cheese, and plodded on. Her feet no longer tripped lightly over the surface of the ground, at every step it seemed an enormous effort to thrust each foot forward. The field sloped, just as the road did on the other side of the bushes, and it took her a long time to reach the top. There the field ended and the downward slope was occupied by a little coppice of larch and beech trees, free, as the ground beneath beech trees always is of undergrowth, and offering easy walking over the soft layers of mast and leaves of many by-gone autumns. Keeping a screen of trees between herself and the road she held a course parallel to it and staggered on.

Suddenly, with the sharp impact of a physical blow, the scent of cooking smote her nostrils. She stopped, lifted her nose as a dog points and sniffed. Rabbit! The pain in her stomach intensified. She laid her hand on it, noticing how sharply it receded between the pointed bones of her hips. Little dribbles of saliva escaped her watering mouth and she gathered them in with a sharp flick of her tongue, before following, like a starving animal, the scent of the savoury food.

It led her away from the road, deeper into the coppice, but it led her unerringly to the spot, where, below a great beech with a smooth, silvery trunk, two wayfarers had made a fire. They were man and woman, and they were squatting on each side of the crackling wood, holding the joints of a rabbit over the heat at the end of long pointed sticks. The lean, long-limbed dog which had caught the rabbit, lay watching them, but as Hester's footsteps rustled in the leaves he sprang up, all the hair along his back erect and his teeth bared. The pair by the fire looked round, their smoke-reddened eyes wary and furtive. Their faces relaxed when they saw that the intruder was only a white-faced and weary girl. The man spoke to the dog, using a tongue that Hester did not know, and the dog, reluctantly obedient, lay down again, joint by joint, keeping his eyes on Hester, to whom, after some words addressed to his companion in the unknown tongue, the man said, "Vhat did you vant?"

"I smelled your cooking. I'm hungry," said Hester simply.

"You vish to buy a piece?"

"I wish I could. But I haven't any money. I hoped perhaps you'd give me some."

"Vhat haf you in de bundle?"

"A few clothes." The man turned and gabbled again to his wife, who took another piece of stick, speared another joint of the rabbit which lay, dismembered and unsightly, upon a broad dock-leaf, and holding one homely toasting-fork in either hand, devoted her attention to the cooking, leaving her man to strike the bargain. The man sat down again and motioned with his free hand to Hester to do the same. Gratefully she dropped to the ground, keeping her bundle close beside her.

"Open it," said the man in his queer sing-song voice.

Shes laid out for his inspection the pitiable little collection, the grey cloak, the crimson dress, a change of underclothes, much crumpled, three handkerchiefs, two lengths of ribbon and the only book she had brought, a small worn copy of *Lycidas*, given her in a moment of rapture by Miss Peck as a reward for being word-perfect in the difficult poem.

Holding his stick steadily in one hand, the man turned over

Hester's things. His hand was so dirty that it left its mark on everything except this crimson of the dress and the grey of the cloak. Without speaking he separated the cloak from the others and pushed the rest together contemptuously. Even in her present state of hunger Hester considered that a meal purchased at the price of her most voluminous and useful garment, rather expensive and voiced her opnion.

"It is the only vun I vant. It vill wrap her," he replied, nodding towards the woman who took this as a sign that she might present the more advanced joint to Hester, and with that scent beneath her nostrils and the sight of the brown, slightly scorched meat before her eyes, she was no longer disposed to haggle.

"All right," she said, hastily, "you can have it." The man now surveyed his portion critically, considered that it was cooked, and from the pile of lumber against the tree-trunk brought out a flat cake of flour and water bread, burnt black on the outside from being baked in the ashes of a former fire. With a nasty-looking knife he hacked the cake into three roughly even portions, offering one to Hester, taking one himself and tossing the third into the lap of the woman who went on toasting the portion of rabbit that she had started to cook when Hester arrived. The man glanced at the bits of pink flesh remaining on the dock-leaf. "Carac," he said, and the dog leaped up and dragged the carcase, leaf and all to some little distance, whence the crunching of bones testified his enjoyment.

Nothing that Hester had ever eaten had tasted so good as that scorched hind-leg of rabbit and rough flour cake. After the first ravenous mouthfuls she began to eat more slowly, trying to make it last, extracting the maximum of satisfaction from every mouthful. She looked at her host and hostess. They were not a pretty pair, small and swarthy and very dirty, smoke-dried as the hams in the smoke house of The Fleece. Their nondescript, dun-coloured clothes were masses of rags and they were barefooted except for clogs which they evidently whittled themselves, for several finished pairs lay, with a number of linen pegs, washing dollies and butter-shapers, in a wide basket woven of withies, and one, unfinished, lay beside the man. They evidently made a living hawking such home-made goods from door to door, and upon the proceeds, the dog's catches and probably a little discreet stealing, they supported themselves. And they seemed content, if not obviously happy.

Hester detached the last morsel from the bone, gnawed even the gristle from its end, and then, not without regret, flung it to the dog. She could have eaten four such portions. The woman inspected the ashes of the fire and lifted a pan of dough from amongst the heap of possessions. She dropped lumps of it amongst the red embers and turned them about with a stick. The man took up his knife again and went on whittling the clog. Hester sat still until a pleasant drowsiness warned her that unless she moved at once she would fall asleep here in the sun.

She began to gather her scattered things, smoothing out the clothes and laying hem upon the crimson dress. Suddenly the woman turned from the fire, and without speaking twitched away the dress, so that the underclothes and the ribbons and the book were distributed on the ground. She held the dress against her body, pulling out the fullness of the skirt and measuring both length and width. Then she spoke with that rapid, hissing, unknown tongue and the man nodded. Hester waited, imagining that some buried feminine vanity was causing the woman to try how she would look in the garment. But instead of returning it she dropped it on top of her heap of jumbled goods, and after a glance, in which triumph and slyness were mingled, went on with her cooking. Hester, still hoping that the woman had merely made an exchange and thinking that the dress was more easily dispensed with, put out a hand to draw the cloak back towards her. But at that the woman, cackling like a pea-hen, seized the other side of the garment and tried to smack off Hester's hands. Hester looked towards the man.

"Tell her please, she can't have them both."

"And vy not?"

"Because it is too much to give, just for one little piece of rabbit."

"So. A little vhile ago you go gobble gobble and make de fine meal, now it is in your belly you say little piece. You are ver' ingrate."

"I'm not," said Hester, placatingly. "It was very good rabbit and I enjoyed it. But if I let her keep my cloak *and* my warm dress I shan't have anything to put over me at night."

He leered at her. "Pretty young girl like you, easy keep varm at night." He gabbled in the strange speech to the woman, who redoubled her efforts and tweaked the cloak from Hester's fingers. Then gathering it and the dress together she sat down upon them, took up the stick and went on turning the loaves as though nothing had happened.

"Wouldn't she like some of these instead?" pleaded Hester looking at the scattered remnants of her bundle.

"All rubbitch," he said scornfully. But on second thoughts he rose, keeping the bright knife in his hand, picked up the petticoat and held it by its band around his skinny waist. He pirouetted round and round, holding the knife hand daintily in the air. The woman suspended her cooking to look up and then rock on her haunches with mirth. Finally he threw it across the fire to her and she pounced on it like a jackdaw and thrust it beneath her. Then he picked up the two ribbons, bought long ago by Ellie from the pedlar. Skirting the fire he joined the woman and laid them, one after the other, across her tousled, ash-flecked hair. They both laughed heartily.

Hester, certain now that she would be left with nothing at all, scooped up the handkerchiefs and the book and thrust them into her bodice. For a moment the man looked at her angrily. The sun flashed on the blade and the thought shot through Hester's mind that she might even be murdered for the sake of the things she wore. Then the man's mood changed back to merriment. He laughed again and pointed with the knife.

"You go now," he said. "Good rabbit, eh?"

For a moment Hester stared at them both, hatred in her heart and a longing for vengeance in her mind. But the man had the knife, he was agile and strong, and the woman had the dry toughness of willow wand. If looks could have struck or hatred killed they would have fallen dead there by the fire; as it was, Hester turned away. And as though to emphasise her defeat the man cried sharply, "Carac, remodi!" and the dog, bounding up, raised his hackles again and came behind Hester, laying his snarling muzzle to her heels. He followed her, harrying, but just not touching, until Hester saw a bit of broken branch across her path. She snatched it up and turned.

"Be off," she shouted, and lunged at him. He paused, gave one last snarl and then, jumping sideways, was gone, running from tree to tree, furtive and crafty as his owner. Hester carried the stick until she was sure he would not return, then she threw it away. She walked until she was near the road again and then swerved so that she could follow it. Presently the wood ended on a field of growing corn, and Hester, unwilling to walk through it and bring down upon herself the wrath of some farmer, got on to the road again and hurried along in the ruts

139

by its side.

Soon she was troubled by thirst. The very ditches were dry and she found no means of slaking until, after mid-day, she saw a woman drawing water from a well in the front garden of a pretty little house bowered in climbing roses. It had a friendly look and the woman who was working the well-handle seemed neat and respectable. Hester leaned over the gate and asked if she might have a drink. The woman looked up and studied her. A girl looked harmless enough, but one never knew.

"Stay where you are," she said, and then, raising her voice called, "Ben, bring me a mug." A half-grown, ungainly lad came out of the house with the mug in his hand. The woman filled it with cool, clear well-water and brought it to the gate. Hester drank it all without drawing breath.

"You were thirsty and no mistake," said the woman. "Would you like it full again?"

"Yes, please," said Hester gratefully. She drank the second mugful less quickly but just as gladly and handed back the mug. "Thank you very much."

"It's thirsty weather," said the woman, looking at the sky. "Have you come far?"

"Not very," said Hester in a voice calculated to discourage further questions, and turned away.

She walked for another hour and then turned aside down a grassy, tree-shaded lane that looked irresistibly cool and inviting, stretched herself out and slept.

CHAPTER VI

WHEN she woke it was dusk in the lane, her dress was damp with dew and there was a sound of crackling sticks in her ears. A fire. She thought immediately of the pair she had left in the coppice and sat up hastily in terror, imagining that they had been following her all day, and certainly for no good purpose. But although a fire of sticks was burning near at hand the flame of it lit up, not two swarthy faces, but one shining pink one, fringed with white hair. It was rather like a ham in a frill, for the white fringe ran across the top of the bald head, down each side of the face and under the chin in a continuous line.

The head belonged to a thin body, muffled against the evening air in an ancient grey coat. Its owner had rigged up two forked sticks, one on either side of the fire, and on the stick that was balanced across them three salt herrings, speared through their heads, were toasting. When Hester sat up the man said in a surprisingly mild gentle voice :

"I was wondering whether I ought to wake you. Are you far from home?"

Hester hesitated. The idea that Job might be trying to trace her made her reluctant to give any information; her memory of her companions at breakfast prejudiced her against her fellow-wayfarers; yet at the same time her stomach's reaction to the scent of the cooking herrings made her unwilling to voice the answer which was formed all ready in her mind, to say, "Oh, no, just over there," and to walk away. The old man noticed the hesitation and said, "Have you a home at all?"

For some reason Hester told the truth.

"Not just now." And she added, as though to explain her homelessness, "My mother is dead."

The old man took it that recent bereavement accounted for her plight, and his voice was even more kind as he said :

"And where are you making for?"

"London."

"Not, I trust, in the belief that the pavements are made of gold. For this is true of no city upon this sinful earth."

"I'm going there to look for work. And I might find that Sam is there too."

"And who is Sam?"

"Someone . . . that I knew," said Hester, moving one foot to and fro across the grass and watching its movements.

Sensing that questions were not very welcome to her the old man asked no more, except to say :

"Unless you have made other arrangements perhaps you would care to share my supper."

"I would, indeed. But I haven't anything to give you. I thought I'd better say so at once because this morning I gave away my cloak for a piece of rabbit, and then the people weren't satisfied and took nearly everything I had. At least, I saved this. You can have it if you care to."

She drew the book out of her bodice, taking care that the

handkerchiefs did not show. She might need them for some future exchange.

"And what is this? Ha, *Lycidas*. A good poem. 'Blind mouths that scarce themselves know how to draw a sheep hook'. As true to-day as the day when it was written. Sit down, my dear, I shall be glad to share my supper with a young woman whose only possession is a book. There, put it back." He laid the book in her hand and reaching to one side, pulled towards him a large canvas bag from which he took a loaf, a knife, two tin plates, and a snuff-box, which, opened, showed itself to be full of salt. Then he slid the herrings off the stick, divided one of them neatly down the centre and laid one whole, one half herring and a slice of bread on each plate. After adding a pinch of salt and closing the box again, he passed Hester one plate with the remark, "I am afraid we must use our fingers. I seldom need a fork, but these fish were given to me." Then, putting his gnarled old-man's hands together he bent his head and murmured, "Lord, we thank Thee for all Thy gracious gifts and for the favour of this food. May the strength that it lends us be ever devoted to Thy service. Amen."

The idea of praying over food was new to Hester, and as soon as she had swallowed the first delicious mouthful she asked, "Are you a clergyman?"

"Oh, no. I'm not one of those who take money for the Lord's work. I'm just a poor preacher. I carry the Word from place to place."

"What word?"

"The Word of Our Lord, my dear. The Lord who said, 'Go ye into all the world and preach the gospel to every creature'. The gospel, that is the good news you know, good news of the forgiveness of sins and of the hope of Heaven. Have you never heard it?"

"No."

"Have you ever been to church?"

"No."

"Virgin soil," he murmured. "But surely someone must have spoken to you at some time about God the Father who gave His only begotten Son that whosoever believeth in Him might not perish but inherit eternal life through Him that hath loved us."

"I know there's a God," said Hester. "In fact I've heard of several, Jupiter and Mars and Bacchus. Miss Peck says they were

142

all gods, in their time. And there was Mithras, god of the morning, and Odin and Thor."

From sheer amazement the old man stopped eating and leaned so far towards Hester, where she was sitting on the far side of the fire, that the smoke met his eyes and made them water.

"My child," he said gently, "where, and how were you raised?" Receiving no answer he proceeded, "I asked merely because I feel that your upbringing must have been very unusual, to result in such a curious mixture of ignorance and information."

"I went to school for six years," said Hester proudly.

"Indeed. Perhaps that accounts for it."

For a while they ate steadily, but at last every bone was clean. Hester licked her fingers delicately, like a cat, before wiping them on her petticoat. Twilight deepened to darkness and the fire had died down to a glow.

"Were you intending to spend the night here?" asked the old man at last.

"No. I expected to wake up sooner than I did and walk again before night. I wouldn't pick such a lonely place to sleep."

"Not frightened of the dark, are you? There is no need to be, you know. God is watchful in the darkness, He will protect you from the terror that flyeth by night."

Hester thought of some of the stories that she had heard by the fire in the kitchen at The Fleece, and said reasonably.

"A lot of horrid things happen in the darkness."

"True, my dear. Very true indeed. That is the kind of thing that those who would undermine faith by sophistry are very fond of saying. But there are two answers to that. One that we have no means of knowing to what extent those to whom the things happen have fixed their faith in the Almighty. And secondly, and more charitably, we must accept the fact that Christ Himself admitted that there was a certain amount of necessary evil in the world. He tells us that offences must come. Besides, I think that when God promises us freedom from terror and evil He is referring to spiritual terror and spiritual evil, and such evil no man and no beast can inflict upon those whose hearts are fixed. But of course these things are hard to understand, especially to one like yourself who does not know the elements of faith. You know how hard it would be to be asked to multiply before you could count.

Suppose now that we take this opportunity of doing God's work, I in my humble way by telling you the good news of redemption, and you by listening. Perhaps, we never know, you overslept yourself this afternoon because God wanted you to share his blessing. And sent me along and spoke in my inner ear saying, 'Jonathan Harper, turn aside here and win a soul to my flock.'"

"You use," said Hester mildly, "rather too many metaphors. Perhaps I should understand better if you just told me plainly what it is you would like me to know. I mean," she blundered on, "if you know the bare fact you can understand the use of the allegorical language, but you shouldn't start off with that."

So Jonathan, struggling to avoid the picturesque phrases in which, from long usage, his message had become entangled, began at the beginning, outlining the story of creation, the history of the Jews, the birth, life and death of Christ. He talked, in his gentle, rather beautiful voice, for full two hours, and Hester gave him the rapt attention that had endeared her to Miss Peck and Mrs. Bridges. Of the whole discourse only one thing struck home to her inner, emotional consciousness—the idea of God as a source of power. That you could, in a moment of human helplessness, as Jonathan assured her you could, cry "God help me," and immediately be sustained by a power from without yourself, seemed to her eminently desirable. Otherwise she received his passionate instruction—just as she had received Miss Peck's dissertation upon the Olympian gods—with interest and a complete lack of emotion. Compared with the others Jonathan's God seemed very well-behaved; but there was nothing in the story to compare for drama with the stories of Europa and the Bull, or Leda and the Swan. When, at the end of it, he asked her to kneel, and got, with a cracking of his old knee-joints into a prayerful attitude himself, and poured out over her an earnest and heartfelt prayer in which he begged God to protect and keep her, to lead her in the right path and to let the seed of instruction this evening planted within her heart, bear and multiply a hundredfold. Hester was amazed and touched by the urgency and emotion in his voice and half expected some extraordinary change to take place within her. But nothing happened : no revelation came; her bewilderment did not give way before a sudden onslaught of understanding. Still in what Jonathan, had he been aware of it, would have called "the outer darkness", she thanked him, yawned, and said that she felt

144

sleepy. He opened his bag again and took out a neatly folded woollen shawl, which with grave courtesy, he offered to her to wrap her arms. She cuddled down in it and was asleep before Jonathan had finished wrestling with God on behalf of her soul.

In the morning he gave his whole attention to her material needs. It was not fit, he said, for a young girl to wander the roads. Her experience of the previous morning had proved that many people on the road were dishonest and there were worse things than plain dishonesty to be guarded against. He had, he said, no money, but he had the means of earning some.

From the bag of his possessions he drew out an old fiddle and a bow, lapped around by many protective layers of sacking. With loving hands he tightened the strings.

"I use this instrument," he explained, "in order to gather the people. They are easily attracted by simple tunes. Then, when they are so good-humoured that they are willing to toss me their hard-earned coins, I tell them that that is not the payment that I desire. 'Lend me your ears', I cry, and then I give them my message. But I think to-day, God, who sees all our needs and takes heed when a sparrow falls, will not be wrath if I let the people pay with their pence before I give them the good news. Our Lord Himself experienced the need for coin of the realm once and sent a disciple to catch the fish with the money in its mouth."

"Where will you go?" asked Hester, determined that nothing, not even the promise of money, should take her a step backwards towards The Fleece. To her relief he jerked his head towards the opposite direction.

"I passed through a little town yesterday evening. I did not stop there because the voice did not bid me. Now I understand why. That is the beauty of committing one's way unto the Lord, my dear. He never makes a mistake. He was bringing me towards you in your hour of need, and saving the good news for the townsfolk until this morning. Shall we go? I regret that we must go breakfastless, but you see, I did not count upon the pleasure of your company at supper, and reckoned that I could have eaten bread and cold herring upon my way this morning."

He packed the canvas bag neatly, and at Hester's offer to carry the fiddle laid it in her arms.

For all his age he walked rapidly, shuffling along in a way that raised clouds of dust, and very soon, from the top of a slight hill they could look down upon the steeple and the roofs of the little town.

It was market day. Around the old Market Cross, from which the symbol had been removed in earlier days, the women were laying out butter and cheese and dressed fowls. In small, hurdled pens the animals were loudly expressing their discontent at their new surroundings.

"A good day," said Jonathan gleefully as they took up their stand. "With God's help I shall be allowed to gather your coach fare and after that many souls to His service." He removed his broad black hat and laid it at Hester's feet.

"Perhaps, if they prove shy, you would carry that round, my dear." Then he took the fiddle from her, tucked his bag behind one of the pillars of the cross, tested the strings, and began to play.

He played superbly: the old fiddle seemed to sing, to laugh and sob beneath his fingers and the swiftly flying bow. As though drawn by invisible strings the people ceased from their buying and bargaining, even from crying their wares, and crowded around the man, rocking on the balls of his feet as he moved his body to the music, and the yellow-haired girl who stared at him enraptured. He played simple jigs and country airs and it occurred to Hester that his audience must find the change startling when he put down his fiddle and took up his preaching. Only, of course, she reflected, to-day he was playing in order to collect money; perhaps usually he played church music and grave tunes. She was wrong in this, for Jonathan, being happy in his religion, saw no incongruity between his merry, worldly music and his grave, earnest bidding for converts. Didn't the psalmist bid us "make a merry noise unto the Lord?" And a merry noise he made. When, obeying his nudge, Hester carried round the hat, she was astonished at the stream of small coins which poured into it. Jonathan played while she made the collection and then stopped, panting, and wiped his wet face.

"I thank you, my friends, I thank you," he cried, beaming upon them. "I'll play again later. I mustn't hold you from your business any longer now."

"Bide a bit until I've sold my cheeses," shouted a stout, jolly woman, "and then maybe I'll spare you one."

"A kindly offer indeed," returned Jonathan, "and very welcome." He wrapped his fiddle, retrieved his bag and packed it. The crowd went back to its interrupted marketing. And as it thinned Hester looked up and saw Dick Tench, with the bit of black leather shaped to fit the socket tied over his eye, leading three young horses into the yard of The Wheatsheaf. The sight was a frightening reminder that she was not so very far from Job's country after all. She had forgotten that, and had, without thought, exposed herself to the view of all these people. How many others in the crowd might not have done business at The Fleece?

She shrank back behind Jonathan and whispered, "Where shall we go now?" He turned and noted her pallor.

"To breakfast, I think. You look as if you had fasted long enough. Come along." He put his earnings in his pocket and replaced his hat. With a hand beneath Hester's elbow he began to steer her towards The Wheatsheaf. As soon as she was certain of his goal she stopped and backed against his hand. "Not there," she said, "not there, please."

"Why?" he asked, in mild astonishment. "What have you against it?"

"Somebody now went in who might know me."

"And that would matter?" His shrewd old eyes searched her face.

"Yes, indeed. He might tell Job he had seen me."

"My child," said Jonathan, gravely, but kindly, "from what or from whom, are you running away?"

"I'll tell you," said Hester, in a burst of confidence. "Only, let us go somewhere else."

The plea was unnecessary, for already he had turned and was recrossing the market square to the corner where his quick eye had seen the sign of The Unicorn; and there, over the shilling market ordinary, Hester told him the whole story, falsifying only one particular, her relationship with Sam whom she called her "friend". As he listened, Jonathan's face grew grave, but it brightened at the end and he assured her that God had her in His keeping.

"And what shall you do in London?"

"Look for work," said Hester. "I can do all kinds of house-work, and I cook most things. And I might find Sam in London."

"I don't think you have any conception of how big and busy that city is, or how wicked, my dear. I tremble to think what might befall you there. And although I hesitate to quench your hopes I must tell you that you have as little chance of finding

Sam there as you would have finding a needle in the proverbial haystack. Have you no friends? No relatives?"

Hester shook her head.

"I am quite alone," she said.

"Then give me your little book."

She handed him the copy of *Lycidas* and he wrote an address on the flyleaf, pondered for a moment and added beneath it, "The Lord preserve thy going out and thy coming in."

"There," he said, handing it back. "There is the name and address of a decent body, who will, if you mention my name to her, give you shelter and help you to find honest work. Now, if you will remain here, out of sight, I will go and inquire in the yard about the times of the coaches."

He returned in a little while saying that there was no vehicle leaving that day.

"So I shall have the pleasure of your company until to-morrow, at least. I rather think that perhaps the Lord is preparing another way for you. He would be as unwilling as I am for you to be swallowed up in the iniquitous byways of Gomorrah. I must keep an attentive ear. But meantime I must return to what I know is my work. You stay here."

Near to the table where they had been sitting was a window-seat, cushioned and padded with worn crimson cloth that matched the shabby curtains. Hester moved across to it and curled up like a cat. A shaft of sunlight fell across her knees and threw into pitiless prominence the dirt and the grass stains on her skirt. She smoothed the folds meditatively, wondering how and when she would ever get a new dress and what it would be like. The vague, muted noises of the market came to her through the window, soothingly. She put her head back against the thick dusty folds of the curtains and passed from meditation to day-dreams, and from thence to light slumber She was never really asleep. The sweet notes of Jonathan's fiddle, plaintive across the dividing air, wove themselves into her dreams, and when they stopped suddenly she came to the surface of consciousness and thought, "Now he is going to preach." Then she sank again and drowsed on until some new and more raucous noises smote her ear.

The window, bulging outwards, gave her a full view of the market. The little Square was full of a seething crowd. In the middle of it, with his back against the Cross pillar, she could see Jonathan—or at least his head and his hands, lifted, outstretched, appealing. And through the air things were flying. He had not mentioned, when he discussed his labours on the previous evening, that in some places people did not take kindly to his preaching, and for a moment Hester stared at the scene without taking in its significance. Then with a burst of knowledge she understood. The crowd had taken offence at something that he had said, and were throwing things. They were not unanimous, for little minor struggles were taking place on the edge of the crowd, and Hester saw the stout jolly woman who sold cheeses swing with all her weight upon the uplifted arm of a man who was about to hurl his cattle-driving stick into the centre of the crowd .

Without another moment's hesitation, unmindful of Dick Tench or any other informer, Hester was out of The Unicorn and making for the Market Cross as fast as her legs could go. Jonathan had befriended her and now he was in trouble! A crazy mixture of gratitude, pity and sheer blind anger carried her forward. Bending her head she burrowed under the arms of the swaying crowd and worked like an arrow through it.

Jonathan's guiding voice had been right in its dumbness yesterday and had made one of its rare mistakes this morning. For as Hester forced her way towards her friend a large round cheese, well-aimed, caught him upon the side of his temple, jerking his head back against the stone pillar. His arms fell first, then, with an expression of almost ludicrous surprise upon his face, he crumpled slowly. There was a mark upon the grey stone of the pillar as though a ripe plum had burst against it. Jonathan dropped to his knees, then doubled over and lay still. Hester screamed as she burst through the front rank of spectators, and after that sudden tearing sound there was a silence, as the assembly realised that the bit of horseplay, so lightly started, had ended with bloodshed. The thin bright stream ran out over the cobbles.

Hester dropped to her knees and lifted the battered head. The cheesewoman joined her. She thrust her big red hand into Jonathan's coat, waited and then withdrew it.

"He's dead, you parcel of swine," she said. "You've killed a man as never did any harm. Benjy Farrow, you flung the cheese, one of mine too that I was saving for him. I'll see you pay for it too, you rotten little sod."

Except for a few mutterings the crowd was now silent. Everyone was inclined to back away, to deny a share in the responsibility. A clear authoritative voice was audible all over the Square as it said, "Now Elizabeth, bad language never helped anything yet."

Cleaving a way through the press of bodies, like a reaper through standing corn, came a robust, florid figure, wearing bright blue breeches, high boots of incomparable lustre and a canary-coloured coat of extravagant cut, and carrying a heavy riding-crop.

The cheesewoman laid Jonathan back against the cobbles and rose. Fiddling with her apron she dipped in a curtsey and said, "Oh, your reverence. I wish you'd been here a while ago."

"What's been going forward?" asked the clergyman. Then, as a whole chorus answered him, he waved his crop, not without menace and said, "You tell me, Elizabeth, without swearing, if that is possible."

Words rushed out of Elizabeth like water from a tilted bottle.

"Well, here was this dear old soul, your Reverence, playing away as nice as nice and everybody listening, damn them all for the ungrateful . . . begging your pardon, sir . . . and then he stops and says, 'You've been good enough to receive my music kindly, but I've better things,' he says, 'in store for you than that. I got a message straight from my Master who sent me to lead you sinners to repentance'. And then Danny there shouts out, 'Who're you calling sinners, mister?' And the old fellow says, as calm as anything, 'You, my friend and everybody else as can hear my voice.' And then the row starts. They don't want him to preach, they want him to go on with the fiddle. So they start to chuck things and make noises. And then Benjy Farrow steals a cheese from me and throws it. You can see for yourself what he did."

"Thank you, Elizabeth. You give a very clear account. And as you say I can see for myself. And we mustn't blame Danny overmuch, you know. There is preaching for such as desire it, in the proper place and at the proper time, Church on Sunday morning. As for Benjy and the cheese—very reprehensible indeed, but I hope his eye will be as good and his aim as true in the match against Little Brampton on Saturday."

Almost everyone in the crowd, relieved at having the disaster dealt with so lightly, cheered at this. The parson in the canary-coloured coat accepted the tribute and those nearest to Benjy were inclined to offer congratulatory words and buffets. In the diffusion of interest the clergyman looked down upon

Jonathan. There was a certain pity in his gaze, but it was the pity of the superior being who considers that a fool has merely reaped the reward of his folly.

"Better remove the victim of this unfortunate accident into the Town Hall; a cell, I think. We'll deal with it later. Now my good people go about your business. You Benjy and you Danny come and finish what you started."

The fiddle lay where Jonathan had placed it before he started upon the second half of his programme. As Danny came forward to lift the dead man's head he set his huge foot on it. It crumpled, much as its master had done, but with a sharp splintering of wood. So much Hester saw through the mist of anger that was blinding her. But as Benjy, from his outer place pushed forward and the crowd, regaining its market-merry spirit, began to disperse, she caught another sight of Dick Tench, gazing with interest into the heart of the crowd. She turned away sharply, presenting her back to him, and when the two men took up their light burden, she stole round to the other side of the cross and sat down upon a step, sick and shaken. Like Sam, a few days earlier, she was oppressed by the injustices of the world. Without going into any great perceptive depths she realised that Jonathan had been truly good, and through doing what he, rightly or wrongly, considered his duty, he had been struck down and killed, just because a good-hearted woman had kept her promise to save him a cheese, and because a young man had a practised aim.

And the accident that had lost Jonathan his life had lost her the first disinterested friend that she had found since Mrs. Bridges had died. I don't seem to be very good for people, she thought, with a sudden rush of insight. My enemies all flourish and my friends meet with misfortune. Mrs. Bridges wanted me to have Martha's place, and it was quarrelling with Martha that killed her. And Sam was thrown out of The Fleece because we were fond of one another. Those people in the wood cheated me, and they're all right, I'll warrant; Jonathan turned back in order to help me, and now he's dead. It isn't fair. It isn't fair.

CHAPTER VII

SHE sat there for some time in a mood of desolation and something that was just not self-pity, since it was tinged with self-disgust. But gradually her spirit hardened and her chin came out. From now on she would manage by herself. And she was the better off for meeting the old preacher, she had the address and the money. There was nothing to be gained by sitting here where every moment might bring recognition. She rose and patted her dress and hair into some sort of order, and then, skirting around the Market Square, struck the main road again and began walking.

For awhile, anxious to get out of town, she walked quickly, and presently overtook a carter walking at the head of a team of three horses which were drawing a heavy covered goods wagon. She passed them and then looked back. The cart had a cover, and the horses, although their pace was slow, would be able to make more continuous progress at that rate than she could do. She walked more slowly and looked back, trying to judge the carter's character from his face. It was broad and red and completely expressionless, but at least there was nothing sly or vicious about it. When the wagon drew level again she said,

"Are you going along this road?"

"Witnesham, nigh to Ipswich."

"Have you room for a passenger?"

"Ah."

"How much will you charge me?"

"Two shilling."

"Then may I get in?"

"Ah."

Since the heavy, iron-shod vehicle took a good deal of starting he made no attempt to stop it in order to let her climb in.

He plodded along at the head of his horses and Hester climbed, with a run and a jump, in over the wagon's tail, and snuggled down on some sacks of meal with her back to a keg. At first it seemed a haven of security and comfort and she swayed unheeding to its lurching.

152

When it was quite dark the man took out the horses and hobbled them, turning them loose by the roadside.

"Got to see somebody here," he said. "I'll be back."

Hester imagined that he had gone in search of supper and wished that she dared suggest that he either let her go with him or brought her something back. But he was so uncommunicative that she was deterred. The wagon had been drawn off the road on to a piece of grassy common. Looking out Hester could see no house or sign of human habitation. With the munching of the horses for company and the memory of her dinner for sustenance, she pulled some of the sacks into a more comfortable position and settled herself for sleep. Once during the night she woke and heard the man's regular snoring from the front of the wagon. She did not wake again until a sudden jerk told that the vehicle was again under way. The world was bathed in the beauty of a summer sunrise. She scrambled down and walked behind the wagon for a while to get the stiffness out of her limbs, and when, at a water-splash, the man halted his team and let them drink a little, she cupped her hands and quenched her thirst at the same source. After that she rode again, more conscious to-day of the bruises that resulted from the bumping of the vehicle. At last the man, still without halting the horses, shouted to her.

"Yon's Ipswich. I turn off here."

Hester alighted and joined him. "Can you tell me where the coaches start?"

"White Horse. Go straight, you can't miss it. Thank you, good day." He took the two shillings, still plodding, and guided his leader around the corner.

Hester walked straight, through streets so crowded that she imagined it must be market day. In The White Horse yard the coach stood, ready to start. She was only just in time. She had a momentary fear that the coachman would not accept her as a passenger, she was so very different from the rest of the passengers. But when, abandoning all hope of having a meal first, she pushed her way through the people and rather timidly made her inquiries, she met with no opposition once she had produced her fare. In much greater comfort, and through the peerless beauty of the summer weather, she made an uneventful journey to London and was at last deposited in the yard of The True Troubadour, in the Strand.

The coach was being awaited by a number of people, friends

of travellers who greeted and embraced those whom they had come to meet, and a group of little barefooted boys who darted like eels between the skirts of the women and the legs of the men, crying, "Carry your bag! Carry your bag!" The others came to lead away the steaming horses, and at this familiar sight a wave of nostalgia smote Hester. For one weak moment she longed for those monotonous, laborious but peaceful days at The Fleece. To be wearing a clean dress and a stiff white apron, helping Mamie to cook in the sunny kitchen, to share the excitement of the incursion of the passengers, the rush of the dishing up, to accept with lordly indifference Phoebe's help with the last tasks of the day, and then to meet Sam! What Heaven that would be. There at least she knew her place, knew friend from foe, knew what each hour was likely to hold in store. Here she was alone and lost, dirty and ragged, and as though to put the crowning touch upon her shame, one of the small boys jostled her rudely, shouted "Carry your bag, lady?" in tones of derision, and was rewarded for his witticism by the guffaws of his mates.

Turning aside slightly Hester pulled her *Lycidas* from the front of her gown. "Mrs. Carter, The Bakehouse, Dove Lane," she read, and below it Jonathan's text which, at this moment, came like the touch of a friendly hand. Heartened, the girl straightened herself, pulled together the gaping rent of her sleeve, and turning to a lad who had just been commissioned to carry a valise almost as large as himself, said, "Can you direct me to Dove Lane?"

"Goin' nearly there meself,' 'he said cheerily. "Foller me and I'll tell you where to turn." He struggled out of the yard, his legs bowed beneath the burden, his body thrown out at a sharp angle to balance the weight of the bag. Because he had addressed her kindly Hester felt sorry for him, and from following, drew level with him and put one hand through the strap of the valise.

"I'll help you, as far as I go," she said. He jerked the bag away from her fingers.

"You trying to nick this poke?" he asked sharply, " 'cos it can't be done, see? Us porters got a signal. I only got to yell out one word an' I'd have friends here in a blink."

"I wasn't meaning any harm," said Hester, drawing back stiffly. "I just thought it was rather big for you to carry."

"Gor. This ain't heavy. Carry two like this, I can. Come on." He changed the bag to his other hand and Hester followed his bowed and struggling progress, until, without turning his head, he jerked a thumb to the left.

"Down there's Dove Lane. Second turn on the right."

"Thank you very much," called Hester after him, and turned to the left. The street here was so narrow that no two vehicles could have passed in it. The houses leaned forward as though confessing some furtive secret to one another. Heaps of filth lay in the gutters and amongst them swarms of squalling, half-naked children played. From one dark-mouthed alley two women came, screaming the foulest abuse at one another and evidently needing only room enough to swing their arms before they came to blows, for as soon as they were both in the open street they fell upon each other with the ferocity of wild beasts, tearing at hair and eyes, screaming, punching, biting. The children near-by moved away a little and went on playing. Other women came to the doors of their hovels and watched, without emotion or interference.

Hester crossed the street and was glad when she must turn aagin, hoping to find Dove Lane an improvement upon its neighbour. It was quieter, but just as dirty and dreary. She walked down one side and up the other, searching for something that remotely resembled the cottage window in the village where the Fincham sisters displayed their plum cakes and gingerbread for the benefit of those housewives who were not gifted in the art of cake-making. But except that the house on the corner had a little bow-window that bulged on to the footpath, there was nothing to distinguish one house from another. And that window was so dirty that it was difficult to look within it; certainly there were no cakes to be seen.

As Hester paused beside it for the fourth time, the door beside it was torn open and a dishevelled, furious female came out on to the step.

"What the hell are you peeping in here for?" she demanded. "Spying for Ginny Joe, I'll take my oath. You —— off back and tell him I ain't harbouring Jim. I ain't seen him for weeks. I don't care if I never see him again, the ——. And I won't have Joe's garbage hanging round here day and night, droring attention."

"I don't know what you're talking about," said Hester. "I'm looking for Mrs. Carter. She used to keep a cake shop here, I believe."

"Then you're wasting your time," returned the woman, slightly mollified. "She's been in hell this three months—mean,

155

psalm-singing old skintflint. Twopence for a blasted bun and pay before you smell it and give your soul to Jesus before you choke on the crumbs. Whadyer want with her?"

"I was sent," said Hester. "I was told that I could stay with her, while I was looking for work."

The woman's face and manner changed completely. She eyed Hester up and down as men eyed Dick Tench's horses before making some sly careful offer of about half the price they intended to give. Hester would hardly have been surprised if she had demanded to look in her mouth. The fury with which she had attacked in the first place, ugly as it was, was more congruous and in a way less terrifying than the crafty look of consideration which now replaced it. Her eyes slid over Hester in a manner that reminded her of her hatred for creeping things.

"So you're looking for work, are you, dearie? And you want a place to stay. Well now, wha's wrong with this? I reckon I could find a good kip for you too, a pretty little piece like you'd be if you'd got the clo'es."

Hester drew back a step. She was weary and hungry and lonely enough almost to be glad of the woman's invitation.

But the sudden change to friendliness; the almost hungry way in which she looked at her, and a distrust bred of this squalid, ugly place, held her upright and aloof for just a moment more.

"You mean that you could find me work?" she asked.

"Easy as kissing your hand. Come on in, dearie, we don't want all the street to know our business. You mustn't judge by the way I called out at you just now, you know. We all has our troubles, and Ginny Joe and my folks have had a row. Nothing to bother your pretty head about."

She held the door wide, and Hester, reflecting wildly that she had nothing else in view and certainly no possessions worth stealing, mounted the step and crossed the threshold.

The room, whose cobwebbed window looked on to the street, was clearly uninhabited and uninhabitable. It was a crowded store-room of what appeared to be a collection of rubbish.

There were piles of rags, bits of broken furniture, rusty lanterns, tools, several casks, coils of rope and some fishing-nets. They were thrown and heaped together and all covered with a greyish film of dust and cobwebs.

But the room behind, to which the woman led the way through a short passage, had a certain sluttish comfort about it. A small fire burned between the high hobs, a kettle was singing. There was a rug at the hearth, several comfortably cushioned chairs, some gillyflowers in a cracked mug and a bullfinch in a cage.

The room, without being very clean or even tidy, contrasted so sharply with the one at the front, and with the appearance of the slatternly woman who seemed to inhabit it, that Hester looked about her with naïve surprise. The woman seemed to sense it.

"You mustn't take any notice of me," she said, still with that false, placating smile. "I was just getting up. I saw you from upstairs. I was up all night . . . nursing somebody as was sick. I came down to put the kettle on and then went back to make myself tidy. But we won't bother about that now. I daresay you're peckish?"

"I am, a little."

The woman poked the fire beneath the singing kettle, reached to the cupboard in the wall beside the hearth and lifted out, one after another, teapot, cups, a basin of sugar, bread, salt and a dish containing some soused mackerel. She made and poured some tea, measuring it far more lavishly than poor Miss Peck, and set one cup and all the other things before Hester, urging her to help herself and to eat freely, with such hospitality that Hester began to wonder whether she had misjudged her. Yet, every time that she looked up from her eating she caught the woman's eye dwelling upon her calculatingly, and each time it slid away in a manner that revived her doubt.

"What's your name?" she asked at last.

"Hester Roon."

"Mine's Sarah. Sarah Bates. Mrs. Sarah Bates. But most people call me Sally. And how old are you?"

"I was seventeen in the autumn."

"Have you come far?"

"From quite a long way. From the country."

On and on went the catechism. Some questions Hester evaded, sometimes by lying; but by the time that her hunger was satisfied Sally had extracted most of what she wanted to know, namely that Hester had no friends, no relatives, could cook, and understood a good deal about domestic matters.

"I know just the job for you," she said at last. "Only, as I say, you'll have to have some different clo'es. Stand up a minute and let's have a look at you."

Hester obligingly rose. The woman rose too and went from

157

the room. She was gone a long time. When she returned she had an assortment of clothes over her arm, a pair of scissors, a needle and a reel of thread in her hand.

"Go on," she said kindly, "finish your food. This'll be too big, I know, so I'll just start ripping."

She slashed into some black material, wielding the scissors in a clumsy and unaccustomed fashion. Then, when Hester had eaten her fill and drained her cup for the last time, she began to fit her, and having fitted, to sew the things together. Hester, seeing the vast loose stitches being made, begged to be allowed to help, and between them, after an hour and a half of work, they had reconstructed two black dresses and a coat to Hester's size. One dress was of rustling silk, with bands of velvet around the skirt and the sleeves, and while trying it on—her delight tempered by its slightly musty odour—Hester said, "I ought to tell you that I have no money. But I'll pay you out of my first wages."

"That's what I mean you to do," said Sally.

Evening fell, darkening the little room.

"There, that'll do," Sally said gladly, driving her needle rapidly over the last inch or two. "Now we'll just nip upstairs and put ourselves tidy." She poured the contents of the kettle into a jug, and with Hester carrying the clothing, led the way up the narrow stairs and into a stale-smelling bedroom, dirty, but comfortably furnished. The bed, too large for the room, even had silk hangings and a panel of cherubs, all of whom had lost most of the outstanding portions of their anatomy.

The woman stripped off her filthy baggy wrap and struggled into a corset. Then she poured out the water into a fine china basin decorated with roses, but chipped all round the edge, splashed in it half-heartedly and afterwards told Hester she might use it. With some distaste— for incomplete as Sally's ablutions had been they had left a grey scum around the edge of the water—Hester plunged head and arms into the basin, afterwards wiping on the towel which Sally passed on to her.

"Does it matter which I wear now?" she asked then, approaching the dresses.

Sally turned from the mirror, with whose aid she was making an elaborate toilet, and said, "Not a damn," so Hester lifted the silk dress over her head. The skirt, very full and weighted by the velvet bands, swung gracefully. The bodice, fitted with some art by Sally's skilful though careless fingers, buttoned smoothly over her young bosom and then, narrowing, hugged her slim waist. She was impatient to get a glimpse of herself, but Sally, with a hare's foot and a lump of swansdown, was busy obliterating the ravages of time and experience. At last, however, she turned away and went to a cupboard, whence she took a vivid and voluminous gown of mustard yellow and green stripes, plastered with lace and ribbons. While she fought her way into this the mirror was free.

Remembering her own injunctions to Phoebe, Hester asked before borrowing the comb; and having borrowed it, wiped it surreptitiously upon the towel. She dragged it through her short, curly hair, worked the parting smooth and straight and wound the curls anew around her fingers. Against the severe black of the dress with the velvet outlining the square of her neck, her flesh looked pale and cool as alabaster; her hair shone, yellow and lustrous. If only, if only, she thought, she had had such a dress while Sam was with her. She whirled round with a swishing of silken skirt and looked at Sally, who, raddled and coiffured and tightly laced, stood with her hands on her bulging hips, looking at her with unmistakable admiration.

"You got looks, you know," she said, half reluctantly. "I ain't sure that I ain't making a mistake." She gnawed her nail thoughtfully. "Still, never mind. There's time for everything. Come on."

Downstairs she mended the fire and filled the kettle. Then she bade Hester set the table while she went out to buy some supper. Hester swooped about the little room, searching for and finding in unexpected places the cloth and the cutlery. She was still bewildered by the change in Sally's manner, and at once appreciative and distrustful of her sudden generosity. But since there was nothing to be gained by wondering about it she shut it away and considered that she might think herself fortunate in having found a roof, food and clothing so easily. She hummed a little tune to herself as she set the table.

A tap at the window made her start. She looked up but could see nothing; the dusk outside seemed black in contrast with the brightness of the room, for Sally had lighted a lamp before leaving. After a moment or two the tap was repeated. Then a dirty curtain that hung over part of the back wall near the stair door, stirred and behind it Hester could see a door, ajar, at this moment. Round its side a man cautiously poked his head. His eyes met Hester's for a fraction of a second, then he drew back. The door shut hastily and the curtain swung over it again. Just at that moment the passage door opened and Sally sailed in, a large jug in one hand, a basket in the other.

"What's the matter?" she asked, following Hester's eyes to the curtained doorway.

"A man tapped twice on the window and then peeped in. He went away when he saw me."

Sally flew to the doorway and called softly.

"Jim, Jim. It's all right."

There was a perceptible pause. Then a voice asked out of the darkness:

"That you, Sal?"

"Yes."

"Who's the wench?"

"Come in and see for yourself "

Again the curtain swung and Sally reappeared, holding the man by the arm. As soon as they were inside she flung her arms around his neck and kissed him heartily.

"God, but I'm glad to see you. I was beginning to think they'd got you, or else you was in the river."

"I was laying low. Ginny been around?"

"Two or three times, not lately. Look, this is Hester Roon. She come looking for old Mrs. Cakey Carter and I went for her like a cat, thinking she was one of Ginny's nosers. But she's all right. I thought she nac ekat Annie's ecalp. What do you think?"

"Too young," said the man, looking at Hester and pursing his mouth with disapproval.

"Aw, rot," said Sally. "All the better. We meant to peek this eno ni the krad, didn't we?"

The queer little words interspersed with the others fell easily from Sally's lips and seemed to be understood by the man, for he nodded and twisted his head to take another sideways look at Hester, who, with a puzzled expression, was watching them both.

"She's looking for a job? Can she cook?"

"You said so, didn't you dearie? You see, we know a job a girl just left . . ."

"Ah, she left it all right," interrupted the man. "Sal, I haven't had a decent bite for a week. What you got? We can talk later on. Is Fussy coming?"

"Yes."

"I thought so," said Jim, scowling at Sally's gown. "I only got to be outa sight for a coupla days for you to go on the bitch again. And I'll warrant you've got him some supper."

Sally opened the basket and laid out jellied eels, pigs' trotters, butter and cheese.

"I'd got company whether you and Fussy come or not," she said a little sharply.

"Let's get on with it, then," said Jim. "Gin!" he added sniffing the jug. "Just come right, I did." He began to eat and drink with avidity while Hester, who had set the table for two, reached down another plate.

Presently another tap on the window heralded Fussy's approach, and he entered by the back door. Hester could understand Jim's jealousy of the newcomer, for Fussy had an advantage over him, both in size, looks, clothing and charm of manner. He also briefly inspected Hester, shot out a stream of the curious words that sounded like English but didn't make any sense, and likewise settled down to his supper. Sally endeavoured to keep the talk from drifting off down strange channels, and frequently tried to draw Hester into it. They all seemed curious to know from whence she came, and why. Beyond saying that she was an orphan—implying, as she had done to Jonathan, that this state was a recent affliction—that she had no friends and had come to London to look for work, Hester told them little. Presently Sally said, "You must be tired, dearie. You slip up and go to bed." Hester, conscious of being dismissed, said good-night and retired. For a while she lay in the darkness, listening to the boom of talk going on in the room below and wondering about the three of them. That they were crafty and underhand she was certain; what job, in a respectable sense, they could have to offer was less certain. But they had, to an extent, befriended her, and upon that thought Hester closed her eyes and slept. To-morrow might make everything clear.

CHAPTER VIII

IN THE morning Sally woke her.

"Come on," she said briskly, "look lively. Fussy's calling for us soon. Your breakfast's ready."

This was a new Sally. The slattern of yesterday afternoon, the painted woman of the evening were both gone. In a sober and fairly clean dress of grey cloth and a severe hat of dark blue with a grey band, she looked like a respectable tradesman's wife.

"I'll put your things together while you eat," she said. She had retrieved—probably from the amazing collection of things in the front room—a small wicker clothes-basket. Into it she packed the silk gown and the coat.

"This yours?" she asked, lifting the *Lycidas*.

"Yes." Sally dropped it in.

"You can read?" she said. "Well, that will be handy. Was there anything else of your own?"

"The dress I came in," said Hester, buttoning the sober black cloth dress on which they had worked yesterday.

"Oh, leave that. I'll wash it and mend it and bring it along to you some time. I suppose I'd better tell you where you're going."

"I would like to know," said Hester.

"You can keep the comb if you haven't got one. You'll have to be tidy, you know. Well, there wasn't much to pack, was there? You'll have to have some more underclothes. I'll see to that, too. Now come on and I'll tell you all about it."

She clumped down the stairs, carrying the basket, lifted the teapot from the hob and poured out some tea for Hester. The remains of the supper was on the table, just as they had been left overnight. A mouse had been making merry with the butter and at the sight of its traces Hester's good appetite quailed, and she fastidiously helped herself to bread, breaking off the crust and eating only the crumb. Sally was too busily engaged in talking to notice.

"Out towards Finchley," she began, "there's an old woman lives all alone in a big house. She once got Fussy to cart her a load of wood and she told him she'd given up having servants because they robbed her so. But she said if he could find her a decent orphan girl, to live with her, for company like, she'd give her a good home and be kind to her. Fussy found a girl, Annie her name was, but she didn't do. So yesterday when you said you was looking for work I thought it'd be the thing for you."

"I'm very grateful," said Hester. "What's the old woman like?"

"Oh, old, and a little queer. Thinks everybody is going to rob her. All the windows are barred and the doors kept locked. Apart from that she's a nice old thing, a real lady, Fussy says. But you needn't stop if you don't like it. We'll find you another kip. There is Fussy, now. He's going to drive us."

Evidently Miss Martineau had been expecting Fussy; for after a lengthy inspection from the side of one of the barred windows, she opened the doors at the top of the steps and came out.

"So this is the girl you promised me," she said in a high, reedy voice. "I did tell you about Annie, didn't I? I suppose you never heard what the matter was."

"Not a word, ma'am. I never set eyes on her since. But this one's called Hester, and she'll be better than Annie. She can read."

"That will be very fine. Here, wait a minute. Take this for your trouble." She pressed some coins into his hand. "And I shall be glad of another load of wood towards the end of August."

Her eyes stared past Fussy and Hester at the top of the steps to where Sally sat in the little cart, holding the pony's reins.

"Your wife is well?" she asked.

"Yes, thank you." He turned to Hester with a sudden change of manner. "Now my girl, you behave yourself and do what the lady wants. Sally and me'll look in from time to time, with your permission ma'am, and see how you're getting on."

The patronising tone of his voice annoyed Hester, who stared at him, coldly sullen, and the old lady did not appear to notice his appeal for permission to visit the house. Instead she drew back a little and laid her hand upon the door. Fussy removed his hat. "Good-bye ma'am. Good-bye Hester," he said, leaped down the steps, rejoined Sally in the cart, and with a flick of the reins over the pony's back went rattling away.

Miss Martineau opened the door and signed to Hester to enter. She turned the key in the lock and shot the bolts at the top and the foot of the door. The key she dropped into the capacious pocket that was tied around her waist over her skirt.

The house had the dimness, the deep muffled silence, the chill that one associates with the tomb. It had not been aired, or warmed or stirred for years, thought Hester, sniffing the atmosphere. They stood in a wide, lofty hall, with shuttered windows on either side of the door, and a black marble staircase winding up into the dimness of the upper floor. The walls were draped with some dark material and decorated with oil-paintings, muted by age and dirt into a uniform colourlessness. The floor of the hall, laid with squares of black and grey stone, rang hollowly as they moved. A trapped and helpless feeling overcame Hester. Outside the summer sun was shining and warming the flowering earth, people moved about in it, talking and laughing. Within these walls all life had stopped, years ago. It was a house of the dead.

Miss Martineau, moving with the stiff agility of a bird in a frost, led the way to the back hall, where, in the shadow of the stairs, three doors stood, side by side, in the wall. She opened the middle one and tapped away down a stone passage, which, curving slightly, debouched at last, through a doorway which had no door, into a large gloomy room that was half sitting-room, half kitchen. There was a dresser with a few old plates and cracked cups upon it, a table half-covered by an old plush curtain, two sagging chairs, a settle against one wall, and a wide stone fireplace, blackened with the smoke of years. A few logs of green wood were smoking and spitting on the hearth and over them a black soot-encrusted pot was suspended from a hook.

This room, although it looked out upon a high blank wall, and its windows were barred, dirty and wreathed upon the outside with ivy, was lighter than the rest of the house and Miss Martineau, taking a stand in the middle of it, said,

"Put down your basket and let me have a look at you." She studied Hester for some moments, her head tilted and her eyes screwed.

"Have you been an orphan long?"

"Nearly five years."

"And were you in the orphanage all that time?"

"I've never been in an orphanage."

"Now don't be silly, child. There's no need to be proud. I like orphans. They haven't been spoiled by high living, and they aren't always stealing out with parcels of food for their families. And who taught you to read?"

"I went to school."

"Well, well. I'm sure that we shall be very happy and comfortable together. We shall live here. I never use the other rooms now. It takes so much fuel to warm them. But I expect them to be kept tolerably clean. I'd better show you over the house, I think. And then you can make some dumplings to go in the broth."

She led a depressed and bewildered Hester from room to room of the great house, throwing back the shutters in each for just long enough to allow an inspection, then closing them again. The house was full of mouldering treasures; beautiful hangings and curtains, ruined by damp and moth, tarnished silver candlesticks and bowls, marble figures covered with dust and cobwebs. In one enormous drawing-room on the first floor a superb Chinese hand-painted wallpaper, still bright with fabulous birds and dragons and flowering almond trees, was streaked in patches by damp and slowly peeling from the walls. The room held also an ivory-coloured carpet with a few flowers of scarlet and jade trailing across its surface, and two lacquered cabinets full of figures in ivory, ebony, jade and rose quartz.

Miss Martineau seemed quite oblivious to the disintegration that was taking place. She glanced around this room with a proud possessive eye.

"My grandfather arranged this room," she told Hester. "He was a great traveller, one of the first Englishmen to penetrate China. He brought these things home. See, this is a Thibetan prayer wheel, and these"—she opened a cabinet and drew out some rolls of silk—"these are the painted story of the conquest of Ti-Lung. They are quite priceless." She laid them back before Hester had time to look at them. But not before she had seen the sinister marks of green mould and the cracks where the silk had perished from long folding.

"I should live in here, if it were mine," said Hester. "It's the most beautiful room in the house, but it's spoiling, you know. Look," she pointed to where the paper bellied and drew a finger over the lacquer to show how the bloom of damp had gathered.

"I know. It's very sad." The thin, reedy voice was quite placid. "As custodian of all these treasures I regret not being able to afford to cherish them properly."

"I could paste back the paper," said Hester. "And if the windows were opened and a fire lighted it would soon dry out. That wouldn't cost much, would it?"

"We'll see," said Miss Martineau. "Come along." For Hester was gazing again at the birds and the dragons and the flowering almonds. The old lady relocked the door.

Finally she showed Hester her bedroom and the one that she herself was to occupy. They were next door to one another and though just as dark and full of heavy furniture, rather less musty-smelling than the other rooms. In the one which was to be Hester's the old lady suddenly referred to Annie.

"She was a very good little girl," she said rather regretfully. "But she just disappeared. For a few days she seemed very unhappy and cried a good deal. I didn't encourage visits from Mr. Fussel and his wife, as a rule, but when they came one evening I was quite glad to let them in, thinking that they would cheer her. However in the morning she was gone. Do you want Mr. Fussel and his wife to visit you?"

"You mean Fussy and Sally? I don't know." Perhaps, she thought, if I stay here long I shall be glad to see anybody. At least they are alive and warm, though I don't like them much, and I don't believe they are married, and there's something queer in his telling the old woman that I was in an orphanage.

"I don't know. I expect Sally will come once at least, to bring me a dress I left behind. She promised to."

"Well, if she does of course you must let her in. But you must tell me when she arrives and when she leaves. Having seen my treasures you will understand my distrust of the outside world."

With or without understanding it, Hester soon recognised it as the most powerful ingredient in the old lady's outlook. For weeks on end the house was entirely cut off from all communication with the world of men and affairs. Behind the kitchen was a larder, always locked except when Miss Martineau went to it for supplies, and it might have been the storeroom of a ship bound on a long voyage. Bags of cereals and flour, small casks of salted meat and fish, bladders of lard and blackened joints of bacon occupied its shelves. Once a fortnight a woman from a farm hammered on the door and handed in a pound of butter and half a milk cheese on a strawbed. Miss Martineau looked from the window, unlocked the door, and paid the woman. The whole transaction was over in a moment, yet if Hester missed it she felt defrauded.

Very occasionally at irregular intervals Hester was allowed to take a basket and go to shop for such necessities as were growing low in the storeroom. On such occasions the sense of freedom and excitement that came upon her as she breathed the open air and mingled with free people in the sunlight, was so powerful that she always felt that she would never go back. But she always did. She had nowhere else to go.

She was almost perpetually hungry, for Miss Martineau doled out her stored provisions with extreme parsimony. Her own aged and withered frame demanded little to sustain it, and she had no regard for Hester's needs. Apart from that she was kind enough and Hester was not overworked. Her remark on that first day about keeping the rest of the house tolerably clean meant nothing. Now and then she would tell Hester to bring a broom and a duster and clean such and such a room. But having once unlocked it she seemed uneasy until it was closed again, and wandered in and out, urging the girl to greater haste. And since every room would have needed a week's serious cleaning to restore it to anything resembling order, Hester could do little more than brush off the surface dust.

"There, that will do for to-day," Miss Martineau would say impatiently. And when Hester passed through the door and the key was turned and put into the big black pocket, she gave an audible sigh of relief.

There was one bright spot in the dreary round. On the ground floor of the house, tucked away at the back and looking out into a small square of completely overgrown and blackened garden, was a library. Someone of Miss Martineau's family, now long dead, had been a passionate reader and collector of books. Many were in languages that she did not even know by name, even more were treatises and learned essays in which she took no interest. But many were readable. There were plays and poems and stories and account of travels; there was, in manuscript, a record, entered almost daily, of the intimate life of one, Joseph Martineau, between the years of 1575 and 1598. He had had what Hester deemed a full and exciting life. He had never lived up to his name over the matter of Potiphar's wife, or anybody else's: he was a self-confessed liar and when he thought necessary, a cheat: he was disgraced because he diddled

Elizabeth Tudor out of her part of a prize cargo, and after that spent some years in piracy : he returned to fight in the fleet that repulsed the Armada, and then spent ten years in trading, in which slaving played no small part. The record ended quite suddenly with an entry giving an account of the Gargantuan meal which he gave to celebrate his sixtieth birthday; oysters, roast capon, sucking pig, patties of mincemeat and Canary wine were provided. "After which we lighted our pipes, and with the brandy many a brave tale shuttled back and forth. . . ." That was the final sentence. And whether he lived to enjoy another birthday, or died in his bed from the result of that one, Hester never knew. But she thought about him a great deal, and even appealed to Miss Martineau for further information. Miss Martineau, however, was completely uninterested in her ancestor : nor did she regard the manuscript as one of the treasures of which she was custodian. Almost two centuries later, when silver candlesticks could be purchased for a few shillings, since labour-saving households had no use for them, Joseph Martineau's Diary was purchased by an American collector for six thousand five hundred pounds, and probably Miss Martineau's bones stirred in the grave at the thought of how often she had allowed Hester to brood over it by a smoking fire.

For with the failure of the summer it became clear to Hester why Miss Martineau, so careful and parsimonious, engaged any servant at all. The little old lady suffered from a most painful and crippling form of rheumatism and was often unable to rise from her bed without aid. And on the days when she did rise she retired early, leaving Hester straining her eyes to read by candlelight.

It was some weeks after Hester's installation, though still summer weather, when Sally called, bearing a large basket on her arm. Her face was as flaccid and dissipated-looking as ever, but she was neatly dressed. She knocked upon the heavy knocker, was inspected by Miss Martineau through the window, and finally admitted. The three sat down in the kitchen, and Sally, slightly ill at ease, endeavoured to make general conversation. At last Miss Martineau rose, saying graciously, "Well, Mrs. Fussel, no doubt you will wish to talk to your protegée, and you, child, will enjoy a chat with your friend, I know. So I'll bid you good night." She touched Hester lightly on the shoulder and went, with her queer pecking step, up to her bed.

Sally immediately relaxed, took off her hat, unfastened the

top of her bodice, and lifted her basket to the table. Out of it she took a squat black bottle, some small crusty loaves, split and buttered, and the breast of a chicken.

"I reckoned you could do with a bite," she said. "Regular old skinflint, ain't she?"

With her eyes on the food Hester said, "I don't think she remembers what it feels like to be hungry. It's very kind of you to bring this."

"Hand us a coupla cups, dearie, and let's set to. I'm peckish myself. Had to walk. Fussy couldn't bring me."

She splashed the brandy out of the bottle into the cups, and divided the chicken fairly.

"You're not married to him, are you?" asked Hester.

"Not on your life, dearie. The old girl cooked up that notion for herself. No, Fussy and me and Jim and one or two others do a bit of work together now and then." She dismissed the subject. "Enjoying the grub? That's right. Thought you would. Come on, drink up." She splashed some more brandy into Hester's cup, and changed the subject again.

"Been over the house yet? Lovely, Annie said it was. I wanted her to show me over some time, but she never would. Said it was all locked up."

"So it is," said Hester. "And she carries the keys about with her. All but one."

"And which is that?"

"The library. She let me have it so that I could get a book any time."

"Anything but books in there?"

"A desk and two chairs. Nothing else. It isn't worth seeing. The Chinese room is the one that is best to look at."

"And what's that like?"

Using every colourful word that she knew Hester described the Chinese room. "I'd live in it if it were mine," she concluded.

"So would anybody with any sense," said Sally, looking with scorn round the apartment in which they sat. "And Annie said that though she never had anything on her table she'd got dozens of silver forks and spoon and plates."

"I believe she has," Hester admitted.

"Bags of money, too, tucked away," said Sally.

"Of that I am not so sure. She's always talking about not being able to afford things."

169

"Don't you believe a word of it, my dear. All lies. You keep your eyes open and see . . . and you'll see that it's all lies. Where's your cup? You carry your brandy well, I will say. Half what you've had and Annie was all at sea."

"I've had it before," said Hester. "I wish you'd tell me about Annie. Miss Martineau said she cried a lot just before she left. She seemed to like her, though."

Sally's face hardened. "She was a silly little drab. I got her this good job, same as I did you." The hard look changed to the shifty evasiveness that Hester had come to associate with Sally's face. "But nothing happened to her. She just got lonely and left."

"I see."

The feeling remained with Hester that there was something mysterious about Annie's departure. Loneliness does not cause a person to disappear.

Sally now began to put, with what subtlety she could command, certain questions about the house, the position of the rooms, Hester answered them non-committally, and after a time Sally stood up to go.

"Ain't there a back way?" she asked, as she put on her hat. "If there was it'd save me all the hill. I could just slip out there down Cook's Lane and be on the road in no time."

"There was one, but it's all nailed up. So is the door in the wall. You can just see the top of it over the laurel bushes from the library window. But you couldn't get it opened."

" 'S a pity. Besides wearing out your shoes for nothing you have to let *her* know every time you come. Me or Fussy could slip in often of a evening and cheer you up a bit, but it's such a to-do having to act the polite every time."

"I'm sorry," said Hester, smiling. "*I* didn't nail it up, you know."

"You got more sense," said Sally, and made her adieux.

Not until she had gone did Hester realise that she had not brought the pink dress. But she troubled little about it, it was worn out anyway, and when she got her wages—Miss Martineau had promised her twenty-five shillings a quarter—she would be able to buy some stuff and make herself a new one.

CHAPTER IX

AT VARIOUS times through the declining, darkening year Sally paid her visits. She always brought a bottle and some tasty titbit. She was always affable and inquisitive. Once Fussy came too, and on that evening the meal developed a party spirit. Fussy also produced a bottle, and through the slight haze that resulted from drinking gin and brandy alternately, Hester was conscious of his admiring glances. They said a good deal about what good friends they had been to her, which she could not deny, and about Miss Martineau's parsimony, which she did not trouble to deny. For Miss Martineau had been in bed for two whole days and had nearly driven Hester crazy, counting her keys and begging for Hester's assurance that every door and window was closed. And when Sally had knocked upon the door the old lady had, with the greatest difficulty, been persuaded to hand over the key.

"Let her go away," she said peevishly. "I don't like people in the house when I'm in bed."

"But Sally isn't people," said Hester reasonably, "and I haven't spoken to anybody from outside for a fortnight. I would like to see her for just a minute."

"Well, get rid of her quickly then. I shan't be easy until the door is locked behind her."

So Hester went down to where Sally was making a repeated attack upon the door, and there was Fussy too. And she made no attempt to hurry them away. Sally had brought, beside the usual brandy, a joint of pork, with crisp brown crackling, some rosy apples and about half a peck of walnuts.

Exhilarated by the food and the drink and the company Hester allowed a complaint of the monotony of her days to escape her. Fussy laid his well-shaped brown hand over hers and said :

"Cheer up, little girl, we'll get another job for you, don't you worry. Just be good and do what we tell you and you'll soon be out of this. Pretty lively girl like you stifled here with that old curmudgeon, it's silly. That's what it is. Drink up to the good time coming."

He glanced at Sally significantly. And as they left the house some time later he said, "Well, that's going to be easy. We might as well fix it with Jim for one night next week."

"I'm not so sure,' 'said Sally. "Did you notice to-night what she put away without turning a hair. And she don't rant on half like Annie used to do about being hungry. And you know how Annie turned."

"We was fools over Annie," retorted Fussy. "Held up and baulked by one silly snivelling girl, that's what we were. I never enjoyed scragging anybody so much. But that didn't get us back inside, did it? Still, this time we chose well."

Hester removed all traces of the meal, for Miss Martineau might be better and come down in the morning. Then she tried to slip upstairs to bed without attracting attention. But the old lady called to her. "You have been a long time. Did you lock the door? And bolt it? Then give me the key."

Hester was half undressed when a querulous voice called again. Going to her employer's room she found her, grimacing with pain, trying to rise from her bed.

"You'll have to help me down to the hall. I must see the door for myself. That's the worst of giving anyone a key. I shall never do it again."

"But I locked it quite securely," Hester insisted.

"I must see for myself."

They made a slow, painful journey downstairs, Hester half-carrying the old lady and almost speechless with fury. The door was locked.

"You see," she said, "you've given yourself all this pain, and me all this trouble, for nothing."

"I can bear the pain, and you are paid to take trouble," said Miss Martineau, calling upon a dignity which she used rarely.

"That's true," Hester admitted. "Come on now, up you go."

The brief exchange of sentences was significant of an understanding of which Sally and Fussy knew nothing.

Next day Miss Martineau insisted upon rising and creeping around the house, hanging heavily upon Hester's arm.

"It's an awful thing to be old," she said solemnly. "For years and years you get up without thinking about it, you enjoy your food without appreciating it, you even wish away time and look forward to the morrow. And what happens to you? Every day is bringing you nearer to the time when you have to be pried out of your bed, every movement is an effort, and even to think is

172

a burden. And then you die." A slow tear squeezed itself from her eye and travelled along a furrow in her cheek. A pang of pity for her made its way through Hester's heart, but hard after it came a feeling of panic and impatience. This old woman, in her sorry summing-up of life's brevity, was right. Time slid away unnoticed. It was going by at this moment, now, as she moved at a snail's pace through this horrible, empty, dead house. This was her life, and it was being wasted. Longing for something unnamed, unnameable, rose in her mouth like a flavour. Longing for movement, colour, excitement: and under that a deeper longing for the pleasures to which Sam had initiated her. She did not long for him exactly; he was gone, sunk away, lost. But for some man, some man to whom it would matter that she was young and ardent, her body slim and supple, her hair yellow. Her full mouth tightened and her narrow jaw set hard. She had been crazy to stay here so long. Just because she was frightened of being friendless and penniless and out of work. Because she had no ready-made ties she had tied herself. Life welled in her, making her breath unsteady. There was all the world for her seeing, seas and ships and coloured countries, and here she was, a prisoner. But it should not be for long. She would escape.

"I shouldn't talk like that to you. You are young. You have all your life before you," said Miss Martineau, brushing her cuff across her chin. And Hester realised that she had done all that thinking in the time that it had taken a tear to roll down the old lady's face.

"I don't mind," she said, taking a firmer grip of the old bent body. "Where do you want to go?"

"To the fire."

She stayed up until the evening of that day, but next morning, although she struggled into a sitting position she could not force her feet to the ground. She allowed Hester to lay her back, saying only, but with great bitterness:

"Well, it's come at last. I'm bedridden."

"You'll have to give me the larder key," said Hester, matter-of-factly. "What would you wish me to get out to-day?"

"Please yourself," said the old woman, and Hester realised that she had turned her face to the wall.

In that week there came the evening to which Sally, Fussy and Jim had been looking forward, and for which they had

173

been working. With sacks folded unostentatiously beneath their arms they arrived in the little pony cart and left the animal tethered to the railings at the corner of the house.

Miss Martineau had had her supper and Hester had read to her for an hour before making her as comfortable as possible with a hot brick to her feet, another to her back and the whole of her body wrapped in flannel.

The night was cold and blowy. Hester laid more than the usual ration of sticks and green wood on the fire, hoping that the flare of the dry sticks would help her to read and take some of the dampness out of the wood at the same time. Every now and then a gust of wind went shrieking round the house and sent a gust of acrid smoke down the chimney. It gave her a superficial nervousness. She was conscious of the size and emptiness of the house, of the locked rooms. It needs people, she thought, one old woman and one young one can't fill a house this size sufficiently.

When the knocking sounded hollowly through the house she jumped so that she dropped the book.

It was too dark to be able to see the steps from the window, so she called through the door, "Who is it?"

"Only me. Sally."

"Wait a minute. I'll have to get a key."

"Be quick then, before I'm blown away."

Smiling, glad of the promise of company, Hester began speeding up the stairs, from the top of which came the sound of the reedy voice : "Hester! Come here at once. Who is it?"

"Only Sally . . . you know, Mrs. Fussel," said Hester, bursting into the room. "Can I have the door-key?"

"No," said Miss Martineau flatly. "I have enough to bear without having the house open at this hour of the night. Tell her to go away and come again when I'm better."

"But she's come such a long way, on such a nasty night. Besides, I want to see her. You may be able to manage, never seeing anyone. I can't. Please give me the key. I'll lock the door and bring it straight back to you."

"I don't want it opened. Mrs. Fussel stayed far too long before."

Renewed knocking sounded from below and Hesters' nerves, strained by loneliness and the sound of the melancholy wind, gave way. She walked to the bed and stared straight into Miss Martineau's eyes. "Give me that key," she said. Both her stare

174

and her voice were more menacing than she knew.

"Stand away then."

Hester backed a pace. With difficulty because of her stiffness, the old woman drew her black pocket from under her pillow. Her fingers were slightly unsteady on the strings, but she singled out the key from all the others and handed it over without further protest. Hester flew down the stairs, two at a time, slithered across the hall and threw open the door. Sally, Fussy and Jim filed in.

"Don't speak. She's edgy to-night and didn't want even Sally to come in," Hester whispered. "Go into the kitchen. I'll just take this back."

The thought that she had taken advantage of the old creature's helplessness made her stay for a moment and ask sweetly if there was anything else she could do.

"Nothing, child. But you did lock the door again? That's all right then. I'm sorry to be so difficult about your friends, but helplessness makes one nervous."

"I know. I'm nervous myself to-night. It's the wind. I won't stay down long. Are you quite comfortable?"

"As comfortable as I shall ever be. All right. Get along down and make the most of your company."

They exchanged smiles as Hester turned away.

Downstairs the three had removed their outer clothing and Sally was laying out the usual repast.

"I've got something to eat to-night," said Hester happily. "Miss Martineau is in bed again and she said please myself about taking out stores, so I took the plumpest piece of ham and boiled it."

She lifted the covered dish from the dresser, pleased to be able to contribute, and laid it beside the pork pie and the pickles which Sally had taken from the basket.

"Now the bottles," said Sally, looking round sharply. Jim Fussy produced them from their pockets.

"You remember Jim, don't you?"

"Of course," said Hester, forgetting that she had thought Jim mean, dirty and ugly."

The pork pie, the pickles and the ham went round. The bottles followed. Hester's dried wood caught fire and blazed with a merry crackle, very different from its usual hissing smoulder. The temperature of the room rose. A slight flush warmed the clear pallor of Hester's cheeks, her eyes sparkled

175

and one curl fell forward between her eyes. She looked quite a young Bacchante. Both Jim and Fussy paid her compliments in looks and words, until Sally turned sulky. There was a great deal of talk about the wonderful time that would be theirs "when this job is finished."

"Do you mean when I have finished here?" asked Hester at last.

"Emit ot emoc otni the nepo?" asked Fussy, turning from Hester and shooting the question rapidly at the others.

"Another drink first," said Jim, leaning over and draining the bottle above Hester's cup.

"What is that talk?" asked Hester over the brim.

"When you've got that down, we'll tell you," said Sally.

Hester emptied the cup and set it down with a flourish.

"All gone," she said rather foolishly, "now tell me."

With one concerted movement the three drew in their chairs. All the brightness and animation went out of their faces, leaving only a tense concentration. Like wolves, thought Hester, looking from one face to another and startled by the resemblance between them.

"Well now," said Fussy, "you're a clever girl, Hester. What do you imagine that we put you in here for? To get a foothold in the house, of course. You just nip upstairs and get the old girl's keys and we'll have the house cleared in an hour and get away without anyone being the wiser. You too. I suppose you haven't managed to worm out her real secret, where she keeps her money, but if you get the keys we'll soon find it. I'll make that my job. I got a nose like a hound. The rest of you can open up the rooms and take anything that looks valuable and saleable. Hester's game, ain't you, duckie?"

"You mean to rob Miss Martineau?" asked Hester, trying to keep her voice non-committal.

"That's the notion. I knew you'd get it. Look sharp now. The sooner it's done, the sooner we'll be away."

The haze of alcohol and good fellowship cleared from Hester's brain. She knew exactly what she must do.

"Keys first, eh?" she said, pushing back her chair.

"That's the style."

She held her chin because it was inclined to tremble.

"It may take me some moments. She hates parting with them, and I'll get them peaceably if I can. So be a little patient."

She walked as far as the curve in the passage and then, lifting her skirts, fled up the rest of it, through the door into the hall, swung on the newel post to change direction without stopping and raced up the stairs.

Miss Martineau, propped up on her pillow, looked at her with approbation.

"Good girl, you haven't been long," she said, and began fumbling for the pocket under the pillows.

"Is there a key to this door?" demanded Hester.

"Of course there is. There are keys to all the doors. What are you so excited about, Hester?"

"I can't tell you. Just give me the key to this door. I must lock it at once."

If the door could be locked on the inside it would be some time before they could break it down, and in that saving interval she could break a window and by shrieking out of it, attract the attention of neighbours, or maybe the watch. But Miss Martineau could not understand that. She was convinced that Hester meant to lock her into her room in order that she and Sally might loot the house at their leisure. She thrust the pocket back into its hiding-place and stared at Hester with a glance in which terror, defiance and cunning were oddly mingled.

"Oh,' cried Hester, "please, please give me the key. I can save you if you'll just trust me." Her voice broke on a sob. "You *bloody* old fool. The house is full of thieves, I tell you! I've got to lock us in."

Still Miss Martineau did not move. Hester shot forward, took the corner of the pillow in her hand and tugged. Twisting around, Miss Martineau brought her hand into view. Her gnarled old fingers were clenched around the muzzle of a heavy old pistol. She had drawn it from under her pillow. Not stopping to right her grasp she brought the butt down with surprising force upon Hester's fingers, just as her hand touched the drawstring of the pocket. A sharp arrow of pain shot through her hand and she drew back instinctively, cherishing her broken finger and turning livid with rage. She forced herself to calm, intending to speak clearly, earnestly, convincingly, as to a child —and then, looking up, she saw Fussy and Jim, with Sally behind them, filling the doorway and knew that the last chance had passed.

"I told you," she shrieked.

Miss Martineau, surprisingly calm now that the moment which she had dreaded so long had actually arrived, steadied herself with one hand against the post of the bed, and levelled the pistol at the door.

"I shall fire," she said, "if either of you takes a step."

"Fire away," said Jim. He stood quite still in the doorway, but Fussy dropped to his knees and crawled rapidly across the floor, shielded from Miss Martineau's fire by the footboard of the bed. Hester saw him. Miss Martineau did not. To her dim old sight there were as many figures in the doorway as before, and her eyes were fixed upon Jim. Hester remembered that Miss Martineau's physical movements were limited. Even if she saw Fussy she could not get into an angle to aim at him.

"Give *me* the pistol," she shrieked.

Without moving her eyes, Miss Martineau said, "Stand away from me."

Fussy had reached the foot of the bed. He rounded it and stood up. Hester screamed again, seized the little bedside lamp that stood on Miss Martineau's table, and hurled it straight at him. The lamp smashed and the flames seized the counterpane, shot up, laid bright hands on the hangings and spread aloft with triumphant cracklings. The room was far brighter than it ever was by day. Hester saw Fussy lean over and snatch the pistol from Miss Martineau's hand.

There was no weapon now but the table. She lifted it into the air, its three feet radiating, a deadly weapon to one who had the strength to wield it properly, but too heavy for her. Before she could strike a blow with it Sally, creeping into the room after the men, had snatched the poker from the grate, and coming behind Hester, dealt her, with extreme satisfaction, a mighty blow across the back of the head. Hester fell forward and lay still.

Ripping strips from the sheet Fussy bound Miss Martineau's hands and feet, pressing a pillow firmly on her face. Then he lifted the key-bag. He glanced towards the window. The heavy curtains hung over it. The flames would not have been seen from the street.

By the light of the burning hangings he emptied the keys into his palm. One dropped close to Hester's head, but its fall was muffled by the blanket that lay there heaped where he had thrown it and he did not notice it.

"God rot it," he cried, "there's a dozen or more and nothing to tell t'other from which. Blast that little rat, she could have helped us. Now we'll have to try every lock in the place."

They ransacked the bedroom first, finding nothing and choking in the smoke-laden air. The posts and curtains were still smouldering; now and then a bit of burning material would fall, kindling a new patch of fire where it fell.

"Let it burn," said Jim, savage with disappointment that the room yielded nothing of value. "Come on, let's try elsewhere."

They scuttled out of the room, unlocking, bursting open, leaving destruction in their wake until the house looked as though a tornado had been through it.

A piece of flaming tinder from the bed-head dropped within an inch of Hester's hand as it lay palm upwards on the floor. It caught the carpet and burned brightly in a widening circle. The heat reached her fingers, and at the fiery touch she stirred and groaned. She opened her eyes and lay for a moment trying to remember. Darkness shot with flame; terrible pain in her head. Was she ill or dreaming? Then memory of the night's doings flooded back upon her. Raising herself on her elbows she turned over and was violently sick, and as she writhed there, retching, there rose, level with her eyes, and seemingly enormous from that angle, a mountain-range of white blanket with a key tucked into one of its valleys. She waited until the wave of nausea receded and then stretched out one shaking hand. It was one of the only three keys she had even been allowed to handle. It was the front-door key. Even the effort to recognise it made her dizzy and sick again. She closed her eyes and let everything spin on a terrible wheel. But some shred of consciousness clung on with the tenacity of all weak things. The front-door key. They couldn't get out without it. Even if anyone saw anything suspicious about the house—and there was no reason that Hester could see why anyone should—the thieves would have time to break out by that nailed garden door before the stout front entrance could be forced.

Front-door key! You've got to get down and open that door and scream until somebody hears you, said Hester's shred of consciousness. I can't, complained her body, I'm hurt.

What is more, persisted the relentless mind, you've got to get Miss Martineau off the bed before she's burned to death, and the curtains drawn back so that somebody may see the light, even if you never manage to reach the door.

Obediently Hester struggled to her feet. Miss Martineau lay where Fussy had thrown her. The fire was mainly on the other side of the bed and the blanket and mattress was burning less rapidly than the hangings. Hester heaved the light body to the floor and dragged it over the carpet towards the door. She paused to be sick again. Now the curtains. One after another, with several weak tugs, she drew them apart. Then, taking the key in her uninjured hand, she set out for the stairs. Reeling and staggering, she felt her way along the passage through the darkness. Sally and her companions had finished with the upper floor. By the door of the Chinese room Hester's toe caught one of the little jade figures from the cabinet and her other foot trod upon one of the panels of the story of Ti-Lung. Halfway down the stairs she paused, listening. They were in the hall.

"One big key left and three small ones," said Fussy's voice. "And that's this door." There was a screech of an unoiled hinge as the left-hand door of the three that stood together in the wall below the stairs swung open.

"A cellar," said Jim. "I'll bet this is the place." They tumbled down, one after another, and Hester, gathering her last dregs of vigour, crossed the hall, slipped back the bolts, turned the key and was out on the steps screaming:

"Thieves! Fire! Help!" repeating the words and punctuating them with piercing screams. A light came bobbing down the road. She screamed towards it. A window went up. She lifted her head and cried in that direction. Then the step on which she was standing began to sink away. It had caved in, she thought wildly, but she might be able to catch the railings and save herself from the depths. But the railings had gone. With one last despairing cry she threw up her hands and let the gulf receive her.

Part Three

CHAPTER I

THE *Worcester* was slipping away down the river with the ebbing tide. On either bank the flat stretches of rough pasture lay numb beneath the rime frost. Through the thin drifting veils of cold mist the sun's face showed, broad and red but devoid of warmth or the promise of cheer.

The vessel moved through the typical English November morning furtively, as though ashamed. A lover of ships would have understood. For the disgrace of age and infirmity was upon the *Worcester*. Once she had been part of the wooden walls of England; once she had hunted down her quarry, been stripped for battle, sent her challenging shot across her enemy's bows. Once, through eddying billows of smoke and flashes of threatening flame, she had sought and found honour. In those forgotten days she had been painted and gilded, proudly and adequately manned, her canvas whole and clean, her ropes taut and new. Now, battered and dingy, her paint faded and blistered, her patched sails dirty and her metal work tarnished, she stole through the cold mists with her load of human debris —a transport ship.

Here and there within the bounds of her creaking timbers there were those who, by virtue of youth, or undaunted optimism or fortitude might still wrest something from life; but the greater portion of the *Worcester's* living cargo was destined to misery and despair, just as the old ship was destined, after another perilous journey or two, to join the hulks in the river. And just as the Navy had discarded the *Worcester*, giving her over to this sorry business, the country of their birth had discarded her passengers—useless, troublesome rubbish. Let them be taken elsewhere.

But at least they were alive. That thought came to Hester as she sat on the bare planks of the 'tween deck and endeavoured, by clasping her knees to her chest and wrapping her arms about them, to preserve a little warmth in her body. It was better, inestimably better to be here, suffering present discomfort, bound for some destination unknown and faced with an uncertain future, than to be with Sally, Fussy and Jim, whose mutilated remains, preserved in tar, were still hanging in chains for the discouragement of anyone else in whom house-breaking propensities might arise.

She had escaped their fate so narrowly that the thought of it could still bring out the cold sweat on her forehead and send icy arrows through her vitals. She remembered, with a hunch of her shoulder and a curl of her lip for the essential injustice of things, how Miss Martineau, who owed her her life and the preservation of her property, had done her best to hang her. Hester, she said, had let in the thieves against her express wishes. Hester had demanded the keys. Hester had tried to take her pistol from her.

The old lady's worst dread had been realised; the thing against which she had guarded all her life had happened; her worst nightmare had been exceeded and she was bent on wholesale vengeance, blind to the truth and incapable of mercy. She had suffered little actual loss because, thanks to Hester, Sally and her companions had hardly succeeded in opening the strong-box in the cellar before they were apprehended; but the house had been desecrated, a plot of long standing had been revealed, and in Miss Martineau's eyes Hester was as guilty as Fussy. She spoke of the girl with damning venom.

But forces more potent than an old woman's ill-considered spite were at work. The judge was in good humour. The gout which had been troubling him for a fortnight had suddenly eased. In the miraculous respite from pain he was in a mood to consider Hester's youth, a thing which he would have ignored on any day during the previous maddening fourteen. With equally unwonted humanity he took into consideration that it was Hester who had given the alarm, and also, since the old lady had not burned in her bed, dragged her clear of it.

These facts, though they mitigated, upon this painless day, her crime, did not excuse it. She had allowed herself to be made the tool of ill-doers. London was full of bad characters, too few of whom were ever caught. Those who were must be punished with ferocity in order that others might be deterred from their evil courses. Sally, Fussy, and Jim were to be hanged, disembowelled, tarred and left to swing in chains. Hester was sentenced to transportation.

A good deal of the hasty trial was blurred in Hester's memory, because the blow on the head which Sally had dealt her had resulted in some slight derangement of the brain. Now and then a veil seemed to come between her and the world and then she could neither hear nor see distinctly. At such moments her speech was hesitant and slurred, so that the judge, surreptitiously moving his afflicted foot beneath his gown and finding no familiar twinge resulting, was inclined to regard her as a feeble-minded creature who would almost certainly get into trouble again. But not, thank God, in England. Pass on to the next case.

So Hester sat huddled in the cramped convicts' quarters of the *Worcester* as the smooth ebb-tide gave way to the choppy waters of the open sea and the shrouded land fell away on either side; and the captain came slowly and reluctantly out of the coma induced by his overnight potations and realised with much bitterness that here he was, committed once again to coaxing this leaky old tug across the Atlantic, with a cargo of taxed tea and manufactured goods in the hold and a hundred transported convicts between decks. A fine job for an officer who had worn the king's uniform! He reflected, as he knuckled his red and swollen eyelids, that the damned ship might sink without causing any regret to anyone except the shippers of the tea. A derelict ship, a disgraced officer, a mass of human wreckage, and some taxed tea about which the colonists who must buy it or go without were perpetually complaining. What a choice burden to commit to the tender mercies of the sea!

But the captain was a sailor as well as a cynic, so he set about doing what was necessary to convey each portion of his cargo safely to its destination, even though it might be unwelcome there. And once the familiar problems had arisen, the difficulty of keeping the convicts healthy in their close quarters and on their scanty diet, the possibility of preventing the men from co-habiting with the women, the outbreak of goal fever—one case of which had been allowed to come aboard—and the delivery of one woman convict of a wailing, ailing baby, he forgot his past glory and present disgrace and showed himself a man of resource and courage. So after a long and tedious voyage the taxed tea reached the teapots of the American housewives who grumbled at its price over the steaming cups, and the convicts came to the sugar islands where their labour, if not their presence, was welcomed, and many of the women found that fate was, after all, not so unkind as it had seemed. For white women were rare enough, especially amongst the poorer sort, and many men were willing to marry them and forget the past. Hester, with some remnant of beauty clinging to her, despite her dirt and pallor, would have found a ready market enough but for an unusual situation that had occurred upon one of the largest and most prosperous plantations in Bartuma.

CHAPTER II

WHEN the *Worcester* was still three days out from the island, old Mrs. Markham of Watershead was entertaining Mr. Alfred Kyne, the lawyer from St. Agnes, to dinner. They were friends of such long standing that they had both almost forgotten the days when the feelings between them had been far warmer than friendship. Alfred Kyne had forgotten the rage and frenzy with which he had heard her old father's dictum, "My daughter shall never marry a beggarly attorney." Constance Markham had outlived the despair and hysteria with which she had begged her father to let affection prevail over sordid financial considerations. The stern old man had hardly noticed the opposition. Constance had, in the obedient manner of her day, married the man whom her father had chosen, made him a diligent and faithful wife, developed from a meek maiden into a household tyrant, survived her husband, brought up her sons and lived to be able to regard Alfred as a good friend and an able man of business.

Alfred had never married, though now he would have ascribed his celibacy to his errant taste rather than to disappointment. He had long since ceased to deserve the epithet "beggarly". Hard work, an elastic conscience, phenomenal luck in speculation, and an uncanny facility for knowing just a moment

184

sooner than anyone else which way the cat was going to jump, had enriched him beyond even his youthful ambitions. In St. Agnes, where he had set up as a poor attorney, his name was now mentioned with respect and a degree of awe. His finger was in almost every pie, testing its temperature, drawing out the finest plum and frequently leaving the less desirable portions to burn the fingers of the less shrewd.

If he ever reflected that wealth had come to him too late, and that his bought loves soon palled, no sign of such uncomfortable thoughts was allowed to mar the rubicund serenity of his face. Nor did it bear, on its pleasant pink surfaces and in its amiable curves, any trace of the guile and callousness for which he was well known. People meeting Alfred Kyne for the first time were always impressed by his benevolent, placid appearance and mild, courtly manners.

Constance Markham was one of the few people whom he had never deceived. There had been troublous times between the death of her husband and the coming of age of her surviving son, and she had always depended upon him for advice and help. But, since the days of love were long past and sentiment never very strong in her, she had always walked warily with him, ready to question and to explain, ready to show displeasure if necessary. She need not have troubled. Sentimental he was not, nor generous, nor weak, but his victims were always chosen with discretion and never, even in her earliest, most infatuated days, had Constance shown any promise of being anyone's easy victim. She would have run away with him forty years before if she had been credulous or easily persuaded.

So now they sat together, elderly people with the greater part of their lives behind them, their minds seasoned with experience, their bodies replete with good food and softened by comfortable living, and they discussed the trivial gossip of the neighbourhood, the current political problems, and the price of sugar.

But presently the old lady leaned forward and a confidential note came into her voice.

"I've just remembered something I wanted to ask you, Alfred. It's quite important, too. I suppose you don't happen to know of a decent white girl who would be glad of a good home and an easy place? I know it sounds silly, but Philippa has taken a fancy for a white girl. She never did take very kindly to the negroes—and in her present condition you know . . . I thought you might be able to help me."

Alfred sipped his wine appreciately and wiped his lips with care before he answered.

"My dear Constance, you might as well ask me if I know where there's a pearl necklace for sale for sixpence."

Mrs. Markham was not discouraged. "What happened to the three Claughton girls?" she asked with a shrewd glance.

"Ah, now I see what you're after." He acknowledged the shrewdness with a smile. Claughton, a never very prosperous storekeeper in the town, had recently been ruined, largely through Mr. Kyne's handling of a mortgage.

"Agatha, the eldest, went to Fairmount to teach the child; but it seems that young Easton was more in need of tuition, and unless his parents do something very desperate quite soon, there'll be wedding bells in the schoolroom. Betsy, the plain one, went with her father to Charleston. And Mary, well, to tell the truth, Mary is at the moment keeping house for me." His mild blue eyes challenged her comment.

"I *see*," she said with habitual sharpness, instantly regretted. And she did see why Alfred had been at the store so often, why he had troubled to arrange the mortgage, and why the unnamed client had been so unexpectedly forced to foreclose. Mary Claughton had always been the prettiest of the three.

She softened her voice and leaned farther forward.

"You could spare her, Alfred, couldn't you? To *me*. Just for the next four or five months. I know its a great favour to ask, but after all I would do as much for you. You have no idea how tiresome Philippa is. Ambrose went up to St. Pierre and persuaded Tabitha Slater to part with Poppy. You remember Tabitha's Rosetta don't you? Lovely coffee-coloured thing. Poppy is her daughter, and must have had a white father, she's really hardly tinged at all. We were *delighted*. It was marvellously good of Tabitha, because Rosetta sulked for days and had to be whipped, a thing that had never been known before. But Philappa didn't seem a bit appreciative. I've reasoned with her, even scolded. But after all I have my grandson to consider."

"Otherwise her whims wouldn't weigh with you?"

"Not a featherweight. So you will let me have Mary Claughton, won't you, Alfred? I'd take as much care of her as I would of my own daughter."

"I don't doubt it," he said, and paused, looking steadily at his hostess across the candle-lighted, flower-decked table. Constance, for whom at one time he would gladly have died. She had worn a dress of white Indian muslin, cut low on the shoulders and bound round her tiny waist with a blue sash. Her curls had been so smooth and flaxen and shiny, her eyes so wide and innocent. Every time she had looked at him his heart had turned over in his breast, and when once, forbidden but greatly daring, he had kissed her, merciful God! what desires had not leaped, what fires not burned.

He could remember. But he knew that no trace of the young man he had been, no vestige or ghost of the girl, remained. He was now a man whose days for pleasure were numbered; she was a woman who was trying to deprive him "for four or five months" of the company of Mary Claughton, who, revelling in sudden luxury was disposed to adore the man who had ruined her father. Four or five months might mean little to a woman who had sixty years behind her. To a man of that age they were of almost deadly importance. He did not dismiss as inconsequent a vision of a little smooth brown mole that decorated the plump white shoulder of Mary Claughton.

"I'm sorry, Constance, but it's out of the question," he said firmly. "For one thing I can't spare the girl; for another I doubt whether she would appreciate being shuffled about from hand to hand; and lastly I don't think you would get on with her. She is domineering and independent. In the kitchen that doesn't matter; in your daughter-in-law's apartment it would."

"In the kitchen!" Constance Markham rapped out the words with scorn. "You can't deceive me, Alfred Kyne, so don't waste your breath trying. For the last twenty years your housekeepers have all been young and pretty and complaisant. Yes, complaisant, God help them. Where's Sylvia Biggen and Caroline What-was-her-name? Or that little French thing, Jeannie?"

"All happily married," answered Alfred comfortably. "It's a way my housekeepers have. Mary will probably marry young Rolfe, who is a likely lad, articled to me. You have to remember that a young white woman is a comparatively rare commodity, especially among the poorer sort. Planters, we know, do beget daughters, but they're deucedly particular that they shouldn't marry beneath them." The quiet voice might or might not have held a jibe. If it did the listener was oblivious to it.

"That's why," he continued, "there are two sides to this very vexed question of transportation. Admittedly some of the women are bad, make bad wives and bad citizens and are bad stock to breed from. But most of them, in my experience, have been transported because they have, in the face of considerable difficulty, endeavoured to keep themselves alive by methods involving dishonesty. With the necessity removed they are often as good as the next. I for one see nothing degrading or horrible in a man taking one, not as an apprentice but as a wife."

"You're so used to pleading causes, Alfred," said the old woman with a wave of the hand. "The fact remains that they are thieves, murderers and prostitutes. If England is so anxious to get rid of them she should either hang them or send them to a desert island where they wouldn't be a nuisance to other folk."

"Could you name, offhand, any transportee who had been a nuisance to you, Constance?" It was a rhetorical question, and he was not prepared for the dull, difficult blush of old age that stained the wrinkled parchment cheek of the woman who forced herself to look him in the eyes and shake her head. He hurried on. "All theft, many murders and much prostitution are due to necessity," he said piously, disregarding the fact that many of his own activities, down through the years, had helped to drive a number of women to one or another of these courses. How, for instance, would an impartial observer sum up Mary Claughton's position? "Look here, failing all else, let me see whether I can't get hold of a decent little convict girl for you. The system has its advantages you know. Bound for a term of years; complete control and practically no wages. And believe me, I can tell by looking at a girl, just what she's like."

"I don't doubt it. My copybook used to tell me that practice made perfect. I never questioned its truth. But even with your skilled recommendation I should hesitate to take one into my home. I think I would rather wait and see whether there isn't another Mary Claughton somewhere who has failed to find a . . . protector." There was just a suggestion of a pause before the final word. It left Alfred Kyne quite unmoved.

"There are more protectors than Marys, I'm afraid you'll find. Still, I'll wish you good hunting. So you're to be a grandmother."

"And about time, too. When you think that I had four sons and that there were seventeen years between Edward and Ambrose. I ought to have been a grandmother fifteen times. Tabitha Slater is."

"Yes. She has probably passed the stage where she would

188

consider her daughter-in-law's whims."

"Tabitha is probably less able to afford to humour her dependants than I am," said Constance coldly.

"And that, like most of your statements, is more true than kind. But the question of expense would hardly arise of you did as I advised. I think, if the English Government should at any time in the near future decide to honour St. Agnes with a load of moral castaways I will take a look at them. You shall have the first offer of my findings; and if you don't like her I shall have very little difficulty in disposing of her to a good home. That, I believe is one of the essentials, a good home, honest work and a chance of moral re-establishment. The English never in any circumstances fail to use pleasant words."

"Well, please yourself, Alfred. But if I am suited, or don't like the girl, or Philippa objects, she'll remain on your hands. And if she murders Mary and then poisons you, don't blame me."

CHAPTER III

THREE days later, out of the twenty-five women survivors of the *Worcester*, Alfred unhesitatingly picked Hester, and having complied with the simple and rather farcical formalities with which the Government satisfied its unclamorous conscience, took her off to his home on South Street, virtually as much his property as the black Minna who toiled in his kitchen.

Thoroughly cleaned, comprehensively fed and wearing one of Mary's discarded store dresses, Hester presented a very different picture from the soiled and tattered waif whose youth and bright hair had drawn the connoisseur's attention. For a moment or two Alfred toyed with the idea of keeping her for himself. Maturer thought deterred him. It was unlikely that Hester and Mary would get on together, and he had not yet exhausted all the latter's possibilities. Also there was a brooding and sulky look upon the younger girl's face which did not entirely concur with his idea of feminine charm. About five months, Constance had said. Now after five months in an easy

189

job (for which she would have him to thank) and five months' good feeding, she would probably look more pleasant, and certainly more buxom. By that time, too, Mary would be a known book. It all worked together very well. He sat down to write a note to Constance Markham, offering her the services of Hester Roon, a comely girl of eighteen years of age, of some education, domesticated, and as far as he could ascertain, transported for the venial offence of keeping bad company. A prompt reply, he added, was desirable, since a number of people clamoured for her services. Garçon, Mr. Kyne's French-trained negro, was dispatched upon mule-back to carry the note to Watershead.

It arrived most opportunely. Poppy had carried her mistress the morning tea. Philippa, languid against the frilled pillows, had become suddenly and sickeningly aware of the scent of musk, and as Poppy bent to set the tray on the table by the bedside the source of the scent became obvious. The little coloured girl had been sleeking her kinky black hair with oil. Each curl shone with it, the scalp almost dripped, Philippa's early morning nausea smote her. She was suddenly and violently sick. Recovering, she smacked Poppy's ministering, coffee-coloured hands, screamed, threw her slippers, one after the other at the girl's head, knocked over the table, tea and all, and then flung herself back in the bed and gave way to hysteria.

Constance, roused from the enjoyment of her own tea by the hubbub, thrust on her slippers, seized her gown and bore down on the scene of trouble. Poppy, huddled in one corner, was mopping away her tears and the blood that flowed from her nose, where the slipper heel had caught her, upon her clean white apron. Philappa was screaming, "Go away! Never come near me again, never, never. You stink. You make me sick."

"Now, now," said the elder woman, "what is happening here? No, don't say anything, I can see. Poppy, go down to the kitchen. Now Philippa, my dear, you really mustn't upset yourself like this. You must think of the child."

Philippa, playing up to her audience, cried louder and gasped out some incoherent phrases in which the words musk, pole-cat, ferret and stinking negress was repeated many times.

"Very well. I believe that she stinks. I believe that it makes you sick to have her near you. And she shall never come near you again. Just stop crying, there's a good girl. Look, here is your wrap; come along to my room, out of all this mess, and

190

have a nice rest on my bed while we get this cleared up. Where are your slippers? Oh, I see. That's right. You'll feel quite better very soon."

Her voice was level and soothing; she gentled the moaning Philippa along, and gave no sign of the rage and impatience which bubbled inside her. What on earth, she asked herself, was this generation of young women made of? Of course she was sick! She'd go on being sick probably right up to the day when she had something else to moan about. The old woman thought, with a sudden jerk of memory, of the morning forty years ago, when she and Anthony, her husband, were to set out for St. Pierre, where they were due to repay a visit which the Slaters had made, two months ago, to herself, the bride. The old Slaters had not accompanied the family, for they were too old to travel far, and the others had carried back reports of young Mrs. Markham's prettiness, vivacity and good sense. Invitations to visit St. Pierre had instantly resulted, and since distances were great and travel slow, the young couple were to stay for a week, at least. And on the morning that they were to leave home the bride of three months' standing had risen and been very sick indeed. She already suspected her state, but had no idea that the nausea had any connection with it. She had told no one. She had rubbed some colour into her ghastly cheeks, hoping that Anthony would not notice it, and she had blamed the venison which she had eaten overnight. She was much ashamed of the childish weakness of her stomach. The journey had been agony, the sun striking up from the polished bits on the harness, the landscape whirling past had driven her sick eyes to steady contemplation of her own gloved hands, pressed together and sweating as they lay in her lap. But upon arrival she had given a praiseworthy imitation of the young, pretty, vivacious and sensible Mrs. Markham whom the Slaters expected. And though the next morning, and the next, seven of them in all, had brought a repetition of humiliation and the whole week had proved to be one of nightmare endurance and subterfuge, no one had ever known. Anthony was even a little annoyed with her because she was not much in favour of prolonging the visit for a further week.

"What in the world would Philippa have made of that situation?" Reluctantly, though not for the first time, Constance Markham reflected that her daughter-in-law was a poor tool. She hadn't even the capacity to keep Ambrose happy, though mercifully nobody but his mother guessed at that truth. And I should suffer from that knowledge, she thought, relentlessly, for after all she had been in favour of the match. Philippa was the daughter of an excellent New England family, she was well-bred, well-dowered, and had seemed meek and amenable. To all appearances it was a fortunate choice and she had supported it wholeheartedly. Now she was not so sure.

When she had settled Philippa into her own bed, had fresh tea brought and reiterated the promise that Poppy should never be in a position to offend her again, the old lady dressed herself with care and, crossing the room to her bureau, sat down to pen an urgent note to Alfred Kyne, begging him again to at least loan her Mary Claughton for a while, or failing that, to pursue his inquiries on her behalf. She folded and sealed the letter and started a second in which she was explaining the situation and begging similar help from her friend Lydia Collins, who also lived in St. Agnes in the centre of things, when Alfred's note was brought to her by the still snivelling Poppy. She began to open it while she said, strictly, "Poppy, stop that, you're merely sulking now. Unless you blow your nose and behave yourself, I shall give you something to cry about." Poppy, pampered daughter of the Slaters' famous Rosetta, thought it safe to risk one last dismal snuffle which Constance, concentrating upon the lawyer's cramped, fastidious handwriting, failed to notice.

The note had all the timeliness that distinguished Mr. Kyne's communications. Constance Markham forgot, as she read it, that she objected to women convicts, that one, long ago, had robbed her of something she valued highly, that the presence of a white girl in a servile position in a household of slaves was calculated to cause difficult situations. She simply saw a trim white maid attending upon Philippa, relieving herself of a task that bored and irritated her, and cheering Philippa along the path that would lead to a safe delivery of that precious grandson.

She sat down without further consideration, thriftily tore off the clean half-sheet of Lydia's letter and wrote upon it that she would be pleased and grateful if Alfred could come over on the following afternoon, partake dinner and bring the girl for her inspection.

She decided not to say anything about Hester to Philippa. She must first see herself whether Alfred's susceptibility had not led him to pick some loose-lipped bosomy female who had got into bad company because she was too idle to make an honest living.

In that case she would be obliged to send her packing, and then Philippa would be disappointed.

She went downstairs and along the covered passage, which at once separated and connected the dwelling with the kitchen quarters, and gave orders for Alfred Kyne's favourite dishes to be prepared. "Mr. Ambrose will be returning to-morrow, too," she said, her heart lightening at the thought of her son's return. "So be sure that there's pumpkin pie as well."

Little more than a year had passed since Job Wainwright had conducted Hester along the corridors of The Fleece to the room where he intended to instal her; but the girl who rode, in the cool of the late afternoon, beside Alfred Kyne in his light cane carriage over the rough road between St. Agnes and Watershead was a very different being from the one who had resented the move into the room over the archway because it was wasting her time.

In that year nothing had happened to promote or restore her faith in human nature. Even the momentary meeting with Jonathan Harper, pregnant with possibilities as that had been, had been cancelled out by the manner of the old man's death. The gypsies in the wood had robbed her, Sally had deceived her, Miss Martineau betrayed her. Without fault of her own—unless youth and credulity are culpable things—she had been punished savagely. The weeks upon the transport ship had outraged every fibre of her nature; the filth, the confinement, the compulsory company of women who were in many cases the scourings of the gutters, the gross and vile approaches of the male convicts, the crew, even the guards themselves, had all borne in upon her alert but immature mind the realisation that the world was a horrible place. The law of the jungle was mighty and must prevail : prey or be preyed upon. And Hester, eighteen years old, observant and impressionable, was determined in future to move through the jungle warily. Nobody, she decided, should ever deceive her again; no one should again easily prey upon her.

Small wonder then that Alfred Kyne's questions, his kindlinesses, his little, automatic advances, met alike with discouragement. Direct questions she answered as shortly as possible, trying the while to probe his motive for this interest in her past. She volunteered nothing. For two days she lived in the comfortable house in South Street rather like a stray cat that has come in from the cold. The comfort she accepted, even gloated over, but the outstretched hand, even when actuated by kindness—and Alfred was capable of kindness when his self-interest was not threatened—was met with instant withdrawal, instant suspicion.

When the time came for him to take her to Watershead he was obliged to admit reluctantly that he had failed to breach her defences, even by ordering her a pair of little blue shoes at which the cobbler had worked far into the night. And as they drove along the road to Watershead he had but little doubt that after dinner he would drive back still in Hester's company, for Constance Markham was the last person in the world to be tolerant of awkward behaviour in one who served her. Ah, well, he thought, letting the lash of his whip drift idly across the satiny rump of his carriage horse, in that case he would take the girl to Marie Devine, the milliner on Saints' Square. She was always in need of apprentices because her girls, working in a close and airless room, breathing in the dust of feathers and velvet and hatters' plush, were always being ill and very readily died. Only, he would stipulate that Hester was not to die, or even be ill. Because—he glanced sideways and took in, with an experienced eye, the significance of that beautiful curved mouth —he was certain that something very delectable could be made out of this girl.

Hester's thoughts, as she sat up very straight beside Alfred in his carriage, her palms turned upwards in her lap so that their dampness might not mar the crisp freshness of Mary's discarded gown, were decidedly less pleasant. Before leaving South Street he had explained to her where she was going, that it was likely that she would stay there to be maid to a lady who was not very well and that it was most important that she should make a good impression upon the elder lady who would interview her first. Without meaning to do so the lawyer had conveyed the idea that Constance was rather difficult to please and Philippa a puling invalid, and Hester, out of her inexperience, was expecting another, fiercer Miss Martineau for a mistress and a bedridden nonentity for a charge. It was not a pleasing prospect. But she decided with a shrug of the shoulder that it was just what *would* happen to her. She had gone to London only to be immured, first in Miss Martineau's home, then in prison, then in a Thames'-side hulk. And now, after the long trial of the journey and a glimpse of St. Agnes, she seemed bound for fresh incarceration.

She had, that morning, accompanied a rather suspicious and uncommunicative Mary into the shopping quarter of the town, and had decided, not without reason, that the scene in the market was the most colourful and interesting that had ever met her eyes. The great piles of strangely coloured fruits, the stiff-leaved palm trees with their scanty angular shadows, the white buildings, the striped awnings, the masses of exotic flowers in the gardens of the houses, the thronging people, of every colour from palest white to ebony, the vivid sunshine and the occasional glimpses of the blue waters of the harbour at the town's foot, had satisfied something that had cried out in her eyes ever since those lonely grey days in the attic when she first learned, from her reading, that strange countries existed.

If Mr. Kyne had been with her then he could have breached her defences. He would have noted the parted lips, the alert, observant eye, the quick indrawing of the breath as a more than usually vivid piece of colour-grouping startled her gaze. He would have pointed out and named the various fruits and flowers; explained why so many of the streets bore names corrupted from the Spanish; taken her to drink coffee in the coffee house that was open to the harbour; discoursed upon the differences between mulattos and quadroons. He could have found a way to Hester's guarded but susceptible impressionism. But he was at that moment busy in his office and Hester was out with Mary, who had been suspicious of her from the moment she set eyes upon her. She hurried her along impatiently, pleading that they must be home before the sun grew too hot, rebuking her for showing interest in a street quarrel between two coloured people, saying that ladies did not stare, whisking her from one shop to another, displaying before her the deference which, as the keeper of Mr. Kyne's house and purse, she was able to demand from the tradespeople. Hester had resented the attitude, asked no more questions, forbore even to stare about her openly. But to-morrow, she had promised herself, she would come out alone, she would linger and stare to her heart's content. As for the sun, who minded it? She at least could never have enough of it. She had hungered for it all her life.

And then, at midday, Mr. Kyne had informed her that she was to be banished to what he called a plantation, to mind a sick woman and obey a strict one. St. Agnes, like London, was to be withdrawn from her after one glimpse.

She took the information with her usual stoicism. Pride forbade even the display of disappointment or dismay. She had no means of knowing that she had only to say, "Oh, can't I have a job in St. Agnes?" or even, "Can't I stay here for a while?" and to shoot one of those sudden smiles in the old man's direction and she need never have gone to Watershead at all. Already Alfred Kyne was aware of her possibilities for charm; one moment's display of it could have unseated Mary even then. But Hester, with stony face and heart resolute if not resigned, accepted his verdict and braced herself to face this new turn of the road.

The narrow track, soft with dust and worn down by the wagons that carried the produce of the various plantations to the harbours, was like a reddish river into which the private roads to the plantations flowed like tributaries. Sometimes the houses themselves could be seen through the trees, all as large as Fulsham Hall, back in Norfolk, but lower and more rambling and all accompanied, at greater or lesser distance, by many other buildings, less picturesque, some with tall chimneys sticking up. Hester's invincible curiosity broke down her silence and she asked what they were.

"Crushing-mills and boiling vats. The canes are cut and crushed and then the sugar is boiled until it crystalises," said Alfred, glad to welcome the show of interest. "You'll see the same things at Watershead. Here we are turning into it now."

They left the main road and turned to the left. For a quarter of a mile the track ran between fields, open to the sun, then came a short green tunnel of an avenue and at its end, set in an open space of green grass dotted here and there with trees and flowering shrubs, stood the house, almost identical in shape and size with some they had passed on the road. Its lower windows were shaded by a verandah that ran around it, broken before the front door by a flight of shallow steps, and on the first floor somebody was drawing up the shades that had been let down over the windows during the heat of the afternoon. Mr. Kyne touched his horse with the whip, so that it broke into a sharp trot which enabled him to draw up smartly with a flourish at the foot of the steps. A small yellowish negro boy ran from nowhere and took its head. Mr. Kyne climbed down and turning, offered his hand to Hester.

Unseen watchers had noted the arrival and the door was open before they reached the top of the steps. Hester breathed a sigh

196

of relief. It was a house with a ready-opening door, then, and there seemed to be several people in it. There was somebody upstairs letting up blinds, the boy with the horse, and somebody behind this door. Thank God for that. It wasn't, it couldn't be, as dull as Miss Martineau's house. In her relief she turned to the little man by her side and gave him, for the first time, the full benefit of her smile.

"Scowl at me if I say anything wrong," she said impulsively. And he, ever responsive, took her hand and squeezed it reassuringly. "You'll be all right," he said.

The hall was wide and pleasantly cool and smelt of polish and the perfume of flowering plants that stood about in little three-legged tubs.

"Dis way, Mistah Kyne, sah, if you please," said the negro who had opened the door, and went towards another doorway at the side of the hall.

"Wait here a moment," said the lawyer, and Hester stood alone outside the closed door, conscious of the gaze of the negro, who, after a lengthy stare, turned and disappeared at the back of the stairway. After a moment or two there came from the same direction the creaking of a door, the sound of breathing and the uncontrollable giggle with which children cheer the knowledge of their own wrongdoing. Hester moved sideways until she could see the doorway in the shadow of the stairs' curve, and saw, peering around its edge, three faces, two very black, so black that in the shadow only their eyeballs and teeth betrayed them; the third, lower down as though its owner were ducking under the shoulders of the others, was pale and creamy in colour. As soon as they became aware of her scrutiny they disappeared hurriedly, leaving the door to swing to by its own weight. Hester moved back to the spot where Mr. Kyne had left her.

Meanwhile, within the room, Constance Markham had risen and greeted her old friend very warmly. She had had almost forty-eight hours of dancing attendance upon her daughter-in-law, and though she would not have admitted it at the stake the strain was beginning to tell upon her. She had dismissed all her doubts about the desirability of importing a convict, a poor white girl, a possible thief. She could, she felt, more easily control and overlook even a mildly vicious girl than she could go up and down stairs, carry Philippa her meals, find her embroidery, fetch her book, watch her sick spells and listen to her everlasting complaints. The fear that she might say something irreparable or even strike her son's wife had been growing upon her throughout the long, hot day. She knew her own irascible temper. When the little lawyer entered alone her heart sank. She was surprised at the depths of her own disappointment. He banished it immediately by saying, "I've left her in the hall. I thought I'd have a word with you first." He sat down and proceeded to make the least tactful speech of his life. He almost begged Constance to have tolerance with Hester, to be patient with her apparently difficult temperament.

"I believe the child has had a very hard time, Constance, and she seems disposed to be sullen and suspicious. I think, if I could have kept her a little longer I could have wooed her to a more happy frame of mind, but your note sounded urgent. So treat her gently at first. She has showed signs of coming round already."

To this cynical listener the speech implied that he himself had fallen under the girl's spell and was anxious that she should be as pampered here as she would have been on South Street. Yesterday morning she would have flashed out some sharp remark to this effect and probably bidden Alfred take his new protégée home and do the pampering himself. But this evening she felt weary and very conscious of her age. So she said mildly, "Well, get her in and let me have a look at her." He rose and opened the door.

Between the doorway and the edge of the carpet there was an expanse of polished floorboards, and as she crossed it Hester was conscious of the noise that the soles of her new shoes made upon it, and of the cool, direct scrutiny of the woman who sat in the satin-covered chair with the high back. She came to a standstill two paces over the carpet's edge, and without lowering her eyes made the little dipping curtsey with which Miss Peck had always insisted that her first morning appearance should be greeted by her female pupils.

So they came together, two strong and vital personalities, more alike than either of them knew or would have admitted; took one another's measure and disliked one another on sight.

Hester saw a small, spare woman, rigidly upright, her naturally white hair, needing no powder, elaborately dressed in the high fashion of the day. Against it her skin looked sallow and darkened, scored with deep lines. Her gnarled, powerful-looking hands rested upon the arms of the chair, the fingers half

198

flexed, not quite at rest. Her gown, fashionably made but of sombre colour, a deep puce striped with blackish purple, spread out over the chair, the hip pads occupying its whole width. Outwardly she looked like any ageing woman who is still mindful of her appearance. But her gaze, the cold, calculating stare of those prominent light brown eyes, the close fold of her thin-lipped mouth, the arrogant, fleshless nose and the erect posture of the head were ageless, the outward and visible signs of a person to be reckoned with. Not, decided Hester instantly, because, as she had feared, the woman was old and crotchety, but because she was more vigorous in mind than in body, determined, proud, critical and observant. There was no slightest trace of scorn or disrespect in Hester's spontaneous dislike for her mistress.

Constance Markham, in turn, studied this young female whom chance and her daughter-in-law's whim had thrust upon her. She saw a tall, thin girl, as upright but less rigid than herself, dressed in a simple cotton gown of pale buff colour and so sharply taken in with tucks at the waistline that where they ended the sudden bulkiness gave a tolerable imitation of the fashionable padded panniers. For some obscure feminine reason this convinced Mrs. Markham that Hester was vain and full of ideas above her station. Actually the tucks had been necessary, for Mary Claughton was far stouter than Hester and although Alfred would have been willing to set Hester up with a new dress, or even two, Mary had insisted that her own discarded frocks, relics of the humble days at the failing store, were quite good enough for one who was to be a servant. But Constance Markham was not sufficiently trivially-minded as to judge Hester very far on her clothing. She noted, just as Hester had done, the upright pose of the shoulders, the proud holding of the head, the level look in the eyes. She decided—and she was used to judging character—that the chances were that the girl was honest, but she thought she was probably impertinent too. And she was, of course, undeniably attractive, with that smooth white skin, those tilted, queer-coloured eyes, that mouth and those yellow curls. Just exactly what Alfred might have been expected to pick.

Still, there she was. A white girl to attend upon Philippa. That was really the essential thing, the one to which she must give her mind. Everything else could wait. She stirred very slightly in her chair and said :

199

"Your name is Hester Roon?"

"Yes, madam."

"And you are eighteen?"

"Yes."

"Well, Hester, you are very young and whatever folly or wrongdoing you have fallen into in the past can be amply redeemed in the years that lie ahead. You know that, don't you?"

Hester inclined her head slightly. It was just the kind of talk, pious and yet condescending, that most affronted her sense of dignity and sent a prickly feeling of shame, degradation and resentment down her spine. Across Mrs. Markham's chair she sent a glance at Mr. Kyne. He was staring out of the window, apparently engrossed in something that he could see in the garden. She appreciated his detachment and her heart warmed to him.

"You will find your duties very easy," the crisp, cool voice was saying. "You will chiefly be required to wait upon my daughter-in-law, and I have had a small room next to hers prepared for you. There are, of course, no other white maids and you may find your position rather lonely at first, but if you give your mind to your duties you won't notice that very much. I daresay Mrs. Ambrose will wish you to do certain things that will require your presence in the kitchen, so, as you are fresh to these conditions, I think I should warn you not to gossip with, or admit any familiarity with, the coloured people there. Remember that while you are there you are Mrs. Ambrose's representative—and preserve your dignity." For some reason it flashed through Constance's mind that she need not have said that, and the thought disconcerted her, so that she cut short her admonition and rose and said, "I will take you up now. Say good-bye to Mr. Kyne." Her voice was that of a person addressing a child and Hester's resentment grew. She turned and thrust out her slim hard hand towards the lawyer and said with immense dignity :

"Good-bye, sir. You have been very kind to me, and I thank you for all you have done." He took the hand in one of his and with the other patted the back of it gently.

"Good-bye, Hester, though I shall see you frequently I hope, and hear good reports of you I'm sure. I shall need no other thanks." She gave him that flashing smile again and then turning, followed Constance out of the room, up the stairs, along a wide polished passage and into a room at its end.

Mrs. Markham signed to her to halt just inside the doorway and herself went forward into the room towards the day-bed that was drawn up beneath the further window. The head of the bed, a wide, satin-covered scroll, prevented Hester from seeing the woman who lay upon it, though she could see the top of a dark head with a straight parting.

"Philippa, my dear," said Mrs. Markham in a voice that was now kind and warm—but the other is her natural voice, thought Hester shrewdly—"I've brought you a present, a surprise." As though from incorrigible habit she paused after this announcement, picked up a piece of embroidery, a handkerchief and a book that lay face downwards on the floor, laid book and embroidery on the wide sill of the window and put the handkerchief on the lap of her daughter-in-law. "It's a white girl," she continued. "Her name is Hester and she is going to look after you. I hope you'll like her and be very happy with her."

The young woman on the bed twisted her head and the older woman beckoned to Hester, who crossed the floor and stood beside her.

"It's very kind of you," said the gentle, melancholy voice. "And so exciting. Exciting for me, I mean, and so kind of you to humour my whim. Good afternoon, Hester."

"Well, I'll leave you to get better acquainted. You can tell Hester what you want her to do, and where everything is, can't you? Mr. Kyne is dining with me, so I will return to him. Hester, your room is through there. Always remember to keep it tidy and set a good example."

She crossed the floor, closed the door behind her and made her stately progress down the stairs, thinking : Well, that will at least give Philippa something new to think about besides herself for a day or two. And I shall be able to be far more patient with Philippa when I don't have to attend to her food and her slops and her whims. I think the girl is detestable, but that is probably an unreasonable prejudice which I shall be able to live down, and anyway, it isn't for ever.

CHAPTER IV

PHILIPPA said rather peevishly, "I can't see you without cricking my neck. Come round to the foot of the bed." Hester moved and stood looking gravely down. Philippa Markham, despite her northern birth and upbringing (she came from Boston) had a delicate, hothouse air, accentuated now by her four months' pregnancy. Her skin had the yellowish pallor of ivory, her hair was black and silkily smooth, and her eyes were dark and far too large for her face, especially now that they were surrounded by sepia shadows. Her face was set in lines that might denote chronic suffering or merely pettish ill-humour, but when she had studied Hester for a moment and realised that her mother-in-law had not tried to foist another Poppy upon her, she smiled, and her smile was surprisingly gentle and sweet.

"I'm not really an invalid," she volunteered. "I mean, you won't have to wait on me as though I were bedridden. I'm only going to have a baby." She turned her head away as she said the last words, the smile was extinguished like a candle and there was a sarcastic inflexion upon the "only". People had tried, Hester decided instantly, to wean her from her sloth and self-pity, by saying, "After all you're *only* going to have a baby." The wrong line to take altogether.

"And you don't want to," she said without considering her words, betraying her knowledge of the truth that had eluded Constance Markham for some months.

"What makes you say that?"

"Your voice, and the way you turned your head away."

"You're very sharp. I hope you're not impertinent. Are you?"

"I didn't mean to be."

The great haunted eyes fixed themselves upon Hester's candid ones. Philippa noted the candour, the pity for the weak which showed in them, and missed the scorn with which Hester's pity must inevitably be laced.

"I'm sure you didn't," she said. "And you are quite right. The very thought revolts me. I haven't been able to think of anything else since the moment it began. And nobody understands. If they haven't had one themselves they can't understand. If they have they pretend not to, they have a kind of spite and like seeing other people in the same predicament. And all the time it's like being in a tunnel, a tunnel that gets darker and deeper and that you have to follow to the end." Her gentle melancholy voice took on a wild note and a rigor shook her body. "Of course my husband is delighted, so is my mother-in-law. She doesn't care what happens to me so long as she has a grandson, a real genuine Markham to inherit Watershead. She didn't bring you here for my sake. She knows that black people make me sick, and that is bad for the child. It's the child all the time. They even say—her friends who come to call—'How lovely that Philippa is going to have a baby.' I assure you there is nothing lovely about it."

"I never imagined that there was," said Hester gravely. She thought of the convict woman on the ship. "But afterwards people *are* glad. I saw one born on the ship. There were so many people ill with a kind of fever that the room they called the hospital wasn't any good, so they let the ill ones lie where they were and moved the woman out into the little cabin. And somebody had given the rest of the women some rum, so most of those who weren't ill were too drunk to do anything. Another girl, called Miriam, and an old woman and I had to do it all. She had nothing, that woman, except what help we could give her, but she came through all right. It didn't last long. The ship rolled all the time. And when the baby came we hadn't anything to wrap it in, except what clothes we could spare from our bodies. I had to give it my petticoat. But when it was over and we laid it in her arms she was the happiest woman in the ship. Happier than I can describe. And it was so tiny, so complete and yet so dependent . . . I believe we all wanted it ourselves."

She stopped abruptly, certain now that she had deserved the epithet impertinent again. But Philippa was staring at her with some unfathomable expression in her great dark eyes. Nobody had ever said anything of the kind before. It was permissible for the other women to congratulate her, even to speak of the baby as the heir to Watershead, the continuance of the Markham tradition. But shyness, or their upbringing or some conspiracy of silence, had made them steer clear of essentials. It had remained for Hester, with unconscious wisdom and chance good fortune, to say that it didn't take long, to describe the happiness that would result, not from the triumphant providing of an heir, but of something tiny and dependent. Philippa's easily led mind took a leap away from dread and terror and landed upon the safer ground of the contemplation of the clutch of tiny fingers, the helpless but urgent tug at the breast. Her resentment receded.

"Did it live?" she asked.

"Oh, yes. It wasn't what I should call a very sturdy baby, but then it's mother had been in prison for six months, with not enough to eat, and no air. But it got on. The captain was very good and used to let one or another of us carry it about on the deck in the sun, until it was time for her to feed it again." Again nervous of the reception of all this chatter she stopped but something made her add, kindly, "You'll be all right. You've plenty of fresh air and plenty to eat." She contrasted in her mind the state of Philippa and of the convict woman who had remained in the fœtid, cramped fever den until the moment her pains began.

Philippa hitched herself higher upon her pillows.

"I couldn't eat. That was the trouble. I can't explain. I'm no good at explaining. There's a cook in the kitchen, her name is Delia and the Markhams think the world of her. They don't notice that she smells, a hot animal sort of smell, and she sweats, ugh! how she sweats. I haven't really enjoyed anything that I've eaten here in all these months. I've been here eight months already. But of course one has to eat something, and I used to wait until I was really hungry, then I didn't think of Delia so much. But since I started being sick I've seen her hands, big black hands with pinkish palms, sweating, all over everything I've had. I guess I'd have starved to death if you hadn't come. You will make everything yourself, won't you? Don't deceive me over that. I won't overwork you or bother you, if you'll just look after my food and . . . and make my bed."

"I'm here to do exactly what you tell me to," Hester pointed out.

"Yes, of course. But I want you to be on my side. To do what I want you to, even when I'm not there to see you do it."

"If I say I will, I will. And I promise you that I'll do what you ask me, whether you're ever likely to find out or not. Hadn't I better do something now?"

Philippa pushed herself even higher upon her pillows. She ran a surreptitious tongue over her dry lips.

"I believe I could eat something now. At the far end of the

passage you'll find some more stairs. Go down them and you'll be in another passage. Turn right and you'll find the kitchen. I want a boiled egg, boiled quite hard and some bread and butter and some tea. I expect you're hungry too. Pick anything you like for yourself. Then come back quickly and we'll eat together and you can tell me about London. I've always wanted to go there."

Considerably cheered by her reception and the discovery that Philippa was not a bed-ridden invalid, Hester made her way to the kitchen, where an atmosphere of passive opposition met her. Young Mrs. Markham's prejudice had, after the manner of such things, become common knowledge and was a source of bewilderment and offence. Poppy in particular, was a recipient of much sympathy over the loss of her nice dellikut job.

" 'Tis'n though Ah wus a dirty field hand," Delia had complained, time and again. "Ah washes mahseff as much 'sanybody. Ah's mos' perticular. All mah pans is clean too. Come sniffin down heah from dose farway parts an' wantin' poah white gurls to tend her. Poah white gurls isn' any cleaner. Ahs seen um wid durty faces."

No one had ever seen Delia with a dirty face for the simple reason that she could have heaved coal without making herself any blacker. But she was right in her assertion of cleanliness. Everything in the kitchen was as scrubbed and as scoured as the things in The Fleece kitchen during the reign of Mrs. Bridges. Hester, observant and experienced in kitchen routine, noted this at once and was relieved, though, after her recent experiences she was not disposed to be fastidious. It had been killed, that squeamishness during the first week in goal.

Noting the cleanliness, Hester next became conscious of Delia, black, shiny and impressive, rocking to and fro with a gentle swaying motion in a chair near the window. The indifference upon her features was exaggerated and assumed. She had been quite as eager as Poppy and Margarita to peer round the house door and study the new arrival. Upstairs Philippa was still puzzling over Hester's casual mention of the baby's mother having been in prison, and wondering where Hester had come in contact with such a person. Downstairs every one of the house slaves knew all about Hester, that she had been in prison, that Mr. Kyne had obtained her and given her to Mis' Ambrose as a kind of special slave. Their knowledge was derived from Garçon who had not spent in empty silence his period of waiting for Mrs. Markham to write her reply. So Delia did not move from her chair.

Hester asked a few necessary questions, which received short answers, but she went on collecting the things she needed until, opening the wrong cupboard door by mistake, she turned and saw Delia watching her with the delighted, malicious smile of a mischievous child. She felt herself go cold with fury. She let the cupboard door slam and walked to the middle of the floor. She said, rather loudly and distinctly, for it was hard to believe that a creature so black could understand ordinary conversational English :

"I think it would be better if you *showed* me where things are for once. Then I should know, and there'd be no reason for you to be amused."

Reluctantly Delia arose and together they mustered the essentials for Philippa's simple repast upon a massive silver tray.

"Now I want an egg," said Hester. Delia, swelling with virtue, pointed to the egg that she had already brought from the larder. Hester looked at it. It was a small white egg and the shininess of its surface gave evidence of age.

"Isn't there a fresher one?"

"Dat is a fresh aig."

"I don't think so." (Surely, even in this strange place hens laid eggs as usual, or didn't they? Was she making a fool of herself?) "This isn't for me, you know. It's for Mrs. Markham."

"Yo mean Miss Ambrose. Mis' Markham is settin' down dis minut to her proper dinnah." Delia's voice underlined the comparison heavily.

"Mrs. Ambrose then. So will you get me a better egg? A brown one if there is such a thing."

Delia lumbered back into the larder and returned, bearing a deep blue bowl in which lay several eggs.

"Yo'd best chose your own."

Hester selected a large brown egg with a matt bloom on its shell and dropped it carefully into the water that was already boiling. She looked up at the clock which wagged its pendulum against the whitewashed wall.

"Now I want something for myself," she said. Delia had reseated herself and the wide-bottomed chair was in motion again.

"Yo'd best help yourself. Dere's plenny of food in de larder, but de big brown pie is for Mistah Ambrose, special. Doan go spoilin' de looks ob dat."

Hester hurried into the larder, found a meat pie already cut and carried it into the kitchen. Hurriedly, with another glance at the clock, she found herself knife, fork, and plate, and was ready to snatch the egg from the water as the fifth minute ended and to make the tea. It occurred to her as she struggled back up the stairs with the tray that Delia had actually made and kneaded the bread from which Philippa's dainty slices had been cut; but she decided not to say anything. If Philippa, after the manner of faddists, had overlooked the crucial point it would only be stirring up trouble to remind her of it.

She set her own viands upon the corner of the table that stood by the foot of the real bed and set the tray on the little low one beside Philippa. She poured out one cup of tea, and then, with the pot still poised in her hand, asked, "Did you mean me to eat in here, with you? And am I to have tea as well?" She could remember the preciousness of tea.

"Of course you are to have tea, and anything else you want. And I meant you to eat in here because otherwise you can't talk to me. Ah, this is very nice. I shall enjoy this."

Hester retreated to the other table, drew up a chair and lifted a slice of the pie-crust and the greater portion of the meat and congealed gravy on to her plate. It seemed to her that except on a few isolated occasions, such as Sally's visits and the two days spent in Mr. Kyne's house, she had been hungry ever since leaving The Fleece. Philippa, daintily eating her egg and small mouthfuls of bread and butter, looked at her with some amusement.

"Well," she said at last, "you're not a very entertaining table companion, are you?"

Hester's rare rapid blush raced to the edge of her hair.

"I'm sorry," she said, laying down knife and fork hastily. "I'm very fond of food. And lately I haven't had very much."

The admission reminded Philippa that she knew nothing of Hester's past. Signing to her to continue her food she began to ply her with questions. One thing led to another, and very soon Philippa was hearing the story which had been denied to Mr. Kyne's professional probing. Hester finished the pie, poured out fresh cups of tea and drank her own almost without noticing, so absorbed was she in the outpouring of her story. And Philippa, who had dreamed girlish dreams of the splendour of

London, finely dressed people with courtly manners, the play, Ranelagh, Ascot and Vauxhall Gardens, listened instead to a story of a London that had nothing in common with her fancies. Out came the whole sorry story, not omitting Miss Martineau's final perfidy.

Hester told it well, wasting no words, making Philippa see the things happening, see the strange dead lonely house, the drip of the water down the prison wall, the thirty sea-sick women in the cramped space on the *Worcester*, the wriggling weevils in the convicts' bread.

Philippa, the easily sickened, ate her bread and butter to the last crumb, regardless of the stomach-twisting moments in the story, and wished that she had asked for two eggs instead of one. But she would not disturb the story; she had lost herself far more successfully than she had ever done in the melodramatic novels which Mrs. Elsa Taunton so regularly produced as an antidote for ennui. The afternoon light faded suddenly into the short tropical dusk and still Philippa listened, prompting a fresh outflow by this question and that. Unknowingly she had abandoned her languid pose, let her lacy shawl slip to the floor and was sitting up, clasping her knees in a way that was both youthful and engrossed.

The sudden opening of the door made both heads, yellow and black, turn sharply, stemmed the speech upon Hester's lips and brought Philippa to her feet with a cry.

"Oh, Ambrose, you're back!" She took a few quick paces towards the man who, after closing the door behind him, came to meet her, took both her outstretched hands and stooped his head to kiss her. She seemed inclined to cling to him, but he put her gently away and asked in his deep musical voice:

"Why are you sitting in the dark? Does your head ache?"

"Oh, no, Ambrose. I just forgot the lamps. I forgot *everything*. Look, this is Hester. Your mother found her for me. And she's *white*. And she's had the most exciting life: you'd not believe. She's just been telling me about it."

"I'm afraid your order to look at Hester is ill-timed, my dear. Let me make a light first."

He took a tinderbox from his pocket, kindled it, and moved deliberately about the room, lighting first the candles that stood on either side of the mirror on Philippa's dressing-table and then the two lamps that stood, one on the table near Hester's empty plate, one on the chest-of-drawers at the far end of the room. While the lights flickered and gained brilliance he drew the curtains across the windows, and then, turning and slipping the tinderbox into his pocket, surveyed Hester as she rose to her feet.

For the third time since her arrival at Watershead she endured deliberate scrutiny. But where Constance Markham's cold apprising stare had filled her with resentment, and Philippa's plaintive friendly look had wakened a responsive pity and desire to please, the lordly indifference of Ambrose Markham's glance sent her dizzy with its sudden appeal to her senses.

He was a very handsome man, with a kind of silvery fairness which he had inherited from the flaxen-curled Constance over whom Alfred Kyne had broken his heart. His eyes, of too pale a brown, were redeemed by the thick lashes and smooth brows, and the slight nervous frown between them lent them interest. His nose was like his mother's, thin and arrogant, with beautifully cut nostrils, but his mouth was softer and weaker than hers, more gently turned, and the compression of the lips upon one another combined with the frown to give an impression of a sensitive nature that had known suffering. He was tall and lightly built, and wore his clothes with an elegant air. He was the antithesis of sturdy Sam with his leathery neck and hard hands, the very opposite of Hester's mental picture of all the men whom she had admired in books. No second glance was needed to tell her that here was no resourceful Crusoe, no heroic Anderson, no indomitable predatory Joseph Martineau. Nevertheless, as she stood there under that distant indifferent gaze, her heart began to bound and beat, now in her throat, now in her stomach, and her hands and feet grew large and clumsy, and strange disintegrating processes took place among her features. It was all she could do to keep her eyes steady and refrain from putting her awkward hands behind her and try not to hide the enormous feet by standing one on top of the other.

The ordeal, which seemed to protract itself through eternity, lasted actually less than a moment.

"So you're Hester," he said, "I've been hearing about you downstairs. I hope you'll be happy here. Take away this clutter, will you?" He indicated the forgotten tray that stood by the day-bed, the empty cup, plate and pie-dish which were on the table.

Hurriedly, with uncertain fingers, Hester collected them, balancing the tray upon her out-thrust hip as she opened the door, sidled through it and pulled it to behind her. The passage had been lighted and she found her way easily to the kitchen where Margarita and Poppy, who had been gossiping like magpies until her arrival, fell silent and stared at her across the bowl in which they were washing dishes.

She set down the tray and returned to the upper corridor, uncertain whether to go back into Philippa's room. She could hear from within it the mingling of Ambrose's deep voice with Philippa's light plaintive tones. He had been away, they would have things to say to one another, it would be unwise to disturb them. She went on to the end of the passage, pushed the curtain away and stood staring into the night. There was no moon and the trees were invisible, but the sky was seeded with a million stars. She stood looking up at them, thinking how foolish she had been to pity Philippa because she looked ill, because her voice was plaintive, because she was going to have a baby, because she lived in a house with that strict old woman. There was no need to pity Philippa; she had everything. She was married to Ambrose Markham. It was his baby that she was making all this fuss about. Good God! Pity Philippa, who was this moment behind that closed door with her husband, probably being held in his arms, being kissed by him. You have been here only a few hours and already you've made a stupid credulous fool of yourself again, she told herself fiercely. But she was rebuking the wrong impulse, regretting the wrong reaction. There was much to be learned, much to be endured before she realised that Philippa was pitiable and Ambrose not to be loved.

CHAPTER V

Two days at Watershead seemed far longer than two days in Mr. Kyne's house on South Street; and at the end of them Hester had acquired a status, which though humble, was sure, and was no longer the stray-cat personality that she had been at the end of a similar period in the lawyer's house. She fell into the niche that had already been made for her by Philippa's aversion to coloured people, and she filled it to the fanciful woman's complete satisfaction.

Before the first morning's toilet had been performed Philippa, with the sudden and unaccountable certainty that so frequently—and sometimes disastrously—visits the shallow veering mind, had attached herself to the new maid : just as the frail but tenacious tendrils of a sweet-pea plant will reach for and cling to anything within reach, so Philippa reached for and clung to Hester. Philippa had always been supported. For the length of her stay at Watershead she had longed for and yearned for support. But her mother-in-law, a strong and vital character, had always detached, by some unsympathetic word or action, those groping tendrils, and her husband had strangely eluded them. He had married her, got her with child, he was tolerant of her weakness and patient with her whims, but he was not the unfailing source of strength and vigour for which her nature thirsted. He was too prone to partake of her mood, or to run away from it. He had too many interests elsewhere. And, although Philippa, being unanalytical, never reached this simple conclusion, he had too wide a streak of feminity in his own make-up, ever to satisfy so feminine a creature as herself.

But Hester . . . Ah, from the moment that Hester had looked down upon her and said in that deep, slightly rough-edged voice, "And you don't want to," and again, "It didn't last long," Philippa's invisible tendrils had begun to quiver. Here was somebody sure and strong, vital and young, sympathetic without being maudlin, bound to her service and anxious to please her. The pale weak stream of the pampered woman's personality ran into the deep dark one of the girl who had stood alone in so many strange situations and was absorbed with hardly a ripple to show the merging.

Philippa had hardly been ensconced upon the day-bed beside the open window before Hester shattered her peace by demanding, "Do you lie there all day?"

"Practically. Sometimes I go down for dinner, but often I don't feel well enough. And I feel such a sight."

"Well, it's very bad for you, and very wrong and you'll probably feel worse and worse. Where I come from the country women bake and brew, and even work in the fields right up to the last minute, and they have their babies as easily as *that*." She snapped her fingers.

"But I'm not a country woman," protested Philippa, but

211

quite without resentment. "And walking makes my back ache terribly."

Hester looked out of the window. Outside there was a whole new world to be explored; and once again, as in The Fleece kitchen and Miss Martineau's sealed house the prison portals yawned. From now to bedtime to spend, mewed in this room with Philippa. Not without a struggle!

"All the same I think you should try. We wouldn't go far; we'd walk very slowly, and you could lean on my arm."

Philippa put her feet to the ground.

Fifteen minutes later, Constance Markham busy with the household accounts, lifted her eyes and looked out of the window as she made a calculation in her head. She was startled to see her daughter-in-law, to whom she had repeatedly and vainly suggested that a walk would do her no harm, walking in quite a determined manner at the far end of the garden. True her hand lay on the arm of the convict girl, but she seemed to be walking easily and lightly. And the convict girl was wearing one of the prettiest of Philippa's shady hats, a wide leghorn tied beneath the chin with a rose-coloured ribbon that matched the flower upon its drooping brim.

"Remarkable," said the old lady aloud, and put down her pen and went to stand by the window the better to watch their progress. A clump of feathery palms hid them and then they came into view. Hester had crossed the sunken ditch that divided the garden from the track and was handing Philippa across it. Philippa, safely over, pointed down to her shoe and said something. The two girls began to laugh, clinging together.

"Well, thank God for that," said Constance Markham, and wrote down, without hesitation, the answer to the sum that she had been wrestling with even as she watched.

Philippa had once made a formal visit to the working parts of the estate. Ambrose had imagined, wrongly, that there might be sights of interest to a girl brought up in Boston. But Philippa, then a bride of a few weeks, had been neither interested nor informed by the little tour. For one thing she was riding an unfamiliar horse and secretly pining for the old mare of her Boston days, which had seemed too old to survive the journey and the change of climate and so had been left behind. For another, she was still brooding upon the shattering revelation

212

that marriage had meant for her. And most diverting of all, she had been so intensely in love with Ambrose that she had listened to the voice rather than to what it was saying. So on this morning she was quite unable to answer any of the multitudinous questions that Hester asked. She said feebly, "I don't know." Or, "Ambrose did tell me, but I forget." Or, "Remind me to ask my husband." A final denial of knowledge caused Hester to say flatly:

"But you should. It's a little world on its own. If it were ever going to belong to me I should want to know how it worked."

Poor old Miss Peck, growing blinder and more captious every day, would have rejoiced in this attitude, for had she not always insisted that curiosity was the beginning of all knowledge. But Miss Peck's pupil, having made the remark impulsively, now bit her full lip and prepared to be rebuked for impertinence.

Philippa said, reasonably, "But I'm not going to own it. It belongs to my husband."

"You might be a widow some day. Mrs. Markham is."

"What horrid things you say. Anyway, then my son will own it."

"It might be a daughter."

Philippa stopped and screwed up her face. "Oh, don't suggest such an awful thing!" she cried.

"But that isn't an awful thing," retorted Hester, forgetting all about the impertinence. All the things over which she had brooded in those far-away days of awakening intellect rushed into her mind.

"That is such a *wrong* attitude. I can't think where it began, or why. Why should it be horrible to have a daughter? And why, because you are a woman, should you never understand anything, and not *mind* not understanding? It's as though we wore our petticoats over our heads, over our eyes and ears—and mouths very often. I've thought about it a lot. Reading, you know. The women never do anything except wait for the men to come home. I don't suppose I shall ever understand it. And I ought not to speak to you like this. I'm sorry."

"Oh, don't apologise," said Philippa. "I like to hear you talk. I've never heard anybody say such things before. Are you proposing that I should ride around with Ambrose and see how the crop is doing, or whatever they call it here?"

"Why not?" demanded Hester. "You might be glad of the knowledge some day. Oh, I know there are times and things you

213

can't get over . . ." She dismissed the whole problem of the the female disadvantages with an impatient wave of her hand. "But I don't see why women shouldn't understand things, that's all. We're not all *that* different. Sam used to say, 'What do you want to know that for, you're not going to be an ostler, are you?' But I used to think I might one day have a horse of my own, and then it would be useful to know things. I like knowing things. Perhaps *you* don't. I expect you forgot what you were told because you weren't really interested."

"I wasn't. I was wondering whether despite my hat I wasn't getting sunburnt. And whether I'd ever get to like that horse as well as my dear old Beauty. And whether I should really get on with Mrs. Markham. And whether Ambrose was still in love with me. We hadn't been married very long."

"I see. Well, I've never been married. Perhaps that does something to your mind. But I think if I had as many husbands as a Cranshi woman I should still want to know all about how they got their livings."

"What are Cranshi women?"

"A tribe Miss Peck once read to me about in a book called *Peculiar People.* They have so few women that each woman has at least three husbands. And when one is in her hut he puts his shoes outside to let the other know, and the others never dream of entering while the shoes are there. Miss Peck said that it might sound very strange but was really no more horrible or wicked than King Solomon's three hundred wives. Oh, yes, and that was very funny, really. The parson's son was at school then and he began to laugh. Miss Peck asked him why he was laughing and he wouldn't say, but she made him, and he said, 'Well, I thought about that bit in the Bible and it made me laugh to think that Solomon had three hundred wives and yet he slept with his fathers.' Miss Peck made him bend over and gave him three strokes with the birch to teach him that some things weren't to be laughed about. But I think she was laughing herself, a little."

"And who was Miss Peck?"

Once more Hester delved into the past and brought up a picture of the old scholar.

"She had a very dull, flat, lonely life and she was poor. And she was like a horse to look at, and latterly she didn't see at all well. But she had the right kind of mind," she concluded," and if all women were like her people wouldn't mind having daughters."

"Men don't marry that kind of woman," said Philippa, recalling in turn *her* early tuition.

"If all women were like that they'd have to. There wouldn't be any other sort *to* marry," said Hester with relentless logic.

Philippa laughed, squeezing Hester's arm in sudden affection.

"You are an odd girl! I've never met anyone like you. And oh, I am so glad you came to Watershead!"

"I'm glad too," said Hester.

They had walked in a circle and were now back in the garden. Philippa had forgotten that she should have been out of breath and that her back should have been aching.

"I'm extremely hungry," she said, as they gained the cool hall. "Go and cook me something really substantial. I don't mind what it is. And I think I'll eat it in the dining-room. It's quite a long time since I sat up to the table."

Constance Markham, coming upon Philippa making a hearty meal in the proper fashion in the middle of the morning, decided that she would refrain from pointing out that any old hat would have done for Hester, provided it was shady. And although she listened to Philippa's panegyrics in a sceptical silence she did not contradict her assertions that Hester was wonderful, clever, witty and altogether peerless. If she kept Philippa happy. . . . And certainly, from what Philippa was eating with such gusto, it looked as though the girl could cook. Unless of course, Delia. . . .

But Delia, discreetly questioned, gave unwilling testimony to Hester's culinary skill. She also, indirectly, informed her mistress that there was no problem in the white girl's orbit touching both the governing and the menial spheres of the house.

"Dat one know de dif'rence 'teen ole an' fresh aigs," she reported. "An' she got eyes dat look clean t'rough yo'."

So Constance, set at ease upon that score, decided that the only danger lay in Philippas' pampering leading to presumption upon Hester's part. She remained alert for it, ready to nip it in the bud. She need not have worried. Hester was, despite her assurance with Philippa, still aware that the world is a jungle. And the predatory animal is seldom presumptuous.

ALL too soon, to Hester's thinking, the new life fell into a pattern of days and duties. Her very adaptability militated against her craving for novelty, and in a short time the strange scenery, the different way of life, the bright weather and the three diverse personalities that made up the family at Watershead, became woven into the ordinary cloth of living.

Of Mrs. Markham she saw less than she had feared. On many days communication between them was restricted to "Good morning, Hester," and "Good morning, madam," exchanged when Constance paid her formal morning visit to inquire how Philippa was feeling, and what kind of night she had spent. But on one occasion when Hester was wearing a dress which Mrs. Markham recognised as one which her daughter-in-law had brought from Boston, she paused and said, "What dress are you wearing?"

"One that Mrs. Ambrose kindly gave me, madam," said Hester, her voice instantly on the defensive.

"Did you lengthen it?"

"Yes, madam."

"You seem to be a competent needlewoman. I shall probably find you a job, one day."

With many people the "One day" would have receded into the distance and probably never been heard of again, but on the following day Constance Markham presented Hester with a pile of underclothes, long disused on account of flounces that needed renewal, or smocking that had worn and must be picked out and gathered. Hester set about it sulkily. It was the kind of dull, tedious task that most bored her. Lengthening something for herself was very different; all the time she stitched away at it she was dwelling upon a mental picture of her appearance in it. But sulkily though she worked, she did it with her usual swift competence. Mrs. Markham looked over the finished work, and said that it was very neat, and laid away the garments in her already overflowing drawers. No shift or petticoat found its way to Hester, who might, but for Philippa's generosity, have been by this time in rags.

216

Philippa, however, growing every day more dependent, more fond, made up for any lack of warmth upon Constance's part : and but for one thing Hester would have spent many months in a state of peace and quiescence.

The disturbing element was Ambrose.

It was, perhaps, inevitable that she should love him. She was eighteen, and in some ways old for her age. She had been initiated very early into, at least, the outer form of love, and had since lived lonely for two years. The first sight of her master upon the night of her arrival, standing in the strengthening candle-glow and studying her with cool detachment, the impact of his physical appearance, had made the first breach in her defences. Strangely enough, fury, helpless fury, widened it.

He had received without much comment, the story that Philippa relayed so enthusiastically. The parts which Hester had told so well, and which had gripped Philippa's inexperienced imagination—the miserly Miss Martineau, the plot to gain entry to the house, the old lady's prejudiced evidence—seemed to him more like a story than an actual experience in real life.

One evening, as Hester sat sewing in her room, awaiting the jangle of the bell that would summon her to make Philippa ready for the night, Ambrose opened the door of the little room at the end of the passage and thrust in his handsome head.

"Your mistress is ready for you now," he said. But instead of bidding her good-night and withdrawing his head, he stood in the doorway, watching her as she stuck in her needle, laid the cottons straight and folded the piece of material upon which she was working.

"Are you happy here?" he asked, and the question seemed to have more than interest in her wellbeing behind it. Without understanding the incongruous element, Hester noted it and said, in a non-committal voice,

"Yes, thank you, sir. Very."

"I wonder, if you happened to leave here in any kind of trouble, what kind of a tale you would tell." There was mockery in the speculative question. Hester laid the work on the table and walked to the middle of the room, so that they faced one another.

"It would depend, I suppose, upon the trouble."

"Exactly. I suppose so too. I only asked because the story of your escapade in England seemed a little too fluent, and—shall we say—entertaining. And after all, one likes to know what one takes under one's roof. So suppose you tell me, in a few words, why you were transported. And mind, I seek information, not entertainment."

"Are they separable?" asked Hester, fixing him with her cold, green stare. "In a few words then, I was a fool, a stupid, credulous, unobservant fool."

He laughed suddenly, and although it was not merry laughter it lightened his eyes and curved his mouth in what Hester considered a highly attractive fashion. She felt, unreasonably, unexpectedly and infuriatingly weak and near to tears.

"The details of the story you have probably heard from Mrs. Markham, who is, you said, waiting for me." She brushed past him without ceremony and hurried along the passage, furious because she had run away, furious with him because he had allowed his incredulity to show, furious with Philippa for holding up her story to mockery.

It was impossible to be angry with Philippa for long. She was too gentle and inoffensive, and before the bed was turned back, the hot milk fetched from the kitchen and Philippa's disrobing performed, Hester's anger had narrowed to Ambrose. She was no longer even annoyed with herself; faced with such a situation and upon the unaccustomed and therefore perilous brink of tears, what could a girl do but run away? But Ambrose had, she considered, taken advantage of their respective situations; he should never be forgiven.

Alas for maturity. Offend the child Hester and take a beating for your pains, offend the girl and ruin your looks for a twelve-month. Offend the woman . . . Alas for maturity.

For several days Hester brooded, seeking out a way in which she could convince her master, as she had done her mistress, of the truth of her story, hoping for the matter to be re-opened, noticing his coming and going, saying little things to Philippa in the hope that they would be repeated, and all the while seeing that fine oval face, those brown eyes, that silvery fairness. Within a week she was direly in love.

It had happened without her knowledge. Asked, at any time during those days, her feeling for her master, she would have said that she hated him because he thought ill of her. And then he went down to St. Agnes and was away for twenty-four hours on business, and returned on the evening of the second day and came to Philippa's room, just as before. As before Philippa stretched out her hands and said, "Oh, Ambrose. I'm so glad that you're back." As before, Ambrose bent and kissed her, and from the sudden lurch of her heart at the sight of him, from the sharp and deadly pang of jealousy that went through her when he bent over his wife, Hester knew that her hatred had been transmuted, by some evil alchemy, into something far more hurtful, and so entered into full knowledge of her state.

She stole out of the room, went to her own and sat for a long time in the dark, her head burried in her hands. Even the verdict of her own heart was not to be accepted without a struggle. Admit that he was tall and fair and handsome, that he was elegant, a gentleman, different in every way from Sam, with his leathery neck and horny hands. Admit that the little frown and the turn of his mouth gave a look of dissatisfaction, almost of wistfulness, that made foolish women—like yourself—long to comfort him. What of it? Admit as well that he is proud and arrogant, that he has everything in the world that he can wish for, that he scorns and suspects you. Most of all, think that he is Philippa's husband. What's the answer to that, Hester Roon, who always got the right answers to all the sums, you, Hester Roon, who, shivering in prison and stifling on the transport, vowed that if once you could be comfortable again you would never care for anything else? You're comfortable enough now, aren't you? You have good food, pretty clothes, the affection of your mistress. So why do you sit here in the dark, nurturing in your bosom the little snake that is going to grow and grow, pitiless, relentless, until it has eaten out your heart? Pluck it out and cast it away from you, now. Dwell on how he mocked you, not on how he looked just now, bending above another woman, his mouth poised to kiss her.

"Oh, God!" cried Hester, addressing with blind instinct the power, un-named, unrecognised, who had let this further disaster befall her, and caring nothing by what name other men had called it. "Oh, God. What shall I do?"

She answered the question herself; rising suddenly and making a light, taking up the hated sewing and stitching away as though her flying fingers could distract her thoughts. In that they failed, but she did stitch into that interminable seam her determination that no one should even guess, by word or sign of hers, what had happened to her, nor would she allow it to colour, in any way, her behaviour to Philippa, who had accepted her and been kind.

Concealment was not difficult, for she was little in his company, and Philippa, engrossed in her own state was even less observant than usual. So the days went past and Hester, struggling against infatuation, was even surprised to find that time did nothing to help her. His step, his voice from some place unseen, could still derange the rhythm of her heart.

It was something quite new in Hester's experience—this disconcerting combination of mental humility and physical instability. The affair with Sam, simple and mutual, had taught her nothing of love save its most elementary form of expression. Sam's kisses had quickened her blood, his cheerful voice about the yard had been just one of the outside noises.

She was doubly unfortunate in the possession of that earlier experience : it had taught her too much and too little. And poor old Miss Peck, now so blind that even the largest pot-hook upon the best-scrubbed slate was only a blur to her, had she known of her favourite pupil's plight, might have thought upon her warning, timidly and indirectly given, about Pan and his power over the unvirginal. For the state in which Hester now found herself is, in itself, no uncommon thing. Few adults, looking back, cannot remember the helpless longings, the hot ardours and cold distrusts of an early, unreturned love. But for most the pangs are blunted by ignorance : they have little knowledge of what they long for; nothing to guide their dreams. For Hester, who had lain in the hayloft with Sam, there was no guardian innocence. Past all externals, beyond all preliminaries her thoughts could forge a path. She knew what lay at the end of the road. When she reminded herself that Ambrose was married to Philippa, she saw them united as she and Sam had been. Even her jealousy was more fully fanged than that of a more sheltered girl could have been. Just as her need was greater. She did not, like a young girl, imagine that all happiness would be hers if Ambrose should one day pause, turn, take her hand, even kiss her some evening when darkness had blotted out the colours of the scented garden. She knew, all too well, that she wanted more than that. She knew that Ambrose's hands were shapely, his voice melodious, his head handsome, but she did not, like a young lover, see the whole man in these.

This sharp, accurate knowledge, increasing the force of her longing, increased too, the danger of jealousy for Philippa. Not this Philippa, heavy, self-pitying and frightened, but that young, innocent Philippa who had, in some past season, been taken by Ambrose, as Psyche was taken by Cupid in the night.

(Hester's mind, at this period, reverted very often to the contemplation of the fragments of classical lore which Miss Peck had prematurely tossed it for consumption. She understood many things now. The vigils of Hero, the agony of Dido, Penelope's long fidelity. They were no longer proof of women's crass folly and weakness, they were the footsteps in the emotional desert which proved that other human beings had travelled here.) And of Philippa, the chosen, the bride, the blessed above women, Hester was sometimes so jealous that it was difficult not to delight in her present discomfort of mind and body, difficult to remain patient and considerate. On some days, when Philippa gave vent to one of her wails of self-pity, one of her bouts of anticipatory dread, Hester would throw her a veiled glance of envy and scorn and think how gladly, how proudly, with what a sense of dedication and fulfilment she herself would have borne Ambrose's child. After such stabbing moments she would be more painstakingly kind to Philippa and make a more determined effort to distract her mind; for Philippa was obviously a very poor thing indeed, unaware of her blessings and totally unfitted for her high destiny.

Matters might have been worse and she might have experienced far more mental torture. For in the present relationship of the young couple there was little to move even the most thwarted lover to envy. They spent little time together, and Ambrose's morning and evening visits were almost as perfunctory as his mother's. Hester ascribed this state of things to two perfectly satisfactory reasons. Philippa was about to become a mother, and Ambrose was a gentleman unlikely to be demonstrative before others. Hester was quite certain that in private he was an ardent and adequate lover; quite certain that once the baby was born her jealousy would find bitter food in plenty. She was determined that immediately after the birth she would leave Watershead: Mr. Kyne would arrange that if necessary.

She did not know—though Philippa's extravagant yielding to herself might have informed her—that her mistress was almost as unhappily in love as she was herself. And when she envied the young, innocent bride who had come, well-dowered and well-trousseaued, out of the North, she was envying as puzzled and troubled a young woman as ever existed. For Philippa had never been able to convince herself that Ambrose loved her. He had, it was true, wooed her and married her, but he had never displayed sufficient ardour to break down the

221

barrier that her own delicacy and self-doubt reared between them. They had never approached within sight of the state of fervent union that Hester had known with Sam. That fact accounted, although she did not herself know it, for Philippa's present resentment. She had been trapped, and although the trap had been apparently well-baited, the tit-bit had not been worth the subsequent pain. She was too innocent, too much in love with her husband, ever to dream of attributing any blame to him; she did not dream that his lack of passion arose from his own apathy, his inability to lose himself even for a moment. She blamed herself, retreated in self-abasement, or made advances that were ill-timed and lacked cunning. Rebuffs were inevitable, and gradually she had become discouraged and considered that marriage was an over-rated business, and that the novels of the beloved Mrs. Elsa Taunton had sadly misled her.

In fact Philippa was more to be pitied than her handmaiden for whom life still held something alluring, something to be desired and striven for. Philippa was chained and doomed and finished, and bound, one day soon, for fresh disillusion. For she was already forgetting her former defeats, and beginning to attribute Ambrose's coldness to her present state; she would return, as Hester suspected, with fresh ardour to her marriage bed, and Ambrose would elude her anew.

Of all this Hester was in ignorance. So she cheered Philippa, to the best of her ability, along the road with the one ending, and dreamed of Ambrose with fiery longing. The days passed; and they were good days when, by guile or wilfulness, she managed to take a share in the mending or arranging of her idol's clothes, those fine rich garments that proclaimed his state and smelt of his tobacco : good days when, coming to pay his wife his formal visits, he passed Hester in passage or doorway, so that she was for a moment in dizzying physical proximity with him, and had to struggle for breath with which to return his careless "Good morning" or "Good night."

CHAPTER VII

THE days passed, until there came a day when Philippa, whose head ached, refused for the fourth day in succession to stir from her room. What Bartumans called the "cold" season had begun and the weather was dry and, to Hester, invigorating. Confinement made her fidgety and, without knowing it, she looked out of the window several times and sighed. Mrs. Taunton's latest story, *The Forbidden Bride*, which she had been reading to Philippa, seemed to her a dull silly story about a dull silly girl who repeatedly found herself in agonising situations from which one moment's clarity of thought and frankness of speech would have liberated her, and Hester longed to throw the book on the floor and stamp upon it. She read on, her voice getting duller and flatter, while Philippa, with a handkerchief over her brow, stirred languidly on the day-bed.

Presently Philippa said, "This is very dull for you, Hester. Wouldn't you like to go out for a little while? I don't mind being left alone." But even as she made the generous offer she threw such pathos into the word "alone" that Hester, the book already slammed, was smitten with remorse.

"I'll go if you'll come as well. Just for a moment, just for a breath. It's a lovely afternoon and we wouldn't go far."

"But my head aches. You've got no idea how it aches."

Hester, speaking with the frankness which the Forbidden Bride so sedulously avoided, rapped out, with truth :

"And it ached yesterday and the day before. It'll ache tomorrow unless you get some air."

"I believe you'd recommend air for a broken leg," said Philippa pettishly, but seeing Hester's face, she added, "Give me my little shawl."

Philippa was heavier now and their walks were more restricted, though Hester, whenever it was possible, tried to direct their steps away from the neat and formal garden into some quarter that promised something of interest to look at. Along the one path that she wanted to explore more than all others— the track that led to the cabins of the slaves—Philippa could never be persuaded to go. It wasn't safe, she said, you could catch things there; besides you saw horrid sights. It was filthy dirty and the children were naked and had sores. From Philippa's point of view these were conclusive arguments, and Hester was obliged to turn unwillingly away from the exploration of this other world which lay so near to the one she knew and was so very different. She did not suggest visiting it to-day, it was victory enough to have got Philippa out at all. They walked across the garden, as far as the sunken ditch and turned, not attempting to cross it to-day.

"Could you manage the shrubbery?" asked Hester solicitously.

"So that you can go through your favourite stable-yard?" returned Philippa, gently teasing.

"Well, I do hate going back the way I came. Is your head any better?"

"Not much. A little, perhaps."

They took the narrow path that led through the flowering shrubs and ended in a small gate giving upon the stable-yard, where Hester was always interested in the negroes who were working there. At the end of the stables there was a low shed with a piece of open yard before it, enclosed by a wall four and a half feet high. Tethered on chains that were fastened to staples in the back wall of the open-fronted sheds were three great dogs, in which Hester took lively if rather fearful interest. They were enormous lean slate-coloured beasts with reddish eyes and hanging dewlaps. They called no man friend or master and were renowned for their ferocity. Each night a wizened little mulatto named David entered the enclosure, slipped the chains from their heavy collars and set them free to roam the yard and the precincts of the house until dawn, when he called them, tied and fed them. Philippa had explained that this was a device for keeping the slaves in their quarters after nightfall; and she and Hester agreed that nothing would induce either of them to risk meeting with Satan, Fanny or Lou in the dark.

By the afternoon the great dogs had slept off the effect of their night's exercise and were hungry and restless, roaming about on the end of their chains like caged wild beasts. But it was Hester's custom, in passing, to address each by its name, hoping one day to see the hackles cease from bristling, a tail wag in recognition. She seldom passed the stable-yard without peering over the wall. So far her advances had met with no success at all.

On this afternoon Satan, inspired perhaps by the weather as Hester herself had been, had lunged against his chain. He had been doing it for years without result, but now, at perhaps the ten-thousandth lunge the staple had left the wall, and after a puzzled moment when it seemed to him that it was wrong to be free and yet weighted by his chain, he had scaled the wall at a bound and was roaming the apparently deserted yard, seeking, like his namesake, what he might devour.

Hester opened the little gate at the end of the shubbery path and stood aside so that Philippa might pass through. Then she latched it carefully behind her, drew level with her mistress and offered the crook of her arm. They walked a few steps.

"Do you want to visit the dogs to-day?" asked Philippa.

"Not to-day. They wouldn't do your head any good."

"You're very thoughtful," said Philippa, walking on with her eyes cast down, as a woman with a headache does. Hester's eyes roamed around in search of anything interesting that might meet them. And suddenly it did. A great dog, loose and alone, standing with its head at an alert angle, looking in their direction, attracted already, either by their voices or their scent.

Hester put her arm around Philippa and turned her, heaving and pushing her towards the gate. But before they had gained it the intermittent smack of the chain on the ground told that Satan was bounding in pursuit and getting nearer with each bound.

"Get through the gate, you've the baby to think of," gasped Hester, giving Philippa a final heave in the right direction. And Philippa, still bewildered and not certain what she was running from, and thinking that Hester was probably mad, was instinctively obedient and managed to make swift, if ungraceful progress to the gate.

Hester turned and faced the hound. The gate clashed behind her and then Philippa turned and saw, and sped on towards the house screaming at the top of her voice.

Hester made one attempt to halt the slate-coloured avalanche of hatred. She said in a loud shaky voice, "Satan, Fanny, Lou," not knowing which might be the magic name. On any tongue but David's they were all meaningless to Satan; but the out-stretched hand with which Hester accompanied the words saved her life. He sprang at that instead of at her throat and then stood, as though turned into stone, the hand crushed in his fangs, the blood from it dripping over his lower jaw. He had done what he had been trained to do, he had caught the wandering two-legged creature and was holding on. If this hold did not serve, if the creature struggled or tried to get away, well, Satan knew a better hold still and could have transferred his grip in less than the blink of an eye. But the creature stood quite still.

Ambrose, from the house, and David at work in the farthest stable, were each attracted by the sound of Philippa's screams. They ran from different directions. Ambrose, meeting Philippa upon the verandah steps and hearing her breathless explanation, yelled for his mother and ran back for his gun. David brought, without knowing why he did so, the pitchfork with which he had been cleaning out a stall. They arrived within sight of Hester and Satan, both as rigid as statuary, at the same time. And David, seeing Ambrose raise the gun, shouted, "Doan shoot, Master! Hi, Satan, drop it!"

That was the one voice. Every morning it called and although it marked the end of freedom it heralded feeding-time too. Satan opened his mouth and Hester reeled backwards into Ambrose's arms. David picked up the end of the chain and led the hound away.

"I can walk," said Hester, hearing Philippa's voice from beyond a turn in the shrubbery path. "Lend me your handkerchief. She mustn't see."

She helped Ambrose to wind the large coloured silk square around her crushed and bloody fingers, and when, the moment after, Philippa, pale and panting, hurried up with Mrs. Markham in hot pursuit, she said, "I'm not hurt. It's only a little nip."

Philippa, with whom of late every emotion had been accompanied with hysteria, threw herself forward, clasped Hester to her and burst into the natural, if noisy, tears of relief.

"You were so brave," she sobbed. "I didn't realise what was happening until I was through the gate, and then I only screamed."

"That was the best thing you could do," said Ambrose calmly. "Come along Hester, we must get the nip tied up."

Already the blood was finding its way through the muffling folds and Hester's pallor was taking on an unmistakable green tinge.

"What I can't understand is why you had to walk this way at all," said Mrs. Markham sternly. "Surely there are plenty of places more pleasant for walking than the stable-yard. I never heard of such a thing."

"Afterwards, afterwards," said Ambrose impatiently, hustling Hester towards the house. Philippa mopped her face and left off clinging to Hester, and mustering a voice clearer and stronger than usual, announced, "It was my idea. To come through the shrubbery and the yard makes a round walk, so much less tedious than going back the way you came."

"Oh, well, if it was your idea," said Mrs. Markham, who had been badly frightened on her grandson's account. Hester, dimly aware of the magnitude of Philippa's lie, turned her dizzy head and halted on legs that were rapidly turning to water and sent Philippa a glance in which gratitude and mockery were oddly mingled. Then she let herself be dragged into the house and dealt with. Ambrose attended to the torn crushed fingers himself, and showed both knowledge and deftness.

"Going into the stable-yard was really my idea," she said faintly, when the worst was over.

"A quite unnecessary confession," he said coolly. "I doubt if my wife had ever been in it before your arrival. And the consequences might easily have been disastrous. However, thanks to you, the worst was avoided, and I suggest that you forget who arranged the walk. Don't go there again, that's all."

"I won't," said Hester, with feeling. He fastened the knot of the scarf from which he had fashioned a sling and slipped it over her head. Then he startled her by laying his hand on top of her curls for an instant.

"You're a very brave little girl," he said. Most of the remaining blood in Hester's body blazed in her cheeks.

"I'll go to Mrs. Ambrose now. Maybe she's worrying," she said. She laid a benediction on the name which was also his. "Thank you so much for dealing with it."

The little episode served to lever the three members of the family still further apart. Philippa was convinced that Hester was a heroine who had saved her life at the risk of her own. She said, with perfect truth and some acrimony :

"You didn't see her push me forward and then stand there waiting to stop it. And it looked like the devil. *Anybody* else would have tried to get through the gate and then we should both had been *eaten*."

Mrs. Markham considered, with some truth, that Hester was

entirely to blame for the occurrence, that she had done no more than she should have, in facing the danger into which she herself had led Philippa, and that she was gaining credit where she should have met with rebuke.

"I have not interfered, hitherto, because I thought that her influence somewhat counteracted Philippa's tendency to invalidism. But now it has been carried too far. It is only by a mercy of Providence that Philippa has escaped a miscarriage. In future I shall attend, far more closely, to what the girls are about."

Ambrose, well aware of the validity of both the arguments, offended both women by disagreeing with each in turn. He held, in his mother's presence, that Hester had showed unusual courage and fortitude, while to Philippa he announced that Hester was a venturesome little fool who had been given far too much of her own way.

The friction was intensified when Philippa announced that Hester must be rewarded.

"She has been," said Ambrose, "she was bitten."

"She deserves a good whipping into the bargain," said Mrs. Markham. But Ambrose softened his verdict by presenting Hester with a guinea; Mrs. Markham endorsed hers by administering several crushing snubs. Philippa set her wits to work.

"Would you like to spend a day in St. Agnes?" she asked. "I'm afraid you'd have to go alone, but David would drive you down and you could look in the shops and buy things."

If she had said "Ambrose" instead of "David" Hester would have accepted the offer with suitable gratitude. As it was, it meant spending a whole day away from Watershead, involved running the gauntlet of Mrs. Markham's displeasure and gained her nothing that she desired.

"It is kind of you to think of it. But I think I'll wait. Perhaps one day I might go with you."

It was the kind of remark—and well she knew it—that flattered and pleased her mistress. Philippa smiled and said most certainly they would spend a day, or even two, in the town together. Heaven knew she would need some distraction and some new clothes when all this was over.

The matter seemed to have dropped. Days passed. Hester resigned herself to gentle amblings about the grounds and dull hours within doors. She discarded the sling (laying it away as a relic because Ambrose had tied it) and wore an old glove upon

228

the injured hand. It had been devastatingly painful and almost as awkward, since the full extent of the injury had to be concealed from Philippa; but it had brought her casual inquiries from Ambrose that were compensation.

CHAPTER VIII

ONE day, as she carried Philippa's clean linen from the kitchen, Ambrose met her at the head of the stairs. He asked his usual question, "How's your hand?" and she, with the usual banging of the heart and uncertainty of voice (apt in moments of stress to find no range between a squeak and a growl) replied that it was better. Instead of passing on he halted and asked:

"Can you ride a horse?"

"I never have. But I could try," she answered, furious because her voice was so small, squeaky and breathless. Would she never get control of it? The thought occurred to her that perhaps he wanted an errand done, a message taken, something urgent that he did not wish to entrust to a negro.

"I'm sure I could," she said (and this time her voice, affected by the uprush of confidence because he had chosen her, was its firm, slightly, rough-edged self.) "I know how it's done."

"It's not so easy," he said woundingly. "Especially if you have passed childhood without trying. But I daresay I can pick you an ambling pad. My wife has the idea that you would like to see the place. She thinks you would find it entertaining. God knows why, or where she got the idea. Would you? Say no if you like."

"There's nothing I'd rather do," said Hester truthfully.

"Very well. Be ready at three o'clock to-morrow."

He passed on, and Hester, in a daze, proceeded to Philippa's room and laid the fresh linen on the bed, preparatory to sorting it and laying it in Philippa's many sweetly-scented drawers.

Philippa looked up.

"I've tried to arrange you a little treat. It's been so dull for you lately. I thought—I daresay it sounds silly, it certainly does so to me—that perhaps you would like to ride round with my husband. He can answer all the questions that you are always asking."

"I just met him. He told me. I should like it. Like it very much indeed. But . . . I'm not sure . . . I mean, I shouldn't like to go if it's going to be a bother."

"Why Hester! I believe you're being diffident. I'd never have believed it. Of course it isn't a bother. He is very glad to do something to show how grateful we are, we both are."

"But there's no reason for you to be grateful." It was the harshest voice. "I only do what I was brought here to do."

"Oh, Hester!" Philippa stretched out her limp white hand and took Hester's thin hard one into her soft clasp. "You know, you *must* know, that if you just waited on me you'd be doing what you were brought here to do, as you call it. And you do so much more than that. You saved my life, and my baby. And you're my friend. And my support. Except my husband you mean more to me than anybody."

Philippa's soft voice was vibrant with sincerity. It made Hester remember painfully her jealousy, her scorn, her avid longing for this woman's husband.

"It's all wrong," she said harshly. "You mustn't think about me like that. I'm just a servant."

With a servant's limitation of service; a servant's privilege of owning private hopes and dreams even if they run counter to the interest of the served.

"Something has upset you, Hester. Perhaps you don't like the treat. I don't think it's at all a good idea myself. But you always seemed so interested in the sugar, and in the slaves. I told Ambrose that if you rode you could probably go past the cabins without catching anything. But don't do it. I'll think of something else."

"You couldn't think of anything I'd like better. But, you see, I don't deserve a treat at all."

"I'm the best judge of that," said Philippa pontifically, and lay back as though the last word had been said.

Hester turned away abruptly and began to lay away the linen. She was angry with herself, and furious with Philippa. Couldn't she see? Couldn't she guess? Had she no imagination at all? To arrange a thing like that, and then to be so sweet and simple that she was making it incumbent upon Hester to take no advantage of the unique opportunity that to-morrow would offer. Making it imperative that she should cast down her eyes and say, "No, sir," and "Yes, sir," and "Thank you sir, for showing me." Oh, hell!

"Open the lefthand cupboard," said Philippa's voice from the day-bed. "Now bring me that green thing. No, the next, the dark green. That's right. Now the pretty box from the shelf. Take out the hat and bring it here. There, see, they match. The best tailor in Boston made the habit, and Mary Ann Tibbit made the hat. They're yours. You are to wear them to-morrow. You can't wear an ordinary skirt on a horse, you know, your legs look so queer. And anyway, I don't want them. I hate all horses except my dear Beauty."

"I . . . I . . ." Hester began. She wanted to scream and stamp, to throw the green habit and the plump hat at the gentle smiling face of the woman who was torturing her, just by being gentle and smiling. Philippa said, "I don't want you to thank me. Go and enjoy yourself in your own funny way. And then come back and go on being patient with me." She passed on to memories of Boston, inspired by the mention of Beauty and the sight of Mary Ann Tibbit's handiwork, and Hester forced herself to take interest in this account of a loved and longed-for life. With especial warmth did Philippa speak of Maggie, her old nurse, and then her maid who had only failed her once in all her life. That was when she said, as firmly as she had said all things, "You may choose to go and live amongst a lot of black cannibals, Miss Philippa, but don't ask me to."

"I was very much disappointed," confessed Philippa. "I thought she would have followed me anywhere. And from that moment I wasn't really looked after until you came. Oh I am glad you came."

In meditating upon the ultimate misery of those who must be looked after or pine away, Hester managed to shut out her irritation.

To Hester's boundless relief, Mrs. Markham left Watershead early on the next day to pay a visit to her old friend Tabitha Slater at St. Pierre. Ever since Philippa had thrust the green habit and the plumed hat upon her, Hester had been dreading that, arrayed in this unnatural glory, she would have to face the question or the cynicism in the old lady's eyes. Constance Markham, Hester dared wager, had never arranged any treat for any female whom she had called friend. She would have seen the implications at once.

231

But she was not there to see. And at three o'clock Hester left Philippa dozing upon the day-bed and emerged by the side-door. With set face and lifted chin, desperate disguise for her fear and tremulous excitement, she made her way to the stable-yard for the first time since her meeting with Satan. Elias, David's son, far blacker than his father, was walking two horses backwards and forwards. They looked sleek and frisky and very large. As large, thought Hester, as the coach-horses back at The Fleece, and six of those could draw a great coach full of passengers and luggage. It seemed unlikely that she, inexperienced and still hampered by her hand, would be able to control one of them. This immediate, practical problem absorbed her attention and gave her some relief from the emotional tug-of-war that had been tearing her all morning, loyalty to Philippa upon one side and love of Ambrose and the knowledge of the shortness and frailty of her opportunity upon the other.

The large white-faced clock over the stable entrance showed that it was five minutes past three. Watching the long hand she could see the jerks with which it went forward; ten past, the quarter hour. Of course he wouldn't mind how long he kept her waiting; he wouldn't mind if he didn't come at all. She closed her eyes at the impact of that thought as though someone had struck her in the face.

Twenty past. And now she was acutely self-conscious. Even Elias was laughing at her, she was sure. Standing there dressed like a lady and being kept waiting like a horse, a slave. The fine green habit seemed to scorch where it touched her. He had meant all along to make a fool of her; saying "yes" to Philippa's fond request, laughing at her averred willingness to mount one of these terribly tall horses, and then not intending to come.

Half past. Suddenly she turned, gathered the long skirt in her hand and hurried back the way that she had come. Let the horses wait his pleasure; let Elias walk up and down until darkness fell; Hester Roon would not. Thank Heaven she had got away in time.

She tore the hat from her head and threw it passionately into the corner, where it lay with its plume quivering as though it shared her rage. Her fingers flew to the fastening of the habit. The bodice had thirty small oval gilt buttons and the fingers of her injured hand were not yet supple. She had reached only the fifteenth when Ambrose's voice rang up the front stairs :

"Hester! Where's Hester? I'm waiting."

Wait on, thought Hester, tearing at the buttons. She heard his step on the stairs, heard him call outside his wife's room and reply to some remark of Philippa's, "She is *not*, I tell you. Elias said that she had looked out and then come in again."

In Elias' timeless existence, half an hour probably counted as looking-out space, thought Hester with curling lip. The last button came through and she was stepping into her own dress when Philippa's little hand-bell rang out its silvery note. Hester demurely presented herself before her mistress, ignoring Ambrose.

"Why aren't you changed?" asked Philippa with widening eyes, "I sent you to change before I lay down."

"I changed back."

"Whatever for?"

"I thought the master had forgotten about me." Most humble words, most defiantly spoken.

Fortunately Ambrose refrained from speech. He stood by the door with his gaze abstracted and the tip of his crop idly tapping the lacquered surface of his boot. Philippa, who had never in her life seen past the externals of any situation said :

"Well, make haste now. My husband has been delayed quite long enough." The words, which might have been an order, were softened into a request by Philippa's gentle expression. Hester looked away angrily and her eyes fell upon Ambrose. The one ray of sunlight that entered the room was directed at his head, outlining hair, eyelashes and brows in gold. The tall lolling figure in its cream breeches and tan-coloured coat made its familiar call to her senses. Without speaking she dashed out of the room and within as short a time as thirty oval gilt buttons could be coaxed back into their buttonholes, was back in the stable-yard.

She suffered the ignominy of being hoisted into the saddle, and being assured that there was nothing to fear. Barby was old and placid as a cow. Nor need she use her injured hand. If she would just sit there Barby would follow the other horse. They set off. For a few moments the unfamiliarity of her position engrossed her and she sat rigid, prepared for almost anything to happen. But after a moment or two she relaxed with a deep breath of relief. It was all right. She was going to manage.

As though knowing that her attention was now free Ambrose said, "You're a mutinous little devil, aren't you? I was ready at three o'clock, then a man came to see me, and I was hoping every moment he would go, so I didn't send out a message. Better people than you have been kept waiting half-an-hour, you know."

"Better people, yes. They wouldn't mind. People in my position are easily hurt."

"There seems to me very little wrong in your position. We're all tied down in one way or another, you know. And all mistresses are not so unexacting as my wife." It was a crushing sentence, but he said it, not crushingly, but sadly, and he ended it with a sigh, so that Hester, far from being angered was softened and interested.

"You don't know much about being tied down," she ventured.

"Oh, don't I? That shows how little you know. There are about one hundred and fifty slaves on this place and I am the most fettered of them all."

"What nonsense," said Hester, forgetting to be respectful for a moment.

"It isn't nonsense at all. I don't want to live here. I never did. I hate everything to do with plantation life. I loathe sugar, filthy smelly stuff. I hate slaves. What kind of life is it, do you imagine? I go for days without seeing anyone except my family. If anyone calls, or I pay a visit, what do we talk about? Sugar, sugar, sugar, the yield, the price, the prospects. It isn't what I expected of life. I had three elder brothers, I never thought that before I was thirty I would be tied down here." The expression of his face showed the origin of the frown between his eyes and the compression of his lower lip.

"What happened?" asked Hester in the quiet voice that invites confidences without betraying curiosity.

"Oh, one tragedy after another. First my father died, comparatively young. I was a baby at the time, my brother Edward about seventeen and the others somewhere between. My mother was a marvel; she trained Edward and looked after the place until he was really old enough to take charge. Then there was the French war and both he and my next brother, Stephen, were killed at St. Agnes, defending the harbour. By that time John was growing up and mother taught *him*. I explained that I wasn't interested in the plantation, and at first mother was glad; divided inheritances aren't desirable, you see. They let me go to New England to study law. I never had such a good time. There were several of us, you see, all young men, with something to study, something to talk about, ambitions to cherish. It was like Heaven." He stopped, staring ahead of him, and seeing, not the cane fields, the stark black bulk of the mills, the rich soil of his inheritance, but the thinning coloured leaves of the New England fall, the pale wind-cooled sunshine through which he had wandered, his law books under his arm, in company with the young men whom he had loved, the witty young men, their minds already tempered with the lawyer's detachment and critical faculty. He sighed again. And as Hester again answered the sigh with a softly breathed "What happened?" he began to tell the story that not even Philippa had heard.

"John was wild. He got into a little trouble over a woman and somebody called him out. Mother tried to persuade him to leave the island for a little while, but he wouldn't go. And he was killed. Mother sent for me."

"And you came?"

"I came. What else could I do? She had had three sons. She had lost them. She was growing old. After all her work and effort to keep the place together for her sons I couldn't say, 'Sell it, give it away, I don't want it.' I did resist for a little while. But—well, she was very set upon my coming back; and I am very fond of her. I came back."

"And regretted it?"

"Every day. No that isn't true. At first I regretted it every day. Now I mind less and less. After all, it doesn't matter where you are or whom with. Not really, I mean. You carry your own ability to be happy, or the lack of it, wherever you are. And I suppose you might as well die of fever or in a slave revolt in Bartuma, as of old age in Boston."

Almost unconsciously he had voiced the dread that had pursued him since the day when he had overheard his elders talking of the horrors of the big revolt of 1753. Those who remembered it seldom discussed it, but it had cropped up in the conversation on this occasion, and the phrases in which it was described had sunk deeply in to the plastic mind of the little listening boy. They had formed his intention of getting away from the island; they had inspired his reluctance to return; they lay at the root of his hatred of his inheritance; they returned in dreams from which he awoke sweating and paralysed with terror; they were responsible for a good deal of the severity with which the slaves at Watershead were treated.

The betraying sentence slipped out, but its significance escaped Hester, whose mind went leaping, as ever, in pursuit of any fresh piece of information.

"A slave revolt. What's that?"

"Hell let loose,' 'he said briefly. "You have to remember that slaves are savages. They have no restraints. Left to themselves they would and could behave exactly as they would in Africa. That is why we set guards at night. O'Leary and Colson never sleep except in the day-time. And there are locked gates; and the dogs."

Still unconsciously he was comforting himself.

"You mean that without these things we shouldn't be safe?" She tried to picture a revolt in the orderly household at Watershead. Delia, wielding her carving knife with murderous intent, Poppy working havoc with her goffering iron. It seemed ludicrous.

"They seem so harmless," she said.

"In the main they are. And of course I am not talking of the house slaves, or people like old David. They're almost human. But the average field hand is little better than a wild beast. If they get a grievance, or imagine one, and then any little thing happens to slacken discipline—well, you get a revolt."

"And what happens?"

"They run wild and burn buildings and kill people. And the white women . . . they'd be better dead."

"And how is it stopped?"

"There are soldiers in St. Agnes. You don't need to worry, you know. There may not be another for years. There may never be another. But it's a thing to be remembered and guarded against. And all the maudlin people who shed tears over the poor black slaves ought to live through a revolt. That'd teach them."

Hester had been four months at Watershead and had never given the question of slavery a thought. Always she had been dimly aware of a world outside the house and the garden, and she had more than once looked curiously along the path that led to the cabins of the slaves. But she had accepted the presence of the slaves beyond her range of vision as she had accepted the coach horses, the cows, sheep and pigs of her native countryside. Once indeed, when Margarita had turned up the lamp in Mrs. Markham's room so that it had blackened the ceiling and scorched the curtain, the old lady had struck her with a heavy ebony ruler which she had snatched from her desk, and Hester, some hours later, had reported that Margarita was still crying and that one of her eyes was closed. That had made Philippa embark upon the question of physical punishment and she had said, "It's queer how you fall into habits. I flung my slippers at Poppy once. If I had done that to Maggie she'd have flung them straight back at me, hard."

"But Job Wainwright often used to hit me," said Hester. "And once when I annoyed him he held my head in the pail until I thought I would drown."

"Then it's different in America," said Philippa. "And of course it's very different here. But they're only slaves, after all."

On that day Hester had pondered for a little while upon the difference between being a slave and a servant, but it had dawned upon her that perhaps she was not so far from being a slave herself, and she had dismissed the uncomfortable thought. To-day, however, Ambrose's description of the slaves in independent action took hold of her imagination, and though she gave him her attention as he explained the processes of crushing the cane, cleansing the syrup, boiling it and separating the granules from the molasses, she found herself more interested in the men and women who were at work, than in the work itself.

They were of all sizes and shapes, tall and short, upright and bowed, young and old. Few were very fat and most of them were more than half-naked, being clad in either short drawers or a kind of overall, according to their sex. Even Hester's curiosity could hardly survive the intense heat of the boiling-rooms where, in huge open vats over great fires, the syrup bubbled and steamed.

Overseers stood about with short-handled, long-lashed whips in their hands, and occasionally they cracked them, aimlessly, as the driver of a team flicks his whip in the air. But when the shed where the final process was taking place was reached Hester saw a whip used to good purpose. Here the granulated sugar, still surrounded by the sticky residue, was poured into cone-shaped receptacles, and Ambrose pointed out how the top of each cone was sealed with wet clay. The moisture from the clay seeped down, he explained, and as it passed through it cleansed the grains by taking the stickiness with it.

While Hester was watching, two slaves overturned one of

the cones and the hot stuff spilt out, splashing their feet and making them shuffle and scream with pain. Immediately the nearest overseer was upon them, lashing his whip right and left.

Hester, somewhat to her own surprise and horror called, "Oh, don't!" Ambrose made a sign. The overseer and the scalded men were suddenly no longer there.

"I think you've seen enough," said Ambrose. "There's time, if you would like it, to see the place that gives the plantation its name."

They went out into the air and found the waiting horses.

"I'm afraid we'll have to trot a bit. You'll be stiff to-morrow, but that won't kill you," he said, helping her into the saddle again.

The rutted dirt-track ended in a piece of pasture, through which ran a small, steady stream. They followed it, Ambrose riding ahead and Barby following without any instigation from Hester. The grass grew scantier and scattered with stones and then ended suddenly at the foot of a slope of bare earth dotted with large boulders, streaked with strange colours, ochre, green and mouldy blue. The horses picked their way delicately between them until Ambrose halted.

"We must leave the horses here," he said as Barby obediently drew level with his mount and stood still. While he dismounted and pulled his rein over the horse's head, Hester freed herself and slid to the ground.

"I would have helped you," he said, coming round to pull her rein forward. "You'll soon ride, though. No nerves to hamper you."

"And no dignity to consider," said Hester, tugging viciously at the long skirt which had hitched itself up in an unsightly manner. "What about the horses?"

"As long as the reins hang that way they'll stand. They're trained." There was an edge of sarcasm in his voice.

He began to lead the way up the slope, turning now and then to offer a hand to help her over a difficult bit. But Hester, with a handful of skirt hitched up like a bustle behind her, scrambled after him as nimbly as a goat. The rocks grew larger as they climbed, and more fantastically streaked and mottled. Presently they reached two, twice as tall as a man, that leaned together as though barring the way. There was just room to squeeze between them, and Hester followed him through. Inside was a space, the size of a large room, enclosed within a rocky wall, broken, so far as Hester could see, only by the opening through which they had come. In the middle of it was a rocky basin, no bigger than a large washtub, and out of it water sprang, gurgling, filled the hollow and overflowed only to disappear again at the foot of the rocky wall.

"See," said Ambrose, pointing. "It flows under there and then comes out again in the stream that waters the meadow, serves the house and then runs on to St. Agnes. That is why this is called Watershead. Pretty, isn't it?"

His voice sounded strange and hollow.

"What a hiding-place," said Hester, thinking of old stories of siege and adventure. "With just some food you could live here for days and no one would ever know."

"If you're ever missing I shall know just where to look," he said teasingly. "Well, having shown you our sights I'd better take you back. It'll be dark soon."

As suddenly as the day gave place to night in this latitude Hester's mood changed. The little jaunt was ending. Philippa's "treat" was over. She had had almost two hours of his company and she had hardly thought about him at all. It seemed incredible. But there it was. She had thought about slaves and sugar! And a good thing too, said her logical mind. Mooning about thinking how pleasant he looked and what a nice voice he had wouldn't have done you a bit of good, would it? It would only have made you feel worse. But now, with devastating suddenness and violence she did feel worse. Standing here looking into that clear water, in this quiet, remote place that might have been the top of the world, she was conscious of his nearness and dearness. They had never been alone together before; might never be again. And they had talked about slaves and sugar. And now they were going back. . . .

Slip off, then, the reins of the mind, the control of reason, the hobble of thought. Let the body, which is so much older and wiser, take charge. Let fly that provocative glance, hold out for inspection that full, ripe mouth. Now, as you draw together in this narrow cleft of the rocks, look up and down, so . . . And then stumble. After all you may never get the chance again.

Like a puppet obeying the pull on its string she obeyed the directions of this fleshy wisdom. Like a puppet Ambrose jumped forward, put his arm around her and pulled her towards him. Every grain of her flesh, every nerve, even the marrow of her

239

bones was clamorous with desire, and they were finding means of communication to his flesh and nerves and marrow, apathetic and slow to respond as they might be. A flirtation with his wife's maid with its consequent demands and complications was not exactly what Ambrose Markham had requested of the gods; but for a moment he was ready to forget everything, even his habitual caution, and the invitation that trembled upon that full red mouth would have taken a stronger, or even a colder man to resist.

He would have kissed her, and the consequences might have been more shattering than he imagined, but at that moment Hester's good angel, small, downtrodden, but sturdy, decided to interefere. A momentary vision of Philippa, her pale face wearing an affectionate smile, presented itself before Hester's inward eye. Two decisive steps sideways took her into the narrow rocky passage; Ambrose was forced to drop his arm and the danger was over for the time being. As a further assurance of temporary safety a loud voice was now heard, echoing amongst the rocks. "Markham?" it called, with a sudden rise upon the second syllable.

Amongst the rocks at the mouth of the passage stood a man whom Hester had never seen before, though she and Philippa had an out-of-the-window acquaintance with most of the callers to Watershead. He was a tall man, but his breadth of shoulder and slightly bowed legs made him seem shorter than Ambrose, beside whose elegance he looked uncouth and ungroomed. His plentiful hair, the colour of a tan terrier's coat, was unpowdered and unfashionably cropped; his cravat was carelessly arranged and his clothes gave the impression of having been slept in. His face, squarish, but thin-cheeked, was tanned all over to a uniform pale brown and across it his bushy eyebrows, rather redder than his hair, jutted over eyes of an amazing, arresting bright grey.

Hester, emerging first from the opening between the slanting rocks, took in all the salient details of his appearance in a swift, slightly disapproving glance. He had snatched off his disreputable hat and now stood, rather taken aback, waiting for Ambrose to follow Hester into the open.

"I'm sorry," he said, "I saw you ride up a few minutes since and thought I might catch you here. I didn't know that Mrs. Markham was with you. I won't trouble you now."

"This isn't my wife," said Ambrose rather shortly. "Miss

240

Roon is staying with us. Excuse us, Hester, a moment. What was it you wanted?"

"It'll do another time," said the man; his manner showed that he had noticed Ambrose's shortness and he turned away, picking a path that led slanting through the stones so that the distance between him and Ambrose increased steadily.

"Come on, Lyddon, out with it. I want to get back to the house."

Raising his voice Lyddon answered, "I know I'm not a good advocate to choose, and I've picked a bad moment as well, but I promised old Methody I'd have a word with you."

"You're wasting your breath, Lyddon. Even if you could convince *me* that his ministrations were desirable you'd never convince my mother, and after all she has had more experience in these matters than I have, or you. We decided that we wouldn't have him on the place. And that stands."

"I was afraid so. But he begged me so earnestly and he's such a decent old fellow, I promised that I'd put just one point to you. It seems that on his last visit he promised to marry some couples and baptise a few babies next time he called. He has a feeling that they'll think he deserted them. Will you give him permission to make good his promises? After all, that can't do any harm."

"Nor any good. The couples are all bedded down by this time and the brats are answering to some name or other."

Hester, glancing sideways, saw Lyddon's face take on an obstinate look.

"It isn't as though his teaching was subversive. Quite the opposite, in fact. And if he does promise them freedom in Heaven, well, Heaven is a long way off, and maybe we shan't be growing sugar there." He gave a short barking laugh. "Ah, well, I've done my best and kept my promise to the old man. Good day to you, Markham. Good day, Miss Roon."

He swept off his battered old hat again and for a second those bright grey eyes, so strangely light in his dark lined face, held hers in a stare that filled her with a feeling for which she had no name. She returned his good day demurely. He strode away, moving swiftly and lightly on those slightly bowed legs, and reached his horse which stood with the others. The animal, a beautiful grey, evenly dappled, with a coat like silk and long flowing mane and tail, almost white in colour belied her first assessment of him as a poor man. Even to her inexperienced eye it was a better, more costly horse than any in the Watershead stables. It came towards him with a coy, mincing gait, stood while he mounted and then, after daintily picking its way through the stony edge of the pasture, broke suddenly into a swift, stretching gallop, checked on the bank of the stream and crossed it with a jump as smooth and effortless as the flight of a swallow.

The man himself seemed to partake of his mount's grace. Once in the saddle he was no longer unkempt and bow-legged, he was part of the picture that showed a superb rider, superbly mounted.

"Damned, upstart black-bailer," said Ambrose angrily, throwing back the reins of Hester's horse and stretching out his helping hand. Hester waited until he had himself mounted and then said, "Who is he? And what is a black-bailer?" Thank God, she thought, for the man's intrusion. There was a difficult moment due to follow that other, and he has helped me to evade it.

"A black-bailer is a local name for those people who are always moaning about the poor slaves, the hard time they have, the cruel treatment meted out to them, and the iniquity of the whole system. And his name is Lyddon. Where he comes from nobody knows, but he's an upstart and an outsider. He bought Joyous Gard when old Pulman died, and he's upset everything and everybody ever since."

"Joyous Gard," repeated Hester, savouring the words. "That lovely name. It was Lancelot's castle, wasn't it?"

"He didn't name it," said Ambrose, jealously ignoring her reference. "Old Pulman did. Lyddon would call a place Pig Stye and be quite happy with it."

He fell silent and once Hester caught his eye resting upon her, speculatively.

"I couldn't help hearing," she said hastily, "so who is old Methody?"

"A crazy, whining old fellow. I believe he was a parson once. He's got an idea that he has a mission to the slaves. Goes round holding what they call 'preachings' and trying to undo all the good discipline has ever done. He talks to slaves about their immortal souls and the brotherhood of man. And he marries them. God knows husbands and wives raise enough fuss if you part them when they've only lived in sin. After old Methody has been at them they drag in the religious aspect too. I ordered him off some time ago. And it won't be Lyddon who will persuade me to let him return."

"I didn't think you seemed to like him much."

"I don't. I'm a placid fellow as a rule, but there's something about him that raises my ire. I believe he's rich, he paid quite a fabulous price for Joyous Gard, and he has excellent stock and plenty of slaves. But he lives like a field hand. I know because I went there once to buy some slaves. He wouldn't sell—or even hire one, though they were eating their heads off, ten deep about the place. Half the place was shut up then."

"Is he married?"

"No. Hullo, what the devil's wrong here?"

They had gained the short avenue that led to the house, and running down it, waving his hands and gesticulating frenziedly was the mulatto, David, followed by Elias.

"Master! Stop! Stop!" yelled David, and as Ambrose reined in, Barby trotted past and then halted so that, as David poured out his story to Ambrose, Elias stopped by Hester.

"Mis' Ambrose. She took mortal bad. Delia say fetchum."

Without waiting Hester tugged at the rein and smacked Barby on the flank. Greatly surprised Barby shot forward, and Hester was on the ground and tearing up the verandah steps by the time David had made Ambrose understand. They tore upstairs one after the other. Delia, moaning and wringing her hands, was keeping watch by the open door of Philippa's bedroom. From within the room there came the sound of other moans, eloquent, not of fretful indecision as Delia's were, but of pain.

"Mis' Ambrose, she doan let us do anyt'ing," cried Delia, rocking to and fro on her flat slippered feet. Hester pushed past her. There, on the middle of the big four-poster, fully dressed, Philippa lay, moaning and writhing. At the sound of Hester's approach she screamed, without turning her head, "Go away. Go away!"

"It's me," said Hester. And Philippa, scrambling up, wallowed across the wrinkled sea of chintz coverlet and seized her arms in a grip of iron.

"It's coming," she shrieked. "Do something! Do something to help me, *please*!"

Hester, still in Philippa's grip, turned her head to look at Ambrose who stood, stricken and white, in the doorway.

"It's too soon. We were going to warn the doctor well ahead.

Now he'll have to be fetched."

"Shall I send, or go myself?" asked Ambrose.

"Go yourself. You can't do anything here."

"Are you sure? Oh, if only mother . . ."

"Get along," said Hester, shouting.

He went away and she heard him going down the stairs two at a time, shouting to David to bring back his horse.

"Leave go my hands, darling," she said then, controlling her voice, so that it was soothing and coaxing. "Everything's going to be all right. I'm here. It'll be all right."

Philippa unclenched her fingers. Hester stepped to the door. "Have you ever had a baby?" she asked quietly of Delia.

"No, ma'am. Ah's alwuss lived propah."

"Ever helped anyone to have one?"

"No, ma'am."

"You're no good then. What about Margarita?"

"She ain nevah had no baby."

"All right. Go downstairs then and . . ." She gave the pop-eyed Delia minute instructions as to what to do down-stairs, and then turned back to Philippa.

The one possessor of first-hand experience, Poppy, who had borne her first baby a year ago, kept this piece of helpful information to herself and proceeded stolidly with her appointed task for the afternoon, grinding coffee for the next day.

Hester closed the door, and with some difficulty persuaded Philippa to allow herself to be undressed and put into the bed. Then she lighted the lamps and suggested that Philippa might like a cup of tea.

The suggestion, smacking as it did of the mundane and everyday, sobered Philippa.

"I can't drink tea *now*," she protested.

"Of course you can. It'll do you good and help to pass the time."

"But there won't be any time. It won't go on like this for long! Will it, Hester, will it?" There was panic in her voice.

Hester forbore to say that her most ardent hope was that it would go on like this long enough for Ambrose to reach Mount Pleasant, where the doctor lived, and return. Helping a husky convict lass in her delivery, even though the ship rolled and the lantern smoked, and the groans of the fever patients penetrated the thin partition, seemed an easier and less responsible task than aiding the nervous, terror-stricken Philippa to produce the heir to Watershead. She had an absurd notion that if she could only distract Philippa's mind she might postpone the crucial moment. So she ordered tea which was brought up by Margarita. But before Philippa had sipped hers she gave a start which sent the cup flying and screamed again, louder, and Hester, setting down the pot from which she was pouring her own cup, ran to the bed and realised with a sinking of the heart and an out-thrust of the jaw, that in all probability she would be sole priestess at this ritual of birth.

The room grew warm from the lamps. Hester struggled and sweated. Philippa screamed and moaned. But the inevitable process went on.

At last Hester said, "I shall have to have Delia in now." Philippa seemed not to hear. Hester rang the bell and Delia panted up with everything that Hester had ordered.

When Ambrose arrived with the doctor, who had been run to earth in a tavern by the harbour at St. Agnes, the baby, crimson, wrinkled, incredibly aged in appearance, was lying in a nest of shawls on the day-bed, and in the four-poster Philippa lay sleeping. Hester was pouring out a fresh cup of tea. The room bore no traces of the recent drama.

The doctor, still breathless from hard riding and exuding fumes of rum, went to look at Philippa. Hester stood at the foot of the day-bed and introduced Ambrose to his son.

"It's a boy," she said, as proudly as though she had produced it.

CHAPTER IX

MRS. MARKHAM, fetched home next day by her son, knew the proudest moment of her life when she could take hurried leave of her hostess, Tabitha Slater, fifteen times a grandmother, on the plea that she must see her grandson at once. On the way from St. Pierre to Watershead she managed, by dint of a few skilful questions, to learn that Philippa had been left alone while Hester roamed the plantation in Ambrose's company.

"Don't tell me, this time, that that girl is a heroine," she said acidly. "If she had been attending to her duty, the doctor could have been fetched in time. It stops my breath to think of what might have happened."

"And would have, if Hester had not been as capable as Satan," said Ambrose.

His mother glanced sideways at him, her face darkening. She said no more. She had not lived to this great age without learning the folly of announcing one's plans beforehand, but to herself she decided that Hester Roon should take herself, her capability and her yellow head, elsewhere as soon as Philippa could be made to see sense.

Just at present, though, Hester was as necessary to Philippa as she had ever been. For Philippa was ailing and slow in recovery, and except Hester no one was allowed to touch either her or the baby, known already as Anthony, after Ambrose's father. Unable to feed the child herself Philippa rejected with the utmost scorn and repulsion the idea that a black wet-nurse should be installed. In vain did Mrs. Markham assure her that it was a well established custom from which no ill result had ever been noticed. Her own first baby had been suckled at a black breast.

"Not Ambrose," cried Philippa, in horror.

"No, not Ambrose," said Constance, wondering whether that were the truth or not . . . . there had been Edward, Stephen, John, and Ambrose, how should a mother remember everything about each one?

"The milk is perfectly good, far better than a cow's. And it has no more effect upon the child than a cow's milk does."

"It would have an effect upon me," cried the victim of negrophobia. "I should never feel the same about him again."

"Never in my life have I listened to such ridiculous rubbish," cried Constance, realising with an uprush of relief that now her daughter-in-law's state of mind could no longer be detrimental to her grandson's existence. "May I ask how you propose to feed him, or is he to starve in accordance with your idiotic fancies?"

"Hester feeds him," said Philippa, with complete faith.

"That is one thing Hester is unable to do," rapped out the old lady.

"Well, she is doing it. She's doing it now with some linen dipped in milk. He sucks it. She saw how it was done when she was on the ship."

246

"Where is this insane business taking place?"

"In Hester's room. She has the stove there to heat the milk, and she said the stove was too smelly to bring in here."

With a sibilant rustle of her silk skirts Constance Markham hurried along the corridor and was brought to a full-stop by the locked door of Hester's room. She rapped upon it sharply.

"Who's there?" asked Hester.

"I am. Open this door as once. How dare you lock yourself in here with the baby? What are you doing?"

The door swung open quietly. Framed within it the irate grandmother saw her grandson, his small red face hidden from view in the bulging bosom of a young negress, the very Cora who had been fetched to the house early the morning after it had been decided that Philippa could not feed her son, and whom Constance had asked to wait in the kitchen until she had talked sense into Philippa.

For a moment there was no sound in the room save the soft swallowing and breathing of a feeding baby. Then Hester said, "You're not to tell her."

Constance Markham looked at the convict girl and for the first time the dislike in her eyes was tempered, if not with affection, with respectful admiration. Then she closed the door. Going back to her own room she unlocked her bureau and drew out a mass of papers. Almost all morning she sat there, comparing, computing, pausing with her quill tip between her teeth and staring out of the window, casting up a column of figures and then referring to some other paper at the bottom of the pile.

When at last she rose and locked the bureau again she had taken a decision that was to have far-reaching effect. Anthony Fraser Markham had made a successful appearance in the world as heir to Watershead. It was plainly his grandmother's duty— and therefore his father's—to see that his inheritance was worthy of him. All kinds of reforms and economies were to be set afoot, in order that he might, at the age of twenty-one, find himself one of the wealthiest young men in Bartuma.

That every one of these economies was going to be practised at the expense of the race of the woman from whom young Anthony was drawing the very substance of life never occurred to his grandmother. Nor would it have deterred her.

Within doors life went on much as before, altered only by the presence of the baby. Out of doors, in a world as full of

hopes and fears, of human love and hatred, of physical sensi-
tiveness and spiritual bewilderment as that within doors, many
changes were made. A ruthless weeding-out of old slaves and
weaklings was made. Some twenty or thirty husky young field
hands found their way to the slave block in St. Agnes, and
those who remained were compelled, by ruthless methods of
driving, to perform the extra labour. Rations were cut down.
The salt mackerel, an honoured institution, served every Friday,
was abandoned. Fish had to be bought. It could be replaced, in
bulk at least, by the plantains that cost nothing. Salt fat pork
was to be issued once a week instead of twice.

Now and again Ambrose, more closely in touch with the
slaves, protested half-heartedly. But Constance Markham was
not the woman to listen to half-hearted protests, least of all
from her son. Hadn't the plantation been working almost at a
loss these six years, since the spread of sugar cultivation had
lowered the price? Did he want his son to live to be a pauper?
Wasn't overfeeding and idleness a fruitful ground for breeding
trouble? Had she ever given bad advice?

Ambrose, disliking the whole business, let her had her way. It
was so much easier than arguing, and there was a dangerous
grain of truth in everything she said. And he, no more than she,
no more than the Slaters at St. Pierre or the Eastons at Fair
Mount, nor half a hundred more of the white lords in their
cool, white houses, had any idea of the movement that was stirring in the depths of the black tide upon which their lives were
founded. For it is a truth that though a volcano may erupt and
bury, or an earthquake shatter, a whole community, the area of
the disaster is not thereafter avoided by the human race. They
build again and hope that for their span at least all will be well.
It was so with the planters in all the islands where the slaves
outnumbered, by a vast degree, their masters. There had been
trouble in the past, oh yes, and in all probability there would be
trouble again, but having taken such precautions as would lull
their most urgent fears, they shut their eyes to the danger and
went merrily on.

And Watershead went merrily on. Constance Markham's fit
of economy did not affect her personal expenditure. There was
a vast christening party for Anthony Fraser, and this was followed by the gay celebrations of Philippa's birthday, which
coincided with her return to the ways of the world. The nearest
neighbour, Bruce Lyddon of Joyous Gard, was not bidden to

either and, for the first time since his arrival in Bartuma, this deliberate exclusion caused him concern.

For Lyddon, who had made his devious way to Bartuma along a path that was hard and dangerous and had as little of the romantic in his nature as any man, had been smitten down, in the thirty-ninth year of his age, by that curious affliction known as love-at-first-sight. He had stood there by those coloured rocks in the bright late afternoon sunshine and seen a girl emerge from the shadow of the rocks as suddenly, as perfectly, as dramatically as Aphrodite came out of the sea. He had heard her name, Hester Roon, and the simple syllables of it had gone ringing through his mind like the trumpet of a herald. And that was all.

He had not arrived in his present position through not knowing his own mind or his own limitations. He knew both now. That woman, once seen, and heard only to say "Good day", was the one woman in the world that he wanted : and there were almost unsurmountable obstacles in the way of his desire.

At least, so they seemed, for he imagined that Hester was a friend of the Markhams possibly on a short visit only; maybe betrothed already; in all probability as arrogant and scornful as the Markhams themselves.

But when he tackled the problem in his usual forthright manner the obstacles (not for the first time in his varied experience) melted one by one.

Judicious questioning here and there gleaned for him the precious information that the girl in the green habit was no guest or friend of the family at Watershead. She was an imported girl, off the *Worcester*, picked by lawyer Kyne and presented to young Mrs. Markham, who was Northern bred and had a queer antipathy to blacks. This sorry history, so repellent to the average suitor, sang in his mind like a peal of joyous bells. But when the first impact of joy was over he realised anew that Hester was as much shut away from him as though she had been a member of an Eastern seraglio. He had not the entry of Watershead, and he would not be likely to meet her in any house where he did visit. Good God, he thought, startled, I might never see her again.

For several days he went about his estate in a trance and at night roamed the empty, echoing rooms of the house, planning the grace and elegance with which they should be furnished, and imagining the beauty of Hester Roon against the background that he planned. He told himself, but without conviction, that he was behaving like a love-sick schoolboy; that this was the vengeance, cunningly taken by the gods, for his long years of cynical philandering. He told himself, rather more firmly, that he had only to wait and time would obliterate the memory of that small white face with the curved mouth above that narrow jutting chin, shut out the remembered light in those slanting, queerly coloured eyes. His mind was willing to give time its chance, but his heart defied the anodyne.

And then, in the unaccountable way in which, having found an unaccustomed word, one finds it again, having heard a name for the first time one hears it drop from the lips of the next stranger, he began to hear things about this Hester Roon. Told half compainingly by Constance Markham to her friend Alfred Kyne, and repeated by him as proof of the fact that he had only to look at a girl to see what she was like, the story of Hester's meeting with Satan, and that of her behaviour on the day of Anthony's untimely birth, had spread abroad, and now reached the ears that were most desirous of giving them welcome. Lyddon's delight at hearing these garbled accounts was only equalled by the intensity of half-desperate longing that shook him afterwards. Undoubtedly this was the woman; but how to prove it?

He meditated the bold—and to him, natural—course of going to Watershead and asking outright to see Hester. The scheme had enormous advantages. It was simple, straightforward and involved no waste of precious time. But it had disadvantages too. His appearance at Watershead would give rise to comment which might easily embarrass Hester; and the request might be refused. Her position in the house was, after all, menial. It was better, he decided, to try to get in touch with the girl herself and ask her to meet him. Having decided that, he lost no more time.

Horribly conscious that the pen was the worst weapon he could have chosen, he nevertheless sharpened a new quill and tore from the big leather-bound book in which he kept his rudimentary accounts, a long, blue-lined page. He proceeded to write in large awkward letters, some heavily scored out, what amounted to his first love-letter.

"Dear Miss Roon," he began, and then, thinking that too familiar, drove three black lines athwart it. After all, he had never spoken to her. "Miss Roon: Dear Madam," a stupid piece of formality. Cross that out too, and leaving the manner of address to those who were skilled in such things, set down what you want to say.

"I have something that I think is very important to ask you. Would you be good enough to arrange to meet me at any place and any time that is convenient to you?"

He read it through, frowning. It sounded abrupt; two, at least of the words looked oddly spelled; but it said what he wanted, more or less, and he knew that he could neither add to it nor improve it. It remained to sign his name. He wrote it and then stared doubtfully at the sprawling letters. Bruce Lyddon. Would that mean anything to her? Would she remember that Ambrose Markham had called him Lyddon? Not very likely. So beneath the signature he screwed in, "of Joyous Gard. I met you the other day by the rocks near the spring."

He was thirty-eight years old; as arrogant in his own fashion as Ambrose Markham; he had made a tidy little fortune in whaling—which took a man to do, at least; he had fought for the East India Company in two nasty little wars, known famine, wounds, and finally prosperity. But his face, as he regarded his finished letter, was the puzzled, dubious face of a child. His vanity, his male self-esteem, urged him to destroy the scribbled paper, call for his horse, ride furiously down to St. Agnes and in Madame L'Estige's comfortable, dimly lighted bawdy house, drown the memory of Hester in an orgy of drunken, purchased delight. For an appreciable time he hesitated. Then with hasty movements of his long brown fingers he folded the sheet, sealed it and bellowed for Andy.

Andy, a very old negro with a face like a wizened monkey, a halo of white hair and the innocent eyes of a child, came running.

"Up at Watershead," said Bruce, "there is a young lady named Miss Hester. I want this," he tapped the folded paper, "to reach her with as few people knowing as possible. Can you manage that?"

"Ah shud say so," said Andy confidently. He forbore to mention that Delia was his brother's wife sister, a close relationship as such things went. He preferred that his master should attribute the successful performance of the errand to his own craft and guile. He had served Bruce before, and knew that rewards awaited the slave who could do apparently difficult things and keep his mouth shut.

About an hour later he shuffled to the kitchen door at Waters-head, was admitted by Margarita and greeted Delia, who was baking bread, with cousinly affection.

"Ah wuz just passin' an' speculated dat Ah wud just call in to say Howdy. My, dat bread smell good, Delia. Ah s'pose yo' wudn't had just a liddle sweet crust for a poah ole man to mumble his gums on, hugh?"

"Ah'm glad sumpin down at dis place please yo'," retorted Delia. "Ah bin led to believe dat nuthin' heah wuz as good as up at yore place." Nevertheless she opened the door of the vast oven, took up the long-handled, shiny bread-shovel, drew out a loaf, tested it by tapping its bottom and holding it to her ear, decided that it was done and broke off a large portion of the crisp brown crust. She set it before Andy, lumbered into the larder and returned with cheese and butter and a mug of ale, and Andy settled down to make the repast as long as possible so that he might have time to consider his next move.

At meetings like this all the gossip of the plantations was exchanged. Andy listened and talked and mumbled his sweet crust and tested Delia to see whether she was a safe messenger.

"Yo' got comp'ny in de house. Mis' Ambrose cousin Ah heah tell."

Delia enlightened him as to Hester's status in a manner that betrayed her lack of friendly feelings towards the interloper.

"Yo' doan appear to hab no great 'fection for her," said Andy. "Yo'd like to see a spell put on her maybe?"

"Yo' an' yore spells, yo' go along," said Delia scornfully. "Yo' cain't put no spells on dat one. She got eyes look clean t'rough yo'."

"Dat's de best sort for spells. Tun yo' head away Delia, whiles Ah wuk a liddle spell. Just a liddle joke, eh?"

Half scornful and half credulous, Delia turned away her head, and Andy, who had been prepared, had Delia spoken well of Hester, to take her into his confidence and entrust the note to her to deliver, bent over, his innocent eyes watching Delia and his wrinkled old mouth uttering strange sounds. Suddenly, with a smack of his hand on the table he bade Delia turn and look. He lifted his hand and showed the folded paper on the scrubbed table.

"Yo' gib her dat," he said, gently smiling. "Dat'll pepper her tea, propah. But doan yo' say a wud about it. Not to anybody. If yo' do de spell woan wuk. Yo' just put dat where she's shore

252

to find him, an' doan know nuthing nor say nuthin'. Yo' and me, we'll get lotta fun outa dis."

He chuckled so maliciously that Delia was at least assured of one thing, the folded paper boded Hester no good. As soon as Andy had finished his meal, set his battered old hat upon his head with his white hair standing up in the place where the crown should have been, and taken his leave, Delia watched until Hester and Philippa went out of the house and then laid the note on top of a pile of clean handkerchiefs on Hester's dressing-table.

Had Delia been present and seen the startled and puzzled face with which Hester read the few earnest words she would have felt certain that the spell was a reality. What in the world could Bruce Lyddon of Joyous Gard have of importance to communicate to her?

She had learned by this time the real underlying reason for the dislike with which the Markhams regarded their neighbour. Philippa had told her the story. It concerned the undefined boundary between the two estates, a matter which the Markhams and the Pulhams, being friends, had ignored. Upon Lyddon's arrival, he and Ambrose, starting off with an initial dislike of one another, had quarrelled fiercely. Alfred Kyne had been called in and had suggested a compromise that left both parties unsatisfied. This combined with the newcomer's blackbailing tendencies and his refusal, in the hour of Ambrose's need, to sell any of his sleek slaves to Watershead (which had a reputation, even then, for hard usage of slaves) had broken off communication between the neighbours.

What then, could Ambrose's enemy want with one of his household?

Hester studied the page again, almost as critically as its writer had done. The script was atrocious. Miss Peck's ruler would have dealt mercilessly with the fingers responsible.

But this critical Hester was the same person as the girl who had once let Death himself into The Fleece because she could not resist her curiosity. This was the same Hester who was always longing for something to happen. In much less time than it had taken the lovesick man to decide to dispatch the note, Hester had written, in her very best hand, "To-morrow, by the spring, at half-past three." Cora, already her collaborator, and the better off by several baskets of provisions given by

253

a grateful grandmother, promised to deliver the paper. For Cora, as Master Anthony Fraser Markham's wet nurse, was excused from all labour and free to come and go as she would between the feeding times.

What other messages the few trusted slaves carried upon their errands between plantation and plantation, only they knew, only time would show. What did Alfred Kyne, for instance, know of Garçon, beyond his nice French manners and outward subservience? Did Bruce, trusting the guileful Andy and even taking advantage of his craftiness, forget that Andy was a slave and a black? And the favoured Cora probably had other things in her bosom beside a fountain of milk. What did the careless white masters know or care?

CHAPTER X

IT WAS easy enough for Hester to announce that she was pining for a really long walk; and if she chose to take it in the afternoon, with the hot season just beginning and sun high in the sky, Philippa was not the mistress to question her whim. The baby slept in his be-ribboned cradle; Philippa dozed beside him on the day-bed. And Hester, so little conscious of the significance of her errand that she did not even change into one of the pretty dresses given her by Philippa, went striding off towards the rock-encircled spring.

It was a long way to walk. Mounted upon Barby she had not noticed the distance. A thin film of red dust, kicked up by her hurrying feet, covered the plain print dress. Her face and neck grew moist. As soon as she reached the shadow of the rocky passage she tore off the hat with the pink ribbon and the velvet rose and ran her hands through her damp, clustering curls. It was cool here. She pressed her hot palms against the striped and mottled surface of the rocks and drew refreshment from them.

She had thought, during the long walk, far more of Ambrose than of the man she had come to meet. Love and jealousy, like a twin-headed snake, had nagged at her all the way. She had hardly any rest from it now, for there were no feelings of pity to mitigate her envy of Philippa. Quite often now there was a hollow in the pillow beside that black head when Hester entered the room in the morning. Such evidence of restored connubial relationships went to her heart like a sword, turned her sick, made her reply to Philippa's friendly morning greeting a triumph of courageous effort. Once Philippa's own pillow had been wet; and Hester, pounding it fiercely, attributed the tears to ecstasy, not to frustration. She would have wept herself—had indeed often experienced a curious tendency to tears in Lownde Wood after Sam's embraces. How much more with Ambrose?

Bruce, pacing around the basin of the spring, heard the step of his beloved; looked up, and saw, stepping daintily into the rocky chamber, not a lovesick woman, but a golden girl with a curving, scornful, scarlet mouth and questioning eyes beneath damp clustering curls.

His heart was pounding so heavily that his first greeting, accompanied by a sweep of the hat and an ungraceful bow, was soundless. Hester was in complete control of her voice and it rang out, brisk and rough-edged :

"Good afternoon, Mr. Lyddon. I'm sorry if you have been waiting. I walked and it was farther than I reckoned."

He looked down at the narrow feet in the rather clumsy little dust-covered shoes and thought that they should never again fall on the unyielding earth, the unworthy earth. The grey mare's foal should be trained to answer to a thread of cotton, should be trained to an easy pace, should carry this light burden with pride.

His head buzzed with emotion, confusion, the unwonted inrush of dreams.

He stood silent, looking like a fool, and Hester drew several unfavourable comparisons between him and *her* beloved.

"Well," she said. "What was it that you wanted to tell me?" She stood, poised like a bird for flight. He must speak quickly or she would be gone, swift and impatient and still unknowing.

He stripped off his best coat, a crude blue with silver buttons, and laid it over an outjut of rock by the lip of the spring. His shirt was unbecoming, yellowish in colour, meagrely frilled and damp beneath the armpits with the sweat of his torment.

"Sit on that, won't you?" His voice was deep, gruff, not musical like Ambrose's, and it sent a shuddering reverberation along the rocky walls.

She sat down, her back very straight, the pose of her head

inquiring, her hands laid together, palm uppermost in her lap. The thin print dress clung to the long slim line of her thigh and fell smoothly over the rounded knee. Once more the thunder of his blood precluded speech. He dropped down on the bare cool rock, not too near her, and fought for speech.

"The Markhams don't like me," he began with apparent irrelevance, "and though I'd have been willing to make the peace, even if it meant putting myself in the wrong—I mean admitting that I was wrong, even then I couldn't have been certain of seeing you. So I had to choose this way. I hope you didn't mind. I mean, it's not what I would have chosen, getting you to walk so far and meet me here. It's not the thing to ask a young lady to do. I know that. And I wouldn't wish you to think that I wasn't respectful."

What is all this about? Hester almost spoke aloud in her impatience. She tilted her head more inquiringly and her lashes made a shadow on the privet-flower pallor of her cheek, and the big man before whom mutinous whalers had trembled, lost all thread of his discourse, and could only think, Great God how beautiful you are.

"I had to see you," he managed at last. Nothing else seemed forthcoming, so Hester said, "What about?"

"I suppose you have no idea?" It was his last attempt to avoid the inevitable fence.

"I thought it might be something to do with Ambr . . . Mr. Markham. A message perhaps."

Oh, you who were so weatherwise, who could hear the change of the wind, who knew to an instant by the change in the rope's tension whether the harpoon had struck or missed, hear now that change of voice as it says "Ambr . . .", the minute confusion of tone as it substitutes the formal title. Hear it, learn from it, make up some trivial message and get away with your heart still unexposed.

"No," he said. And this time the voice was better modulated. "It was about you and me I wanted to talk. I'm not a very good talker, so I'll be brief. I saw you, Hester Roon, down there by the rocks, and I fell in love with you, like that." He smacked his hand on his knee. "I mean it, I'm serious. I want to marry you. Wait a minute, please. You don't know me. I'm nothing to look at or to listen to, and it isn't to be expected that you have any feelings about me at all. But if you'll marry me I'll give you anything you ask for, and I'll look after you properly. If I'd

256

had any means of seeing you properly I wouldn't have blurted everything out like this. I'd have waited and wooed you a bit at a time. As it was I thought this way was best." His sudden burst of speech ended abruptly, but it conveyed what he wanted to say, and he rose to his feet and stood like a man awaiting his sentence.

Hester, more surprised than she had ever been in her life, stood up too. Her hands fluttered upward until they rested, clasped, beneath her breast, and she darted her tongue over lips gone suddenly dry with astonishment. But her eyes were steady and her voice under control.

"I shouldn't have come if I'd known *that* was what you wanted to say. I'm afraid I can't marry you." The two little sentences had a brutal ring, and the lines in Bruce's face deepened.

"I expected you'd say that, at first. But won't you think it over? I was impatient to tell you—and God knows, if the answer was the one I wish I'm impatient for that, too. But I want you to take your time. I know it's a serious business." He floundered on, unmanned by her nearness and the level stare with which she was regarding him. But he looked at her so earnestly and humbly, and what he was saying was so pleasing to her pride, that she was disposed to treat him with a cavalier kindliness.

"I'm afraid no amount of time or thinking over would change my mind," she said.

The unaccustomed humility which had been bothering him ever since he had seen her first, began to give way as soon as it met with opposition. He threw it off as he might have done a tight garment.

"Why?" he demanded. "Are you betrothed already?"

"No," said Hester, meeting frankness with frankness, "but I am in love. I couldn't marry you like that, could I?"

"Good God, no! It's the last thing I'd ask. I ought to have thought of that before. I believe I did once. Then I forgot and blurted out all the other without thinking. Well—I hope you'll be very happy."

"I don't suppose I shall," she said, with a shrug of the shoulder. "You see, he's married."

She had no idea why she was confiding like this in a man who a few minutes before had been a stranger to her. But it was a profound relief to tell someone. For the first time she understood why the maids at The Fleece had held such long whispered conferences, of which the passer-by could only catch, "And I said . . . And then he said . . .". There was a queer bitter-sweet pleasure in talking about the person one loved, and there was no one at all at Watershead who could be treated as a confidante.

"Oh," said Bruce, conscious of a lightened heart. "He's married. And do you intend to stay single all your life because of that?"

"I suppose so." Sweet statement of fact and faith.

"Nonsense," he said. "You're . . . How old are you?"

"Eighteen." So young. Half his age.

"You'll fall in love half a dozen times more, I expect. And you may—I don't say will—but you may live to wonder why ever you refused a decent offer on his account." He could smile at her childishness. The stories had led him to expect someone harder, more mature. He thought hard. Who would the man be? Whom would she have met? It was fairly recent, this passion. She was still rather surprised at it herself. Not Ambrose Markham. He repudiated the obvious answer even as he asked; "Ambrose Markham?"

"Oh, I couldn't tell you," said Hester, blushing scarlet. "I don't know why I have told you so much. At least, I did because . . . well, so that you would understand that it wasn't any use . . . you and me, I mean. You wouldn't tell anyone, would you?"

My dear child, he thought, tenderly, if you go about turning that colour at the very sound of his name nobody has to be told.

"Of course not. Besides, remember you hold my secret. Now, I'm going to say something that will annoy you very much, I know. All the same I'm going to say it. This fellow that you imagine you love isn't worth anything at all. Even if he wasn't married he's not the man for you, nor for any woman who has blood in her veins. Look how his mother leads him on a string. That's always a bad sign. He's over thirty, and still a pretty boy. Why you, Hester Roon, are twice the man he is."

She was too startled and angry to deny the truth of his assertion. She did not even pause to ask herself how he had guessed.

"You're horrible," she said furiously, "horrible. Oh, I'm sorry I ever came here, sorry I ever told you anything. I know you hate him and now I suppose you're jealous as well. Well, you needn't be, because even if I'd never seen him I should . . .

I should . . ." She searched her mind for a term hard and hurtful enough to fling at him.

"Never think of marrying me? I suppose not, if your taste lies in the direction of pretty boys. I'm surprised at you, Hester. I'm disappointed. So I'm jealous, am I? Well, a disappointed and jealous man has to be allowed a little licence. Has he ever kissed you?"

Hester hesitated. She did not wish to answer the impertinent question, and yet she wished that she could have said yes, thousands of times.

"No? I always thought he was a fool. Well, I'm going to kiss you now, so that when he does you'll have something to compare with it."

Before incredulous astonishment would permit her to move he had reached out, lifted her in his arms and set his mouth on hers. It came down, hard and powerful, and in his arms, for all her wiry strength, she was no more than a puppet. It was worse than being a puppet, for that would have no feelings, whereas she was rent apart with shame and fury, and beneath, oh, traitorous flesh so ready to betray the outraged mind, a strange voluptuous pleasure. She went suddenly limp and at that, just a moment too soon, he set her down. They stood for a moment breathless. Then Hester dragged out her handkerchief and ostentatiously wiped her mouth, hard. But her eyes no longer met his squarely.

"That," she said venomously, "is the way that you would treat me because I am a servant and fool enough to come here alone. Let me go. Let me out of this."

But he planted his body across the entrance and held out his hand.

"You're not to go, thinking that," he said solemnly. "I don't care what you are, where you come from, whether you're queen or kitchen maid. I told you I loved you. I don't mind what you say to me, I deserve it all, but I can't bear you to think that I've insulted you because of some trumpery bit of class distinction. Take that back. If you don't know that I kissed you because I couldn't help myself you don't know anything at all."

He looked and sounded as though he might kiss her again. She must escape.

"All right," she said, more calmly. "I believe you."

He reached for her hand and turned it over in his own. Little firm worker's hand with thin fingers and hard palms.

"Listen," he said. "I think we can say now that we know one another. If there is ever anything that I can do for you I beg you to let me know. And if ever you change your mind—as you will —about your pretty boy, think of me. Give me a chance. I'm too old now to change mine and I tell you, once and for all, that you are the woman I want for my wife. Is that clear? Then good-bye."

He bent his tawny head and kissed her hand, first on the palm then on the backs of the fingers. And again that sudden thrill ran through her. She drew her hand back sharply, said, "Good-bye," without looking at him, slipped through the rocky passage and escaped. He followed her into the open and watched, for as long as he could see it, the slim hurrying figure in the print dress with the pretty rose-decked hat swinging unheeded from its hand. When, a mere dot now, she leaped the sunken ditch and was lost in the garden he turned away with a sound that was half laugh, half sigh. He forded the stripling stream and regained his own ground. With his own impatient hands he saddled Blanche, the pale mare, shouted to his overseer to lock up his house, and before darkness fell was seated in Madame L'Estrige's plush-filled, mirror-decked haven of the lost, drinking steadily and regarding with a new and scarcely veiled dislike the plump dark charms of the inoffensive girl who considered him, not without reason, her special property.

Hester hurried back to Watershead full of very mixed feelings; but by the time that she had reported to Philippa that the walk had been delightful, smuggled Anthony out to Cora, made Philippa's evening meal and put the room ready for the night, the familiar atmosphere of the place that had become her home had closed around her, soothing and Lethe-like. This meeting with Bruce Lyddon, who changed so suddenly from humility to violence and then back again, meant nothing, was nothing, altered nothing. Almost gladly, almost happy to have withstood this test of faith, she lifted her old chains and hugged them. She loved Ambrose; she served the woman whom she envied more than any one on earth; she waited for something that she could hardly name. Now and again the memory of that deliberate forgotten kiss touched her in her dreams. But it was always Ambrose who kissed her, never Bruce, it was always Ambrose who murmured words of love, and it was to Ambrose that she gave, even in sleep, the full response of a passionate, half-awakened nature.

CHAPTER XI

TIME ran smoothly past and the day arrived when Mrs. Markham would celebrate her seventy-first birthday. A number of friends and neighbours had gathered to congratulate her and dine at her table on the occasion. For the first time Bruce Lyddon had been bidden as a guest, and, to the faint surprise of both the Markhams, had accepted the invitation. The concession in his favour was to mark the end of the feud about the pasture rights. Bruce had, as Ambrose expressed it patronisingly, "admitted himself in the wrong, like a man.' The Watershead cattle now roamed the disputed pasture, and the fence, advised in his wiliness by Mr. Kyne, had been broken down. So now Bruce sat, watchful, hopeful and disappointed, at the table, laden, as the meal ended, with fruit and flowers and wine.

Constance, at the head of the table, wore a grey silk dress, very stiff and full and plentifully decorated with bows of purple ribbon. She looked along the table to where her old friend, Tabitha Slater, sat beside her old friend, Alfred Kyne, and enjoyed the warm glow of knowing that she had both worn better than Tabitha, and made more of a success of life. Even now, at this age, she held the reins of the estate. Probably Ambrose didn't fully realise it, but it was obvious that he took her advice, never disobeyed, though he always contradicted her, and entrusted her with the accounts on the plea that he had no head for figures. Of course he hadn't, poor darling, nor had his father before him; but one head for figures was quite enough in one family, and she intended to manage the accounts until she died. Tabitha, being a sentimentalist, had allowed first her husband, then her sons, to bully her. Even Rosetta bullied her, and that was why she was at this moment wearing a dress that had been turned, and ribbons that were limp and frayed. And Tabitha herself looked very old and weary. She drooped in her chair.

I may be old, but I am not weary, thought Constance, drawing back her shoulders and stretching her waist until the whalebone in her bodice creaked. Seventy-one, of course, is a great age, but my family is long-lived, and apart from that silly little pain in my side I enjoy good health. She caught Alfred's eye and smiled graciously. He had given her a sack of very precious bulbs for her garden.

Alfred, also looking about the table, turned his connoisseur's eye upon Philippa and wondered why she was so limp and unhappy. She'd been a pretty, sweet little thing two years ago; now she looked much older, flattened out, dimmed. Ambrose certainly wasn't the husband that Alfred would have chosen for his daughter had he had one. Too much mothered; it took the stuffing out of a boy. Yet Ambrose, slightly flushed with wine, was a handsome sight, and maybe after all it wasn't his fault that his wife looked as though life had cheated her. Coming from the North perhaps she found the heat trying; it had been hot enough to-day in all conscience.

Bruce Lyddon sat and listened to the chatter and wondered whether, by abasing himself to Ambrose, he had done his cause any good. Here he was, certainly, an accepted guest under the roof that sheltered Hester; he had even heard her name when somebody congratulated Philippa upon the tasteful arrangement of the table's centre-piece. Philippa's face had lightened suddenly and she had said, "Oh, that was Hester's work." But although his pulses had missed a beat at the sound of her name, he was already regretting the pasture rights which he had sacrificed. Hester was in this house, but as far away from him as though a sea divided them.

With a rustling of silks and a scattering wave of perfume the ladies retired. The men closed in to the table, refilled their glasses, lighted cigars and began to talk about the subject which was nearest all their hearts—except the demented Bruce's—sugar, its price, prospects of harvest, sugar, sugar in all its aspects. Somebody mentioned Old Methody.

"I hear Brett has forbidden him High Hurst now. You'll soon have the monopoly of his ministrations, Lyddon."

"Damned, dissenting old bastard," said young Slater. "I can't think how you endure him."

"Preaches red revolution, so Brett said," added another man.

"That doesn't agree with what I hear," said Bruce, leaning forward. "The last preaching at my place was on the text, 'Servants, obey your masters.'"

"So you were told," jeered Ambrose.

"But I know it for a fact."

"How?"

"Because I always listen to the preachings. After all, I don't mind his coming, if it gives them any pleasure, but I must keep a check on what he says."

"Well I'm damned," said Alfred Kyne. "Are you by any chance Methody yourself?"

"Not in the least. But that isn't Methody's fault. One piece in every discourse is directly aimed at me." Bruce smiled rather sourly as he recalled Methody's dig about the evils of whoring after strange women. He had doubtless seen Blanche tethered in Madame L'Estrige's yard.

"You'll regret it before you've finished," said Alfred Kyne judiciously. "All this kind of thing is definitely unsettling. I can remember the good old days."

"Some pretty nasty things happened then, if I hear aright."

There was a sudden cold silence. Of course Lyddon was a comparative newcomer and not to know; and he was an astute man of business and it made things easier that he and Markham were no longer at loggerheads; but really he should have learned by now that that kind of thing wasn't said at a table where almost every man had lost brother, father or friend in the rising sixteen years before.

Young Slater, with tact worthy of an older man, stepped into the conversational breach while everyone was clearing his throat and trying to form some diverting sentence.

"D'you know, Markham, I've never seen your heir. I didn't get down to the christening, you remember."

"And I was in Havana," contributed another man.

"And I was abed with fever."

"I'll get him in now," said Ambrose, reaching for the bell-rope. "Joseph, ask Miss Hester if she'll bring down Master Anthony without saying anything to the ladies. Philippa has some notion about tobacco smoke being bad for him," he added as explanation to his guests.

"The nurse girl is worth a look, too," whispered Alfred to his nearest neighbours. "I picked her out from a cargo of twenty-five, and had hard running to snatch her from under Madame's nose. A loss to the community, I think you will agree with me, but after all, friends come first." The garrulous little man became aware that Lyddon, upon his left, was looking at him with great ill-favour. Of course the fellow frequented Madame's and probably hated to think that he had missed anything. 'But this girl hadn't the nature to make a successful *fille de joie,*" he added comfortingly. "Not elastic enough." And to-morrow I shall take my business away from you, thought Bruce, and I'll warn Gibson what you're after and lend him some money myself, you filthy-minded little usurer.

The door opened and closed softly and Hester stood there, Anthony, flushed and heavy-eyed from sleep, upon her arm. "Carry him round, Hester,' 'said Ambrose. And Bruce winced at the easy familiarity of his tone. "He screams if I take him."

Moving slowly, her body braced against the child's weight, Hester circled the table. Complimentary words to Ambrose and inane attempts to attract the baby's attention circled with them. Hester's heart was singing because, for a second, as Ambrose had bidden her carry the baby round, he had put his arm about her, casually, meaninglessly, merely drawing her into the room and starting her on her way around the table. But it was enough to lighten her heart, to pour a stream of heartening false hopes into her blood and to restore the charm that had been lacking when she entered the room. In fact Alfred Kyne, looking at her pale, grave face, had thought, What can be the matter with this house? Constance is the only woman who flourishes in it.

Bruce, too, had noticed the pallor and gravity of Hester's face; he had also seen the carelessly stretched arm and the sudden change that resulted. He was horribly willing to believe that perhaps by this time Hester had captured Ambrose's attention. It was impossible, he thought, that any man should live in the same house with her and not love her.

He hardly glanced at the baby, but looked past its round downy head, caught Hester's eye and held it for a moment. The memory of that shameful afternoon assailed her like physical sickness and she turned away her head. The hot colour rushed to her cheeks, blotting out the delicate flush that had tinged them as Ambrose's hand fell upon her waist. She had not expected to see Bruce there, had hoped that she might never meet him again. And yet, under the mental Hester, who was in love with Ambrose and despised Bruce because he lacked the qualities that she admired in her master, the old fleshy Hester stirred uneasily, remembered the strength of his body and the thrill that had gone through her as he kissed her. Once more she retreated from it, hurrying past that corner of the table, leaning forward so that little, rheumatism-stiffened Mr. Calligan might touch the baby's cheek with one gnarled finger.

Then, thankfully, she carried Anthony away to his cradle.

Five minutes later Philippa, whose female friends had hit upon the same idea for passing a few dull moments, rang the bell and summoned Hester and the baby to the drawing-room.

This time his mother carried Anthony round, and Hester, standing just inside the door, saw her wrinkle her nose, inquiringly, bend low and sniff the child disapprovingly. Then, just as she presented him for Tabitha Slater's inspection, Anthony gave a wail and was sick.

Philippa muttered an apology, and moving with unwonted vigour, carried the child from the room, followed by Hester.

"Why does he smell of cigar smoke?" she asked sharply.

"Mr. Markham sent for me to take him to the dining-room."

"Well, I never. And you took him without telling me. You knew perfectly well, Hester, that smoke is bad for babies. Now he's been sick right in Mrs. Slater's face. I'm so ashamed."

Her voice rose to a wail, and Constance, excusing herself, rose and came rustling into the hall.

"What is the matter?"

Tearfully Philippa explained. Her own private troubles and the heat of the last few days had frayed her nerves. Her temper had been querulous. Hester knew, but it had never been directed against herself before.

She said stubbornly :

"What else could I do? Mr. Markham sent for him."

"Don't answer back," snapped Constance. "The obvious thing to have done was to consult us first. You're too fond of acting on your own initiative. I'm very tired of it. I think it's time you realised your position here. There, take him away and change his clothes. I shall have more to say about this in the morning."

Constance, the mother of four children, knew full well that babies were often unaccountably sick; and she did not share Philippa's morbid suspicion of cigar smoke. But she was not going to miss so golden an opportunity of widening a breach between Philippa and the girl whom she so much distrusted. There had never been the slightest rift before; by morning Philippa would have weakened; so as Hester, inwardly fuming, climbed the stairs with the baby, Mrs. Markham, in a few sibilant words, managed to convince Philippa, before they returned to the drawing-room, that Hester was thoughtless and stubborn and that the two qualities might easily threaten

Anthony's welfare. After all, thought the old lady callously, the child was weaned now and Hester's connivance was no longer required to deal with the feeding question. Let her once get gone and an ascendancy over Philippa would be easily established which would give Anthony into his grandmother's hands. And whose were fitter?

Philippa, regretting her mother-in-law's intervention, and repenting her own sharpness with Hester, had decided, long before the evening ended, that of course Hester should stay. In the morning she would feel stronger, more able to resist the indomitable old woman; for the moment let it go.

Upstairs, Hester, shattered by Philippa's words, and seeing the significance of the concerted attack, resigned herself to the idea of being sent away, probably to-morrow. It was clear that if Mrs. Markham could keep her daughter-in-law annoyed with her for so much as twelve hours, that span would measure her remaining time at Watershead.

Anthony, washed, re-clad and sleeping peacefully, lay in his cradle. Hester sat by the lamp, her work still folded on the table within the yellow circle of light and her head propped up on her linked fingers. Perhaps, she thought miserably, it would be just as well if she did go. In a new place, with new work and fresh people to think about, she might have a chance of recovering from her infatuation. For a moment the thought was comforting, but it was succeeded by a feeling of the most utter desolation. Never to see him again, never to hear his voice, never to hear his voice, never to come into touch with him through the meticulous performance of intimate little duties, such as the mending of the frill of that shirt which she hadn't started yet. It was not to be borne. She laid her hand on the soft cambric of the shirt. It was a link. There were several such. To have them broken would kill her.

In the dining-room the excellent products of the Markham cellar had gone round several times. An argument arose over an article that had been published in the *St. Agnes Gazette* three weeks before. Ambrose made a statement which Alfred Kyne questioned.

"I kept the paper," said Ambrose, getting rather unsteadily to his feet. "I'll fetch it. Go in to the ladies, will you? They're waiting for you, Slater, to give them some music. I'll bring my copy of Aggie's Rag into the drawing-room."

266

The door between his room and Philippa's where Hester kept vigil by the cradle, was open, and showed the yellow lamplight. No need to light a candle, then, he could find the paper in a moment. He looked into the room.

"Bring that lamp here, will you Hester, and hold it while I look in this drawer." Obediently she lifted the brass lamp and carried it into his room. He was slightly tipsy, and after the ring of wine-flushed faces around the table, Hester, paler than usual with the agony of thought, looked spectral to his eyes.

"Are you feeling ill?" She shook her head. "Then what is the matter?"

"I'm in disgrace," said Hester, and told him why. He found the paper and tucked it under his arm, slamming the drawer shut. The trivial story hardly reached his consciousness. As he turned he saw her face in the yellow lamplight, the shadows of the lashes long and tremulous, the mouth full and firm. She looked at him. And for the second time the alchemy of one person's desire worked. He took the lamp from her, set it with unsteady hands upon the chest-of-drawers, took her in his arms and kissed her.

It was the action of a constricted nature loosened by wine, the action of any half-tipsy fellow faced by an attractive girl who will obviously not resist him; but to Hester it was as though God Himself had stooped out of Heaven to kiss her. Her mouth, her arms, her body, and her mind all embraced him; and this time there was no vision of a gently-smiling Philippa to reproach and check her. It was Ambrose himself, startled by the passion he had evoked, who loosened her hands and freed himself.

"Must I go to-morrow, now?" she asked, imagining that she had found a champion capable of routing with a word both the women ranged against her. The question fell upon Ambrose like a dash of cold water. God, how right he had always been about women, leeches every one of them, save only his mother. A casual snatched kiss—did the little fool imagine that that was going to change anything?

"Don't you think it would be better if you did?" he asked craftily. Hester took the question as he intended her to.

"Maybe it would. If I didn't have to go too far away."

"That's right," he said. "We must find you a place not too far away. Then everything will be all right. Look, I must go now. They're waiting for me. I'll tell Joseph to bring you up some wine to keep you company." Maybe if she drank enough to get fuddled and then went to bed she would be unlikely to remember much in the morning. My God, he thought, hurrying down the stairs, what a firebrand. And what some man who liked that kind of thing was missing!

CHAPTER XII

ALREADY drunk on a vintage more potent than the fruit of the grape, Hester neverthless consumed, because he had sent it, the greater portion of the bottle of coarse Marsala which Joseph reckoned good enough for "dat poah white gurl." And with every mouthful she grew more elated and more lucidly certain what she was going to do.

To her, Hester Roon, who had never had anything, in the last weeks everything had been offered.

"Some place not too far away. Then everything will be all right." That meant that he would come to see her, or arrange some place where they could meet. What else should it mean to a girl with her head buzzing with the mingled fumes of love and Marsala?

And what place was nearer than Joyous Gard? Where else would she be so welcome, or so free? Where else would she be able to secure the clothes, the little feminine accoutrements that helped to hold a man?

After all, it wasn't wronging Bruce Lyddon much. He'd have her at any price. He had told her to come on her own terms. He had said he would wait. And wait he would, until the day of doom, while Hester, who had never had anything, lived in luxury at his expense and met Ambrose regularly by the spring. It all seemed possible, feasible, so easy in arrangement and performance that she felt herself freed from all mortal considerations and limitations. She could do anything she chose. She had Bruce for a slave and Ambrose as a lover; Philippa and old Mrs. Markham could go to hell!

She carried the rest of the wine into her own room. It was a precious elixir; sent her by Ambrose to keep her company because he had been obliged to leave her. She would drink it before she set out; and it would protect her from the terror that walketh by night; from her horror of crawling things : it would carry her through her monstrous proposal to Bruce, it would guarantee her omnipotence.

She laid her cloak ready on the bed and changed into her thick soles.

There were sounds of the party breaking up. Old Mrs. Slater, who could not travel back to St. Pierre until to-morrow, came upstairs. There was a confused sound of horsehoofs and leave-takings. At last Philippa came to bed, exhausted and rather ashamed, so that she deferred making her peace with Hester until the morning. It would not, she reflected, do any harm to let Hester see that she was not to be disobeyed with impunity. A few words, her usual affectionate smile might even then have softened Hester's mood; one has to be very debased to steal from a generous giver. But Philippa went to bed in silence and Hester, her tipsiness undiscovered, her clumsiness attributed to sulkiness, went to her own room, gulped her wine, snatched her cloak, and was out of the house within five minutes. Because of the guests, Satan, Fanny and Lou were not loose to-night. Everything was arranged for her benefit. Everything was ordained—her escape from The Fleece, her London adventure, her undeserved punishment. They were just steps that were leading her to this night, this wonderful night.

She took the long way to Joyous Gard, round by the road, because the short path led past the stream where the frogs croaked in the shallows, and despite her demented haste the journey took her almost three-quarters of an hour. Bruce had been home for a considerable time; but he had let himself in by the kitchen door, and had sat down beside the embers of the fire, thinking and dreaming and cursing himself.

The last part of the journey had been, for Hester, beset by fears; perhaps Bruce, too, set fierce dogs roaming at night. The shifting of a shadow, the rustle of a leaf made her start; but she never once contemplated turning back. By good fortune, as though her guardian angel was really watching to-night, instead of slumbering, she arrived at the back of the house, having missed the main entrance. The kitchen window showed as a square of light, and when she tiptoed to it and craned her neck to look within, her feeling of inspiration reached new heights. For there, sitting by himself, was Bruce. She tapped on the door.

It occurred to Bruce, as he crossed the floor and shot back the bars, that one of the Markham's guests had decided not to make the journey home and had called here in search of hospitality; or else perhaps one of the slaves was ill. Enough light spilled out from the kitchen to show a cloaked female figure with a white face; by all that was holy, Hester Roon.

"Can I come in?" she asked breathlessly. One hand fluttered from her breast to indicate the interior of the kitchen questioningly.

"But of course," he said, standing aside. "I hope there's nothing wrong."

"Oh, no; nothing wrong."

He noticed that her face was now even whiter than it had been before Ambrose's touch had coloured it; and her eyes were strange, a glassy green with the pupils shrunk to mere pinpoints. He shook up the thin shabby cushion of the kitchen chair in which he had been sitting, and Hester sat down, throwing back her cloak. She must wait until she had regained her breath. It must be the fast movement that was making her feel so unsteady and strange. The distant corners of the kitchen seemed to be swaying round and round, and it was only by fixing her stare upon a steady object near at hand that she could defeat a queer feeling of dizziness.

She needed all her wits about her, too. She realised that. The thing which had seemed so easy when she thought of it was not to be so easy of execution. Bruce, drawing up a stool and sitting down upon it, his hands clasped between his knees and his steady stare questioning her, was different from the man whom she had imagined. He was very big and solid and real. A slight sense of panic shot through her. She ignored it and said, with a brittle brightness quite new to her, "It's a funny time to call, isn't it?"

She discovered that the moment she unclenched her teeth her lower jaw began to shake with an uncontrollable tremor. She bit off the question, set her teeth, and propped her chin on her fingers. For the first time since her entrance her fixed stare wavered and took on an expression, faintly surprised, puzzled, and a little furtive.

"It's never too late or too early to call upon a friend," he said, leaning forward so that his face seemed to lurch at her suddenly and she drew her head back against the top of the chair.

270

"That's what I thought," she replied, trying to force her stiff mouth into a smile. He leaned back, satisfied. The words had come to him in a gust of wine-scented breath. She had been drinking. That explained the queer manner, the fixed stare and that betraying tremor of the chin.

"Well?" he asked.

The moment had arrived. She braced herself, defying her own dizziness, the thickness of her speech, the rolling spaces of the kitchen.

"I came to tell you that I have changed my mind." There, it was out. But still he said nothing; did not leap up delighted and take her into an embrace which she had expected and schooled herself to endure. He just sat there, looking at her kindly, but sceptically, as though the words meant nothing to him at all. "Well," she said, impatiently, "have you forgotten? You asked me to tell you if ever I changed my mind. About marrying you, I mean."

She thought suddenly and rather sickly of the bottle of Marsala; of that last glassful, hastily gulped. Was is possible that she was intoxicated? Not speaking clearly? Not saying what she intended at all? Mastering chin and tongue again, she demanded:

"Don't you understand me?"

"Oh, yes," he said. "I understand. Tell me, have you been drinking?"

"A little. I took a little wine with my supper." She waved her hand to indicate the negligibility of her potations.

"And had the wine anything to do with your change of mind?"

"You're very rude," said Hester rebukingly. "I suppose you have changed yours and now want to get out of it by pretending that I am not sober. I am. Perfectly sober."

An idea struck him. He resisted it for a moment and then succumbed to the temptation of its unique possibilities. After all, it was important that he should know what had brought her. A very short time ago, the casual touch of Ambrose Markham's hand had set her all aglow; a very short time ago she would not even look at him, whom she was now proposing to marry. What had wrought the change? He thought he could find out, and although his heart bled for her he decided to try.

"You've had a long walk. It's very remiss of me not to have offered you some refreshment. I'm afraid I have only brandy in

271

the house. Could you drink that?"

Still shrewd enough to see through the trick, but not confident enough to refuse to be taken in by it, she said :

"I should very much like some brandy."

He left her alone in the kitchen while he fetched bottle and glasses, and she spent the time opening and shutting her mouth, and since her chin was still rebellious, smote it hard with one hand.

My poor dear, thought Bruce, pouring out a liberal portion, you'll hate me in the morning, but we must have truth between us. He handed her one glass and then, holding his own, went back to the stool.

Hester drank, choked, recovered herself and drank again. The immediate effect of the spirit was good. Her chin left off shaking and confidence returned. She'd show him whether she were sober or not, nasty suspicious person. Brandy, what was that? Hadn't she drunk brandy with Sally and Fussy and Jim, and wouldn't she have outmanœuvred them but for an old woman's crass stupidity? She set the glass on the floor. It was empty, though she could only remember that first choking gulp. Bruce waited, his heart aching with tenderness as he watched her fight the weakness of her flesh. Oh, to be able to take her at her word. To carry her away and lay her between the cool sheets, with a pillow beneath the head which would presently ache fearfully. He could imagine the joy of the morning that would find her waking beneath his roof. But first this mystery of the change of heart must be laid bare.

"Now," he said, leaning forward. "Tell me everything that has been happening at Watershead."

"Well, I'm in disgrace. I ought not to have taken the baby into the dining-room without asking his mother's permission."

Nothing very revealing there.

"And so . . . ?"

"So Philippa—that's Mrs. Ambrose, but I call her Philippa when we are alone—was very cross with me. And once she stops standing up for me the old woman will have me out. She always has hated me. You see"—her voice grew confidential and she leaned forward, reeled to the side and then sought the support of the chair-back again—"she has always been the one who knew everything and ordered everything. She hates it that Philippa should more mind what *I* say and think about things. So she wants me to leave Watershead."

"And do you want to leave?"

She shook her head.

"Oh, no. It's the only place in the world to me, though sometimes I think . . . I think poss'bly I ought to leave."

"Because of Ambrose?" A shot in the dark that reached the centre.

"Yes. You see, always being there, seeing him and hearing him. It's very hard. And sometimes I am so jealous of Philippa I can hardly be civil to her."

"You still love him, don't you?"

"Yes, I do. Somebody once said that it wouldn't last. Did you say that?" She wrinkled her eyes at him, but there was a mist before his face and a dull roaring in her ears. "It doesn't matter," she said fatuously.

"Just tell me this, and then you shall lie down. You'd like to lie down, wouldn't you?"

"I would rather. I'm a little . . . tired. But I can tell you anything."

"What made you come to Joyous Gard?"

"Oh, that's very easy. After they'd both been so nasty Ambrose came up. And I told him that I must go away. And then he kissed me, and he said I must find a place not too far away so we could see each other. And this was the nearest. I do feel funny."

Bruce rose from the stool and put one arm around her.

"So you came here and thought you'd marry me and go on seeing him. Is that right?"

Of course, she had known that, sooner or later, he would hold her and possibly kiss her. She mustn't mind.

"That's right. So now it's all right, isn't it? And can I go to bed now?"

"Yes. I'll take you."

He stooped and raised her in his arms. She was very light and her bones were small. She seemed to crumple in his clasp. The frailness of her and the soft tendril of the curl that just brushed his chin melted him with a tenderness the like of which he had never known and which convinced him that he had been right in thinking that this was the other woman. Naughty, self-willed, obstinate little creature she might be, but she was the dearest thing in the world.

He laid her upon the sofa in the room which, beside the kitchen, was all that he used on the ground floor. Then he ran upstairs and snatched pillow and blankets from his own bed. He tucked her up securely and wished her good night.

"Good night," mumbled Hester. "You've been very kind."

He returned to the kitchen and sat for a few moments deep in thought. Then, after peeping in and finding her asleep, he went to his own room.

CHAPTER XIII

HESTER had whirled round violently upon a dizzy wheel of which her head was the pivot and then gone to sleep as though she had been stunned. Almost immediately, it seemed, she was conscious of a rattle of a cup, and stared up thinking that Poppy had made the tea because she had overslept. Philippa must never know, she thought, or she won't drink any. She opened her eyes and cried out at the pain which shot through them. "Oh," she said, shutting them tight. "Oh!"

"It's bad, is it?" asked Bruce. "Well, I've brought you some tea. Have it while it's hot."

More cautiously she opened her eyes, lifted her head and saw him by the side of the sofa. He held a tray in his hand, and upon it stood a fine china cup of delicate design and a coarse brown plebeian teapot.

She pushed back the topmost folds of the blanket and pressed her hands to her temples. Her head felt as though it must burst. Thought was out of the question, but memory assailed her relentlessly. She remembered the trick and how she had walked into it, babbling fool that she was. Her face was like that of a trapped animal. What now? it seemed to ask. Bruce poured out a cup of tea and handed it to her, scalding hot. He said nothing. But he crossed to the window and threw back the shutters so that the room was full of the grey dawn light. Then he blew out the candle, whose little flame had struck her shrinking sight with intolerable sharpness. When it was gone the greyness stole about the room, revealing, despairing.

He waited, still without speaking, until her cup was empty, then he refilled it and perched himself at the foot of the sofa.

"Can you remember anything about last night?"

She started to nod her head, but a loose cannon-ball inside her skull crashed forward on to her forehead.

"Don't talk about it, please."

"But I must. You see, when you refused my proposal you gave me a good reason. I can't well do less in refusing yours."

"Oh, please forget it," moaned Hester, only just resisting the temptation to pull the blanket over her head and cower down, out of sight and hearing.

"You sound very penitent, and you look very penitent. It's to be hoped you are. I hope you realise, Hester Roon, that you came here, flown with wine, to make the most infamous proposal to a man who was silly enough to think well of you. Suppose I'd been blind enough not to notice what was wrong with you. Where should we have been this morning? Ask yourself. A change of mind, indeed! Merely a change of tactics, fooling your friends now. I wonder what I have ever done to you to make you even consider such a thing."

"Let me go," said Hester, pushing aside the rest of the blanket and scrambling to her feet. Her head hurt atrociously when she stood up, but she straightened herself and pushed her fingers through her curls, pressing her palms to her temples at the same time. "I'll go away and I won't ever see you again, so you won't be reminded."

"But that will be punishing me for your wrongdoing. I don't want you to go away for good. I still hope that one day you will come again, sober, and look me straight in the face and say that Ambrose Markham is nothing to you. Because that day is bound to come, you know; and I should like to celebrate it properly."

Her patience gave way suddenly.

"Well, that day will never come. I've let you say what you wanted to, because I *was* wrong to come here as I did. You don't have to point that out to me. But even if I did change my mind about Ambrose I'd never tell you. I'll never come near you again. Never."

"You'll make your head worse." His voice was still kind and the sound of it maddened her.

"And whose fault is it that my head aches? You talk about me playing tricks on you. Look what you did to me. Giving me all that horrible stuff to drink and listening when I didn't know what I was saying."

"When wine is in, truth is out, you know. And my word, it

came out with a vengeance. By God, if it was anybody else than that stuffed nincompoop you'd deserve to have him. But you'll get over it, as I tell you. And I shall be the first person to know. Now if you go upstairs you'll find a kettle of hot water by the wash-stand. You can bathe your head and make yourself tidy while I saddle Blanche. I'll let you ride home, though it's more than you deserve."

"I can get home by myself, thank you."

"You came in your own way. You'll go back in mine. That's only fair."

She waited until she heard the kitchen door close behind him, then she unlatched the window and stepped over the low sill. She hoped to be able to run, but the errant cannon-ball smote her such thudding blows that she was obliged to walk, and gingerly at that. She was still in the drive of Joyous Gard when she heard the thud of hooves behind her and the pale mare, spectral in the grey light, passed her and was reined across the path. Bruce dismounted and lifted her into the saddle.

"Unlike you I mean what I say," he said. Taking the mare's bridle he began to walk. Blanche, surprised by the lightness of of her burden and the slowness of the pace required of her, tried to toss her head, minced for a step or two and then re-signedly settled down to a delicate elastic tread that hardly jarred Hester at all.

Neither she nor Bruce spoke again until, across the tree-dotted, fragrant garden the shuttered windows of Waterhead could be seen.

"You're in good time," he said, and lifted her down. He held her for a moment with her feet off the ground.

"Remember, I'm still waiting," he said and released her. Without a word Hester began to walk away.

Bruce mounted, and despite Blanche's impatience, remained stationary until Hester had crossed the sunken ditch and was lost amongst the trees. Just as he turned away the sun came up in sudden triumph and the sky blazed with cyclamen, daffodil and rose. He sighed and gave the mare her head.

Hester groped in her pocket, found the side-door key, let herself in and locked and bolted the door behind her. She gained her own room without meeting or hearing anybody, locked that door on the inside and threw herself on the bed. Shame and fury such as she had never known consumed and sickened her. The empty Marsala bottle and the glass with a spoonful of wine still in it stood on her table and mocked her. She had lost the most daring and brilliant throw of her life because she had been tipsy. Never again, as long as lived, would she drink anything.

Poppy tapped on the door. She croaked, "Go away." Presently Poppy returned and her soft velvet voice said, "Mis' Ambrose askin' about yo,."

Mrs. Ambrose! Philippa, who had lavished affection upon her because of one whim, and then withdrawn it because of another. Cigar smoke is bad for babies. Fiddlesticks! Well, she had served her turn. She was finished. Let her make her own tea.

"I'm ill," she answered. "I shan't get up to-day."

Poppy padded away. After fifteen minutes the door resounded to a rapid rat-tat that could only be Mrs. Markham's.

"Hester! Are you really unwell or just sulking? Open this door. If you're ill you must have some medicine."

"I don't want any medicine. I just want to keep quiet. Leave me alone."

Presently the softest tap, the most diffident voice of all.

"Hester. It's me. I've brought you some strong tea and my smelling-salts and some Cologne. Let me in."

"I don't want anything, thank you,"

"Hester. I'm sorry that I spoke to you like that last night. Are you still angry?"

"No. I've got a headache."

'Shall I make you a vinegar bandage?"

"No. Leave me alone."

"Oh, Hester, I'm so distressed."

"So you should be, you started all this. I shan't speak to you again."

Mrs. Markham's brisk voice : "Philippa, quit fussing the girl. She'll come out when she's hungry."

So you think, thought Hester viciously. I shall never come out. I shall lie here and die. I'd be better off dead.

But Philippa was evidently still outside the door, for presently Constance Markham could be heard again, speaking in a low sibilant whisper, full of fury.

"Philippa, how can you make such an exhibition? Mrs. Slater is just leaving. Come and take leave of her properly and don't let her carry such a ridiculous story home. Say you were feeding Anthony."

After that there was silence at the end of the corridor. Twice during the rest of the hot day Philippa came weeping to the door, but Hester was sleeping the first time, and the second time merely repeated, "Go away."

The short dusk gave way to night. Hester woke from her second long sleep and stared into the blackness. The house was silent. Her head was better and she was conscious of extreme hunger and thirst. She was herself again. As she rose from the tumbled bed, found her tinder and lighted the lamp in which just a little oil remained, she knew an uprush of hope and confidence that equalled the morning's despair. She was still alive. She was still the girl whom Ambrose had kissed and bidden find a place not too far away. Everything would yet be all right. Mr. Kyne would find her a place. There would be no Mrs. Markham to watch her perpetually with suspicion and the sharp eyes of dislike; there would be no Philippa to cling and smile and undermine her resolution with the weak tools of affection. All would yet be well. But not unless she found something to stay the pangs of hunger. Ruefully she reflected upon the cynical truth of Mrs. Markham's words about coming out when she was hungry. Well, she was hungry, and she was coming out; but with any luck the old hag need not know it.

The kitchen stairs opened from her end of the corridor; she need pass no other door. She reached the long passage, designed to keep the dwelling-house apart from the scent and heat of the cooking, and there she moved and breathed more freely. She reached the kitchen door, closed it softly behind her and looked up at the wag-tail clock on the wall. It was almost eleven o'clock. She had not eaten for twenty-four hours.

Intent upon the larder, her mouth already damp with anticipation, she was half-way across the kitchen before she noticed anything unusual. Generally the kitchen never lost the stored warmth of the day's activities; to-night it was cool. The door was open and thin drifts of the mist that often followed warm days in Bartuma were creeping over the threshold. That was strange, she thought. Joseph always locked and bolted every door and it was the invariable custom of either Ambrose or his mother to inspect them last thing at night. Oh well, she would close it later on. She must satisfy her hunger first. She set the lamp on the table and crossed the floor to where, on the far side of the kitchen, three doors stood side by side. One led to the part of the house where Joseph, Margarita, Delia and Poppy slept, the second was the larder door, and the third, usually padlocked, opened upon the cellar steps.

As she neared the doors she became conscious of the raw reek of spirits and, peering forward in the dim light, saw that the darkness which she had taken for the cellar door was in reality the yawning space of the opening. The door, white-washed upon the inside, was hardly visible upon the white-wash of the kitchen wall against which it was thrown back. A broken bottle lay on the first of the shallow dark steps.

Had someone broken in? or had Joseph gone mad and rifled the cellar in order to make merry with his friends outside in the cabins? Interested now, her hunger momentarily forgotten, she passed the middle door and pushed open the one that gave upon the short passage from which the slaves' rooms opened. Running back for the lamp, she carried it over the threshold which never in all her months at Watershead she had crossed. There was complete silence, no sound of breathing broke it. The rooms—only two bore traces of occupation—were stuffy, untidy, smelly and quite empty.

Fear, uninformed and formless, began to move down her spine on cold, swift feet. Something was wrong. What, and how wrong she had no means of knowing, but the silence of the place, the empty rooms, the yawning mouth of the cellar and the kitchen door open to the night, began to gather a dreadful significance. She ran to the door, meaning to close it swiftly.

The key was not there, and hoping to find it upon the outside of the door, she opened it again and held the lamp to its outer side. As she did so she saw, dimly illumined by the failing light, a sight that turned her to stone. Tangled together in a sprawling mass of limbs, canine and human, lay David and one of the big dogs that he tended. No living creatures could lie together in such intricate intimacy; both were dead. The lamp began to shake in Hester's hand. Stepping back on feet that seemed to have taken root in the doorsill, she closed the door and shot home the bolts. As she did so the lamp, empty of oil, went out.

She had never known such a moment of horror as this, in the sudden dark, with that horrible thing just on the other side of the door, and terror of the unknown but half-comprehended battering at her brain. But she forced herself to calmness. There was nothing to be feared in the kitchen, she told herself, and she knew where Delia kept tinder and candles. In a moment she was shielding a little flame with a shaking hand. And then, as though the flame had taken wing, the unshuttered kitchen window was illumined by the light of a great tongue of flame that shot into the sky. It was hailed by a deep, far-away mutter that seemed to voice a devilish satisfaction.

In less than a moment Hester was along the passage, back up the stairs and battering upon the door of Ambrose's room. She beat it with her clenched fist and then tried the handle. The door was locked. Perhaps, too, he was spending the night with his wife. She beat upon the next door and called frenziedly, "Ambrose! Ambrose!" She was not conscious that she was using the name by which she always thought of him.

Behind the closed door, Philippa, lying alone, was dreaming of her girlhood days in Boston, before she knew anything of marriage or of Ambrose. The shouted name mingled in her dream and seemed to herald his coming. She stirred in her sleep and sighed voluptuously. Even Hester's savage opening of the door did not wake her to full consciousness.

But Mrs. Markham, sleeping the light and dreamless sleep of old age, heard the cry, knew Hester's voice and came storming out of her room in her trailing bed-gown.

"What is the matter? Have you gone mad?"

"Ambrose," said Hester again. "Where is he? The slaves are burning things. David and Satan have been killed."

The old lady reeled back against the post of the door and laid her hands upon her heart.

"My son is not here," she said in a whisper. "He is spending the night at Mr. Kyne's. Oh God, what shall we do?"

And Philippa, awake and aware at last, echoed the foolish question.

"I know where we should be safe," said Hester rapidly. She lighted one candle from another and thrust one into Mrs. Markham's hand.

"Get some clothes on quickly. You too." Oh, thank God that she herself was dressed, fresh from sleep, able to think.

On flying feet she dashed down the front stairs, threw open the door of Ambrose's study and snatched up the lighter of the two guns that stood in the corner. Devotion had given her a knowledge of his habits and belongings that Philippa would never have. She found powder and shot in their places; Ambrose was a pernickety man where possessions were concerned. She laid the things together near the front door and forced herself down the kitchen passage again. The little stick-basket stood by the stove. She tipped out the sticks and ran to the larder, where she snatched a loaf of bread and a portion of cooked fowl. There was no time to exercise selection. If there had been ten minutes to spare she could have collected many things that would have subscribed to the comfort of their exile; as it was she dared only grab and run. Already the muttering, like an incoming tide, was drawing nearer.

When she reached the front hall again, Mrs. Markham and Philippa were just coming down the stairs. They had slipped their shoes on to their stockingless feet, put skirts and cloaks over their bed attire. Philippa carried the baby, bundled in his shawls. Hester measured in her mind the relative weights and awkwardness of a gun and a basket and of a sleeping child. She decided that Philippa had better carry Anthony. She swung the gun under one arm, laid the powder and shot with the other provisions in the basket and slipped her arm through the handle, wedging the basket against her hip. Then she opened the front door, noting as she did so that it, too, was unlocked.

The little cavalcade crossed the lawn and reached the screen of trees just as the foremost ranks of the mob, mad with lust for fire and blood, reached the stable-yard and the back of the house.

CHAPTER XIV

THE night was dark, but Hester, plodding ahead, found the spot where the sunken ditch was easiest to cross, the very place where she and Philippa had stepped over and laughed on that first morning. She breathed a sigh of relief when, having seen the others over, she stepped down herself and felt that there was another slight barrier between them and the danger behind. Philippa, a slow and lazy walker at the best of times, began to breathe in short heavy gasps as though her chest were full of stones, and the old lady said, "Give me the baby."

The exchange was made with hardly a pause and they reached the dirt-track that ran between the cane fields. At exactly the right spot again Hester turned aside towards the pasture, and they made better pace over the turf than through the deep slithering dust. Suddenly the old lady said, "Take him a moment, Philippa," and seemed to collapse. Hester halted.

"Make an effort," she urged, "it isn't far now."

"I'm—just—touching my toes—for stitch," said Constance, straightened herself and set off again.

There was another silence, broken only by the sound of their labouring breath and the brushing of their skirts, until Hester said, "Be careful now. There are stones."

Progress over the boulder-strewn piece was slow and heavy going. The climb was steeper than Hester remembered, either from riding or running up it. First Mrs. Markham and then Philippa fell behind. The old woman looked back once and said, "They've fired the house," in a heavy stunned tone, as though this were some evil that had come upon her by accident, not through her own greed and cold-heartedness.

"Never mind that now," said Hester, grunting under her burdens. "We're nearly there."

For the first time Philippa asked, "Where are you taking us, Hester?"

"To the spring-head. I don't think they'll look for us there. And even if they did, with a gun, we can hold the opening forever."

The big scattered boulders and masses of rock were not coloured now, but black and forbidding. It was difficult in the darkness to find the place where the two rocks leaned over the passage. Hester set down her burdens and halted her party while she felt about with her hands, scrambling this way and that, until she found the place.

"Now," she said to Philippa, "you come first. Give me the baby, and walk carefully, because the floor is very uneven."

Shielding the child carefully, least his head should scrape upon the rocky wall, she edged her way into the rocky chamber. Philippa followed and took the baby. Hester returned and led Constance by the hand, and then went back once more for the basket and the gun. When everything was within she drew in and expelled a deep breath. The most urgent danger was passed.

The spring chamber was as cool as a deep well, for even at midday the sun never reached the bed from which the spring rose, and the rocks upon which they must sit or lie were icy cold to their touch. After the rapidity of their flight they were grateful for the coolness at first, but soon Philippa began to shiver.

"How long shall we be here?" she asked.

"I don't know," said Constance. "It depends upon whether they've risen in other places. If they haven't we shall be looked for to-morrow."

"But suppose we are not! Oh, why did I ever come to this horrible place?" asked Philippa dolefully.

"You'll be all right. We shall be rescued to-morrow," said Hester, and the words were not spoken out of an empty desire to comfort. It was the simple statement of her own faith. When Mrs. Markham had so abruptly informed her that Ambrose was from home her heart had sunk; the responsibility had seemed so heavy; but she had shouldered it, and now that they had gained some measure of safety she was glad of his absence. For he would come to-morrow. A burning house cannot be long hid; someone would carry the tidings and Ambrose would arrive, quell the rising, and set them free. And he would find wife, son, and mother safe, safe through her. Could any woman offer more to the man she loved?

The three woman huddled together, pressing close to one another to conserve the heat of their bodies, bunching their skirts beneath them to defeat the sharp chill of the rock. Once Hester detached herself and went to the mouth of the opening. Over Watershead the sky was red, and, outlined blackly against the glare, the palm-trees at the bottom of the garden looked like grotesque figures, lifting stiff arms in a dance upon the brink of hell.

Had other estates suffered the same fate? She left the mouth of the passage and climbed a boulder, looking east and west. A pink glow lay over Fair Mount, but it might be only a reflection. She decided not to mention it to the others. After all, even if Fair Mount burned that didn't mean that St. Agnes was affected; and it was from St. Agnes that Ambrose would ride, swift and certain, to their rescue. She went back, bunched her skirts again and welted into the little group. She leaned back against the wall of living rock and drew Philippa's head on to her shoulder. Mrs. Markham sat for a while rigidly upright, then her head began to nod, nearer and nearer her daughter-in-law's shoulder. They dozed uneasily.

Waking from one snatch of sleep Hester saw that the sky was light above the rocks. Looking up, as from the bottom of a well, she watched the daylight strengthen until the rocky chamber was full of the familiar green gloom. To-morrow had arrived.

They moved about stiffly, uncricking necks and joints, enduring the painful return of feeling to limbs numbed from cramped positions. Hester, now consumed with hunger, produced the basket of provisions. With sure eager fingers she tore the fowl into portions, the loaf into chunks, and then paused. There was nothing here for the baby. The same realisation struck Philippa, who had been watching. Her eyes met Hester's across the food. Neither spoke for a moment.

At last Hester said, "He can chew a crust. It will do his gums good. It won't be for long."

"The Fair Mount people will have seen the fire," said Constance. "We may have to wait while they collect help, but they'll reach us to-day."

Daylight had brought courage. They spoke to one another confidently. They watched Anthony chewing and swallowing the sweet, crisp crust. After her long fast Hester felt that she alone could have eaten a whole loaf and half the chicken; but she thought of the pink glow over Fair Mount and restrained herself. She watched the others eating. Mrs. Markham had always had a hearty appetite, Philippa's was capricious, and this morning she was ravenous. It was impossible, reflected Hester, moving uncomfortably, to subscribe with one breath to the general opinion that help would come to-day, and then in the next to bid them make spare with the poor provisions. And yet ... if ...

"We'd better save a little," she said at last. "We may have to spend the day here."

"How shall we know when help arrives?" asked Mrs. Markham suddenly.

"I'll keep watch," said Hester. She knew the boulder behind which she could sit, shielded from any eye that might be watching at Watershead, yet able to see the road. She drank deeply from her cupped hands, gave Philippa her cloak which she would not need in the sunshine, and stole out to her post.

All day she kept vigil. The sun was hidden behind a veil of cloud and the rain came down and soaked her. The earth lay as though in a steam bath. Sometimes the downpour was so heavy that it hid the road from her. Sometimes it stopped for a few moments, the sun gleamed out and she could see not only the road but Watershead itself. A good deal of activity appeared to be going on. The house was smouldering still, figures moved about the garden; she was startled to find that she could see them so clearly and drew more closely behind the screening boulder. Shreds of song and music and laughter came to her upon the still air. Once a party, raucous and capering, came out, driving the mules and horses before them into the fields of young cane. They slashed at the purple, jointed stems, stamped them into the rain-soaked earth, drove the frenzied animals to help in the destruction.

Once a shrill squealing of pigs rose into the air and went on, rising and falling for an hour. Hester, watching and listening, wondered critically about the slaves. What were they thinking? What were they hoping? What benefit did they imagine they were deriving from these few hours of freedom? They must know that it couldn't last; that terrible vengeance would be exacted. Yet they were doing nothing sensible, merely taking a childish delight in destroying the things that they hated, the big house, the mills and boiling-sheds, the canefields. They should, she thought dispassionately, elect a leader and all work together to fortify the place. But even as she planned for them she realised that nothing that they could do could save them ultimately; they were careless because they were, at heart, hopeless. They must enjoy themselves while they could.

Nothing stirred upon the road. The bright periods grew shorter and fewer. The warm heavy rain blotted out the view. Dusk came, almost instantly followed by darkness. Soaked to the skin Hester went back to her charges.

The towering rocks, high enough to keep the sun from reaching the narrow floor, did not exclude the straight-falling rain. Only the baby, wrapped in his shawls, was warm and dry. There was no confidence in either woman now. Philippa, frankly despairing, coughed and shivered, rocked the baby drearily to and fro and moaned from time to time. Mrs. Markham, huddled near her, spoke openly of other risings of which she had heard, of plantations cut off from one another for as much as a week; of people whose fates were never known.

"Why don't people learn?" Hester demanded, as they shared their supper of damp bread and shreds of fowl. "If it has happened before, why don't people take precautions?"

"But we do. We did. The gate in the fence round the cabins was always locked at sunset. There were the dogs. And O'Leary and Colson, both white men and armed, were supposed to do

285

little except see that the place was safe at night. David too. He was faithful, I know. And I would have trusted Delia and Joseph with anything I had."

"But they were black," Hester insisted. "And even I, though nobody talked to me, and I only spent one afternoon amongst the slaves, saw things that made me sick. For a moment I felt like revolting. It looked to me as though everything you had, Mrs. Markham, was bought with blood. And I'm white. How do you think the black people felt?"

"They don't think like we do." The old voice was quite firm as it voiced its creed.

"That is what Am—Mr. Markham said; and I believed him. He laughed at me, and told me not to be a black-bailer. Oh!'"

"What is the matter?"

"I've just thought of something. That word reminded me. We've thought so much about Fair Mount. What about Joyous Gard? That's even nearer. Couldn't they do something for us?"

"I should think Mr. Lyddon is dead in his bed. If this is a planned, widespread revolt, as I am beginning to fear, he won't have had a chance. Black-bailers never do. They don't take precautions at all; they trust to their slaves' good feeling." Her voice was harsh and scornful.

"Bruce Lyddon isn't a fool," said Hester, scrambling to her feet. "I'll go to Joyous Gard this minute."

"But you'll get lost. You don't know the way. And it won't be any good. If he had been alive and able to move, he would have come. Even he would have done that when he saw the fire."

"Don't go, Hester. Don't leave us. I feel better when you're here. If anything happened. . . ." Philippa's voice broke.

"Nothing will happen, I promise you. And I do know the way. I can get there in half an hour from here." She felt her way to the spring again and drank. "I shan't be long. But if I should *seem* to be, take that as a good sign; I might be collecting help. Sleep if you can."

Two nights before when she had made the journey to Joyous Gard, the night had been fine and dry. To-night the rain was so heavy that to walk through it was almost like swimming, and her feet sank into the mud and came out again with sounds like little gun-shots. She tried not to think consciously about her errand, or the way she should go, but let her instinct take control and direct her. Because of this she dared not make any divergence from her path, even where puddles had joined and became running streams she splashed through them, sometimes knee-deep. She could hardly be wetter, she thought, and took comfort.

She arrived, as before, at the back of the house. She drew a great breath of relief as she saw its mass, still standing, whole, solid. But there was caution and alertness in her step as she crept towards it. Who knew what that comforting appearance of ordinariness might hide? There was no light anywhere. She decided to tap upon the kitchen door first.

At Joyous Gard the slave cabins were almost half a mile from the house, but had Hester come earlier she would have heard the inmates, crowded into an empty shed, lustily singing "Washed in the Precious Blood." For Wednesday was Old Methody's night for preaching at Joyous Gard, and rumour of trouble on other plantations had not prevented the old man from riding his moth-eaten mule to the one where he was certain of a welcome. And his faith had been rewarded. He was disappointed to learn that Bruce was not at home, but he found the plantation quiet and orderly. He had a successful meeting, with two quite serious cases of conversion-hysteria; and he had christened three babies Bruce Methody or Methody Bruce. He had rebuked two wanderers, betrayed by a fellow convert as being detected in fornication, and promised to unite them in holy matrimony next Wednesday if they could offer proof of having lived chastely meantime, and he had prayed with an old woman confined to her bed with elephantiasis of the legs. He had had a very successful hour. At the end of it the slaves went, orderly and a little exhausted from the violence of their worship, into their compound, a neat square surrounded by cabins, that vastly exceeded, both in newness, cleanliness and comfort, those of any other estate in Bartuma, and the old man halted to have a word with the overseer who was locking the gate.

"Mr. Lyddon isn't home?"

"No, sir," said the overseer, a hard-bitten little Welshman, who had followed Bruce through many vicissitudes and been rewarded with what he considered very high office indeed. "And sorry indeed I am. He went off sailing early on the Tuesday morning and said he might be three or four days gone. A big responsibility it is to be left with the place to run in times like these. I suppose you've heard nothing from Watershead?"

"Unfortunately Watershead and I are hardly on speaking terms," said the old man sadly. "What has happened there?"

"There's no telling. Joe Beaver said, though, that he saw the sky red above it last evening. He wanted to go over but I told him—under me he is, with the master away: 'Your duty lies here, so it does,' I said, 'and Watershead has been no friend to you and yours in the past.' But it was curious I was and wondered if you had heard anything."

"If it shared the fate of the Cities of the Plain, I should not be surprised," said the old man gravely. "But even so perhaps we should investigate. I will ride past on my way home."

"It's careful you ought to be then," said Llewellyn, doubt in his voice. "I'd come with you, so I would, but that I should not leave the place."

"If there is trouble there two men could do no more than one," replied the old man, getting stiffly on to his mule. "We'll hope that Joe Beaver was speaking in his cups, from which I have never been able to wean him."

Llewellyn, after a last look-round to see that all was well, retired to his own house, where Megan, a pretty little coloured girl—of whom Old Methody knew nothing—was cooking him his favourite supper, pigs' trotters and dumplings. Old Methody's mule, almost as stiff as his master, fought a losing battle where the road branched to Watershead and reluctantly turned away from his stable.

By this time it was quite dark and raining hard. The old preacher could still see nothing, either good or bad, as the mule ambled along the avenue of limes before the ruin of the house. But he had lived in Bartuma long enough to have developed experienced nose and ears. The one brought him evidence of a considerable quantity of pork having been roasted recently; the others took in and understood the significance of the singing, laughing and quarrelling that was going on. And then, compared with the darkness of the avenue, the garden seemed light, and across it he could see the stark, uneven, serrated walls of the big house where flames and the smouldering had been checked by the rain.

He asked himself, as always in an emergency, "What would Jesus do?" And was slightly disconcerted by the answer. The Master would undoubtedly have ridden round to the scene of the feasting and merrymaking and quelled it with a few stern yet gentle words and the magic of His eye. He would have called the sinners to repentance, and inquired what had happened to the members of the family.

But the Master, argued Old Methody, had power denied to common mortals. For one of them, white, old and feeble, to venture to investigate at this moment would mean certain death. And though he would have walked through a burning building to save a life, he reckoned, by the look of the ruined house, that those who had lived in it were past human aid. Sad, very sad, but after all they had brought it on themselves; everything was peaceful enough at Joyous Gard where the slaves were well-treated and his ministrations welcomed.

He turned the mule's head.

As though ten years had fallen from its age the animal cantered forward Again, at the cross-roads, it pulled towards home, towards the warm stable, the filled manger, the well-earned rest. But Old Methody bore on the rein, at imminent risk of losing the battle, for the harness was mostly of string. However, it held together, and the mule and Old Melody went on together, down to St. Agnes to rouse the town.

CHAPTER XV

BUT St. Agnes was roused already. There were no plantations there, but there were the boat slaves, sturdy fellows who went to and fro from the anchored ships to the waterfront, with boats so heavily laden that they shipped water at any careless stroke. And there were small companies of slaves in the warehouses and stables. They were sufficient to keep the soldiers occupied for three or four days, while the citizens kept within doors, locked their own black retainers in cellars and shudderingly waited upon themselves. To the student of history the little yellow-paged, leather-bound book entitled *A Brief History of Bartuma* offers, in its heavy crooked type, the following summary of the event:

"The revolt of 1775 surpassed all previous ones, in the craftiness of its planning, its ferocity, and the wideness of its reach. In parts of the island the terror reigned for twelve days. It is estimated that half the white population lost their lives and the value of the property destroyed has never been accurately computed. The prosperity of the island was seriously affected and had hardly recovered before the Act of Abolition dealt it another blow."

Like all other upheavals and disasters, it produced its heroes. On a dozen of the scattered plantations members of the dispossessed and down-trodden race stood by their masters and by their loyalty either saved them or shared their fate. Mrs. Slater's pampered Rosetta, often the subject of a barbed sentence from Constance Markham, carried the old lady out bodily from the burning house, hid her in the woods, went back and joined in the general jubilation, but slunk off twice a day with food and comforts for her mistress. There were many such. And there were, of course, plantations untouched by the conflagration. Joyous Gard was one. Old crippled Mr. Calligan's was another. If his slaves, remote on the isolated plantation, ever knew that revolt was pending they had no knowledge of the outbreak. Neither did he until the time came for his monthly visit to St. Agnes, when, to his great astonishment, he found the stables where he always baited his horses a mass of ashes and charred wood. But these were happy exceptions, and Hester, knocking more loudly upon the kitchen door at Joyous Gard, had no means of knowing that she stood on one of the blessed spots. The darkened, unresponsive house, and the silence that swallowed up each sound she made, convinced her that although the house had been spared, its master had shared the general fate.

She crept around the house, trying every door and window. There was, as far as she could see, no means of entry. Bruce had said, "Shut up the house," and Llewellyn had done it, as he did all things, thoroughly. When she had rounded it twice, pressing and pushing and peering through the darkness, and found no means of ingress, Hester began to whimper. The sense of danger, of alien eyes watching her, which made her stealthy and cautious, left her. She thought of the rugs and blankets, of the foodstuffs that might be left in the deserted house; she thought of her damp, shivering dependents who would be hungry to-morrow, and her efforts to force a way into the building became reckless and desperate. But they were unavailing. Moaning with fury and disappointment she turned away at last.

She left Joyous Gard, which had, not so long ago, offered her everything, with nothing more valuable than a chipped basin in which, every morning, Bruce's cook put out milk for the cat. She had struck her foot against it as she turned from the door for the last time, and took it with her because she thought it would simplify the problem of giving Anthony a drink of water.

She occupied the dreary journey back to the spring chamber by racking her memory for records of people surviving for long periods on water alone. Captain Martineau had dealt with the subject in his journal, she remembered; but the number of days escaped her. And he and the men who were with him in the boat on that occasion were rough hardy sailors, used to privation, not an old woman, an ailing pampered one and a young baby. Her mind, as she climbed the slope and found the mouth of the entry, was as uncomfortable as her wet, weary, hungry, mud-caked body.

Mrs. Markham and Philippa were both awake. Philippa's greeting was ecstatic with relief.

"I don't care," she said when Hester confessed the bitter failure of her errand. "Now you're back I don't care." For during Hester's absence Philippa had come face to face with another problem, the partial failure of her mother-in-law's mind. From talking about the past, as she had done during their scanty meal, she had slipped back into it. She had addressed Philippa as Tabitha and Judith, had demanded to hold Ambrose and then, when the child was laid in her arms, had said suddenly, "No, I forgot. This is Anthony, isn't it," and had given a foolish little laugh.

She seemed to recover her sense of time when Hester spoke of the silence and the deserted house at Joyous Gard.

"They wouldn't burn the house unless they thought their master was in it," she said. "They probably all went over to Watershead to share in the festivities." Her voice was bitter. "But they'll regret it. My father is a very strict man. He is very severe even with me. I put on my best dress and pulled forward my curls and pleaded with him on my knees to let me marry Alfred. But he would not. And I dared not cross him. Nobody dare cross him. If I were a man I should be like that too. Ambrose isn't. He doesn't take after his father at all." She gripped Hester's knee. "You know what is the matter with Ambrose, don't you? He should have been a girl. I wanted a girl so much. Three boys I had, so lusty and sturdy, and I thought they would all marry and leave me. A girl I could have kept; she would have stayed with me always. I'd made all preparations for a girl, pink ribbons on the cradle and fresh clothes on the doll that I'd had as a child. And then it was Ambrose. But he should have been a girl, he has a girl's nature underneath. I know. I've had to be the man of the family since John died. Poor John, so headstrong and violent. That's why he died." She began to weep quietly.

"Don't talk about it now, Mrs. Markham. Try to sleep."

But sleep was more difficult to find to-night than on the night before. They were not so hopeful now. Their damp clothes increased the feeling of cold and discomfort. The night seemed longer than her whole lifetime to Hester, as she looked up, time after time, searching for some sign of light in the sky. It came at last and brought with it that same uprush of hope and confidence. After all this was only the second day. If news of the fate of his house had reached Ambrose yesterday it probably had taken him all day to make his plans and gather help. No man who was sane would walk into a hornet's nest without taking some precautions. He would come to-day. The weather might be sunny, and if they were careful perhaps they would creep out one at a time and sit behind her boulder, keeping watch, and at the same time dry their clothes and warm themselves. Inspection of the basket showed that there were still a few flakes of meat upon the chicken carcase and the few crumbs of bread, though damp, were edible.

She was, however, worried about the baby. He had chewed his crust manfully yesterday morning, but at mid-day he had been sick, and although they had made an attempt to feed him with shreds of chicken in the evening he had wailed a good deal and moved his lips as though he were drinking, telling them as plainly as he could that he missed his milk. As she thought of it, Hester's eye fell upon the cracked basin. She looked at it thoughtfully, gnawing her fingers. The two women were lolling together, the leaning weight of each body supporting the other, their mouths were open, their eyes closed. They were asleep.

Carefully she washed the basin in the spring, and then, tiptoeing, found her way to the opening and stepped out. After the rain it bid fair to be a nice day, the sky to the East was placid and faintly yellow with the upcoming sun. Hester scanned the surrounding countryside. It looked deserted. Down in the cabins no doubt the slaves were sleeping off the effects of their orgy. It might be safe to venture forth for a little while.

There were often cows in the lower reaches of the pasture, down where the stream widened and the lush grass grew. Even to look for them meant leaving the shelter of the rocks and boulders and crossing the meadow in full view of anyone who might be watching. But given a cow, or the possibility of one, a cracked basin and a hungry baby, something must be risked in order to bring the three together.

The cows, unmilked since Tuesday evening, had strayed to the extreme end of the meadow, crowding round the gate through which they were usually taken to be milked. Their over-full udders had streaked the long grass with milky streams. Hester had little difficulty in persuading one to stand while she filled her pathetic little basin, emptied it down her own throat and filled it again. When she rose from her knees and raised the basin, and with hurried cautious steps, took her way back to shelter—indirectly, lest by any chance one might be watching—the other cow showed an inclination to follow her. She encouraged it. But when the stony ground began the cow tossed its head and went lowing back. Not daring to follow it again, Hester cursed herself for not having caught and tied it with something—a stocking would have done—though to what she could have tied the stocking remained uncertain.

For a short time after they had eaten their breakfast the sun shone. Philippa resisted the suggestion that she should go out and sit in the sun.

"I'm so slow and clumsy. And I daren't go, anyway," she said. So Hester squatted outside behind the boulder, watching the road and turning from side to side, until her own clothes were dry. Then she changed dresses with Philippa and repeated the process. Mrs. Markham, led out next and shown where to sit, said with immense dignity, at the mouth of the opening, "I think I must go home now. Thank you so much, it's been very enjoyable." Plainly she could not be left outside by herself, nor could she be trusted to watch the road. Hester crouched beside her while she dried and then hurried her back into shelter.

Shortly afterwards down came the rain, a curtain of prismatic colours in the unobscured sunlight. Hester kept watch behind the boulder, on the slope down which the streams of water slid smoothly, dividing wherever a rock or stone challenged their path. All day she watched the road. No one stirred on it.

When darkness hid the track she went back to the spring-head with despair in her heart.

Philippa refused the crumb of soaked bread, the last yield of the basket.

"My throat is so sore," she croaked. "I couldn't swallow. And my bones ache so. I wish I were dead. We might as well have been killed, Hester."

"There's still time," said Hester hoarsely out of her own pain-stiffened throat. "Even if they come to-morrow we'll still be alive."

"But who is to come?" asked Mrs. Markham, back for the time being in the present. "Ambrose is dead. Everybody is dead. We are the last people left."

She had voiced the dread that had been in all their hearts. Suppose that were indeed the case? Suppose the island had fallen completely under black domination?

"We can't be sure of that, yet," said Hester as stoutly as she could. "And when we are we must go down and, if we're not killed on sight, say that *we* will work for *them* if they'll let us live. We could watch for a chance to escape."

"You don't know what you're saying," said Constance harshly. "They wouldn't kill you intentionally, now. But one after another they'd rape you until you were dead. That has been known to happen."

They were the last sensible words the old lady said that evening; but she said them with the assurance of experience, so that even Hester was quelled, and in the darkness Philippa fell swooning against the wall, and Anthony rolled from her knee and began to cry. Hester reached for him and soothed him. They did not know, because they could not see, what had happened to Philippa, but after a time she came round and croaked :

"Hester."

"Yes?"

"Can you shoot?"

"I never have. But I could load the gun and try. You needn't worry."

"Then shoot us, Hester, please. Do that last thing for me. Put us out of our misery and spare us any more."

"I can shoot," announced Mrs. Markham loudly. "I used to go shooting with my father. I could shoot wild duck, and they're very difficult indeed. He said once, 'Constance you should have been a boy. I wish you were.' I wish I were too. Then I could marry whom I liked. I don't really care much for the man father has chosen. Oh, Alfred, why are you so poor? And so dear."

"We're not going to talk about that, yet," said Hester firmly, ignoring the interruption. "We've got aching bones and sore throats, that's all. But I promise you when all hope is gone I will do it, Philippa. Does that content you?"

"If you promise."

"I do. But I think first that I ought to go down to Fair Mount, or one of the other places. Even St. Agnes. You see, if they've heard that Watershead is burned they might not think of looking for us."

"Ambrose would. Surely he would. If he were alive he would have come," moaned Philippa Hester bit back the words that sprang to her lips in retort. Ambrose might be dead, but there might be others alive. And as she thought of the words their import smote her like a blow. Ambrose dead—herself alive. She was surprised and a little appalled to discover that, admitting the possibility, she did not fall dead herself. No. Her mind went on wriggling like a bait worm on a pin, as she tried to think of some way out, some desperate way by which she might save herself and those who were with her. The desire for life had become a habit, not easily broken.

But desire for life, she decided, sitting there in the darkness, was not enough. In Philippa it was not even very strong now, and a further period of waiting in what was virtually the bottom of a well was not to be contemplated.

She stood up.

"I'm going out again." Her lips and tongue formed the words but they made no sound. She swallowed fiercely, cleared her throat painfully and began again. "I'm going out. If there is help to be had I will find it and bring it back. If not I'll come back, Philippa, and keep my promise to you. But I may have to hide to-morrow morning, so don't worry if I'm not back until after dark."

Philippa began to cry and plead with her not to leave them. Mrs. Markham, whose muddled mind some meaning of the words had reached, said clearly, "Rats always desert sinking ships."

"Let us come with you," begged Philippa, clutching at Hester's knees.

"Three couldn't travel so quickly or quietly," said Hester, in a hoarse whisper that racked her throat. "You must be brave for just this little while longer, and look after the baby—and her."

For the last time she edged through the narrow opening and stole down the slope. She had exhorted Philippa to be brave. Now she knew she needed more courage than she possessed herself. She thought of Jonathan Harper and breathed her first prayer, "Oh God, give me courage. Let me find Ambrose. Oh God, help me. Oh God."

CHAPTER XVI

LATE that afternoon Bruce Lyddon had beached his small sailing boat in the cove where he kept her and set out along the path that led into the town. Three days and two nights of complete solitude had given him back his senses. He was determined that he would fetch Blanche from the stable where he had left her, ride straight to Watershead, take Hester by argument or force if necessary, sell the plantation and leave Bartuma. Neither Ambrose Markham nor Hester's love for him should stand in his way. Once out of the island she would forget. He would show her what love meant. He would uproot this sickly girlish infatuation.

He strode along impatiently, brushing the gleaming raindrops from the drenched pink-and-white ginger flowers on either side of the narrow path. It ended in some roughly hewn steps that led into the street. At the top of them he stopped. Two dead black men lay on the stones and the blood had run down in trickles and pools, congealing blackly. A mass of flies buzzed around the bodies.

Bruce looked at them. Against the strict letter of the law slaves were killed frequently; but not so openly as this; nor were their bodies left upon the public road. Had they been fighting and killed one another? Even so someone would have given the order to remove the corpses. He bent over them, disturbing the flies. No, both had been shot in the head, at pretty close range too.

Straightening himself he looked about him, noting first the

296

unusual emptiness of the little street, then a broken window or two, and then, at the corner, a shop that looked as though it had been looted and fired. Some incongruous things—a broken oar, some bits of women's clothing, a smashed chair—lay on the path. He turned the corner. Three white men and a half-caste, all with guns under their arms, were hurrying along the opposite side. He knew one of them by sight, but before he could hail them one of them shouted, "Lyddon," and the four stopped, still keeping together.

"What's been afoot here?" he asked.

"Slave revolt. Hell's business, as you can see," replied the man who recognised him. "How've you fared?"

"I've no idea. I've only just left my boat. I went sailing on Tuesday morning."

"Well, it's odds then that you won't find much left when you get home. It broke out on Tuesday night, sudden as a thunderstorm. I guess it's quelled now, but my God, it was a filthy business while it lasted. Eight warehouses burned to the ground, the boat-houses wrecked and God knows how many folks killed. Poor old Easton . . ."

"And Tom Walker," added one of the men.

"Scores," said the third briefly. "Well, come on lads, we musn't stand here talking. We're on our way to Phillips' place. Nothing's been heard or seen of him.'

They fell into step again and hurried off. Bruce took to his heels and ran to the stable. The door that led to the yard was splintered and half off its hinges, and there were more puddles of blood at the foot of it. But the stables inside looked as usual, and as Bruce stepped through the splintered doorway Miles, the man who owned the place, came out of a loose-box with a pail.

"Well, glory be to God that you're alive and well, Mr. Lyddon, sir. Has this business touched you?"

"I don't know yet. I've been away. My mare all right?"

"Thanks be to God, she is, and the rest of the beasts as well. I got warning in time. Eh, but it's been a terrible business. I do hope your place is all right; though both your neighbours are done for, I guess."

"Watershead?" asked Bruce, dry-mouthed.

"Aye, and Fair Mount. Old Methody brought us the news last night. Ah, but now I recall sir, he said he left your place as peaceful as could be. Fancy me forgetting that." He rubbed his hard hand on the seat of his trousers, seized and wrung Bruce's in a frenzy of belated congratulation. Bruce shook him off impatiently.

"Get my mare," he said. He followed the man into the loose-box, cuffed back the delighted, caressing nose of the whinnying mare, helped throw on the saddle and buckle the girths and was out of the yard before Miles recovered from his bewilderment. "Well, that's a way to take a bit of good news, I will say. You'd have thought he'd have said thanks be to God if he didn't thank me," he mused, picking up the pail.

"I sent her back. *I* sent her back." The words rang through Bruce's brain as the mare, fresh from three days in the stable, went smashing up the street. He did not look about him; saw neither armed civilians, nor the wearied, dirtied and often wounded soldiers who were still patrolling the streets. Even when Blanche lifted her haunches and jumped over a pile of black bodies, hastily collected and thrown anyhow in the middle of the cross-roads, he did not notice them. Hester had been at Joyous Gard on Monday night. If he had let her stay she would have been safe still. He had shamed her and mocked her and sent her back. And the next night Watershead had been burned and it was a thousand chances to one against her being alive at this moment. He groaned aloud and the sound sent Blanche leaping forward even faster.

Darkness fell, but he hardly checked the thundering pace. The mare could be trusted to pick her way. She slackened of her own accord after the first six swift miles and settled down to eat up the distance between her and home at her usual regular loping trot.

At the cross-roads where Old Melody had fought the mule they turned on to the side track, and so missed, by about a quarter of a mile, the gasping, stumbling girl who had set out to run to St. Agnes.

Now, with the most familiar part of the journey before her, her second breath gained and her own stable beckoning, Blanche broke into a gallop again and drew up, blowing and sweating but far from being foundered, in the quiet stableyard at home.

Her master behaved queerly. He threw his coat over her and went away. She found her way to her own stable door and stood outside it, making impatient noises.

Bruce ran to Llewellyn's house. There was a light within and the door gave to his hand. The overseer sat at the table, his supper just served and the coloured girl leaning over his shoulder giving him a kiss to savour it. He pushed her away and jumped to his feet.

"Mr. Bruce! Glad indeed to see you back I am. And don't look so distressed, man, everything is well."

"*Here*, I know it is," said Bruce, for the second time ungratefully brushing away the information that any other man would have given his ears to hear. "But what about Watershead?"

"It's burned, I hear it is, and the slaves rampaging about all over the place. Old Methody looked in upon it last night and this morning called in on his way from the town with the news."

"Is anything known of the people?"

"The family, you mean? That young Ambrose is sitting weeping for his mother down in St. Agnes. He was absent that night. The women were alone in the house, so they were. All dead I should say they are."

"Well, we've got to find out."

"Joe Beaver said much the same. But I bid him be still. 'Them black devils will cut your liver,' I told him. 'And what call have you whatever to have your liver cut out on account of the bloody Markhams and them dead at that?'"

"There's just a chance that they might not be," said Bruce, turning away. "I'm going over to see."

"And I'm coming with you, indeed. And Joe Beaver and Leonard will."

"They've both got wives and children," said Bruce. "It's only you and me, old man, who're as free to lose our lives as ever we were."

(Ambrose, sitting in Mr. Kyne's house, said, "To go there with less than twenty men would be suicide. If the soldiers can't be made to go, can't they be bribed? Not that I care about the place, if my mother is dead, as I fear she is.")

"Indeed we are so," said Llewellyn. "But Old Nick won't want us yet. There's still sin in us. Get my gun, Megan girl, while I make the lantern."

They went out together into the night.

"Joe Beaver and Leonard will never forgive me, if I go without telling them. It's itching they've been to go ever since Joe saw the fire on the sky. I'll not dare face him in the morning. And if two are good, four will be a lot better."

"Very well," said Bruce. "Call them while I get the guns."

299

For the second day in succession, in hot, damp weather, the slaves had eaten to satiety of scorched fat pork. Few, when the darkness fell, had energy or desire for anything but sleep. There was nothing to do but eat and sleep and wait for the coming or the orders, of the Leader, the unknown, mysterious person who had organised the revolt. For months now, by some secret channel, the mingled stream of orders and promises had been pouring and had been passed about by whispered word of mouth. They were to rise at a certain time, burn, kill and take possession. Then they were to wait. When the revolt was successfully accomplished the Leader would take charge and tell them what to do. The island was to be theirs and all the good things that it grew. There would be no more labour, no more starvation, no more whippings. He had promised, this unknown Leader, everything that every revolutionary has ever promised his followers. Meanwhile they were not to go wandering about or quarrelling amongst themselves; they were to rest and enjoy themselves.

He knew, this black revolutionary, the value of segregation, and how the mob, once started, is difficult for even the mob ruler to gather again In this way he was a genius, and he might have held Bartuma for a little while and made himself a king. But he had, unlike many of his ilk, led the van of the attack and he had been killed by an angry white woman, the wife of the storekeeper, his employer, who was lying abed with a broken leg. She was terrified, that woman, but she had loaded the gun at her husband's instruction, and taken a wobbling aim through the window, and the tremor that had shook her as she aimed had proved fatal for the black Moses who had intended to set his people free. So no orders had reached Watershead, and the revolt was already broken in St. Agnes; and when four white men rode up suddenly, with lanterns, two apiece, tied to their saddles, and had fired into the night and shouted and made noise enough for a multitude, it was virtually over at Watershead as well.

One Koromantee, it is true, lifted the gun that he had taken from the dead O'Leary and fired, almost as blindly as the woman who had killed the Leader, between two of the lanterns. And the bullet went through Bruce's shoulder, shattering the bone. But he failed to load the gun again and of steady resistance there was none. Into the cabins, into corners, behind bits of the house ruins and into what canes were left standing, the leaderless, the defeated, the doomed took their way.

And Delia steped forward, and with commendable boldness and no veracity at all, lifted her face to the lanterns and said :

"Include me out ob dis riff-raff, genemen. Ah's bin a prisonah mahseff."

"Shut up," said Bruce. "What happened to the people who were in the house?"

Delia began to sob :

"Oh, mah good mistress an' oh, de poah liddle baby! Oh, oh, oh! Dey's in Hebben now Ah fear me."

"Stop that blubbering. Did they have any time at all? Could they have got out?"

"Dat riff-raff come for me an' smudder me in a blanket an' take me away," lied Delia stoutly. 'But Ah put up a great fight. Dat make some noise Ah assure yo'. Ah hoaped dat somebody might heah me. Mebbe dey did. Mebbe dey's hidin' some place."

"That is possible," said Bruce. Another order, "Comb over the place. Fire your guns again and shout."

Up by the spring-head Mrs. Markham seized Philippa by the shoulder.

"Wake up," she said, "the French have come."

"Who?" croaked Philippa, springing to her feet. "What did you say?"

"The French," repeated her mother-in-law. "They've been attacking St. Agnes for days. Oh, my poor Edward, oh, my poor Stephen, their sacrifices were all in vain."

She began to weep noisily.

"Sh!" hissed Philippa. "Yes, that was gun-fire, and that. Oh, it must be Ambrose at last."

She leapt into the passage-way and stood in the opening. Then her natural timidity asserted itself. Oh, if only Hester were here to speculate sensibly on what this could mean. Left with a baby and a crazy old woman, thought Philippa. If ever I get out of this I shall go to Boston and never, never come back.

More shots shattered the night silence, and then, faint and far away, she could hear voices calling, indistinguishable at that distance, yet rising to a note that sounded urgent and interrogative. Still bound with the bonds of doubts and fear, Philippa waited until she could see lights bobbing, rising and falling at shoulder-height, and one, higher, being waved as though to signal.

One thing only could give Philippa enterprise—the motive of a greater fear. And now it came. Suppose these were really friends, searching and calling? And suppose they went away, disappointed? Then she, Anthony and Constance would be abandoned, left to starve and moulder in the dim dampness of the spring chamber. The thought prodded her to action. At least she would steal down near enough to hear what they were calling. Hurrying back she laid the baby upon his grandmother's knee. Useless to try to explain anything, she thought.

"Mind him for a minute," she said, and slipped away.

Down through the boulders, without sense of direction or caution, barking her shins, ricking her ankles, bruising her elbows, over the stony ground she went, down on to the level, easy-going damp pasture land. Now she should be able to hear them. She halted and held her breath.

"Hester! Hester Roon! Ahoyoy!"

Philippa opened her mouth. She put more force into the cry than she had ever expended upon anything in her life; but the sound was hoarse and flat, with little more carrying-force than a whisper. Desperately she began to run towards the nearest light. It moved sideways, eluding her. She cried again and the light stopped. Screaming now, squeaky, hoarse screams one after another, she ran forward and the light came to meet her. She seized Joe Beaver's booted foot and swayed forward.

"Up at the spring," she gasped, and fell prone.

Joe Beaver roared out through the darkness that he had found one. He lifted Philippa and laid her across his saddle and the four white men cantered towards the spring.

Already faint and dizzy from pain and loss of blood, Bruce flung himself from the saddle where the stony ground began, and roared to the others to dismount or they'd break their horses' legs.

"Stay with them, Joe," he shouted and began to stumble forward. If Hester were in the spring chamber he must be the first to reach her. He swung the lantern that he had snatched from his saddle from his elbow and clutched his shoulder with his hand. God, he couldn't fail now. Llewellyn, spry on his feet and unwounded, was gaining on him.

"Go steady, Llewellyn," he shouted. "You'll break a leg, you don't know the ground." The little Welshman gave no heed, but he ran wide of the opening, which Bruce, swinging his lantern, found easily. Breathless with hope and haste, he edged his bulk through the passage—here, in their first meeting place —here. The lantern light illumined the little rock-bound space; showed Mrs. Markham, her face blank and smooth, sitting on the edge of the spring, her skirt and the edge of the child's shawl trailing in the water, showed the baby's face, a little pinched and shrunken under the folds of the grimy shawl, showed the emptiness behind and beyond. With his good hand Bruce seized the old woman by the shoulder.

"Hester. Where is she?" he spluttered.

"Quietly," said Constance with dignity, "you will wake the baby. It's very unusual, you know, to have a baby at my age. Do you know how old I . . ."

"Mrs. Markham," said Bruce, leaning forward. "Listen. Where is Hester Roon?" By God, he had leaned too far forward, he had lost his balance. His feet scrabbled at the damp, slippery stones, but it was no good, the rocky edge of the spring hit him between the eyes.

"Well, by Davy!" said Llewellyn, pushing himself into the little space. And "Well, by Davy," he said again five minutes later. "Two unconscious, a mad old woman and a baby, and all to be got to Joyous indeed. I didn't know he'd been hit, did you Leonard?"

"I doubt if he knew himself," said Leonard.

("If six men are all you can spare we may as well save ourselves the journey," said Ambrose. "There's nothing we can do, after all.")

CHAPTER XVII

IT WAS twelve miles, they reckoned, to St. Agnes, thought Hester, toiling along. But then, of course, she had turned aside at Fair Mount and damned nearly gone too far. It was not until she smelt the stench of burnt wood that she realised that what she had imagined to be sheds was really all that was left of the house. Behind it there were sounds that terrified her, and a dog barked. She hurried back to the road.

All her bones ached, and all her joints were stiff, even the swift movement to which she forced herself did not serve to liberate them. She decided to make no more visits of inspection. She had tried deserted Joyous Gard and ruined Fair Mount; there was no reason to hope that other plantations had been more lucky. Or St. Agnes, suggested her relentless mind. What is there to hope for at St. Agnes? She reminded herself that more white people lived in the town and that there were soldiers stationed there. She had seen them on that morning— so many centuries ago—when she had gone shopping with Mary Claughton. Then, asked the sceptic, grinning in her head, why hasn't Ambrose come? If St. Agnes is all right. . . .

It's no good crying, said Hester to herself. It's a waste of breath and you can't spare any. You've got to think about Philippa and the baby back there with that daft old woman. You've got to get to St. Agnes. Stop thinking about anything. Count your steps. Count a thousand steps. Say a step is a yard, twenty-two yards are a chain, ten chains are a furlong, eight furlongs are a mile. Bless you, Miss Peck, you and your ruler! Then ten twenty-twos are two hundred and twenty and eight times that are one thousand seven hundred and sixty. Say two thousand, in case your steps aren't quite a yard. Count two thousand steps and you'll have done a mile. You ought to have started counting at the beginning, then you'd have known when you were getting near the town.

But she knew, without counting. The Captain in charge of the soldiers, an embittered little man who was constantly demanding his Heavenly Father to inform him what he had done to deserve so dull a post, had, in the last two days, come gloriously into his own. Not only his own men, but the fellows whom he privately called "Gold-grubbing money hogs"—that is, the burgesses of the little town—had obeyed his slightest word. He had given them orders aplenty, and amongst them was one that he had for a long time wished that it was within his province to enforce—that every shop and private house, every warehouse and stable, should hang out a lantern at nightfall. The citizens, hearing every hour of whole families wiped out and houses burned, felt a deep though temporary gratitude to the soldiers and their officers to whose efforts much of St. Agnes' immunity must be attributed. Wherever life remained a lantern hung, as though in celebration. And Hester, looking down from the hillside above the town, saw the little points of light shining, bright as stars, but steadier.

She descended the hill cautiously. She had never heard of the town being lighted, and whose victory the unusual illumination celebrated she had no means of knowing. It might be the blacks'. But the streets were all empty and quiet. It was getting late now, and the people's nerves had been shattered. They barred their doors and stayed behind them. She saw no one as she slipped from light to light along the streets, her broken shoes flapping, her body bowed and spent with weariness, lack of food, anxiety, sleeplessness.

She found, without much difficulty, though it was one of the darkened ones, the only house in St. Agnes that she knew, Mr. Kyne's, and tapped gently upon the door. Then she darted into a patch of shadow behind the porch and watched to see who opened it. There was no sign from the house that anyone had heard the timid knock. She entered the porch again and rapped louder. There was no reply. The house stood dark, silent, unresponsive, just as Joyous Gard had done.

The complete emptiness of the street gave her courage. She lifted the lantern from its nail at the side of the porch of the next-door house and, holding it in her hand, went round to the side of Mr. Kyne's. Two windows, stoutly shuttered, that was all on that side. She crept into the deeper darkness at the back of the house, thinking desperately that if any one leaped, as she dreaded they might, out of the shadows, she could use the lantern as a weapon. But nothing stirred. The back door, too, was shut and bolted, the shutter at the kitchen window was in place. Perhaps Mr. Kyne, she thought, had heard a rumour of trouble, shut his house and and gone away. But Ambrose was supposed to be staying here. Once again she experienced a pang of concern as to what had happened to him.

But that must wait, she thought. Here was an empty house, with whose geography she was familiar, and there was certain to be some kind of foodstuffs within it. Mary had shown her, with obvious pride, the store-room full of dried and preserved fruits, jams and jellies. If only she could reach it. She would put some food in a rolled-up blanket and she would carry it back, something to show for her long walk and absence. She lost her sense of inimicable eyes watching, of hurtful hands stretched out, as she grappled again with the problem of supplies. The store-room window, she remembered, was beyond the back-door of the house, in an arm of the building that ran back, enclosing, with the stable, woodshed and well-house, a small rectangle of cobbles. She set off towards it, holding the lantern low now, forgetting its lethal qualities and heeding only the light that it gave. Something lay on the cobbles a bundle of straw, perhaps, or a heap of manure. She steered clear of it, but as she drew level and the lantern light touched it, she gave a loud, hoarse scream and jumped away. Two human bodies—she knew there were two because one face was white and one black —lay there together, quite still, quite dead.

She stood for a moment almost as still, except for the rigor of horror that crept through her marrow. Horrible. Was everyone in the town dead? Was she alone in a lantern-speckled town, the only living soul?

Well, even so, she thought at last, when the horror had run through her bones and ended with curious prickling sensations in her toes and fingers, better dead men that live ones who might question her business and resent her presence. Carefully avoiding even a glance at the place where Mr. Kyne and his perfidious Garçon lay together in the close embrace of death, she passed on to the store-room window. The living must always be considered. . . .

The store-room window had been forgotten, or neglected. The small square was blocked only by a thin screen. It pushed aside when she attacked it. She set the lantern inside and heaved herself after it. A glance around told her that the provisions were still there, but the sight of them sickened her, and she passed on with her lantern to the store-room door, which opened easily. She must first see whether Ambrose was within. She had asked God to lead her to Ambrose—suppose she found him dead! And she must have a blanket. With this double intention she went through the house, moving swiftly and freely until she came to the bedroom nearest the stair-head.

She opened the door and walked towards the big four-poster that stood like a monument in the middle of the floor. The curtains were drawn, and as she put out her hand to pull one back and snatch a blanket, some sixth sense warned her that she might see something within, and she was not really surprise to see the body of Ambrose, fully dressed and booted, lying athwart the bed. She thought he was dead and all the breath went out of her body; and she stood there, shocked into immobility, too distressed even to make a sound. But there was a sound in the room, she could hear it in the silence, a gurgling, breathy sound. He lived, he breathed, he was wounded. She stood the lantern on the pillow and with strength that she did not know she possessed, pulled him over, so that his face was no longer half-hidden in the cover. It was the colour of clay and there were doughy folds beneath eyes and chin, and the mouth, no longer compressed, had fallen open loosely; the lower lip quivered with each soughing breath. His head was not injured. Assured of that she went over him carefully, pulling aside the crumpled clothing, examining every limb with trembling anxiety. There was no sign of a wound, not even a bruise upon him. But as the first sharpness of fear receded she became aware of the smell of spirits, as sharp and reeking as that which had come up from the broken bottle in the Watershead cellars. She looked down at the side of the bed, near her own feet. Two bottles lay there, both on their sides. One had not been quite empty and the contents had run out, making a little pool on the carpet.

She leaned back against the bedpost and clenched her hands. This was what she and Philippa and Constance Markham had been trusting in, saying, "Ambrose will hear and bring help"; "Ambrose will come to-day." The house, with its locked doors and the body on the bed, told the whole story, too plain for doubt, too definitely for contradiction. There had been some trouble, and Ambrose had locked the doors, drunk himself insensible and gone to bed.

Anger came upon her, scorching her flesh. She seized him by the shoulders and shook him mercilessly. His head lolled, a narrow streak of light-reflecting eye, red and blood-shot, showed for a moment between the puffy lids. His lips moved and mumbled something, but there was no sign of any real return to consciousness. As soon as she released him he fell back like a sack upon the bed, his head lolled over sideways and the steady gurgling breathing began again.

I'm wasting time, thought Hester. She dragged off the warm white blanket which was intended to wrap Philippa's shivering limbs, and turned away, leaving Philippa's husband uncovered and indecent, his clothing deranged from her frantic searching for a wound. She folded the blanket, tucked it under her arm, picked up the lantern and made for the door which she slammed viciously behind her. She knew no one else in all this deserted town, nobody knew her. She had seen soldiers on her brief visit to the town but she had no idea of where their headquarters were. She felt bitter and defeated and terribly tired. And the man in whom she had put her trust, the man who had knowledge and wealth and influence, all of which would have helped to raise a rescue party, lay there, hiding behind locked doors and drawn curtains, dead drunk.

Her own mind was not working clearly now. She had only one idea, and that, in the circumstances, not very good or very helpful. She must get back to her helpless little party. She had promised that. Beyond the keeping of the promise she had no thought, no plan.

That there were other houses than Mr. Kyne's in St. Agnes, that there were other men than Ambrose in the town, were facts that escaped her. She had ceased to think, had become an obedient animal which had been given a direction—"To St. Agnes"; and now received another—"Back to the Spring."

Everything had narrowed down to the making of the effort necessary for the return journey, all else was darkness. Working like an automaton she selected some food from the store-room, wrapped it in the folds of the blanket and tied it with a piece of cord that she took from a box. There was no need, she decided, to clamber through the store-room window, she could leave by the front door and so avoid passing the bodies on the cobbles. She did not even bother to lock the door behind her; she no longer cared what happened to Ambrose Markham, and she had no time to waste. She had twelve miles to walk before sunrise. She kept the lantern in her hand, swung the blanket over her shoulder, holding the cord against her breast, and began to walk.

She was much less tired now than on the outward journey. Her head was numb and empty, light as a bad nut, but it seemed to remember the way. Her legs on the contrary were numb and heavy, senseless as wood, but they seemed to move forward, first one and then the other, making, one by one, the twenty-four thousand steps that were needed to carry her back to the spring-head. When the cord cut unbearably into one shoulder she changed it automatically to the other; when both were rubbed to equal rawness she clutched the unwieldy bundle in her arms. Grit and stones found their way into her broken shoes, and the friction of them raised blisters. She was just conscious of these new outposts of pain, but she walked as a hen walks after its head has fallen by the block, except that she walked with purpose and direction.

There was a full hour of darkness left when she climbed the slope between the boulders and began to clear her throat so that she might tell a good lie about being unable to reach St. Agnes and the robbing of a house on the road. She had been walking for almost eleven hours and would probably have gone on until she fell dead.

"It's me, it's Hester," she croaked as she pushed the bundle before her through the passage. There was no answer. Perhaps they were sleeping. She would try to put the blanket around Philippa without disturbing the blessed unconsciousness. She stumbled forward into the empty chamber. And as she did so, as though it had granted her the respite and could wait no longer, down came the rain.

She sat down by edge of the spring and cried helplessly and hopelessly for quite a long time. After all that effort. She never doubted that they had gone wandering off, probably impatient at her long absence; or else because Mrs. Markham had taken a sudden crazy fancy into her head and Philippa had not been able to restrain her. She discovered that she was much fonder of Philippa than she had imagined, loved the baby, and did not hate Mrs. Markham so much as she had thought. She had been quite a brave old thing until her mind wandered. Now all three were gone and God alone knew what had happened to them.

At first she cried for them and her tears were hot and angry. But gradually, just as the chill of the cell-like place crept through her body obliterating the warmth of exertion, her spirit grew cold with a sense of greater bereavement, more utter desolation. She realised that all that she had done and endured in the past hours of trial had been done for Ambrose's sake. Yesterday, to-day, this evening on the way to St. Agnes, she had not been striving for the women's sakes alone. She had not known then that she loved Philippa and admired the old lady. She had been pressing on towards that day, that moment, when she would meet Ambrose again and hand over to him his family, intact and safe, preserved by her for his sake. And she had met him again with the evidence of his uselessness, his cowardice, his weakness thick upon him. That detached plaintive spirit that she had so much admired had failed in the test; the body she had longed and yearned after had shrunk away, hidden behind locked doors and drawn curtains and sought senselessness through brandy. It was as though, after martyr- dom, a Christian should find Heaven empty, mere space about an untenanted throne. Her tears were slower now, wrung from some lower depths, more painful of extraction and devoid of balm. But she cried until every one of them was shed, until her aching swollen eyes were dry and sheer weariness laid its calm- ing hand upon her. Thought returned. Soon now it would be light and then she would search for them. The thought of the wild black men down at Watershead should not deter her. The trust was now a bitter farce, but she would carry it through to whatever end might lie in wait. In the meantime she would stretch her tired bones upon the floor, draw the blanket around her for warmth, lie on her back and watch for the morning to lighten the patch of sky visible between the rocks.

Within five minutes she was sleeping the sleep of the emotionally and physically exhausted.

CHAPTER XVIII

AWAY over the stream, down at Joyous Gard, much activity was going on in the deserted house. Llewellyn's Megan and two other women made fires and heated blankets, and while the overseer, helped by Joe Beaver, put Bruce to bed, the refugees were laid in the parlour. Mrs. Markham, still under the impres- sion that the island had fallen to the French, expressed constant delight and surprise at the kindness meted out to her.

"I always understood that the French were courteous," she said, accepting hot soup from Megan.

Philippa, returning to consciousness to find herself warm and dry and safe, seemed not to notice that the soup was proffered, probably cooked, by the black hands that she had so dreaded; or that Anthony was being held in a capacious lap by another black woman, who was feeding him hot milk from a little cup.

But as soon as her mind cleared she began to fret for Hester. Hester had promised to return, and if she did so and found the sanctuary deserted she would be distraught. Not one of the three black women took the slightest notice of her questions and wailings. They had never heard of Hester and rated Philippa's babblings with Mrs. Markham's meandering chatter about the French.

Leonard, despatched by Llewellyn, set out to ride in search of Old Methody, who had considerable reputation as a surgeon and medical man. Llewellyn and Joe Beaver, having cut Bruce out of his blood-soaked coat and pulled off his other clothes, roughly plugged the wound and applied simple restoratives. When he too returned to consciousness and began talking of Hester, they concentrated upon keeping him in his bed, which difficult feat they accomplished with more thoroughness than gentleness.

Leonard arrived back with the old preacher just as the sun was rising and Llewellyn felt himself at liberty to step downstairs and inquire of Megan how her cases were faring.

"Dey's both silly," said Megan bluntly. "De old woman keep talking 'bout de French, and de yong one cain't say nudding but 'Hester, find Hester,' oll de time."

Llewellyn pushed his way into the parlour.

"Mrs. Markham," he said, stooping above Philippa as she lay on the floor—Constance by the irrefutable right of seniority having been given the sofa—"Who is Hester? And what has happened to her? Mr. Bruce is bothering about her too."

"She's my maid, Hester Roon. She saved us all. And she left us last night. She said she was going into St. Agnes to get help and see if she could find my husband. I'm so worried about her. Isn't there anything we could do?"

"I'll see," said Llewellyn. "You can leave it to me and rest your mind easy."

Upstairs, Old Methody had called for basins and hot water and linen, a supply of wood and a sharp knife. He set to work on Bruce with a will, only speaking in order to tell him to move a little, this way or that, and to congratulate him on the triviality of his wound.

"It's your collar-bone, not your shoulder joint, that is splintered, God be praised. The skill does not rest in human hands to mend a shattered joint."

When he had finished he stepped back and regarded his handiwork with pride. He had fixed Bruce into a contraption that resembled the yoke upon which milkmaids carried pails, except that it was more complicated. One end of the nicely whittled wood projected beyond his shoulder, two others crossed behind the back of his neck, and a short piece sticking up beneath his ear prevented him from turning his head.

"A nice job, Mr. Lyddon," he said complacently. "Thank God again that I was at home when your man came." His face shone. Something in his character prevented him from taking pride in his spiritual conquests; he rejoiced in them, but very humbly. But whenever he bled anyone and the patient was relieved, whenever he prescribed successfully for a fever or dealt with a broken or dislocated limb, he was conscious, and not unhappily, of the pride that is supposed to be an attribute of the devil.

"It may look nice to you," said Bruce ungratefully, unclenching the teeth which he locked upon the groans of pain wrung from him by the rough surgery, "but I can't move about in it."

"All the better," said Old Methody as he emptied the basin of bloody water through the window and rubbed his thin old hands on the towel. "Nobody wants you to move about. In fact it is most desirable that you should not. If you move or excite yourself the blood will inflame. And since God has been so good to you in making the wound slight and help early available, it would be impious to work against Him."

"Impious be damned," said Bruce roughly. "I've got a job to do. We collected two of the Watershead women, but the third, the best of the lot, is still missing. And if I don't find her I hope I do inflame. I deserve to. But for my pigheadedness and stinking pride she would be safe here now. If ever you want to set foot on my property again, Methody, you'll help me into some clothes. There's a clean shirt in that drawer. Cut the arm out with that knife. That's right. I won't bother about a coat, but I'll have those buff breeches."

Muttering to himself Old Methody reluctantly settled to the undoing of his own good work. Bruce had hit upon the one threat that had the power to move the old man. If his spiritual work came into conflict with his surgery of course the flesh must be sacrificed. He even stooped and helped Bruce into his stockings and boots. He was wrestling with them when Llewel-

312

lyn came in to say that he had found out that Hester had gone into St. Agnes.

"Do you hear that, man? Hurry!" cried Bruce, smiting the bent shoulder. "She'd been looking after that helpless crowd since Tuesday night; it's odds if she had had any food or sleep, and she set out to walk to St. Agnes. Twelve miles in the dark and God knows what dangers on the way. Here, Llewellyn, you deal with the other boot."

CHAPTER XIX

THE changing light woke Hester and she pushed herself free of the blanket. She was annoyed to find that she had been asleep at all, and slightly ashamed to discover that the sight of the stores, which she had thrown down haphazardly in the dark, waked ravening appetite in her. Her mind might be as bruised and desperate as ever, but the body was asserting its intention to survive if possible. She crammed food into her mouth and swallowed hastily, wincing as the insufficiently masticated portions rasped her sore throat.

Still chewing, she pushed her way into the open and studied the ground. It offered no clue of the whereabouts of her charges, for the rain last night had washed away all trace of the foot and hoof marks. She shaded her eyes from the brilliance of the sun and looked towards Watershead. Had Philippa and Mrs. Markham wandered that way? Or had they been found? Killed? Or worse? Could she, even by going down there, discover anything of value? If they were there would she do any good by sharing their fate? The fiery resolves of self-immolation with which she had thrown herself down an hour or so ago began to waver. And then she thought again of Ambrose. Was she going to match him in cowardice? It was bad enough to discover that you had loved, worshipped, dreamed about such a one. She began to walk steadily down the boulder-covered slope. Before she reached the pasture's edge she saw something moving along the road. It was of peculiar shape and seemed to be moving with

313

difficulty and yet determination. Careful study revealed that it was a person with a big bundle on its head and another clasped in its arms. Apart from the slaves who had moved, mere dark dots in the distance, and Ambrose, who had lain, a senseless log, it was the first person outside her own party whom Hester had seen since the trouble began. One person, she decided, could not hurt her. She changed her direction and went towards it. Soon she could see that it was a female, black, stout. It was Delia.

Recognition was mutual and they hurried towards one another, meeting like long-lost friends. Delia dropped her bundles and reached for Hester's hands.

"Oh, Miss Hestah," she cried. "Ah sure is glad to see yo'. Dey wuz collin' an' collin' oll ober de place fo' yo' las' night."

"Who were? What happened last night, Delia? Tell me quickly."

"Mistah Lyddon an' two-three ob his men come down an' soon put dat riff-raff to rights. An' dey found Mis' Ambrose, an mah deah ole mistess up at de springhead 'tother side ob de pasture. We's oll hid ourseffs an' watched. Not dat Ah had nuddin' to be 'shamed ob. Ah's bin a prisonah mahseff, as Ah tole Mistah Lyddon. Ah's now on mah way to Mistah Lyddon's place. Ah just cain't wait no longer to see mah deah mistress. Ah just manage to sabe a liddle ob de best silvah and a few dem best linen sheets." She indicated the bundles with her bare muddy toe. "Ah's gonna 'splain how dem udders put de blanket ober me. Ah didden want no hab-to-do wid no Leader. . . ." She paused from lack of breath. Her shifty little eyes watched Hester to see how the story had been taken. It was lucky that she was having another chance to try it out. Mr. Lyddon hadn't really listened to it last night. Miss Hester was very little better. She uttered neither commiseration nor approval. She was staring into the distance over Delia's shoulder in such a strange way that the double traitor glanced round uneasily. There was nothing to be seen.

Delia picked up the smaller of the two bundles and set it on her head again.

"Yo' comin' wid me?" she asked. If so it was possible that Hester would offer to carry the other bundle. After all she was only a poor white girl, a thing that Delia had forgotten in the first ecstasy of greeting. But Hester shook her head, and Delia,

314

with a sigh, raised the parcel of linen—destined only a few hours before to be a goodwill offering to the unknown Leader when he came.

"No, Delia. I think they can manage without me now. Tell them that I am safe and well and I shall go back to St. Agnes."

"Ah'm gonna humble mahseff in de dust," said Delia.

"I daresay you'll do it quite successfully," said Hester, with a glance that made the stout negress slightly uneasy and sent her waddling off wondering whether there were possibly a flaw in her story.

Hester turned towards the main road. If the spirit is really released by death it must, as it leaves the body and turns towards the new existence, feel much as she felt at that moment. The Markhams were safe. She was as free of them as she was of Ambrose. Everything was finished. The revolt was over. There was no need to die. But she could not go back to Joyous Gard. She could not face Mrs. Markham and Philippa, knowing what she did about the man in whom they both had placed their trust. Nor could she face Bruce Lyddon. He had said that she would discover the truth about Ambrose, and that, God knew, was true enough. But she was not going to take a walk in order to admit herself in the wrong.

Yet, even as she set herself to walk away from Joyous Gard, her heart rose and sang at the memory of Delia's story. "Mistah Lyddon an' two-three ob his men." He had finished, and finished well, the job she had begun. In a book she would have hailed him as a man after her own heart; but this was not a book; this was life, and whatever he might do or be he remained the man who had fooled her, the man who had said, "You will come". she was determined that if ever they met again it would because he had come in search of her. Which, of course, being the man he was, he would not do. Very well, she thought, she could live without him. She could live without anybody. She was adult now, the foolish infatuation for Philippa's husband had been the last symptom of childishness.

She straightened her weary body and plodded on.

Behind her suddenly the sound of hoof-beats broke upon the morning quiet. She paused for a moment to listen. That might be the pale mare's easy rhythmic tread, but she could not be certain. Hurriedly she began to walk again without turning her head, but her heart beat faster and the faint colour stained her pale sunken cheeks.

A voice cried, "Hester!" Yes, that was Bruce, there was no mistaking that gruff urgent voice. A faint smile curved her full mouth. The tattoo of hoofs grew more rapid, drew nearer. And although she kept her face forward and her tired feet in motion, the smile that deepened upon her face held other elements than triumph.

THE END